4/24

The
Patron Thief
of Bread

For Clementine

Copyright © 2022 by Lindsay Eagar

First edition 2022

Library of Congress Catalog Card Number 2021947138
ISBN 978-1-5362-0468-1

22 23 24 25 26 27 LBM 10 9 8 7 6 5 4 3 2 1

Printed in Melrose Park, IL, USA

This book was typeset in Minion Pro, WT Mediaeval, and Grand Baron.

Candlewick Press
99 Dover Street
Somerville, Massachusetts 02144

www.candlewick.com

The
Patron Thief
of Bread

LINDSAY EAGAR

CANDLEWICK PRESS

Some people are nobody's
enemies but their own.

—Charles Dickens, *Oliver Twist*

PRELUDE

All the gargoyles on the unfinished cathedral in the dusty market district of Odierne face east except one.

Which means that all the gargoyles are insufferable early risers who begin their gossiping the moment sunshine hits their stone faces. Except one.

"Did you hear?" says one of the east-side gargoyles. "The tanner's wife caught him buying a pint for that saucy new laundress!"

The rest of them chortle. "Well, which would you choose? One smells like fresh linens, and the other one stinks like the entrails of a boar."

Only one gargoyle on the cathedral roof faces west, thereby avoiding the morning departure of the pigeons from their roosts, which means there is only one gargoyle who does not get coated in bird grime. Only one gargoyle who does not have to wait for the rain to wash the smelly splatters from his horns.

And that gargoyle, in faith, is me.

"Serves you right, you noisy scummers!" I hoot the minute I hear the *slap-slap* of white pigeon poop hitting the heads of the east-side gargoyles. "One of these days, you'll get a special delivery right in the chops—that'll teach you to talk so much!"

"Bite your tongue, ugly!" the east-side gargoyles screech back at me. "No one likes you!"

I chuckle to myself. Always to myself. Their words roll off my back like water.

There are five of them, of uniform size and shape except for their monstrous heads, which are chiseled to look like various beasts from God's green earth.

They have a decent view of Odierne's best streets, the vendors, our city's front gates, the count's manor. My ledge overlooks the Sarluire, a river of little color that winds between Odierne and an expanse of barley fields beyond. The water carries the city's refuse, which tends to bunch at the nearby canal bridge. After ninety years of this view, I weary of it.

I weary of the gleam of the Sarluire at high noon, angled right into my eyes.

For ninety years, I have been blinded by that river.

For ninety years, I have had to listen to those east-side ninnies speaking about things I cannot see, their voices so loud I cannot hear anything else.

They were made by a different sculptor. Perhaps that is why it is so easy to argue with them. Or perhaps it is because there is little else to do up here except spin new ways to insult each other, new cruelties to shout across the roof like sermons.

Every day is the same when you are waiting. Tomorrow we will call each other guileless toads, wart-faced nanny goats, great horned devils. I will growl for quiet; they will refuse me my request.

And above, the sun will burn a trail across the sky, and the moon will rise vapors from the sea. Time marches on.

Ninety years.

They call me ugly—but we are gargoyles. We are all ugly.

And ugly has never once stopped the birds. They roost in the eaves, in the bell-less belfries, safe from weather and wind. And when there is no more room in the hollow places of our unfinished frame, they try to roost on top of my head. Every time one of these feathered rodents steers too close, I bite at them, hard as I can.

"Fly south forever!" I shout. "Get plucked!"

At night, when the birds think I am snoozing, they bring their sticks and leaves and pieces of straw to my mouth, hoping to construct a nest before morning. But I snap my jaws shut, aiming to squash them, and end up with dirty feathers between my teeth.

"I hope someone roasts you with fennel and rotten potatoes!" I call as they flap into the darkness. It's a good thing I do not sleep, or else they would make a birdbath out of me.

The pigeons are enough of a plague, and my fellow gargoyles make me wish I could chip my ears right off my head, but they are nothing compared to the abbey next door.

The Glorious Congregation of the Sisters of Mercy, it is called, and its sisters are a bunch of white-cloaked old hedge witches. After their morning prayers, which drone on and on, they stand in their garden and blend together in chant, as if each of their voices is a string and they must musick them into a benedictory banner that hangs above Odierne for all the town to hear.

It makes me sick. It makes me wish for a working spout so I

could spit water and pretend to be throwing up whenever they start their singing.

"*Praise God, from whom all blessings flow,*" they sing.

"*Praise butts, from where all droppings flow!*" I sing back, as loud and triumphant as I can.

"Grow up!" the east-side gargoyles scold. "You're revolting."

So revolting, I have alternate verses for every hymn in the Glorious Congregation's repertoire: "All Glory, Farts, and Honor," "Sing to Him in Constipation," "Of the Fathers Doves Were Smotten."

I do not think God minds. I like to think He is on my side.

After all, God made the silence to be enjoyed.

Ninety years I have watched the river from my ledge.

Ninety years since I was chunked from a strange mountain and chiseled into shape and hauled onto this rooftop to keep our cathedral safe.

"A gargoyle is made to protect," said my maker as she brought her tools up to my horns. And that is what I am supposed to do. Protect.

Ninety years since they started working on our cathedral. But I still remember.

How my stone fizzed with excitement when I saw where my perch would be—so high up, I could see all the way to the horizon. How our structure came together in bursts and bits, block by block, slathers of wet mortar and piles of split timber. All of Odierne came out to witness the birth of a new cathedral, a once-in-a-lifetime spectacle. How I could not wait to keep watch over them. Whatever came through the city walls—sieges, storms, spirits—I would guard the people as my own.

And I remember when the workers left for a midwinter feast day and never came back. The hay they had stuck between our stones to keep the mortar from cracking in the cold was there for many winters and summers alike, until the mice carted it off for their burrows.

Odierne was able to forget. They forgot about us long ago. They stopped seeing our stones as potential walls. Now they look right past our deserted structure as if we are invisible. They walk around the foundation to get to the butcher, to get to the river, as if we are something fixed in the earth like a tree. We are an eyesore, an embarrassment. They have learned to ignore us the way you learn to ignore a festering pockmark on your chin.

And every evening, when we are silhouetted with the rest of Odierne's skyline, I wonder if we will ever be finished? Or are we destined to rot up here for eternity?

"Someday they will come back and finish this box of bricks," I tell myself when the taste of righteous longing overpowers the usual flavor of my tongue, sun-warmed lumière rock. "They will finish the choir. They will finish the last wall. They will put in the windows. This will be a functioning cathedral, and we will protect the city. I will be a functioning gargoyle—"

"You're a functioning monster already." Harpy, one of the east-side gargoyles, a real delight with an eagle's head and the temperament of a snarling boar, can never pass up a chance to harass me. "You're so ugly, you scared the financiers away!"

Gargoyles are supposed to be ugly. *Ugly* does nothing.

We are all ugly.

Someday I will be a proper spout, I tell myself. *And the water will come rushing up and out of me, and I will wash away this loose stone pressing into my rump. Those clucking east-siders will be so impressed by my power, they will be speechless.*

Maybe then I will finally have some peace and quiet. And then I will be able to do what I was made to do—protect.

When I feel extra crackly and heavy-lidded, I mutter this to myself like a spell. Almost like a prayer.

Always to myself.

Only one gargoyle on the roof of the unnamed cathedral faces west. Only one gargoyle can see the sunset.

Light splinters into a stained-glass window—purples, peaches, reds. The last rays of the day skip golden across the ripples of the river, and then the disappearing of the sun—slowly, then gone, like a doused flame.

Shadows. And then it is night. The east-side gargoyles turn in early. They let out gusty, dramatic, overtired yawns, as if sitting on their rocky butts spying on the streets below wears them out. They are snoring by dusk.

Me, I am for the night. When the moon hits the water in a reflection that is whole and then broken and then made whole again, and the stars wink, and it is quiet—really, finally quiet—I breathe out.

Another day. My grimace softens; my horns relax.

It is a clear night for stargazing. Above me, the heavens glitter against the black sky. I do not sleep. Instead, I watch the stars spin.

I could stare up into the sky all night—my neck is already made of stone.

I watch and I wonder.

I wonder when they will finish building our cathedral. I wonder what will happen if they do not. I wonder how hot a fire my stone can withstand. I wonder what it would be like to sink to the bottom of the river.

I wonder if I will be here long enough to count every star. I wonder what would happen if I were pushed off my roof. Does it matter if you are made of rock or glass when you are dropped from such a height?

I wonder what is inside the other gargoyles. Are they solid stone, like me? Or were they constructed piece by piece, claws formed and then fastened to legs, fastened to bodies, fastened to heads? Do they have stone organs? Stalactites for ribs? Does Harpy have a pebble for a heart?

I wonder if their makers ever thought of them. I wonder if my maker ever thought of me.

I do not remember much of my maker except for her hands. Dry and crackled from scrubbing away plaster, but warm on the cold of my slab. I remember that she liked to whisper to me as she blew the dust away from my form: "You will watch over so many others. You will protect them all."

That is why I do not sleep. I do not close my eyes, not even for a moment. Not even when I am so sleepy, I feel like I have become a mountain again. It is my duty to watch.

Once our cathedral is finished, I will be a proper gargoyle, watching over my parishioners—but in the meantime, I keep watch over the moon as it climbs the sky. I watch the river pour past our churchyard, and I watch the horizon. My whole little world.

When midnight strikes, I ignore Odierne's parish bells and whisper twelve chimes for the bell tower that lies scattered behind me. I wonder and I worry and I watch by myself.

Always by myself.

When it rains, we gargoyles are the first to know.

For ninety years, I have been pelted with hail, blanketed with snow, and blasted with the rays of the summer sun. But I will remember this rain tonight as the worst I've seen in all my days on top of our Cathedral Sans Nom.

This is what I call it, my stone tongue in my stone cheek. Our no-name cathedral. We almost had a proper name once.

Unfinished cathedrals do not keep their names.

The sky has been gray since dawn, with clouds thick as dyed wool hanging low above the city. All the birds stay tucked in their roosts, their dry feathers twitching. The river rages in the wind, which blows the waters to whitecaps and steely peaks.

When the rain began, just before vespers, it sprinkled lightly; now it pours down as if heaven has its own gargoyles draining the chilly water through their spouts onto the Earth.

I deepen my frown. If the cathedral were finished, I would be properly fixed to the gutters so I could siphon water off the roof, but instead it pools around me, splashes onto my claws. I furrow my eyebrows until my head hurts, trying to keep the droplets from running down my face, but to no avail.

It has been an unusually quiet day. In the distance, villagers work to secure the Sarluire's plentiful northern bank from flooding the main thoroughfare. Homes are dark and still. Not a single candle flickers from the street lanterns.

Quiet, except for the east-side gargoyles, who talk even louder when it rains because their ears get clogged with water and they cannot hear themselves. They squawk like upset hens, their voices echoing off the wet cobblestones below.

"It's been ages since we've had a good downpour like this," Harpy says. "My skin's been positively parched."

"Good for the horns, too," Goathead adds.

"Yes, that's the stuff," Harpy purrs as the rain intensifies. Fishy, Scales, and Snout all murmur in agreement. "Wash all that bird scum away."

"Pipe down, beauty queens!" I call. "Some of us are trying to enjoy this without your commentary!"

"What kind of storm would it take to wash you away? Hmmm?" Harpy fires back. The others snicker.

I almost point out that we are made of mountain, harvested from deep beneath unknown hills, and so every time it rains, we become a little more weathered, a little more crumbled, a little closer to becoming dust. But I do not.

Let those east-side ninnies gargle the rain and marvel over the feeling of slick, cleaned stone. Let the water slowly wear them down. Let it wear down their mouths first, please.

A cluster of vagrants runs past our yard, all of them soaked like rats.

If our cathedral were complete, they would have a place to sleep. If our cathedral were complete, we would have a kind-eyed priest to push open the doors and usher in lost, drenched souls. "Come inside," he would say. "Come get dry by the fire. You are safe here."

But there is no priest at the Cathedral Sans Nom. In some places, there are not even walls.

On a night like tonight, it is easy to feel like there is not even a God—

A noise. Wet footsteps on the concrete.

I strain to listen beyond the *pit-a-pat* of raindrops on my ledge.

Footsteps dash up our half-finished porch. Footsteps that hurry, footsteps that do not linger in our hollow chambers but run up the scaffolding.

Someone is coming up to the roof.

"Be still, you miserable clucks!" The east-side gargoyles do not hear me above their blabbing, but they shut up when a hooded figure dashes to our rooftop, clutching something tightly to its chest with both hands.

The figure catches its breath, glancing over my ledge. We are eighty feet up, the river coursing beneath us. A dangerous fall for humans and gargoyles alike.

The person removes their hood, shaking the excess water from their face. Gobs of fire-red hair are instantly soaked by the rain.

A woman. Her cheeks are puffy, her eyes frantic and wild as she lowers her bundle to inspect it.

"Mmm-ba," says the bundle. Inexplicably, my stone feels lightened. A baby.

The baby is pure rascal, a giggle in its eye. The woman wrings the rainwater from its wrappings and spares the child a smile—

But her lips tighten. There is noise and movement below.

A group of men, a dozen or more, and greyhounds on leashes, cutting through the fields. My eyes focus through the blur of the storm. The watch. Sent by constables or even by the sheriff himself.

They move so quickly, the rain cannot douse their torches. Something inside of me clenches when one of them shouts, "She came this way!"

The east-side gargoyles stay silent for once—here, at last, is the quiet I have been waiting for, but I cannot enjoy it. Not with this sensation of nerves in my haunches, all needles and pokies. Not with the fear on the woman's face, plain as ink. Not with us grotesques holding our breath, even though we are made of hardened clay.

The watchmen charge past the city walls, making their way through dark doorways and the alleys of the market district, illuminating windows, the hounds nosing every corner.

"Ma ma ma," says the baby, and then makes a noise that borders on a whimper.

"Shhh." The woman tugs her hood back over her head and hunches over, trying to stay hidden. Tendrils of her wet hair cling to her face.

My haunches stir; my fangs itch. The first time someone has set foot in our cathedral in so many years, and she needs protection.

Someday our stone slabs will be reset and plastered. Someday there will be glass in our windows, and the geometric faces of the Loving Mother and Saint Odile will glow blue and green against the night. Someday the sun will pour through our great panes and shine a perfect, colorful light inside our walls. We will be an oasis for the poor, the contrite, anyone in need of a haven from the storm—

And I, the biggest, oldest gargoyle, will protect them all. As I was made to do.

A growl waits in my throat. I am ready to spring forward, scare away, attack—

But for now, all I can do is watch. I was made to protect, but I am useless to her. Until our cathedral is finished, I am useless.

The watchmen move through the rain-bathed streets, the collective tread of their boots coming nearer and nearer.

The baby thrashes in its blankets, bored and weary of the rain. The woman tries to rock it calm, but the small creature's tiny voice rings out, loud enough to be heard over the storm.

The watchmen pause. They hear.

And then, like some sort of machinery, they turn as one. They march up the cathedral porch, up the steps, stealthy as cats even in the storm.

Inside me, something stirs.

"Can the roof even support them?" Harpy whispers. None of us answers; we just listen to the sounds of the watchmen climbing, up the scaffolding, up the hidden stairs that were never meant to be used by anyone except the framers and the masons, stairs that might be rotted to the core.

Up, up, and up.

Up to us.

The baby gums at its fist with a certain teething fury. The woman scans the roof, eyeing each of us, the busted-up bell tower, looking for somewhere to hide, and in a last-minute scramble, tucks herself on the ledge beside me, using the shadows to her advantage.

"What is she doing?" Harpy hisses. "That ledge is slick as moss!"

"She's going to tumble to her death," Snout adds. And I will have to watch, I think—but the woman does not slip. She steadies herself on the ledge, crouched low, folded almost in half, her baby in her arms.

Even in the rain, she smells like the woods, like pine. Like something baking.

The baby, pressed against her chest, breathes in the comfort of her scent, yeast and flour and sweetness, and stops its cries, content.

My own stone is warmer—

"She's up here somewhere!" The voices of the watch arise mere seconds before they do, and then they are on our roof. They spread themselves around, sniffing along with their leashed dogs.

If I were coated in fur, it would rankle. I feel the gargoyle's instinct—to scare away, to keep safe, to protect.

I forget about the rain, how it trickles down my eyes, making tears for me even though I am made of stone and cannot cry. I forget that the east-side gargoyles woke me up even before the fishermen were baiting. They woke me with a conversation about current trends in Odierne's hat fashion that was inane even for them, and so I am tired as well as drenched. I forget that I am missing muscles and bones and a heart, and I tell my claws to please, please move.

One claw.

If that is all I can lift to protect this woman and baby, then I will never again complain about our unfinished cathedral. Or if I do, I will match it with gratitude for this moment.

I am made of mountain and mineral and heat. But still, I pray for a miracle.

The rain doesn't soak the watchmen as they search our roof—maybe they, too, are made of a kind of stone.

Beside me, the woman glances down at the river. The currents churn like a bouillabaisse at the height of its cooking.

Her head is right next to mine, her eyes cast down. The baby is tired of this hiding game now, and it will not be reasoned with. The woman is bouncing it, jostling it, singing to it softly enough that the rain muffles her voice, but the baby is one deep breath away from a tantrum.

"Find her!" the constable in charge calls. "And when you do, cuff her at once! She's a slippery one—don't let her get away this time!"

I look at the woman with new eyes. What did she do? It must have been something truly terrible to have the constable chasing her in such a storm.

I wonder what happens to babies if their mothers are thrown in the dungeon. I wonder if the Lord ever ranks sins according to their gravity. I wonder if it's possible for this woman to find some wiggle room.

And what of my sacred charge, to keep safe, to protect? Should a gargoyle protect someone who committed a grievance against another? Should a gargoyle watch over a sinner?

The long-suffering baby gets a fat raindrop in the eye. Startled, offended, the babe turns red and wails.

Even above the din of the storm, the sound is impossible to miss.

"There!" shouts one of the watch. "Over by the grotesque! I see her!"

"Arrest her at once!" the constable commands, and they rush toward me.

The constable's face is softer than I expected it to be, and younger; perhaps he is a father of small children himself. He eyes the woman as she balances on the ledge beside me. In a crack of lightning, I see panic flicker across her face, just for a moment— but it is replaced with brazen defiance as more and more men surround her.

"You're done for," the constable tells her. "Step down. Time to face the music."

He extends his hand, a false rescue—he'll save her from a fall only to lock her up in irons.

She ignores him. She whispers something to her baby, as if the two of them are alone on the roof.

"Come away from the ledge now," the constable repeats, smug, "and we'll make sure your cell is cleared of toads and vipers before you're shut inside."

A cell. Imprisonment. She must have done something horrible.

The woman's face pinches with emotion, as though she is holding a whole universe inside of her. But still she does not move from her perch.

"If you're hoping for a miracle," the constable jeers, "you'd best look heavenward. You'll find no mercy here. Not for you."

But the mother does not look up. She looks right at me, right at my grimace. And I look at her. She does not know it, but I am looking right at her. Whole universes, in those eyes. As big as cathedrals.

Criminal or no, I must save her.

I would give both my horns to have our doors in working order so they could be closed and barred. I would trade every one of my claws to see the watch stopped and questioned by the bishop. If we had the authority of the church, the authority to give sanctuary, I would never look at another star again.

But this cathedral is an empty belly. It is two and a half walls of decrepitude. It is ninety years of failure. It is exposed vaulting like the jutting rib cage of a fleshless skeleton. It is a wound.

A humiliation.

And I am not a proper gargoyle. Water does not pour out of my mouth, making a rightful spout of me; it floods around my feet. I am not even worth my weight in gravel.

Pray, pray, I should pray. That's what a bishop would tell me to do. That's what the Sisters of Glorious Mercy would suggest.

But I've said many prayers. I've prayed for our cathedral to be finished, prayed the builders would return, prayed that I'd be a real gargoyle. Praying is as good as wishing; wishing is as good as whispering your needs into water so the river can drown them. Every prayer I've ever uttered is just like me: useless.

"What are you waiting for?" The constable sounds desperate now, as though he would sprout his own wings if he could and snag her off the ledge. "We have you surrounded—there's nowhere else for you to go."

I must scare away those who wish her harm. This is why I was created. This was the charge given to me by my maker. *Protect.*

But there is nothing I can do. I cannot move, not enough to chase them away. I cannot growl, not loud enough for them to hear. I can only pray. And that is not enough.

In a burst, the constable lurches forward, grabbing for the woman's hood—

But the woman leaps off the roof and into the river, baby and all.

I was made to watch. And so I watch.

I watch.

I watch.

SUMMER

Eight Years Later

Our Daily Bread

"All right, Crowns, line up!"

In a crooked alleyway along an unmapped street in Odierne, a group of dirty children scrambled to form a single-file row, facing a wall of sunburned bricks.

If you thought they were orphans, you'd be more or less correct. If you tried to count them, they'd scatter and dance around until you lost track of their exact number.

If you thought they were poor, needy beggars desperate for alms, then you ought to check your pockets.

They'd have gotten you.

The eldest of the children strolled before his ranks. Gnat was a scrawny lad of a murky age—he could pass for as young as eleven or as old as twenty, but when he spoke, his was the already-broken voice of those in-between years.

"Saturday," he said. "Today's the day that Master Griselde pulls forty dozen freshly baked loaves of bread from her ovens, which means—" He stopped and held aloft a coin for all to see. "Today, we get to eat."

The bakery's panels were still closed, but the children could already detect the yeasty smell of the loaves hardening in the ovens, even above the more unpleasant sunrise odors of the butcher and the fishmonger.

The glorious smell of vanquishment.

Gnat wiggled his fingers; in a flash, the coin was now a wooden copy of a coin, carved to mimic the penny in texture, pattern, and heft. A perfect representation—except it had been carved from an old wagon wheel.

They'd flipped many of these false coins into the hands of unsuspecting merchants, and now that they'd arrived in Odierne, they'd do it again.

An old trick for a new city.

"Who is it going to be?" Gnat glanced down at them as he paced—he seemed to tower above them all, even those who were technically taller than he was. "Which one of you is going to bring us the bread?"

The row of children twitched.

Gnat would never lead them astray. Never had any of his schemes failed. Never had any of the Crowns been caught by constables or locked in the stocks.

To trust in Gnat was to get your belly filled, your thirst slaked.

So when he looked over his legion of seven, half of them were already raising their hands, volunteering.

"Me! Me! I'll go," said a rosy girl with frizzy copper hair—they called her Fingers, and true to form, her digits were already fluttering to life. "Come on, it's been so long since I got to lift—"

"You swiped a potato from a cart just a minute ago!" one of the other Crowns put in.

"Potatoes don't count," Fingers started, quickly hiding the offending tuber in her tunic.

Gnat's "No" was sharp as a riding crop's snap. "It's time to give someone else a chance."

At the far end of the line, the youngest child tried to hold still.

She was a pale and grimy girl with dull hair, dark eyes, and a tiny mouth, which she kept closed as much as possible.

Her name was Duck, so dubbed because the Crowns had found her floating in the Sarluire as a baby. "Our little duckling," Ash liked to say, and since he was the one who had fished her out— not to mention the one who had stolen goat's milk to feed her as an infant and mashed up his own food for her as she grew—the rest of the gang respected it.

She kept her head tipped up, her gaze on the wall of the alley. The buildings on this side of the street were older, so they tilted slightly, leaning like tipsy nuns. In a few years, the roofs would be touching. Moss grew between the bricks, a vibrant green that Duck always associated with this time of year, the end of the rainy spring and the triumphant entrance of summertime.

A happy green.

The palm holding the two coins—one tarnished silver, one wooden—stopped under Duck's nose.

"Today's your lucky day." Gnat pitched the coins into the air and walked back down the line as they fell.

Duck fumbled to catch them.

It had been days since they'd eaten anything as solid as bread. They'd been gobbling up whatever they could forage—rotten onions, unripe berries, the occasional squirrel they roasted on a spit. (Surprisingly sweet, with a hint of nuts.)

Yes, it had been a rough month since they'd left their former territory behind. Once a city was played out—once the Crowns noticed they were picking the same pockets and rotating among the same shops—it was time to move on.

Duck knew she was not the only one whose stomach was empty as a drum.

"What do you say, Garbage?" Gnat angled himself against the wall so his right hand was tucked away. This was a familiar pose; even around the Crowns, Gnat did not like when his right arm was visible to the world. "Can we count on you?"

The two coins were heavy as rubies in Duck's fist.

So far, she'd only participated in the background of the Crowns' various scams. As the youngest, Duck was always stationed as a lookout, but she'd been both waiting for and dreading this day—Gnat did not abide freeloaders in his gang. Every Crown had to pull their weight.

And Crowns did not say no to Gnat. That would be saying no to food. Saying no to your livelihood.

"Aw, Gnat, she's no good at this stuff," groaned a wiry boy called Frog Eyes. "No offense, Duck. But someone else should go."

"She'll lose her nerve before she even gets to the counter," a girl named Spinner added. "And then we'll starve."

"I'm not eating any more rats. Send Fingers," said Drippy.

Duck lowered her gaze, wishing the moss would grow beyond the bricks, spread through the alley, and gulp her up whole.

The others were not wrong.

She'd practiced swapping out the real coin for the false one in her palm over and over, trying to make the motion smooth, but her hand was always just a little too sweaty, a little too slow.

If anyone would mess this up, it was Duck.

Gnat's shrug wasn't particularly friendly; neither was his defense of Duck. "She's a Crown. So she'll get that bread, or she'll die trying." He looked at Duck for confirmation. "Right?"

Duck looked at Ash, the oldest Crown after Gnat, a tall and rumpled boy with dark skin and hair. When she met Ash's eyes, Duck gave him the tiniest of nods.

"She'll do it," Ash announced to the rest of the Crowns, which was as good as Duck saying it herself. With Ash around, there was no need for Duck to speak. With Ash around, Duck could always be heard.

"Here, then, put this on." Fingers passed Duck a fraying straw hat, the kind a farmer would wear. "Lower, so your eyes are shaded. Good."

"Remember, give your order to the baker only, not to her journeyman," coached another Crown, a round and pink-faced boy with floppy, overgrown curls whom they called Le Chou— the Cabbage. "The baker's the one you talk to. No one else."

All of this Duck knew.

She knew to pace herself. She knew to avoid using eight words when five was enough. She knew to be at once likable but forgettable, and to be on her guard for watchmen at all times.

As the quietest member of the Crowns, this should be an easy job for her.

But this was the first time Gnat had ever entrusted her with their bread. She looked down the row of Crowns, looked into their faces.

Deep inside her, something quivered.

"Hold on a minute—we need to send you off proper." Ash grabbed Duck's hand and placed his on top of it. The rest of the Crowns, resigned, put their own hands in the circle.

"Our fingers be nimble!" Ash started.

"To our graves, be swift!" shouted another Crown.

"And on every head a crown!" they chorused as one.

"There, now." Ash clapped Duck on the back. "Go bring us back our bread."

Duck tried to breathe normally. With a final reluctant smile for Ash, she poked her head out of the alley.

"Keep your wits about you." Gnat's breath on her neck was hot and earthy. "Pay attention to what's around you, but don't be twitchy. Oh, and Garbage? If you lose that penny, don't even bother coming back."

With that, Gnat shoved Duck into the square.

Dawn bells had rung prime only a short while ago. Already Odierne's streets bustled with the noise and motion of people trying to get their carts, their animals, and themselves to where they needed to be. Hammers chimed, hay bales thudded, horses whinnied and clomped on the cobblestones. Housewives and maid-servants dodged the piles of offal and swarms of flies swimming in said offal to get to the food shops, which were cranking open their front windows at this very moment.

The sounds of summer, music for city and country folk alike. Duck and the Crowns had many reasons to favor summer above all other seasons: They could sleep anywhere, for one thing, instead of spending cold nights in unlocked cellars and stables. They could feast on apricots snatched from orchards and squash rinds taken from unattended hog troughs. They could take dips in streams and rivers, as long as they steered clear of the spots where the dung piles leached into the canals. They could chase butterflies and lie in the sunshine.

Summer was also perfect purse-snatching weather. Everyone in Odierne went out on the streets for festivals, for market days, for no reason at all except that they longed to bask in the sun's pleasantry—the ideal swiping conditions.

Not that it mattered for Gnat. He alone was good enough to thieve a pearl choker from under a duchess's fur coat in the middle of January, even though he was one functioning arm poorer than the rest of the Crowns.

Gnat was better than any of them could ever hope to be.

Duck knew she wouldn't impress him today, but she wanted to at least avoid disappointing him. He called her Garbage, "because that's where we found you, floating in the river like garbage," he always said. And then he'd add to the other Crowns, "No one else is allowed to call her that. Only me."

Funny, Duck often thought while chewing on her lip, that while pennies were scant, she had more names than she needed.

Master Griselde was late opening her shop this morning.

Already the fruit peddler was nearly out of cherries, and the butcher's shutters rattled shut—he'd sold the last of his chopped ham moments ago.

But people couldn't scurry home yet. People needed their bread.

So they hovered at the crafters' booths, buying trinkets they usually only sniffed at, much to the delight of the crafters, whose income fluctuated greatly depending on how spendthrift the general population was on market days.

Duck was pleased to see that today, money was moving from person to person like the nits. A nice, healthy economy.

Always linger with a purpose. It was one of the most basic of the Crowns' rules, and one of their most efficient—the last thing you wanted to do when running a scam was to bring attention to yourself. Fortunately for Duck, she avoided attention like it was a malady.

Unfortunately for Duck, it was also against her nature to step forward, to speak for herself, to engage. Her instincts were to observe and to obey. Today, though, she would have to sing out.

A booth with beautiful daggers and embroidered leather sheaths caught Duck's eye. She strolled to its tables, trying to peruse with an innocent, lollygagging manner that matched the rest of the crowd.

"Is there something special you're looking for?" The woman selling the goods appeared above Duck like a bird of prey shading its next meal.

Duck fought the urge to whip her hands guiltily behind her back and shook her head. She was just browsing, she reminded herself. Waiting for bread, like everyone else. She had every right.

"Did you forget your voice at home?" the woman said with a good-natured smile.

It wasn't that Duck couldn't speak.

Just . . . with Ash around to speak for her, she rarely needed to use her own words. After so many years of letting Ash be her voice, the Crowns now just looked right at him when they asked her a question. Ash always knew her answer.

She offered a word to the woman now, a little one, just to prove she could: "No."

But the woman was inspecting her anew, taking in Duck's dirty cheeks, her ragged tunic, her bare feet, and the woman's demeanor suddenly darkened. "This booth is for customers only," she hissed, covering her wares with her sleeves. "Get your little beggar hands off my table before you spoil everything."

Heat climbed Duck's neck.

Immediately an idea came to her, sharp as a blade—she could pretend to be counting the coins in her pocket, show the woman a glimpse of her silver penny, then walk to the next booth. Let the woman think she had missed a decent sale; maybe then she'd hold her words before she said such rude things to someone again.

Stay calm, Duck told herself. Petty vengeance was a quick way to get remembered.

"The pebble that makes the slightest splash is the easiest to forget," Ash would say if he were here. And then Gnat would roll his eyes and tell Ash he was talking like a monk again, and the rest of the Crowns would chortle and tease. Ash couldn't help it—such fancy sentences and wisdom fell out of him the way walnuts tumble from trees in autumn. Maybe if he'd been born to a pair of merchants, he'd have learned to read and write. He would have made a splendid scholar.

But then he wouldn't have been a Crown. And baby Duck, floating in the river? She would have been fish food.

Ash was the voice in Duck's head, and so she didn't stick around to teach the mean-tongued woman a lesson.

And Gnat . . . Gnat was the pulse in Duck's neck. Gnat would have vanished, folded himself into the crowd like it was a lidded box, and so that's exactly what Duck did now. She disappeared.

When the crafter recapped her morning at the end of the day, the image of the greasy child with threadbare clothes would be sunk too deep in the trenches of her memory to be easily fished out.

Behind Duck, there was a click and whirring sound.

The deep-green panels of Master Griselde's shop front furled up like scrolls, revealing baskets of long pleated baguettes, rows of hot cross buns, rye and barley loaves, squares of unleavened bread, and, behind the counter, a confectionary of colorful, delicate pastries almost too tempting to look at.

The bakery was finally open.

Master Baker

"Fresh bread! Come get your fresh bread, rolls, and buns!" The bakery's journeyman, a young man wearing a cap on his curly dark hair, clanged the golden bell that hung from the frame of the shop. He then picked up a tray of round, fat trenchers and turned toward the crowd.

In an amorphous movement like a glob of fish, the people pressed toward the loaves.

And then it was mayhem.

Duck's stomach lurched. She clutched the penny and the wooden coin in her pocket.

The squares of unleavened bread were the first to go, even though they required teeth hard as an ogre's to chew through the crust. But they were the cheapest, and above flavor, customers wanted cheap.

Next to be picked clean were the baskets of moderately priced baguettes, though within moments of their disappearance a new batch was available, piping hot, steam rising from the crusts in tempting curls. Rye and barley loaves were six a penny, and though Duck had seen slightly lower prices for bread in her days, she'd never seen loaves as hearty as these. With her mouth watering like a horse's, she inched closer, into the frenzy.

While the journeyman worked the crowd with his overflowing trays, the counter, the baskets, and the confectionary were all handled by the master baker herself.

Duck had not yet seen her in person. Gnat had gone alone yesterday to case the city's modern square while the rest of the Crowns napped in a miller's loft.

But now that the baker was in front of her, she understood Gnat's description when he'd said, "Think . . . cow."

Griselde Baker was a bull of a woman, tan-skinned, standing tall as a cornstalk. She'd probably easily look the count in the eye, and he, the most powerful man in the region, would likely be ashamed of his own baby-soft face in comparison to hers; the whiskers that sprang from the baker's chin looked sharp enough to carry thread through cotton. Her rusty hair was fading, streaked with white.

Her hands were strong, speckled rough like an animal's hide, from hauling baking trays in and out of the ovens. No wonder she commissioned her loaves so large; standard-size breads would seem like grains of rice in those paws.

The behemoth baker's back was turned as Duck reached the counter. A new stack of barley loaves, still hot from the forging, sat plump as hens, waiting to be devoured.

The baker's personal seal, a halo of laurel wrapped around a flat outstretched hand with the letters GB—for *Griselde Baker*—was pressed into the domes of the loaves.

Out came the shining silver coin from Duck's pocket.

"And for you?" Griselde Baker leaned over the counter to address Duck. "What will you have?" Her hickory-deep voice didn't surprise Duck, but her eyes did—both orbs unfocused, cool blue, but glazed over with a milky opaqueness.

Someone jostled Duck, reaching for the last oatcake, and she tried to remember what she was supposed to be doing, what she was here for.

The baker tilted her head slightly. Lips pursed in amusement. "Did you leave your shopping list at home, then?" she boomed. "We've all done it. No shame in that."

"I . . ." Duck's words dissolved, unheard, in the sound of commerce around her. She tried to take in a breath and form a word, any word, but it was as if an entire castle were pressed on her chest.

"Sing out!" Master Griselde leaned even closer. "You're little more than a specter to my eyes, but I can still hear you just fine. I'm listening."

At those words, the realization dawned on Duck—the baker was blind.

Those clouds in her eyes were storms in her vision.

Master Griselde frowned slightly at Duck's silence, and though she hadn't yet directly met Duck's gaze, she did so now, tucking her chin down so it rippled against her neck.

"Bread?" the baker said simply, and lifted up a loaf as a reminder.

The divine scent of the baked crust hit Duck, and she managed to squeak out, "Six grain loaves." Tipping her hand sideways, she opened her clutch and let the sunlight reflect off the coin.

Master Griselde stacked the massive loaves on the counter in front of Duck. "One penny, please."

Duck clenched the coin and raised it above the baker's hand.

"*Misdirection*," she could hear Gnat whispering in her mind. "*You either wait for a chance or you make it yourself.*"

She watched Griselde's eyes carefully—the baker was facing her, waiting patiently, as if Duck were the only customer in the world and all the others pressing up to the counter behind her didn't count. But it was difficult to know where exactly those milky eyes were looking.

If they could see anything of the coin at all.

In the secrecy of her outstretched fist, Duck shuffled the coins. The silver penny moved flat against her palm, and she held it there, tucked under her thumb.

The wooden coin went between her fingers.

No need to wait for misdirection, she decided, when the mark is blind.

And then, with a single breath, the false coin went into Griselde Baker's hand.

The baker closed her fat fingers around it.

"Good morrow, Master Baker!" A man leaned above Duck's head. She looked up, and her heart dashed into her throat.

"Good morrow, Constable Deveraux!" Griselde Baker pocketed her wooden coin; Duck tracked it the whole way into her apron. "Can I tempt you with some sweet honey rolls?"

Above Duck, the constable pretended to hem and haw. "I really shouldn't . . ."

"What if I told you I baked them for you special?" Griselde

took an already-tied bundle from behind the counter that smelled of orange zest and beehives. "What if I told you I couldn't possibly sell these to any other customers, on account of they're just too delicious?"

She passed the bundle to the constable, who hesitated before accepting it.

He peeked inside the bundle and murmured. "Well, now, would you look at these?"

"Would if I could, Constable," Master Griselde replied with a grin that crinkled her eyes.

It was all very rehearsed. Duck sensed it was a weekly routine.

"You say hello to the missus for me," Griselde Baker said, and the constable nodded his thanks and left.

Then Duck wondered: Had she just witnessed a bribe? She hadn't seen Constable Deveraux pay.

She couldn't wait to share this information with Gnat. He kept a running list of such exchanges between law enforcement and villagers everywhere they went—a bit of blackmail in their pockets, just in case. He'd be thrilled with Duck for uncovering their first one here in Odierne.

Master Griselde looked back down at Duck without losing her grin. "Something else?"

Duck blinked. Strewn behind the baker was the confectionary, all of the pastries far greater glittering jewels than she was expected to bring back to the Crowns.

But something was tickling Duck's chest—the spark of victory and a bit of excess bravery that had nowhere else to go.

Should she try to get her hands on some of the pastries, too?

But a better idea sprang forth—from the baker herself. "Of course!" Master Griselde slapped her forehead. "I forgot your change! You gave me a coronet, did you not?"

Duck had not. She'd baited the baker with an old penny and had given her an old chunk of wagon wheel instead.

"One coronet minus a penny." The baker reached into the till and held out a stack of coins. "Here's your change."

Eleven pennies.

Eleven pennies in her hand.

Duck held her breath, mentally counting the steps between her and the alleyway: one, two, three . . .

"Does that look right to you?" Griselde studied Duck with her hazy eyes.

Duck didn't even glance at the coins as she took them; she didn't say another word to anyone.

She gathered her six loaves in her arms and put the pennies in her pocket as she pushed her way out of the crowd.

Then she ran.

The exit is as tricky as the lift itself—you should walk away as if you are as innocent as a spring lamb.

Duck knew she should slow down, but fear overtook her legs.

If the bread loaves were stacked end to end from the ground up, they would be more than half her height; they thumped against her chest as she left the square.

And in her pocket, the silver penny she'd brought to the bakery jingled like a song as it hit the other coins she'd tricked out of the baker.

When Duck was certain there weren't footsteps following her—that the master baker hadn't sent that chummy constable or her journeyman after her—she let herself walk.

Twelve pennies—that was an entire coronet! Twelve times the amount of money they'd brought with them to Odierne. This would be a fortune to the Crowns. They'd never had a whole coronet among them. Not all at once. Not in a single day.

They could get fabric for new tunics. They could get leather wrappings for shoes. They could get Drippy some of the fancy new spectacles Duck had seen rich people wearing to correct their poor sight—then he wouldn't have to squint with his good eye to see farther than a stone's throw.

And they could eat, of course. Eat well, eat long.

They could even get a full deck of playing cards. They'd been collecting individual cards on the streets for years, one lost card at a time. They were still missing a Five of Acorns and a Telgarian Trumpeter.

Duck had never been so aware of the power of a single penny.

She'd also never been so aware of how many places there were to lose a coin. A penny could fall through a gutter slat. It could be kicked by a boot, sliding behind the wheel of a parked cart. It could disappear under a stall. A bird could carry a penny off, or a rat— or a penny could simply slip out of her sweaty hand and roll away, lost forever in the labyrinth of Odierne's streets.

So she hitched the bread higher in her arms and scurried down the Rue Grande as quick as she could without looking suspicious.

The Crowns couldn't afford to have one of their own get caught.

Getting busted as a thief was bad enough on its own. The watch was not known for its leniency, even if the criminal was technically a child.

Prison, though, was miserable—dark and dank, with no fresh air or clean water, only mush for food, cells full of bugs and toads and real criminals: outlaws and cutthroats, conspirators and murderers.

The Crowns were criminals in the way sparrows were predators—to the worms they snatched out of the ground, yes, but did anyone ever bemoan the death of a worm?

But sparrows, hawks, bears—to the watchmen, they were all the same. And if the Crowns ever got snagged, there would be no hope of mercy. So Duck stuck to the safety of the shadows as she made her way to the secret meeting place, a dusty abandoned cathedral in the western quarter of the city. Only pigeons lived there, along with random remainders of human passersby: chicken bones, empty wine jugs, a lonely shoe buckle on the porch.

Remnants from the cathedral's halted progress were scattered everywhere, too: piles of loose stones, splintered lumber, half-finished tapestries that had never been hung. There was a foundation for a lesser bishop's palace that had likewise been abandoned, souring yellowed weeds poking up between the stones. No need for a bishop without a cathedral.

"It's perfect," Gnat had said yesterday when the Crowns had scoped it out. "Near enough to the shops in the square, far enough away to avoid suspicion. There's lots of good places around here we could hit. Plus," he'd said with a nasty smile, "there's plenty of garbage for you, Garbage."

A few other Crowns had snickered, and Duck had gotten the feeling it was mostly out of relief that they were not the targets of

Gnat's antagonism. Duck never knew how to react when he made such jokes, and he seemed to be making them a lot more lately. He teased the other Crowns, too, make no mistake—but it was never with the same barb that he reserved for Duck.

Was it because she was the youngest? Was it because until now, she'd never run a scam of her own? Was it because she'd handled only smaller swipes, and reluctantly—coins out of purses, pears out of baskets?

Or was it something else?

The cathedral sprawled along a street otherwise occupied by a few shops that never seemed to be open and a run-down abbey.

Beyond that, the Sarluire, recently unfrozen, made a lazy springtime trickle, weaving past the cathedral and on to better things.

Duck readjusted the loaves steady under her chin. Their scent was so intoxicating, their crusts a hard warm comfort against her body as she walked out of daylight and into the chilly morning shade created by the towering cathedral. She inhaled, and a note of something unexpected hit her nose.

Rosemary.

That was the herb that always found her. Rosemary.

A curl of steam escaped from a slight crack in a loaf's crust. She followed it up until it faded against the roof. No clock tower, no spires. Only a haystack of wooden slats and stones piled into an imagined steeple . . .

She leaned back, squinting. Five granite figures hunched on the roof—gargoyles, particularly nasty ones, all of them crackling and crumbling on their perches. Ugly little watchmen.

But they didn't seem to mind the Crowns. Perhaps they were happy for the company, Duck thought as she climbed the steps of the porch and went through the arched doors.

The inside of the cathedral was even more of a mess than its decrepit exterior, but the Crowns had stayed in worse places. They'd made shelters in dark, rocky caves, beneath bridges, in piles of rancid hay, in drippy underground holes more suited for rats than humans, in dangerously high towers that were one windy day away from toppling into ruins.

Maybe other orphans would have given themselves over to the church, or else found farms and manors to work for—a lifetime of dedication to a friar or a lord in exchange for room and board.

But the Crowns preferred the streets. The streets meant freedom. Meals were never guaranteed, yes, and sometimes they went hungry for far longer than any of them could stand, but they were their own masters. Beholden to no one.

And that was far better than a full gut.

Yes, Duck could sleep anywhere—but she found a peculiar feeling come over her as she stepped under the clean, unfinished ribbing of the vaults.

A sense of pride. Of belonging.

Of security.

Was that simply the feeling of unspent coins in her pocket?

Or could this cathedral possibly be home? At least for a little while?

Three Cheers for Duck

"She's back!" The Crowns were gathered in the nave. A great hole in the unfinished northern wall, where a rose window should have been installed, meant the chamber was open, swimming in daylight, making the cool blue shadows in the cathedral even more pronounced.

Duck kept one still-piping loaf under her arm and set down the rest of them on a long pew that needed to be sanded before any worshippers could put their well-upholstered rears on it.

Everyone was sitting or sprawling around a toppled pillar except for Gnat, who leaned against the far wall, his expression unreadable. He had all sorts of ways of leaning like this, to mask his shriveled right arm, which clung to his body like a gnarled vine. He pivoted his right side toward the stones; his left hand was busy working on a new knot. Gnat carried a length of rope with him everywhere and could tie complex knots and bows with five functioning fingers quicker than anyone else could with ten. "The right knot at the right time could save your life," he loved to preach. But for now, he spotted Duck and said coldly, "Did anyone see you?"

Duck shook her head.

"Did you circle the block before you came in?" he asked, pushing away from the wall as he put away his rope. He took the loaf from her hands.

Duck nodded. She had gone around the block twice, just to be careful.

"So quiet. Did you forget how to quack, little duckling?" Gnat tore away a chunk of bread and sniffed it before eating.

She held her breath.

It wasn't that Duck couldn't talk.

It was just—words didn't come as easily to her as they did to the other Crowns.

Spinner and Fingers, the other two girls in the gang, were not as talkative as Drippy or Ash, but they could still string sentences together with no trouble. Even Le Chou, who didn't say much, said enough.

No one said as much as Frog Eyes, who talked enough for all of them, and no one said things the way Gnat did—Gnat didn't flap his gums constantly, but when he spoke, he said the right things. When he spoke, people listened. Duck knew she would never be able to say anything like that.

But still.

Duck always managed to say enough. She very nearly opened her mouth to say just such a thing to Gnat now—but then she realized what he'd called her.

He'd called her "little duckling."

Not "Garbage."

Still not her name, but an improvement.

Gnat swallowed the bread.

The Crowns surrounded him, all of them watching, waiting for the worst. Gnat always tested whatever they brought in first, just in case.

Always ready to save them, Gnat.

"All right," he said after a minute. "Seems fine. Dig in."

The bread was parceled out as evenly as possible—four of the six loaves were split in half to make eight chunks, one for each of them.

"Oh, yum!" Frog Eyes tore off a chunk with his teeth like a starved puppy. "Fank you, Lord, for dis food," he said, his mouth stuffed.

Spinner chortled, reaching past him to grab her own share of bread. "You want to thank someone, thank Duck."

Duck quickly looked at her feet.

She wanted them all to think she'd done a good job. But she didn't want them to . . . to *thank* her like that. To make such a fuss. She'd just done what was needed for them to survive. She'd just done what a Crown had to do.

"These loaves are monstrous!"

"Honestly, this'll keep us full for days!"

The clamors were highly approving, with bonus praises to Gnat for finding this bakery in the first place—it was amazing how empty tummies made all these ruffians so grateful.

Two loaves were left over. One of them was wrapped up in muslin to save for emergencies; if it got too hard, they could always soak it in stolen ale to soften it again.

The other loaf was called the king loaf, which always went to that day's lifter as a payment for risking their skin.

And today, for the first time in her life, that was Duck. Half a loaf just for being a Crown, and a whole other loaf to her name. But Gnat held the king loaf over her head, out of her reach.

"Go on, Gnat, let her eat," Ash prodded.

"Hang on a minute." Gnat lifted his chin and eyed her. "Where's the penny?"

Duck's heart clamored. The other Crowns stopped cheering, sensing blood as she reached into her pocket.

She had been practicing this very move in her mind the whole walk back from the bakery.

She held the tarnished silver coin between her thumb and forefinger and gave it to Gnat—the same penny he'd sent her with this morning.

When he looked down, a whole pool of coins spilled out from under the single penny.

Ash's reaction didn't disappoint. "Holy bones! What'd you do, Duck, pick pockets?"

"No!" Duck rushed to say, seeing the gleam of venom in Gnat's eye. Fingers was the only one allowed to dip into purses and pockets with abandon. Fingers and Gnat. Fingers was fast enough; Gnat was clever enough. Everyone else had to get permission before they even tried it.

"I shortchanged the baker." Duck let this confession roll out of her mouth unabashedly.

"Brilliant!" burst Le Chou.

"Well done!" Ash clapped her on the back. "Now we have enough to feast for weeks!"

"Feast! Feast! Feast!" chanted the other Crowns, giddy with victory, until Gnat shot them a look.

"Brilliant? Or reckless?" Duck imagined Gnat asking, and her insides lurched. What if her stunt with the coins had made her too memorable for the baker? They'd have to find a different mark for their next scam. Or what if someone had noticed her swap and followed her back to the cathedral, and any minute, the place would be swarming with constables? Gnat was never going to give her another job again. No—even worse, he was going to kick her out of the Crowns.

Duck had no one, nowhere to go—how would she survive without them? Her breath grew spiky—

But instead of a tongue-lashing, Gnat handed her the king loaf. "Nice job, Garbage," he said. "Looks like you managed to pull it off—this time, anyway."

"Wait a minute!" Frog Eyes reached for one of the pennies. "Just wait a minute—yes! I knew it! We've swiped this coin before! Look at it—this divot, right here. It kind of looks like a butt. See?" He held it up, and everyone leaned in—yes, the way the silver was dented, it did look like a butt. Duck couldn't verify that it was a familiar butt, but Frog Eyes was convinced.

He placed it back in Gnat's hand, smug. "That coin followed us all the way from Perpinnet. We used it on sausages, remember? And now it's here. That's a good omen, that is."

Yesterday's dinner had been a single bowl of beef stew, swiped from a merchant's windowsill and shared between the eight of them.

The day before that, their dinner had been the dream of dinner.

Now they all sat or lay along the pews, nibbling with contentment. Duck pictured the bread filling up all their hollow parts— bellies, yes, but also their heads, their legs, their big toes.

Ash was the first to finish his portion. He brushed the crumbs from his tunic, licked his fingers, and sighed. "I haven't been this full in weeks."

"These are the biggest loaves I've ever seen." Drippy, a pipsqueak of a boy with a perpetually runny nose, sniffled and held up the bread to examine his last bite with his weak eyes. "As big as a constable's left boot."

Duck was reluctant to claim the king loaf in front of everyone, but Ash nodded encouragingly at her, and so she tore out the softest, fluffiest section from the heart of the loaf and took a bite. It tasted like yeasted clouds.

"I'm saving half of mine for tomorrow." Spinner shoved her leftovers into her pockets.

"And this place is a paradise!" Le Chou leaped onto the stacks of stones as if he were claiming it for the queen of Avilogne.

Gnat tilted his head back to survey the rough beams of the ceiling, the glassless windows, the dried mud and construction dust that formed a carpet on the floor. "It is kind of charming, isn't it?"

"It's waterfront property." Frog Eyes pointed to the steely-blue Sarluire, visible through a great big hole in the wall.

"And look—the place is clean." Ash wasn't referring to the actual cleanliness of the cathedral, which was far from godliness—he was talking about the fact that there were no other markings, no signs that other gangs had claimed this as their territory.

Gnat grinned and handed him a sharp rock. "Do us the honors, then."

Ash chose a spot that was easily visible from the porch but would also require effort to erase, a real demonstration of malice—he climbed to where the altar would have been, had this been a functioning, finished cathedral, and he drew their symbol on the stones with the rock. A five-point crown, messily rendered—what it meant was more important than how it looked.

"There." Ash leaped down from his perch, flushed and beaming. "A little decoration."

"It's been a long time since we had a wall to draw on." Gnat spread his left arm wide. "Welcome home, Crowns."

Warmth flourished in Duck's chest.

Home.

"Our fingers be nimble!" someone started.

"To our graves, be swift!" another added.

"And on every head a crown!" the rest of them chorused.

Though the bread she'd swiped was delicious, Duck had been craving this moment, right here, for much longer.

She had almost forgotten how it felt to be able to exhale, to rest, to stop longer than was necessary to rub the grit off the bottoms of her feet. For a month, they'd slept in shifts, roamed, crouched in tunnels, divided their scraped-together meals into tiny sections that only echoed in their tummies like pebbles dropped into dried-up wells.

Some gangs were little more than feral dogs, guided by their noses, disorganized, undisciplined—but not the Crowns. Gnat ran a tight ship. There were rules and procedures and oaths.

Not a day went by that Duck didn't feel lucky. She'd been adopted into the Crowns as a wee baby. She'd had Ash to vouch for her.

Ash had wanted her.

Even if Gnat hadn't.

The harsh reality was that if Duck found the Crowns now, as a recently orphaned child on the streets, Gnat probably wouldn't let her in. He'd tell her to eat snails.

Sometimes he looked at her like he was going to say it now.

It wasn't his fault, not entirely—Gnat had been stressed lately. They all had. It killed him to drag his constituents around like this, from alleyway to bridge to lodge, scanning for potential places to live, only to find a stallion or a pair of crossed axes or a chalice chalked onto the walls, a sign that another gang had already claimed the area as theirs.

The Crowns had been pushed all the way to Chatoyant County, all the way out to the sheep lands. Odierne was their last chance at city life before they would have been forced to break apart, find jobs on farms.

Life as a Crown was a life on the move. Duck always woke up with the possibility that she might be falling asleep somewhere else that night.

But maybe now things could be different.

Duck found a dry corner of the cavernous nave and settled on her knees, chewing on her bread. It was so hearty, one of the best they'd ever stolen.

She allowed herself to feel the teeniest bit of triumph—she'd pulled off her first real job, and she'd done it with a flourish.

Extra coins and bread to fill everyone to the gills.

Everything was going to be all right.

"A moment of your attention, Crowns, and then the day is yours." Gnat hopped onto an old barrel, waiting for his underlings to settle. "We seem to find ourselves, for the first time in recent memory, with a surplus of goods and money—"

"All thanks to our very own Duck!" Ash clapped, and the rest of the gang hooted and cheered. Duck blushed with pride but was sickened when Gnat narrowed his eyes at her as though she were the enemy.

"Let's not name names," Gnat said. "We all played a role. Anyway, the point is that now we have eleven extra pennies, and I've got a proposal for what to do with them." He paused and glanced at each of them. "The hot fair."

All the Crowns looked at him with wide eyes.

The fairs of Chatoyant were famous far and wide—the cloth-producing merchants of the Lower Countries brought their wares up along the ancient roads to sell in open-air markets. The first hot fair started in mere hours and would last for a fortnight, ending with a bonfire feast on the Eve of the Splendid.

They were the very heartbeat of rural Avilognian commerce, these fairs—a boasting of colorful wares, endless food stalls selling shiny produce and spiced meats, an absolute holy grail for the seedy, hardworking thieves of this kingdom. But sadly, these bustling spectacles had never set up anywhere the Crowns called home . . . until tonight. Tonight, the Crowns would finally get to see one—but not as thieves. As *customers.*

"We're coming to the close of some difficult times, Crowns,"

Gnat's speech went on. "I say we go out tonight and celebrate in style. Who's with me?"

The Crowns erupted in cheers—all except Duck, whose thoughts were a jumble. She'd been a Crown all her life—raised on their stolen food, clothed in the outfits they'd yanked off the dangling lines between buildings. Today, for the first time ever, there was a surplus—and Gnat wanted to *spend* it?

Gnat, their fearless leader, who catalogued every crumb they swiped, now had a gleam in his eye that was completely unrecognizable to Duck. He rolled one of the pennies along the knuckles of his left hand.

"Then it's settled," he told his gang. "We meet back here just before sundown for the fair. Feel free to wander, Crowns—sightsee, run around, squabble over which corner of the cathedral will be yours. But keep your noses clean, do you understand? Absolutely no lifting, no scams, no picking pockets. No trouble."

The Crowns needed no further instruction. They were a ruthless scraping street gang, yes, but they were also children, and now that their guts were full, their egos boosted, and their heads brimming with the dreamy possibilities the night held—eleven extra pennies! A whole coronet! The hot fair!—they scattered. They climbed the broken pews like mountain goats, jumping and swinging and playing.

They crawled up the walls like spiders, leaping onto one another's backs. They wrestled, they hopped down the stairs two at a time, they found sticks to use as swords and split into fighting pairs, joyfully making whacks that could be heard all the way down the road.

Happy, feral children.

Most of them *were* still children, technically. Gnat and Ash stretched the definition of "child" at around sixteen. Spinner and Frog Eyes were fourteen, Le Chou and Fingers thirteen. Drippy was only eleven, but that was still older than Duck, who, at eight years old, was still a baby compared to the others—and they made sure she never forgot it.

Duck watched her fellow Crowns leave in pairs to explore the surrounding neighborhood.

Across the cathedral, Gnat found a new spot on the wall to lean against, his left hand tying a knot in his rope as he chewed the last of his crust.

Another oddity—Gnat never horked down his daily bread; he usually nibbled at it, an inch a day, keeping it in his pockets until it was nearly too stale to suffer.

Surviving on the streets required caution. Gnat pounded this into the Crowns with rules and systems, especially because most of them were like unleashed beagles. But caution grew inside Gnat like an organ.

So then why was he so freely gobbling up his entire share of bread today instead of hoarding it in case it would be his last meal for a week? Why was he taking them to the hot fair to spend their coins, as if money could easily be fished from the Sarluire with nets?

Gnat looked up at Duck just then, his features pinching with suspicion, and Duck gathered the rest of her king loaf and marched up the spiral masons' stairs, up to the roof.

A good omen, Frog Eyes had said of the butt-imprinted penny, and at this moment, Duck hoped he was right.

Ash and Dust

Duck had been on roofs before. She had seen the views from atop western facades in Perpinnet. She'd seen the stars glitter while perched on barns in Tortues. She'd seen the sunrise, seen the morning birds pepper the sky in sheer black clouds while crouching in trees that belonged, like the Crowns, to nowhere in particular.

She'd seen the best and most beautiful views in Avilogne, ones typically reserved for aristocrats' balconies or sacred spires.

This was not one of them.

The view of the river winding east behind the unfinished cathedral was ordinary. The opposite end of the roof showed all of Odierne, but was obscured by the blunt plainness of the city's other rooftops—the thatched straw of the burghers' homes, the slate tiles of the wealthy nobles' manors, the steeples of the churches.

To the south of the cathedral, there was a laundry, a square brick shop with a large yard that was open to the Sarluire. Inside the yard were wooden troughs full of tablecloths and bed linens soaking in wood ashes and soda, cauldrons of water boiling over fires, buckets of soft soaps made from glistening animal fat. Sheets were stretched out on tables, drying in the sun.

To the north of the cathedral, there was a simple abbey, cozy cells and covered cloisters surrounding a sprawling, vibrant garden. That was about the only beautiful thing she could see: those wattle fences hung with honeysuckle and fruit trees and ornamental flowers, flashes of color against Odierne's dullness. It felt like a secret, one only she had uncovered.

A mangy gray cat darted through the empty churchyard on quick feet; it settled in the shade of the cathedral's porch and stared out into the street, whiskers twitching, before heading to some unknown hiding spot.

It was a quiet corner of the market district, a quiet rooftop. The only sounds were the trickle of the Sarluire and the trills of pigeons roosting in the eaves, gentle enough to be soothing.

Quiet enough that Duck could finally hear all the thoughts in her head.

She loved being a Crown. But sometimes she needed to be alone, just for a moment.

The only other ones up here were the gargoyles on the ledges. Duck walked past all five of them on the east ledge, pausing to lean over and look at their grimaces, some of which were so exaggerated it was comical. They were covered with white splotches of bird poo, but beneath that, their stone reflected the light in little glints and sparkles as the sun shone.

One gargoyle, though, was not lined up with his friends. Duck crossed the roof to the huge, hulking gargoyle who faced west and took in the sight of him. He was a grouchy, grandfather-esque grotesque whose thick eyebrows, easily weighing five pounds apiece, were scrunched down on his forehead, creating shady awnings over his eyes.

Those eyes . . . they were made of stone, and yet there was something charged about them, a heat beneath the cold. Almost like if she glanced away, he would blink.

She tested it once, just in case—but when she looked back at him half a moment later, his eyes were still stone.

Duck sat beside this gargoyle, peering over the ledge, and watched the river beneath, the flow of silt and ripples, the water absorbing the early afternoon light and taking it away, taking it somewhere else.

"All hail the king!" Ash came bounding up the masons' steps and leaped over the colossal pieces of an unassembled bell tower. "Would you like to know exactly how much you won for me today?" He came up next to her and spread a collection of items on the ground between them—an almost-gone spool of blue thread, a hard cube of salt, a fork with one tine missing, some old peach pits, other oddities and knickknacks. "Behold, my spoils."

"Gnat says we shouldn't gamble," Duck said. Her tongue loosened in Ash's presence—she was always able to find the words she needed when she knew he was the only one listening.

"Gnat knows the rules are meant to be bent." Ash pointed to several items in succession: "That I won from Le Chou when you didn't wimp out and buy the bread with our honest coin. That I won from Drippy when you didn't try to squirrel away a loaf for yourself. That I won from Frog Eyes when you didn't get lost coming back here. And all three of them had to give me the peach pits when you didn't get yourself arrested."

He found a pebble on the roof and threw it, trying to reach the river, then grinned at her.

Maybe someone else would have heard all these wagers against her and felt like the pebble, sinking into the water. But Duck looked at all the ways Ash had bet on her to succeed and felt like she was flying.

He tossed another rock into the river, and the two of them arched over the ledge to watch the ripples as they cascaded out and blended into the still, cool blue.

"She's blind," Duck said after a moment.

"Who?"

"Griselde Baker." She rested her chin in her hands.

"Blind." Ash swatted away an overly aggressive fly. "Huh."

Duck looked at Ash. "'Huh?' That's all?"

He put up his hands. "I'm sorry! Why does it matter?"

She paused. "Should we be stealing from someone who's blind? Isn't that taking advantage?"

"We don't steal. We relieve people of their excesses, remember?" Ash was only jesting—Gnat would lecture them until Doomsday if he heard them talking like this.

There had been many attempts to moralize their way of life over the years—*People lose coins all the time, so why shouldn't they fall into our outstretched hands rather than onto the street? Food is thrown away every day, so why shouldn't it go into our mouths rather than rotting away in gutters? We're helping; we're restoring balance.*

We're curbing the potential disintegration of the wealthy immortal souls. We are cleansing the city of greedy ruin—but Gnat always shut such comments down.

"You're all thieves," he told them. "You'd steal the last drops of milk from a poor baby's bottle if you could get away with it. You're not divine, you're not balancing anything, and if you'd prefer a more ethical allotment in life, go turn yourself in to a bishop— I guarantee you'll eat better as a Crown."

When Duck didn't smile at Ash's joke, he nudged her. "Aw, I'm only ribbing. Look, don't feel guilty. We're just seizing an opportunity, aren't we? The same as if we took the bread from anyone else."

Duck replayed the morning in her mind—the milky films over the baker's eyes, the wooden dummy in her pocket, the transfer of coins from the baker's huge hand to her own small, clammy one.

"It felt . . ." Duck needed a moment to find the right word. Ash was patient as he waited. "Wrong."

For a moment, the two of them listened to the calm stream of the river, the pleasant trill of a pigeon. Yes, wrong. That was the best way to describe it.

But now it all made sense—why Gnat had selected Duck for this swipe in the first place. Gnat had picked the easiest target in Odierne, and using the false coins made robbing the baker as effortless as falling off a log. A scam so simple, even Duck couldn't possibly bungle it up.

"Wrong, huh?" Ash scratched his head. "I don't know, Duck. Maybe you're not ready to lift."

She shifted her legs. Maybe he was right.

For years, Duck had heard the other Crowns talk about that

feeling, when pulling a scam, when you realize you've successfully done it—the thrill of plucking what you need from someone as easily as picking berries from a bush. That spark of fear, and the excitement and the freedom when you walk away unseen . . .

She would feel it any moment. She had to.

"Did it feel wrong to you?" she asked. "When you made your first lift?"

Ash pursed his lips, glancing up at the sky as he thought. "I guess I felt a little strange about it. Gnat had me take a goose— not cooked, still alive," he clarified. "I remember looking at the goose in my hands," he said, "and wondering if it knew it was being stolen. I wondered if it missed its owner, and if the owner missed it." Honestly. Of all the Crowns, Ash would be the one to ascribe free will to a goose. "The guilt went away the minute Gnat traded the bird for a nice fat rack of bacon."

Duck looked up at the gargoyle, trying to focus her thoughts. What then, if she couldn't lift anymore? Gnat didn't tolerate free-loaders. Would he let her go back to one of her old jobs? Backup or marking or casing? Or would he kick her out? No one had ever been kicked out of the Crowns. They were a team. A family. Gnat made threats to all of them when they were behaving out of line, but he couldn't just decide she wasn't a Crown anymore . . . could he?

The gargoyle's eternal scowl seemed to mock her—*Stop your stewing, girl. You're a Crown through and through. So start acting like one.*

Duck knew she was different from the others. It wasn't that she was a girl—Fingers and Spinner were girls, too. Maybe this would create waves among the Crowns in the coming years—Duck had picked up enough knowledge on the streets to understand the changes that might one day create a chasm between the girls and the boys—but that was a problem for future Duck to worry about when the time came.

It wasn't that they'd found her as an orphan. None of the other Crowns had had families—though to be honest, none of them could remember that far back.

"You're Crowns now," Gnat loved to remind them, "and that's all that matters." Gnat's principle was that your origins were annulled as soon as you took your first bite of stolen bread.

But Duck, being the youngest . . . they all remembered that night.

Still, she'd been as parentless as the rest of them, so it was something else, then, that set her apart. Something she only felt every once in a while. Something she noticed in the corner of her eye or between the beats of her heart. She was happy to be a Crown—they were her family, all she'd ever known. But she often wondered if they felt like she belonged with them as much as she did.

"Ash?" Duck made her request with the slightest flutter of nerves. "Will you tell me? About the night you found me?"

It was not the first time she'd asked to hear this story, but you wouldn't know it by the excitable gleam in Ash's eye. He cracked his knuckles, preparing for his speech as if he were a bishop on Easter. "Picture a quaint little town, kind of like this one. It was pissing rain that night. So dark and stormy, you couldn't see a silver penny if it flew past your nose."

The discovery of the baby in the river had become lore, a tale retold as often as the time Gnat stole a whole drum of oil from a moving cart, or the time Le Chou fell asleep while on guard duty, rolled out of a tree, and landed in a barrel of overripe plums.

"Eight years ago." Ash shook his head as if he were old enough to be nostalgic. "You were just an itty-bitty face poking out of the reeds, and we pulled you out."

"*You* pulled me out," Duck said.

"Good thing I did, or else you would have paddled on down the river like a little duck and some other gang would have snatched you up for themselves." Ash kindly steered around the truth of what would have happened if the Crowns hadn't found her—the only thing that would have snatched her up was the eels. "But lucky for us, we found you. And you know what?" He got real close to Duck and whispered, like no one else could know this: "I knew, even back then, that someday you'd surprise us all."

Gnat said it didn't matter where you came from. What mattered was that you were found.

And it was Ash who had found her. Ash who had cleaned the river muck off her. Ash who had dressed her in suitable rags. Ash, who was a child himself, probably no more than seven or eight years old.

It was Ash who had kept her.

"How long until the fair?" Duck asked.

Ash shrugged. "A while. We've got all day. Want to go explore the block?"

"Yes." Duck inhaled before she added, with a bit of force, "I want to scope out some new places to hit when it's my turn to lift again."

Ash's eyes lit up approvingly. "I'll go see if Frog Eyes and the Cabbage want to come." He swept his collection of winnings into his pocket and climbed down the scaffolding.

Duck stayed on the messy roof for another minute. If the rest of the Crowns approved, she'd like to claim the roof as her room.

Sometimes all those wild children smelled like gutters, especially the boys. It would be nice to have a break from the stink. And yes, the Sarluire was exceptionally odorous in the summer heat, but the breeze up here was fresh and light.

Furthermore, something about this big, burly gargoyle made her feel safe. He was large enough to hide behind, large enough to cast a shadow twice the size of Duck. She gave him one last pat on the horns and blew all the city grime and sky dust from his crevices.

He couldn't speak, but that suited her just fine. Silence was a fine companion.

And speaking of silence . . .

Duck hadn't asked Ash about Gnat. She'd meant to—she wanted Ash's take on Gnat's apparently newfound high-rolling ways. She had a hunch Ash might dismiss it as simple generosity on Gnat's part, ignoring the fact that generosity was not one of Gnat's strong points.

But still. Ash hadn't brought it up, so maybe Duck was fretting over nothing. She trusted Ash. And Gnat had never led the Crowns astray.

Getting to her feet, Duck reflected on the coronet, split eight ways like a loaf of bread.

Maybe Gnat was so willing to spend the coins at the hot fair because he knew Odierne would be a lucrative enough city for them to simply replace those coins. Maybe Gnat looked at the coins not as invaluable resources to be hoarded like treasure, but as the flotsam and jetsam of an ever-bountiful river of commerce.

The tide gaveth and the tide tooketh away, and these coins that had washed ashore into their palms today could, if they wanted to throw them back into the waters at the hot fair, be swept back into their hands again in one way or another.

"Enjoy the view," she told the gargoyle, then bolted down the stairs after Ash.

Night at the Fair

Duck had never realized how heavy a single penny could feel in a pocket.

As though she were carrying a brick.

It wasn't just her pocket—the coin also weighed heavy on her mind. With every step, she was reminded of its presence and wondered if the rest of the world, the strangers she passed on the streets, knew she had it.

So this was how it felt to be a mark. Vulnerable. All it would take was one wrong move. One moment of lowered vigilance, and the coin would be gone. She knew well how quickly it could be taken.

Duck couldn't remember a time when she'd had a penny of her own—but now that she'd experienced it, she wasn't sure she cared for it.

As soon as the sun began its descent into the distant hills, the Crowns had all lined up on the cathedral steps.

Gnat had passed out their allowance—one penny apiece. The rest of the money, he'd announced, was going into savings, which they'd all agreed was a smart idea. They'd never had a rainy-day fund before.

"Live it up, Crowns," he'd crooned. "These coins are yours to do with as you like. Buy yourself a new pair of hose. Gorge on turkey legs and apple cider. Go see a mud squad—whatever you want. The night is yours—"

"Wait," Ash had called out, and raised Duck's hand in the air. "I think it's only fair we give a cheer to Duck! Patron Saint of Gluttony, the financier of our gala!"

"To Duck! To Duck! To Duck!" they all sang out; Duck tried not to notice Gnat's half-hearted sneer of "Garbage, Garbage, Garbage."

Her hair made a cave around her as she hung her head, shy; she looked down at the penny in her hand, seeing the imprint of the butt in its metal. Her first time lifting for the rest of them, and she was so squeamish about letting these coins go. What if she couldn't do it again? What if today's triumph was just pure luck?

She squeezed the coin tight, warming it. *It came back to us once*, she thought. *It could come back again.*

"All right, you louses," their leader finally said. "The fair awaits. Tonight, we spend like kings!" And the Crowns had run down the cathedral steps and into the streets of Odierne like puppies newly freed from their leashes. Duck followed behind them and glanced back once at the unfinished cathedral—the growing darkness made silhouettes of the gargoyles on the ledge.

Keep it safe while we're gone, she asked silently of the stony monsters, and quickly skipped to catch up with her people.

⁂   ⁂   ⁂

The Crowns had been wandering around Avilogne for all of Duck's life, and in those eight years, they had seen many things. They'd watched *Le Mystère d'Adam* on an outdoor stage in a southern churchyard where a sheep had played the role of the devil. They'd dunked their heads in the public baths in Sainte Lucienne. They'd eaten pears in the Perpinnet free-for-all at Michaelmas. They'd had front-row seats to the great Illyon goat disaster of 1248, when a runaway cart had broken a fence penning a couple dozen goats and loosed them onto the streets at Easter. They'd roamed the eerily empty town when Florellis was on lockdown during the almost-siege by the Throgs.

But Duck had never seen anything like the hot fair.

First, the lights.

Lanterns were strung between hoisted poles; lamps staggered along the edges of the roads. Everything was aglow, turning the village green picturesque and magnificent.

A cornucopia of booths and stalls sprawled from road to road. From almost a block away, Duck could see vegetables, fish, and other goodies—she instinctively curled her fingers around the penny in her pocket but also felt an excited fluttering in her stomach.

"You've been keeping this secret from us for far too long, Avilogne," Ash whispered. His eyes were all bugged out at the sight of a table full of puzzle boxes, which Duck knew he coveted but had never been able to swipe. Maybe tonight, with an entire penny to his name, he'd finally be able to haggle his way into owning one.

Vendors of both perfectly legal and possibly illicit goods lined the green. There were, of course, the staples of such markets, only heightened in quality and far more numerous in selection, but there were also extraordinary wares, the stuff of dreams.

Cloth hawkers held up bolts of fine silk, wool, cotton, all patterns, all textures. Samples of heavy brocade hung between the booths in a kaleidoscope of colors—vermilion, rose, gold. Keepers of the fair strolled up and down the rows with their iron rulers, checking measurements against the lengths trimmed by the merchants from Virian, upholding the standard.

The next cluster of booths Duck could smell before they reached them.

Garlic Row. The spices.

"Behold, cinnamon sticks!" one merchant called. "Birds of Khazia build their nests with this aromatic fruit—come take a whiff, and you will see why!"

"Peppercorns, fresh peppercorns straight from the Silver Sea!" another one cried out. "Packed through snowy mountain passes, caught by the Ptolomians themselves in their fishing nets and sold to longshoremen like pearls—every housewife's dream! Get your peppercorns here!"

"Cassia from lakes guarded by winged beasts!"

"Saffron gathered by brush from the royal sunlit boughs of Pasha!"

Duck wanted to stay and smell every jarred spice, every herb bundle hung to dry.

But there was too much to see still, too much to take in.

Other booths sold precious stones, unpolished and crackling with shiny hard edges, like they had been hammered out of the mountain only hours ago.

A blanket spread with glittering jewels, which looked like a galaxy—were they real gems? Or clever imitations?

Racks of tall beaver hats, sold in the same booth as baskets of stockfish and cockles and eels.

Carved chess sets from the south. Cabrian leather shoes.

A bookseller, a corker with wine, and doves.

Telgarian ornaments. Angollian yarn.

And the food, oh! The food. "Many a pie! Beef, four a penny, pork, three for one!" the pie man shouted of his lovely stock, pies stacked in long lines with browned crusts and slits for curlicues of steam to escape and tempt the passersby.

Other mouthwatering booths sold roasted parsnips, bacon on sticks, every flavor of cheese, and cubes of sugar.

And the entertainment! Somehow, Duck hadn't anticipated the hot fair would have such a cache of underground jugglers, fire-eaters, and sword dancers, but they were everywhere. Pipers and puppeteers and trained greyhounds and storytellers, and more. The Crowns stopped collectively to watch a man invite people from the crowd to add items to the broom he balanced on his chin—a bottle, a plate, a spoon.

"I want to learn to do that." Frog Eyes marveled at the man singing and playing the lute who paused between words to catch currants in his mouth.

"You'd never go hungry," Ash said. "Rich is the man who can fiddle for his bread."

Next to Duck, Fingers suddenly froze, her jaw dropping. "It's . . . it's her," she stammered. "It's really her!"

Duck followed her gaze across the row to a knight dressed in emerald-green linens, chain mail, and armor so silver, it practically shone in the dark. Men and women alike tossed flowers as the knight signed autographs, gripping a swan's feather quill in her metal gauntlets.

"It's the Green Dragon," Fingers whispered, her hands twitching with excitement as she stared at the celebrity knight. "Winner of six tournament grand championships. This is the greatest living sword fighter in Avilogne, do you understand?"

"And currently standing only twenty feet away from you." Ash gave Fingers a gentle nudge.

Fingers took a step forward, then stopped herself, shaking her head. "No. I wouldn't know what to say! I can't just—just say *hello*. It's the Green Dragon!" She trailed away, but gave the knight one last longing glance over her shoulder.

Duck knew Fingers was itching for an autograph. Fingers had always been a fan of the jousting sports. She followed the tournaments every season, gleaning the highlights from eavesdropped conversations outside of pubs.

But it was probably best that Fingers didn't stand in line to meet the Green Dragon. It would call attention to the Crowns, this ragtag group of children with coins to spend.

What a shame, Duck thought, a blaze of injustice coursing through her as she and Ash followed Fingers away from the knight's bustling crowd of adorers.

With or without money, there were still some things the Crowns couldn't have.

Still, every Crown was enchanted by the offerings of the hot fair, but none so much as Ash. He wore his penny out, and fast.

Instead of spending it all on a puzzle box, he bought himself a meat pie, some ale, a couple of paper trinkets, and a trio of pomegranate tarts that slicked his teeth red.

The other Crowns did just as well with their coins. They bought new dice, pastries, a little tin of salt, honey-water, fabric scraps, a knife, and a worm, which was definitely meant to be fish bait, but Frog Eyes had already grown attached and named it Ringer.

Duck made a great orbit of the fair, fascinated by and desirous of most of the things she saw, then found herself back in Garlic Row with Ash, who tried to rush her past a Hamish spice stall run by twin mustachioed brothers—but the smell of rosemary hit her like the north wind.

She picked up a sprig, bringing it to her nose.

"You haven't spent your penny yet," Ash pointed out, chomping into his third tart. "You gonna grind that up? Put it on your bread?"

Duck wished she could disappear into this scent.

But the penny in her pocket felt too heavy to lift. She took a good long whiff, then set the rosemary back in the stall.

She was definitely hungry—they'd passed a woman roasting a game fowl on a stick, and the sight of the glistening meat had made Duck's head spin—but she wasn't sure it was a good idea to make promises to her stomach that she couldn't keep. It wasn't like she'd be able to eat this way again tomorrow night. Tomorrow night, it would be back to scraps.

Anyway, she still had bread at home. She drooled at the memory of how it had tasted—like coming inside to a fire after being outside on a blizzardy day.

By now, most of the Crowns had looped through the hot fair once or twice and congregated in the place where the village green split in half to let the canal serpentine past, their legs dangling off the dock.

She and Ash joined them, and Ash pushed an apple into her hands.

"You need to eat something," he said when she tried to protest, and so she bit into it—sharp and yummy.

"What do we think of our new neighborhood, lads?" Gnat was the only one who wasn't munching, but he looked around at them as if he had personally procured their meals for the evening.

"I'm ready to put out a welcome mat," Frog Eyes said, licking the sausage grease from under his fingernails.

"If we can pull off scams like that every week . . ." Fingers said, and Duck's gut flip-flopped. She liked the feeling of having money, liked the part where she could walk through a market and buy something. Even though she hadn't spent it yet, just knowing the coin was hers . . . It was such a comfort. Imagine living like this all the time.

Bread and apples every week, if they ripped off that blind baker on Saturdays when the market opened.

And rosemary . . .

Maybe she should have bought it after all. She could have kept it in her pocket, brought it up to her nose, used her hands to make a little dome to block out the city's other fumes and foul scents— chamber pots that were emptied in a heap not far from the canal, the tannery that blew around the warm, salty aroma of rotting innards, a surefire way to ruin any long inhale—all of that would go away if she sniffed at that sprig.

A rosemary-scented world.

She glanced up at the other Crowns, who were laughing and farting and talking. Those who were still eating looked entranced, faces full of hope. Content. But something still nagged at Duck. They were seven pennies down, a small fortune gone in a lightning strike, and what did they have to show for it? Full bellies? Toys? The satisfaction of having indulged?

"We're looking at a pretty sweet setup." Gnat leaned back on the dock, using his left arm to prop himself up. "Especially if Garbage can get her hands on a coronet a week."

Duck's insides hollowed out. The baker's milky eyes . . . The feel of her big soft hands against Duck's. The sound of her deep voice, bright as morning, jolly as fruitcake.

Frog Eyes took one look at her gaping mouth. "Oh, no, Crowns, I think Duck has caught a bad case of the scruples." He said this in a teasing, brotherly way, as if a moral code were some kind of plague that required rinsing with vinegar—but he was right. As a thief, the last thing Duck wanted to catch was a sense of right and wrong.

Then she'd never be able to thieve again.

"You know the only way to get rid of scruples, don't you?" Gnat started, and Duck braced herself for something particularly nasty.

But Gnat suddenly sat up straight, as though something had bitten him. "Do you see that?" He squinted across the canal at a pool of amber lamplight.

At the entrance of the hot fair, a trio of figures stood, absorbing the light.

Older boys, older than Gnat and Ash, but not quite men. Their hair was trimmed short, molded against their heads. Their clothing was dark, neat, uniform.

On their right hands, they each wore a crimson glove.

Duck's blood ran cold.

Behind her, Gnat swore as he got to his feet. "It's them. Red Swords."

And then he added, "Run."

Swords

In any city, you got your fair share of pests and rodents. Fleas and lice were common stowaways in hair and fur alike; mice and rats were never far away; bedbugs nestled into every mattress, straw or feather. Pests were a way of life, and as such, the Crowns moved through the world as the pests they were—quietly, shiftily, best undetected for their own survival.

The Crowns were not the only pests in Avilogne. No, there were plenty of other street gangs—the Black Pigs, the Innocents, the Halfpenny Pegs. And when the Crowns ran into another such gang, it was to the benefit of all that they part quickly, slip back into the shadows of the city without a tussle in the same way that rats dared not congregate out in the open streets but rather scuttled in the darkness.

But the Red Swords did not keep to these rules.

They moved about the districts of Avilogne with the boldness of rats emerging from a riverbank to march right across the cobble-stones without pause. They did not live by daylight or moonlight alone but came out to do their work at all hours, in any light, whenever they pleased, curfew be damned.

Rumor had it they ran their gang like a ruthless monastery—once you were in, the only way to break your vows and get out was death.

Rumor had it they'd all tie cannons to their feet and jump in the Sarluire before they'd succumb to tattling on one another. There was no such thing as bad blood in the Red Swords; if you went bad, you were no longer blood.

Rumor had it they had the watchmen in their pockets in every city they inhabited—a commission per job, and the watch would look the other way as the Swords robbed and ravaged.

So far, the Crowns had heard tell of the Red Swords only through the whispers that pests passed on to one another between lifts—but the rumors were enough to scare them. The Red Swords were violent and vengeful, to be avoided at all costs, and their leader, Jacques, the so-called Jackal of Avilogne—there wasn't anything he wouldn't tear apart.

They were also as territorial as dogs; if you so much as saw them, it was already too late.

They would always chase you down—but still, the Crowns couldn't help but try their luck.

Duck followed the other Crowns, running as close behind Drippy as she could without tripping on his heels. She tried to hold on to her apple, but it slipped out of her grasp and fell into the canal with a splash.

They slipped into the market with the haste of hounded foxes but with the grace of spooked chickens—Le Chou took a corner too sharply and knocked into a stall. His momentum got the better of him, and he barreled right into a jeweler's table, sending beads flying everywhere.

"You careless oaf, get back here!" the stall keeper cried. "You'll pay for this!"

But the beads were already a blur behind them.

Next Ash rammed into a barrel of live eels as they fled past; the eels flew up, their rubbery bodies flexing midair, and landed on the grass. The owners squatted to recover their goods as people rushed to pocket the squirming fish.

Duck thumped into and pushed off strangers. She ran through a band of musicians, causing a piper to bleat a screeching high note when she shoved into him.

When she dared to glance behind her, tracking their pursuers, there was no one, only a trail of furious merchants and a mess.

At last, the Crowns ran clear of the fair and out of the green altogether and into the quarters of the old city.

Remnants of the dilapidated legionnaire walls remained, though only at half their original height; beyond their moldy, crackled bricks were the homes of the wealthy elite, the count's castle, the watchtower, the mill. Windows were lit, but this section of Odierne felt instantly chilly, even though the glow of the hot fair was not far away. The streets were cold, and though the houses themselves were vibrant with paint meant to show the lower classes that these owners could afford the things no one else could, such as blue exteriors and bright-red roof tiles and purple trim, the colors themselves were lifeless in the moonlight.

All Duck's senses were heightened—heart pounding, she could

hear the wind turning the rusty weather vanes on the rooftops, she could smell every ripple in the canal, she could see every individual cobblestone on the road.

Ash slowed to a stop, looked around. "Hey," he panted. "I think we lost them."

"That's the second-stupidest thing you've thought all night." A boy in a black tunic and hose and a single red glove stepped out of the shadows before them. He was shorter than he should have been, considering what a legend he was. "The first, of course, being that you could come into Sword territory and live to tell the tale."

Jacques. The Jackal of Avilogne, in the flesh.

Duck swallowed hard and tried not to cry.

Behind them, more red-gloved figures dropped from the rooftops of the surrounding buildings, falling into the streets like drops of rain. Duck stopped trying to count them after twelve—more startling than their numbers was the fact that they were dressed uniformly in all black, each with a single red glove on their right hand. Did they have someone specifically manufacturing only right-handed gloves? Or was there a stockpile of discarded left-handed gloves stashed somewhere in Avilogne?

Either way, it was disconcerting how similar they all looked: dark silhouettes, hair trimmed close to their heads, eyes gleaming in the night.

And of course, they all wore their famed sabers at their belts.

"The Red Swords were in Perpinnet last we heard." Gnat kept his chin high as he leaned against the wall, his withered right arm tucked casually against his body as if he were merely tired and not surrounded by a sea of vicious killers. "Since when did you move west?"

"Since we wanted to." Jacques was a sharp-jawed, white-blond young man with a scar across one cheek. "Odierne is ours now. Run home to your mommies."

"Says who?" Gnat replied, and Duck wished he hadn't.

Jacques smiled. He lifted up his gloved hand, crooked one finger, and in a swift, choreographed, terrifying movement, the other Red Swords surrounded the Crowns in a tight circle.

Duck searched for a place through which to slip and escape, but found none. The Red Swords had become a wall, a fortress, a prison.

Jacques grabbed Gnat's right arm and pressed it behind his back. Gnat tried not to wince, but Duck could see he was in pain. Her stomach twisted in sympathy. "Says us. This area is ours."

Gnat opened his mouth to argue again but gasped instead— Jacques twisted his shriveled arm around until they all heard a crack.

Duck closed her eyes.

"Lucky for you," Jacques went on, "Red Swords don't fight *children.*"

Again, Gnat tried to speak—no Crown wanted to be labeled a child, even if that's what they were—but he wisely stayed quiet.

"So here's what you're going to do," the Jackal said. "You're going to go back to whatever hole you've been sleeping in, and you're going to gather your pathetic belongings, and you're going to leave. No stopping back at the market, no pulling one last job, no picking pockets. I don't want you so much as looking for loose change around the fountains, understand? This is our town." With a jerk, he shoved Gnat free; Gnat immediately pulled his arm back against his side and stretched his shoulders, rolling his neck around. He looked very much like he was trying to act as though he hadn't been hurt, but sweat dotted his forehead.

"If we see you pulling jobs here again," Jacques said, "we'll show you exactly why they call us the Red Swords."

And then, as quickly as they had arrived, the Red Swords vanished, not even a whisper or a shadow of them on the streets. The night was warm again, the rush of the canal ordinary.

The Crowns, shuddering, exhaled, all of them finally loosening up. Ash put his hand on Gnat's back and said, "Are you all right?"

Gnat shrugged Ash off with more force than was necessary. "I'm fine." But they could all see the single tear on his cheek that had not yet dried.

"So where are we going now?" Fingers said.

"Guess that's goodbye to our cathedral." Frog Eyes kicked at a loose stone. "Damn. It was perfect for us."

"But where do we go?" Fingers repeated. "We can't go back to Perpinnet." Her hands twitched as if she were hoping she could steal them a new home out of thin air, just like that.

"We can't leave," Drippy said. "This is home."

"Home is wherever the coins are," Frog Eyes said. "We've robbed our way across Avilogne—maybe it's time we pick the world's pockets clean."

"We could keep going east," Spinner suggested. "Go to Wisinburg."

"I'm not going to Wisinburg," Le Chou said. "Too much cabbage."

"Then they'll love you there," Ash teased.

"We could go back to Illyon," Fingers said. "I like goats."

"No, let's go to the ocean," Frog Eyes said. "I've always wanted to live by the ocean—"

"We're not going anywhere." Gnat still glared at the place where Jacques and the Red Swords had stood before they disappeared into the night.

"But you heard what they said," Ash put in. "They said—"

"They said no pulling jobs," Gnat said. "No robbing. No picking pockets. We're not going to do any of that."

"We're not?" Ash said, and looked to the other Crowns, gauging their reactions.

Even Duck was confused, but Gnat had something on his mind. Some scheme. Duck just knew it—and Gnat always looked out for the Crowns.

Gnat closed his eyes, then cleared his throat and said with a newfound calm, "Back to the cathedral. Time for some shut-eye."

"The cathedral? But Jacques said—" Frog Eyes started.

"Yes, I know what he said." Gnat bit his bottom lip as he rubbed his elbow. "I just . . . need some time to think. I'll figure this out—I promise. But for now, back home. We're done celebrating for tonight."

The Crowns followed the canal, preferring the openness of the stinky water to scurrying between buildings where Red Swords could be hiding, waiting to ambush them.

Duck trudged along with the rest of them; she glanced down at the ripples once and spotted her apple on the far side of the canal, drifting with the current, bobbing, only a single bite missing.

Gnat's Plan

When Duck woke up the next morning, Ash was leaning over her, his face inches from her nose. Crusts of sleep were still stuck in the corners of his eyes, but his grin was at least fifteen minutes old.

"We're not dead!" he shouted.

Duck pushed his face away, disoriented—his fuzzy teeth were stinky enough to scour a cauldron clean. Her stomach was roiling for food already, almost painfully so. Usually her hunger sneaked up on her slowly throughout the day, but yesterday's indulgence with the bread had ramped up her gut's grumbling.

She hadn't slept much, either. Her head felt as malleable as butter. "What are you talking about?"

"I thought for sure the Jackal of Avilogne and his cronies would find us and stab us in the night," Ash said, "but they didn't!" He leaped over her and did a kind of heel-toe dance on the stones. "We're alive, we're alive, we didn't die—" He suddenly halted, looking thoughtful. "Of course, we still have to find a new place to live, because we've been forbidden from stealing food or picking pockets, so we'll starve if we stay in Odierne. But still—we're alive!"

Duck pushed herself up to sitting. The dawn was coming soft and purple over the canal. Down the Rue Grande, a crowd of people watched the barber extract a tooth from a barrel-shaped man who was screeching like a banshee in anticipation.

And here, along the east-facing edge of the cathedral roof, the row of gargoyles still grimaced at the world below, pigeons bobbing for crumbs at their pedestals.

The western-facing gargoyle, the ugliest one of them all, was stoic; the sunlight shone behind his head like a daytime star.

"Wonder where we'll go." Ash stretched, arching his back like a cat. "The Red Swords are already pushing their boundaries as it is. We'll have to walk for days to get out of their territory. Maybe we really will have to leave Avilogne."

Duck tried to imagine this. Of course she knew there was a world beyond Avilogne. There were other countries with villages and roads and cathedrals, valleys and mountains and fields. Other larger kingdoms—as far as Duck understood, the world kept right on going until the horizon became stars and the sea fell off itself.

If they had to, the Crowns could keep running; as long as there was someone to swipe from, they could thrive.

But Duck didn't want to leave Avilogne. She didn't want to leave this cathedral—not now, not so soon after Gnat had called it home.

"Maybe we should reach out to other gangs, band together with them," Ash went on.

The very thought made Duck supremely distressed. "But Gnat

always says that other gangs would kebab us if we so much as asked—"

"I know. But the Swords can't have all of Avilogne. They've got to leave some crumbs for us mice."

"Crowns!" Gnat called from the cathedral porch. "Gather up! We need to talk."

"Don't worry too much," Ash said so only Duck could hear as they went down the spiral stairs to the main chambers. "No matter where those Swords fling us, at least we'll be together."

Ash's words brought Duck enough comfort to slow her pulse, and she was able to sit down on a pew like a regular churchgoer—until she saw Gnat, and the dark circles under his eyes flipped her insides.

He looked, in a word, awful. His hair was sticking straight up, as if he had slept even less than she had.

He absentmindedly reached for his shriveled arm, rubbing his shoulder, and Duck thought about how Jacques had cranked Gnat's arm behind his back as though he were tugging a rope.

Some mornings, Gnat's arm was stiff, aching all the way through his body. On those days, he could usually predict rain, since it made his wrist bones reverberate and echo with pain like they were the catacombs.

If a new arm were something Duck could pickpocket for Gnat, she would get him one for every day of the week and a spare for Sundays.

"What's eating you?" he snapped as he stifled a yawn.

Duck bit the inside of her cheek. "Rough night."

"Join the club." Gnat dropped his arm and shouted, "Hey,

Crowns! Get in here already! You're lucky I let you sleep in until sunrise!"

The others plodded into the main chapel with snoozy faces; their bodies, too, were not used to waking up so sated.

"How many turnovers did I eat last night?" Le Chou held his stomach with a regretful, sickened look in his eyes. "Actually, don't tell me."

"Here." Fingers offered Le Chou a turnover from her pocket. "Hair of the dog?"

Le Chou sighed, took the turnover, and ate it—then immediately winced and grabbed his middle again. "Why'd I do that?" he groaned, and lay flat on the closest pew.

"Gluttony is a sin," Spinner said, but she, too, had the wrung-out look of someone who had drunk a little too much cheap ale last night.

Duck positioned herself on one of the urns as Gnat called for order. "Well, Crowns," he said once they'd all piped down, "we've had a good long run. Coins, jewelry, fruit, knickknacks . . . we've swiped lots of fantastic things. I believe we were getting close to picking every pocket in Avilogne at least once. But now, Crowns, it's time to say goodbye."

The other Crowns opened their mouths like caught fish, but Duck frowned. She knew better than most that words could be tricky sometimes.

"Yes, it's farewell to the good times of lowly pickpocketing, sprats. Farewell to the sticky-fingered life." Gnat paused, and his sly smile was all that Duck needed to see to know—he was baiting them.

He had a plan.

"So . . ." Ash leaned forward, his hands open, ready to catch whatever explanation Gnat tossed out. "How will we eat, then?"

"Yes, where will we get our bread?" Frog Eyes added. "Our milk? Our ale? Our eggs? Our fruit? Our—"

"Now, now." Gnat was enjoying this, Duck could tell. "Of course I won't let you suffer. We are simply going to shift from one line of work to another." He reached into his pocket and pulled out a roll of parchment. "Get ready, Crowns. We're about to become domesticated."

Domesticated?

That word buzzed around their heads like a bloodthirsty fly.

"You mean . . . housebroken?" Ash was incredulous.

"That's right," Gnat answered. "Actually, to be clear, only one of us is going to become an inside cat, and they'll slip the rest of us everything we need to stay alive."

It was silent enough in the cathedral that they could hear the sound of the farrier pounding horseshoes against an anvil with a metal hammer—*clink, clink,* turn, *clink, clink,* turn.

Duck made eye contact with Ash, searching for answers, but Ash shook his head and shrugged.

"For as long as we've been Crowns," Gnat continued, "we've been going after the small stuff. Just one or two coins at a time. A single loaf of bread, split into sections. Nothing that would make a big splash."

"Don't get noticed," Frog Eyes recited. The most important of their rules—for the Crowns, it was law.

"But going after the small stuff means a very small way of life.

And it requires so much hustle—too much hustle to sustain. But we can't get bolder. We can't risk it. Especially not with the Swords breathing down our necks." He paused to look at each of them; Duck looked away before his eyes could find hers. "So we'll have to get smarter instead." He held up the scroll. "One of us is going straight. One of us is going to be an apprentice."

"An apprentice!" Frog Eyes guffawed.

"Fancy!" Ash added. "Only . . . what does that mean, exactly?"

"It means one of us is going to have to move away," Spinner translated, and Duck's insides tied themselves in a knot. The Crowns, split up? She didn't like that idea, not in the slightest. At least if they went to prison, they would all be there, all together.

Gnat was even-tempered as he explained, basking in his genius. "Every trade worth its time belongs to a guild, right? Sort of like a club for all the laborers in that line of work—it gives them group protection. Together, they can set their prices, establish industry standards, create a monopoly."

The other Crowns nodded as if they understood, but there were a lot of words Duck didn't totally understand. Industry? Standards? Monopoly?

"I get it," Ash suddenly said. "The guilds are like gangs. Like us."

"Exactly." Gnat touched a finger to his nose. "To get into a guild, you start young. You work as an apprentice to a master, who trains you. You sleep in their house and you do whatever they say— all the lowest chores of the job. Scrubbing floors. Hauling firewood. Dealing with rubbish. Whatever they tell you to do—but eventually you work your way up, and then one day you're the master, and you're hiring your own ankle biter to work as an apprentice for you.

Now, a little bird told me that someone in this very city is looking for a new apprentice at this very moment."

"Who?" Le Chou asked.

"Griselde Baker," Gnat announced. "She of the massive, fat, foot-long loaves herself."

A fierce wisp of rage dashed through Duck like a summer wind. She didn't like Gnat talking about the baker. Some instinct within her wanted to keep them apart under any circumstances. Yes, Griselde Baker was a grown-up, and yes, grown-ups could usually take care of themselves, but around Gnat, all grown-ups became marks. Targets. Little more than animals. And Griselde Baker was like a big naive cow, grazing in a pasture of her own false security.

Gnat was more than a gnat. He was a snake in the weeds, a leech in the pond. He'd find a way to latch on and bleed that baker dry.

For some reason, that made Duck's stomach lurch.

"So, what are we doing?" Frog Eyes scratched his head. "We're going to find her new apprentice and take his papers? Rob him rotten? Steal his clothes and hope the baker doesn't look too close at our mugs?"

Gnat unfurled the parchment and showed it to them—a folio, official-looking, with the writing sectioned in thirds. From her spot on the urn, Duck could see through the rag sheets that script flowed in neat lines, and a stamped red seal, the wax bumpy, was pressed into the bottom of the page where a signature was required.

None of the Crowns but Gnat could write, and most of them could read only a lick, just enough to decipher a road sign here and there.

Gnat must have made this last night—that's what he'd done instead of sleeping, Duck figured. Getting this parchment, procuring ink, writing it out perfectly so it looked genuine.

"Application papers from the guild," Gnat said. "These are perfect copies. I even put the officers' signatures here and a strong recommendation that the baker hire our Crown to be her apprentice immediately. All we need to do is present these to Master Griselde herself, and we'll be set. Our Crown will pass us all the free bread and coins she can from right under the baker's nose. A coronet every single week, Crowns. Picture it."

"Wait a minute," Ash said as the other Crowns swooned at the thought of their incoming assets. "You said 'she.'"

Gnat smirked. "I sure did."

Duck's heart plummeted into her guts. Her hand went into her pocket, feeling the penny she'd brought with her to the hot fair last night. There were three girls in the Crowns, so there was a two in three chance that it wouldn't be her—

A canvas apron was draped ceremoniously around her neck. Her penny grew hot in her palm.

Some of the others hooted in delight.

"Say hello to the baker's new apprentice." Gnat's expression, when Duck looked up at him, was smug but ironclad. She wouldn't be able to wriggle out of this one.

But she'd be damned if she didn't at least try.

"She's a runt!" Fingers spat. "She's only eight!"

"Masters like their apprentices young and impressionable," Gnat said. "The rest of us are too seasoned."

Duck's inhales were coming in short, stabbing bursts. So Gnat was only using her because she was the smallest? That made her feel . . . mystified. Being the youngest was in her favor, for once—or it would be, if she were the kind of Crown who pined for a serious scam like this.

Duck looked to Ash in desperation.

"What if the baker remembers her? From the other day?" Ash asked.

"Then you'll have to convince her. Tell her you're just such a big fan of her bread, you marched right over to the guild and begged them for your papers." Gnat rolled up the parchment and held it above Duck's head, almost as if he were going to thwack her with it if she misspoke. "If you really won't do this, Garbage, let me know. I can put another Crown in your place. I'll age Frog Eyes down a few years—and you can wander the streets of Odierne alone and hope the Swords don't find you and use you for firewood."

Duck breathed in slowly, glancing at the other Crowns, who watched her solemnly.

All she'd have to do is slip them a coin here and there. A coronet a week, Gnat had said. And smuggle some bread into their hands, too.

A coronet a week would be peas to the baker, or to any other craftsman, but to the Crowns? A coronet a week, split among them? That would be enough to keep them fed. Two meals a day. Vegetables, too, if they wanted them. They could buy more than one set of clothing apiece if they pleased. They could scrape up enough to rent a room somewhere, or a little shack outside of town. Nothing fancy, of course, but it would be enough to keep the rain off their heads . . .

And she could be the one to give it to them.

Yesterday the Crowns hadn't thought Duck would be able to get their bread—but she'd proven that she was more than capable . . . wasn't she?

Gnat touched her shoulder. "You're the youngest," he said, "but you're also the quietest. That's the real reason I'm sending you. I could persuade Griselde Baker to take any one of us, regardless of age. But you won't blab the truth about why you're really there. I can't trust anyone else to keep their mouth shut. So, can you do it? Can you be our quiet little duckling?"

Duck considered his words.

Ash couldn't do it—he was too friendly, too earnest.

Frog Eyes was too obnoxious.

Le Chou didn't have a subtle bone in his body, and Drippy was not very good at keeping track of which things were secret and which were not.

Spinner was more than smart enough—probably too smart— and Fingers would be decent, but would she be able to resist swiping more than just coins and bread? Yes, the other Crowns were unsuited for this job, all except Gnat. He was the only other one who would make a decent apprentice.

Yes, he'd make a very good apprentice, Duck decided. There was nothing he couldn't talk his way out of. He was so good at thinking in twists, thinking on his feet, thinking in slimy and backward ways—and surely whatever hovel the baker used to house her apprentice would be a luxury compared to this old cathedral.

If anyone deserved it, it was Gnat.

But she looked at him now, his right arm tucked against his side like a broken wing, and she realized the truth.

He couldn't do it.

Not because he wouldn't be able to—Duck had no doubt that he'd prefer to just handle this whole apprentice business himself—but because a guild wouldn't send an apprentice with Gnat's particular impairment. That arm of Gnat's was a liability.

Her heart panged; he would be perfect for this role, but a guild would look at him and see him only for what he lacked.

There really was no one but Duck.

Gnat raised his eyebrows, waiting.

Duck peered at Ash.

"She'll do it," Ash started, but Gnat shook his head.

"You won't be able to speak for her in there, Ash. I want to hear her say it herself."

Ash gave Duck an apologetic shrug.

Duck tied the strings of the apron around her, folding it up at the waist so it wouldn't drag when she walked. "I'll do it," she said, the words snagging in her throat.

The rest of the Crowns were reverent as Gnat passed her the parchment. She took it gingerly—just holding it felt like more responsibility than she'd bargained for.

"All right, then," Gnat said. "Today's the Sabbath, so the bakery's closed. But consider this your last day as a free Crown. First thing tomorrow, we'll get you settled with your new boss."

A New Home

This time, Gnat didn't just shove Duck into the square alone, as he had on market day. He himself marched her around the back of the bakery to the staff entrance, both his hands tucked into the pockets of his tunic.

Duck had left the Crowns with a swift goodbye, and perhaps that was best—when Ash had embraced her, he'd whispered, "We'll see you again soon—don't you worry," and Duck had clenched her eyes shut and thought of puppies to make sure she didn't cry.

"Um . . . Gnat?" Duck asked as they walked across a small fenced yard to the back porch. "When am I . . . um . . . ?"

"You'd better stop that twitching and stuttering," Gnat warned, "or the baker'll turn you away before you get to the end of a sentence. You always take a century to spit out what you're trying to say."

Duck fussed with her apron strings and focused on the question that had been nibbling away at her since yesterday. "How long am I going to be here?" she managed to say, and Gnat halted in front of her.

He narrowed his eyes. "As long as it takes" was his cryptic answer, and then he rapped on the back door.

Duck tightened her grip on the parchment.

"Now remember," Gnat whispered to Duck, "do not, under any circumstances, ever—"

But before he could finish, the door swung open.

And there was the baker.

She was even bigger than Duck remembered. Almost large enough to belt on a harness and pull a cart over the cobblestones. Duck found herself frozen, staring up at the master baker, taking in the details.

Things like the width of Griselde Baker's nostrils, the way they flared out as she smiled. The ease with which she did smile, as if she believed as a principle that smiles were free and therefore should be distributed abundantly. The way she held herself—open and relaxed and settled, her massive arm muscles and broad shoulders wide, as though she expected a hug from everyone she met.

She was unlike any woman Duck had ever seen—and quite remarkable when compared to all the men Duck had ever met as well.

"What can I do for you?" Master Griselde boomed, and her voice was as loud as the wind. "Both of you, if you came together. Each of you, if you didn't." She looked just above their heads, and Duck got a glimpse of her milked-over eyes. How much could the baker see? Sometimes Master Griselde seemed to focus on objects, and other times she blurred right past them, as if her eyes liked to pick and choose which things were visible and which were not.

"Sent by the guild." When Duck wasn't looking, Gnat had put

on an apron identical to hers, crisp white and smelling of fresh laundry. "We're applicants for your new apprentice." He made his voice high and nasal, almost grating, and his face was twisted to look bored, annoyed at the world and specifically uninterested in any of the goings-on here at the bakery.

Duck caught her own face before it flashed with confusion—what was Gnat doing, pitting himself against her? What kind of game was this? Was this how he was going to dismiss her from the Crowns? He'd take the apprenticeship for himself, and she'd be on her own, wandering the streets of Odierne?

Gnat handed a roll of parchment to the baker—his own paperwork, Duck surmised. Prompted, Duck did the same, though her hands were shaking.

The baker took both scrolls but didn't even untie them. "Come in, come in," she said, standing sideways in the doorway, ushering them past her bulbous stomach. "Come in, and let's see what we've got."

The bakery was dark. Duck's eyes needed a moment to adjust.

Griselde pushed the two Crowns gently down a hallway toward an amber glow.

"Sorry about the lights," she said cheerily. "We're winding down for the day, and I try to reserve our candles for the wee hours of the morning. You don't mind waking up before the sun does, do you?"

Gnat hooked his mouth down in a genteel grimace. "I much prefer to let the morning wake me."

Griselde Baker snorted. "Well, anyone around here who isn't out of bed on time gets a bucketful of cold water right in the face."

Duck trailed behind Gnat, trying to figure out what he was

playing at—he loved mornings! He was always the first one up! Even if his arm didn't wake him with an aching pain, his brain often pulled him out of sleep with another great scheme—so what was he doing, telling a whopping big lie like this?

Griselde Baker led them into a wide room that Duck immediately recognized was the heart of the whole building: the kitchen. It smelled of warm yeast, sticky-sweet honey, and other things that Duck couldn't place but that made her mouth water. The baker showed them to a long bench against a wall, and she herself took a chair near a farm table that stretched nearly the length of the room.

Behind her was a huge brick structure—the oven, so large Duck would have fit neatly inside.

"Now then." Master Griselde laced her hands together in her lap. "Let's address the obvious fact first. No one wants to be a baker's apprentice."

A defensive heat rose in Duck's cheeks. Who wouldn't want to learn how to bake? Was there anything in the world so lovely as a fresh loaf of bread?

"The other guilds fill up with applicants first—painters, metalsmiths, glassmakers," the baker went on. "That's why you're here, isn't it? Everything else was taken."

Gnat scoffed. "That's right. The wait list to get in with the blacksmith is about a year long, and the butchers were all booked up. So it's either one of the lesser trades, or I age out waiting."

Lesser trades! Duck's mouth went dry. There was no hope for Gnat now; the baker was going to drag him out of here by the ear for such disrespect.

"How old are you?" Griselde Baker inquired, her eyebrows furrowed.

"Twenty next month." Twenty! What was Gnat doing? Hadn't he told Duck that the younger the apprentice, the better their chance of being chosen? His diminutive size, his hunched posture, the way his face so easily soured like a child's . . . all of that would strip years off his age so believably, so why would he *add* years to—?

Suddenly it dawned on Duck. Gnat was trying to make himself look awful in comparison to her. A nasal voice that would be wretched to listen to day and night, morally opposed to early mornings, disinterested in a career in baking, too old for the baker to mold in her image—even if Duck completely botched her own interview, the comparison with Gnat would make her the less moldy of two cheeses.

Smart, smart Gnat.

Sometimes it terrified Duck how smart he was.

"And you? Why are you interested in baking?"

Duck jumped, realizing the baker was staring right at her, waiting. She swallowed, resisting the urge to squeak out, *I don't know!*

Griselde Baker's expectant eyes reflected the dim gleam of the single rushlight across the room.

"When I bite into your bread," Duck said meekly, looking only at the wooden slats of the bakery floor, "I feel warm all over. Even if the bread has gone cold. I—I want to make everyone else feel like that. Warm."

When Duck glanced up, she looked to Gnat, who was doing

an excellent job of staying in character—except for a tiny break at the corner of his mouth. A signature Gnat smirk, accompanied by the slightest of nods.

He probably thought that Duck had been so quick on her feet, she'd composed just the right horse-dung answer to convince the baker.

But that's where Gnat was wrong.

Duck had stated the truth.

She'd said what she felt. Only the truth.

And maybe that meant she was one step ahead of even Gnat.

Griselde Baker tilted her head sideways, inspecting Duck. "You're young, aren't you? You sound young. Younger than most apprentices."

"Eight," Duck affirmed. That wouldn't be a liability in the baker's eyes, would it? Now that Duck was actually inside the bakery, she felt extra small, eclipsed by the oven, the tables, the barrels, and the baker herself.

"Hmmm." Master Griselde considered the parchment Duck had given her, still rolled up in her fist, and Duck's nerves twisted in her side like a knife. Griselde Baker was going to reject her, send her away—

"Master Baker, if I may," Gnat spoke up. "'This child"—he said the word *child* the way others might say *moldy turnip* or *maggot*— "is nothing but an orphan. No family to speak of, nothing to distinguish her as fine. On the other hand, I am from people of quality. Merchants and craftsmen for generations, and a pedigree that stretches all the way back to the first prince of Avilogne himself." He sneered as he leveled the baker with his gaze, and Duck marveled at how quickly he was able to brag about such a thing. She couldn't have made that up so easily.

"So, as you can see," Gnat went on, "there's nothing left to debate. I am clearly your next apprentice—"

"There's not a whole lot that these eyes can see anymore." Griselde Baker set Duck's parchment on the table. "Least of all whatever fancy qualifications you've insisted they list on your application. Meaningless trollop, if you ask me; I don't give a rat's wormy tail who your family is, so long as you can shovel dough into ovens. But I've heard enough." She bowed respectfully to Gnat, holding out his scroll to him. "Thank you kindly for the consideration, but I'm afraid you aren't quite right to work here in my bakery."

Gnat's mouth scrunched up as if he'd smelled something foul. He seized his parchment. "My father won't be too thrilled about this! He'll boycott your shop, and he'll tell all his friends what a fool you are for turning me away—"

"Wonderful!" Griselde Baker clapped her hands. "We hate having single-minded fops eating our bread. Now, on your way, young man, and may you have better luck with your next endeavor."

With that, Gnat muttered a few choice phrases under his breath and vanished down the hall. Duck heard the back door slam behind him.

So that was that. Gnat had made an ass of himself, and through sheer elimination, Duck was now Griselde Baker's apprentice—

No, she realized suddenly. The baker hadn't said those words. She could dismiss Duck right now, too, just as easily as she had Gnat.

"Shall we get you settled?" Master Griselde boomed.

Duck stared blankly. Her mouth refused to move.

"Are you still there, little one?" the baker pressed. "Or did you sneak out with the angry nobleman?"

"Here," Duck whispered.

"By the by, what is your name?"

"M-my name?" Cold panic flooded Duck—she didn't know if there was a false name on the parchment that she should be using, one that Gnat had assigned her.

"A name, yes," Griselde Baker said. "You can call me Griselde, for example. Master Griselde, I suppose, but that's a mouthful. What should I call you?"

Duck answered truthfully again; it had worked well for her earlier.

"Duck."

Griselde nodded once. "Excellent. It suits you. Let me show you to your quarters."

Duck's chest was bruised from all that heart-hammering today, but she willed herself to calm down as she followed the baker down the hallway.

The hard part was over.

Now all she had to do was act like an apprentice for the next . . . however long Gnat decided to keep her here.

It already felt like forever since she'd entered the bakery.

She gritted her jaw, the way she'd seen Gnat do whenever he was faced with a dilemma, and felt like a proper Crown.

It was difficult to pinpoint where, exactly, the bakery stopped and Griselde's home began.

The kitchen was huge—cavernous as a church, with wooden cupboards, benches, and counters lining the brick walls and that long trestle table right next to the ovens. The floor was dirt, but covered over with boards that made every footfall echo or scuffle.

Down the hall, the one that led to the back door, there was a storeroom, chilly and bare but for shelves and barrels and burlap sacks of supplies. Root of hellebore was ground up and sprinkled along the edges of the closet—"Because of the mice," Griselde said, "but a fat lot of worthless help it's been. They just step around it now. I swear, I hear them laughing at me sometimes. If you see any rodents, you have my permission to bash them right on the head."

Beyond that was the counting room, which held a simple desk messy with calculating boards, wax tablets for record-keeping, unrolled parchment letters stamped with the seals of various merchants flung everywhere. The candles were few, the dust great, and the strongbox, where Griselde kept the bakery's income, was on the windowsill beside the desk—bound with iron, fastened with a lock.

"You keep an eye on that strongbox," Gnat had told her last night as he'd laid out all his shining plans for her new job. "That box is going to be your new best friend."

Duck stared at it as if it were a holy relic. How much money was in there now? Enough that she'd be able to skim a coin a week off the top and the baker wouldn't notice?

Griselde Baker's bedroom was just behind the kitchen. "I stay on the ground floor," the baker explained, "so I can sniff out any potential fires before they spread beyond the ovens." Fires, she warned Duck with uncharacteristic severity, were what regularly took down bakeries, so there were buckets and barrels of water stationed around the building just in case.

Upstairs were the servants' quarters, including a tiny bread box of a room where Duck would be housed. "I don't regularly keep an attendant anymore, since it's only me," Griselde explained, "and I'm perfectly capable of dressing myself."

As small as the room was, it wasn't the most cramped place Duck had ever slept. And best of all, this space was hers, all hers. No smelly Ash feet in her face. No chorus of Crown flatulence to keep her awake all night. No feelings of loneliness after everyone else was asleep and snoring but she was still wide awake, watching the moon.

The room even had two windows. Griselde tugged back the curtains on the one facing east so Duck could see the view—not the sprawling scene she'd witnessed from atop the abandoned cathedral, but she could see directly into the market square.

Beneath the window was the awning that stood above the bakery's storefront—only a short drop, and she could be out of this house without a fuss. Not that Duck had any plans to leave, but it was always a good idea to know the quickest escape.

Her training as a Crown trumped all other instincts.

The other window faced the city walls, and if Duck were to leap out this way, she'd land right in the Sarluire.

"Blankets are there." Griselde pointed to a one-drawer armoire. "The oven keeps the place pretty warm, even at night, but when fall and winter come around, you've got this." She kicked at a copper bed warmer that was nudged under the bed frame. "You can fill it from the hearth downstairs."

Fall and winter.

Did Gnat expect Duck to stay here at the bakery through winter?

Until next summer?

Or even longer?

"Duck?" Griselde leaned over, her forehead crinkled with concern. "Would you prefer to sleep in the storeroom?"

Duck shook her head, and then chided herself: *She can't see, which means you're going to have to speak up.*

"No," she said.

"Wonderful!" Griselde Baker fanned a fly out the open window. "Now, about your uniform." She produced a stack of clothing from the armoire. "There are two sets here, one for work, one for rest. Thursday is laundry day."

Duck unfolded one of the outfits—a tunic and a pair of loose linen hose, both of them white. The hose were so big, she could probably fit into one of the legs, and the tunic came all the way down to her knees.

"Well?" Griselde's hands were on her hips; her eyes were soft and unfocused, aimed at the wall. "Will it work?"

Duck didn't want to sound ungrateful. "Um . . . if I find some string, I can tie up the pants."

"Don't be silly!" Griselde boomed. "Leave the pants up here and just wear the tunic. You'll be more comfortable with your legs bare, anyway. It gets miserably hot, working the ovens in the summer."

Duck studied the baker's own clothing—she wore a similar pair of wide-legged linen trousers, the sort a man would wear, with a thin tunic and a sleeveless, beltless surcoat on top of that, all of it faded white. Much less clothing than women of her class usually wore, Duck noticed. The baker left her head uncovered, too.

"You'll meet Petrus tomorrow," Griselde said as she led Duck back downstairs. "My journeyman. He's already left for the day—we take short days on Mondays, since we're open so late on Saturdays. He and his wife live there." She pointed out the back door to a little cottage beyond the fenced yard—thatched roof, quaint-looking green bricks. "They just had a little one. Hugo. Perhaps if you're lucky, you'll meet him, too."

Duck recalled the handsome young journeyman who had issued out baskets of rolls for Saturday's crowd. A jolt of unease went through her.

It was one thing to sneak bread and coins out from under the baker's nose. But the journeyman would be another pair of eyes on Duck, another person for her to lie to.

Another person she'd have to convince.

Griselde Baker lingered in the hallway, as if reluctant to leave Duck alone—but her tour and orientation seemed to be finished.

Duck, suddenly desperate to be alone, took a step backward.

"So . . . dawn?" she whispered, dismissing herself.

"Hold on just a minute!" The baker puffed up her chest. "Are you my apprentice or aren't you?"

Chided, Duck squeaked out, "Yes?"

"Good!" Griselde clapped her hands together. "We still have to clean the ovens before we bed down for the night. Get changed, and then I'll show you how it's done!"

Duck the Baker

Griselde threw Duck right into the thick of things, and her tendency was to throw first, give an explanation second—or never. The baker definitely liked to talk, but she didn't give Duck any step-by-step instructions.

Instead, she thundered stories about times when things went terribly wrong: when the peel caught fire because of all the ground-up pieces of dough that were stuck to it, or when her third apprentice, Roger, forgot to pour water in the steam pans so the hot cross buns came out hard enough to trick a stonemason—and also, unsurprisingly, caught on fire.

"This place is like a tinderbox," Master Griselde said. "We must be vigilant at all times. Keep an eye on every flame, every spark. No draping sleeves. No dangling hair. And be careful where you set the peel."

Duck had learned what a peel was only moments ago—a long, flat, shovel-like paddle used to push dough into the oven and pull bread out. She nodded to show she would be alert at all times and watched the ovens with a renewed wariness.

There was one big oven with a mouth like God's, several smaller ovens with grins like demons', and one minuscule oven barely the size of a loaf of bread. This last one was shallow and square, the roof inside low.

"That's the gingerbread oven," Griselde Baker said. "You never, ever bake gingerbread in a standard oven."

Duck was so delighted by the idea of a separate, special oven for gingerbread, she heard herself blurt out, "How come?" and then immediately wished she hadn't. Her voice echoed in the kitchen, sounding much louder than she'd intended.

"If you cook gingerbread in the regular ovens," the baker informed Duck, "it'll come out all cushy and bendy—which is fine, I suppose, if you've got soft teeth, but in my mind, gingerbread should snap when you break it and crunch when you bite it." She smiled at Duck, her eyes focused near Duck's face but not quite on it. "That was a very good question, by the way. Do you have any others?"

Duck inhaled, her mind racing with dozens of questions, but she said nothing.

"I'm sure you'll have lots of other good ones," Griselde said, holding out one of her giant hands, "a smart girl like you."

The hand waited.

Duck stared at it.

"For now, I'll bet you can figure out a few things for yourself," the baker went on. "Like what we use to sweep out the big oven, for instance. What do you think? Can you find what we need?"

Hanging sideways on the wall was a broom. Duck fetched it

and set its handle in Master Griselde's outstretched hand without saying another word.

The oven was blazing hot. Every time Duck tried to get close enough to sweep it, the heat blasted her in the face, making her eyes water and her nose hairs crimp up. So Griselde had to reach into that fiery maw with the broom and scrape and gather and pull.

"You'll get used to it," she reassured Duck. "I think your height will be an advantage. You won't have to bend down to see all the way to the back."

The baker told Duck that the ovens accumulated so much ash, crumbs, and burnt crusts over the course of a single week that they filled up an entire dustpan. Griselde showed her how to clear them out and scrape the peels clean.

Then she showed Duck how to fill the steam pans and where to find firewood, water, scales, and scrub brushes.

Also, importantly, where the privies were located—there was one in the yard, a garderobe off the counting room, and upstairs, a chute over the cellar.

"We run a tight ship," Griselde Baker said. "Mornings, we mix dough, prepare tins, begin the bakes. The shop opens just after dawn bells ring—just trenchers and barley bread during the week, but don't let that relax you. Folks will buy them faster than we can pull them out of the ovens."

After selling hours were done, they always scrubbed the kitchen, had a nice tuck-in, and went to bed before sundown.

Saturdays were market days, which meant more variety in loaves and more stock—and since they had to bake everything fresh the same day it was sold, they went to bed extra early on Friday evenings.

"We clean the ovens on Mondays, do inventory on Tuesdays, buy stock on Fridays, and close on Sundays. Are you religious?"

The question landed in Duck's lap like it had been catapulted there. She widened her eyes. "I . . ."

"Regardless, I think we can both agree that the greatest thing the church ever gave us was the Sabbath." Griselde flung a towel over her shoulder. "All right. That'll do for today. Let's wash up for dinner." She paused. "Unless you're not hungry. We tend to eat much earlier than most."

Duck blushed, staying silent. She'd been raised to be a regular seagull—always scrounging, always hungry, always prepared to go for long stretches between meals.

But her stomach spoke for her, letting out a loud growl, and Duck hunched over, seizing her middle, horrified.

Griselde laughed. "No need to be shy about a hearty appetite around here, my dear. Here, you are in the land of yeasted bread; I don't want you to ever feel hungry while you are in this house." Griselde picked a round-bellied loaf of white table bread from a basket in the storeroom; the sound of its crust crackling had Duck's attention. "Come along, now. Soup's been on since before you showed up."

Duck lingered near the storeroom, counting the baked loaves scattered on the shelves—half a dozen.

The same amount of bread that Duck had brought to the Crowns the other day—and here it was, sitting in a dark corner of the bakery.

Griselde wouldn't miss it, would she, if Duck were to gather the loaves in her arms now and run for the door—

The smells distracted her.

Ale. Onions, garlic, cabbage, or something closely related. Parsnips, which had a tricky, almost minty scent to them, and something gamy—Duck couldn't tell if the baker had actually cooked meat today or if it was the remnants in the broth that she was detecting.

But something else hit her nose, and she breathed it in.

Ah, there it was.

Rosemary.

That scent always found her.

She backed away from the storeroom.

Gnat had placed her here to steal more than just old bread, so she'd resist snatching up the low-hanging fruit and wait for the chance to swipe something grand.

It would never be easy for a Crown to walk away from untended bread, but she made herself do it, the rosemary guiding her forward like a lantern in darkness.

Another summer.

All I want is to be left alone. But there are new-comers in our cathedral. Street urchins. I have seen so many of their same shape and snout over the years, smelly and starved and reckless.

They have come here for sanctuary—but they should have made for the canal bridges or taken their chances in the forest. Our cathedral has never been a safe place for those who want to hide from the world. Our cathedral was left to rot on the riverbank, near haunted waters. No priest. No altar. Not even proper gargoyles.

I have seen more summers than one could ever need to see. Ninety-nine of them. Each time the season rolls around, it finds us a little dustier. The gold of sunlight is a little more visible through our broken walls. We are a little closer to rubble.

Perhaps I once thought that summer was a miracle, but now the heat makes me cranky. The sunshine on my horns threatens to crackle my stones.

"Best get it over with," I growl. "No point in me sitting here, blocking the sun."

I wait and I watch by myself. Always by myself.

The children have scared the birds out of the eaves. Now the pigeons flap skyward, searching our roof for places to nest. Just when I thought the birds had learned to leave me alone.

For generations, they have chirped it to their babies as soon as they popped out of their pearly eggs: "Keep away from the ugly old horned gargoyle with the chip in his left claw. Fly on the east side of the roof. Build your nest somewhere else."

But now the pigeons cannot get to their usual hidey-holes. They are disrupted by the presence of these giggling, jumping, farting kids, and so they flap for our roof. My ledge.

One bird in particular heads for my mouth, straw and leaves clutched in her beak—the makings of a new nest.

As soon as she is close, I growl, "Got your beak!"

The bird flutters down to the ledge, catching her breath. I see that she is rounded with motherhood, ready to lay her eggs.

I do not feel any guilt for nearly squashing her flat. Perhaps if I were a real gargoyle atop a finished cathedral, I might be willing to let her make a nest out of me. I might be able to protect her nest, watch over her eggs.

But I am no protector. So I will snap at the birds until they go away.

The bird tries again to land on my ledge; I grumble until my stone shakes, and she jumps back, agitated.

"That's what you get!" I crow. "Now shoo! You do not want to find out how hard I can bite!"

"Quiet, ugly!" Harpy barks from the east side of the roof. "The birds molt when they're scared. There's fluff everywhere!"

"Not enough to cover you up!" I shout back. *Ugly* does nothing. We are all ugly. And every time I think Harpy cannot possibly get uglier, she opens her mouth and speaks.

The pigeon looks down at my left claw and cocks her head. My claw is chipped, a wide-open hole in my toe where the stone has crumbled. Just the right size for a bird.

"Don't you dare," I tell her. "Don't you dare do it."

But she does. She backs into the space, tail feathers ruffled, and she sets down her straw and leaves, tickling my toe.

There is nothing I can do. If I were capable of such movement, I would have done it eight years ago.

"I will not stop growling at you," I warn the pigeon. "I will not leave you alone for a second."

But she flaps away from the ledge, off to fetch more fixings for her nest, and there is nothing I can do but wait and watch for her return.

I do not care about unwashed children living in our pillars. I do not care about the twigs in my toes. I do not care about the sun overhead; it has shone on my horns for ninety-nine summers, and one day, when we are nothing more than a pile of gravel, it will shine on our dust.

I do not care—

As long as it is quiet.

The pigeon's nest is finished.

She shapes it with her beak, pushing and nudging until all the straw and sticks and leafy mulch is to her liking, and then she sits.

"Don't you dare get comfortable," I grumble. "I want you out of here as soon as this wind dies down."

It is a blustery day, the kind that blows hot city grit into my grimacing mouth. The fruit trees in the abbey garden are stripped of the pink blossoms that have lingered since springtime. The reeds along the Sarluire whistle and moan as they are bent.

I have sat atop this roof long enough to feel the wind from every direction. Winds from the north bring the mossy chill of the forest, winds from the south push the unfortunate scents of the tannery to my ledge, and winds from the east put Harpy and the other east-side gargoyles on full blast, as if they are gossiping through trumpets.

This wind comes from the west and blows the brackish taste of the Sarluire right into my mouth. The bird flutters her wings inside my toe.

Across the roof, the east-side gargoyles talk above the noise of the wind, and inside my broken toe, the bird rustles and shimmies. The itch of her wings in my toe and the howl of the wind across my stone is more than I can bear.

"Enough!" I command. "I cannot take any more of your twitching! Get out of my toe now, or else I—"

The pigeon stops. She holds perfectly still. Her eyes watch the horizon—

And then she moves again, and I can see them. Three perfect eggs, deep within the nest. Round and white, a pearlescent sheen to their shells.

The mother preens, gives a proud coo.

"Well," I sniff, "congratulations. But I told you not to get comfortable. I will give you until tomorrow morning to gather your things, and then . . ."

I pause when I look down at the eggs again. I have never seen anything so small and so fragile. I have never *held* anything so small.

"Tomorrow morning," I repeat, a strange warmth fogging my brain. "Tomorrow evening at the latest."

The mother bird tucks her wings around her and falls asleep, and the wind seems to calm itself for her sake.

Down the sun goes, reluctantly. It will be back tomorrow with a fiery vengeance.

The mother sleeps, and the eggs sleep, but I am awake.

The eggs have such fragile shells, even though I know they are stronger than they appear. And I, made of stone, am turning to dust.

Dinnertime

Griselde served a meal of perpetual stew, cold roasted chicken with mustard, a strange, chewy fruit that tasted a little like dirt, and two large cups of weak ale. They used the bread to mop up the dregs of the broth.

Duck wanted to gorge on all of it, lick up every last smear of mustard—but so rich and plentiful was the feast that she found herself filled to the neck after only a little bit of everything.

She worried about offending the baker, but Griselde, in between smacks of her lips, said kindly, "You eat about as much as an actual duck, don't you, Duck?"

Duck took another bite of the sweet, doughy bread, despite her belly's warnings. She couldn't help it. Every time she promised herself it would be the last slice, well . . . there was always more bread, and she couldn't stop. It was too good.

"That's our prize loaf, that is." Griselde Baker tore a chunk of bread with her hands. "People love this white flour. I personally think it has all the good stuff beaten out of it. All the flavor's gone."

"There's flavor." Duck swallowed her crust and reached for more. She wasn't trying to fluff up the baker—this bread was absolutely flavorful. It tasted of salt and oil. And of coziness. Coziness and a full belly.

Griselde considered Duck with a sparkle in her eye. "Wait here." She fetched a stack of loaves from some cupboard, all different sizes, shapes, and colors, and set them on the table before Duck. "Black rye, whole grain, maslin, malted, and spelt. The fancy folks like the purest white flour. It's a trend—that's all. Makes them think they'll be pure, too, if they eat enough of it. You wait and see: next year they'll all be clamoring for rye again. These other loaves are much better."

Duck was full to the point of exploding, but at Griselde's insistence, she tried a bite of each variety . . . and found that the baker was right.

The white round table loaf was so deliciously fluffy, it melted in your mouth—but the whole grain lasted. It was instantly hearty. Filling. One bite of this would have kept a Crown fed for half a day. And every chew was slightly different—the bread was chock-full of seeds and nuts and other surprises.

The rye, too, was surprising—a bit sour, and sharp. It awakened all her senses.

She didn't care much for the malted. It was fermented, almost. It tasted the way beer smelled.

But when she bit into the maslin, something shifted.

Inside. Something shifted inside.

This was the same loaf she'd taken from the baker the other day.

The same kind she'd brought home to the Crowns. She could

never forget her own king loaf, the massive square with the criss-cross slashes on the top and Griselde's special seal branded into the crust.

Still warm, even after carting it to the cathedral and up to the roof . . .

Our fingers be nimble!
To our graves, be swift!
And on every head a—

"Duck?"

Griselde's eyes were pointed out the window at the bright sun, but the sides of her mouth pulled down. "Are you all right?"

Did Duck reek of despair? Had her heartbeat slowed down? Had she stopped breathing? How did the blind baker know that Duck was spinning with panic and contemplation?

"Ah." Griselde leaned back in her chair with a knowing, pity-ing smile. "I've had many an apprentice over the years—I recognize this particular silence. It's your family, isn't it? You're missing them."

"I don't have a family." It both was and was not a lie, and it was like a punch to the ribs to say it, but Gnat had been firm. Duck had a part to play, and there was no role for the Crowns in it.

"Of course you do!" Griselde chuckled. "You came from a children's home, didn't you? Over in Marilon? The nuns, the other kids, the teachers, even the rats in your chimney—they're as good as your family, aren't they? Family's more than just blood. It's . . . it's who you break your bread with."

Ash's face suddenly surfaced in her mind. Duck pinched her leg hard to make him go away.

"It's only natural that you should miss them—" Griselde Baker started.

"I don't miss them." Duck rubbed her nose, trying to pass it off as an itch when really, she was keeping her eyes from spilling over. "It's just . . . my first night away."

Her first night sleeping alone. As intrigued as she had been by this earlier, now she couldn't fathom it—how did anyone fall asleep without the comfort of other humans sawing gourds around them?

How did anyone bear to be by themselves, even for a day?

Griselde nodded. She'd been nodding this whole time, in fact— she was like a marionette, with an invisible puppeteer jerking her strings so it looked like she was actively listening.

She *was* listening, Duck realized. The baker was hanging on Duck's every word.

Duck had never been listened to like this except by Ash, and even he was usually one runaway sheep away from turning his attention elsewhere.

Duck had never had so much to say before, either—but the baker was the last person she should open up to.

This was why Gnat had chosen her: Duck knew how to keep her thoughts locked up inside.

She'd turn the key again. Right now.

"Would you mind lighting the lamp on the counter?"

Duck rose to fulfill Griselde Baker's request, but she hesitated before reaching for the matchlock.

The baker was blind, wasn't she? Then what use did she have for lamps?

Griselde laughed, sensing Duck's bewilderment. "I'm not

entirely without sight, you know. I can see things—they're just blurry. In this dim light, there's practically nothing there—I might as well close my eyes." She pointed at all the walls in succession. "Hence all the windows."

Duck unclenched her fists. Some part of her had been ready to run.

"Sometimes it seems like the Lord might be giving me back my sight," the baker went on. "I'll have weeks when I swear I can see things clearly again . . . and then, after a day or two, it's back into the darkness once more." She punctuated this with a chuckle. "Just as well. I count myself lucky to still see what I can."

"What happ—?" Duck started, and then realized it was probably a terribly rude thing to ask.

But Griselde waved a hand and answered her anyway.

"Too many years spent staring into those ovens. You can see that they're all scarred over." She tilted toward Duck, opening her eyes wide. Yes, Duck could see the huge, cloudlike film covering the iris of each of Griselde's eyes. They had once been blue, Duck was pretty sure.

"It took a long time for it to get this bad," Griselde said. "My Symon tried to warn me. He was always pulling me away from the ovens, telling me to take two steps back before I stuck my nose in— but I liked watching the loaves rise as they baked. There's something supremely satisfying about watching the fruits of your labor. Now I pay the piper. Symon," the baker added, her face glazed over with reminiscence, "is my late husband. He's been gone six years now."

Duck felt like she'd gulped down a stone.

Not late as in late for dinner.

Late as in he would never be on time again.

"You would have loved my Symon. Everyone did. He could spiral dough into a morning bun with one hand and shape baguettes with the other." Griselde shook her head free of the memories, clearing her throat. "Anyway. You're not the only one who is missing someone, Duck. I want you to remember that, in case you need to talk about it. I'm here."

The hand, again, extended toward Duck.

Only this time, it wasn't a tool the baker was looking for.

Duck's instinct was to pretend she hadn't seen it, but a strange curiosity drew her to set her own tiny hand into Griselde's big one, which enveloped hers like an oven mitt. It was surprisingly soft, considering how solidly muscular it was, and there—Duck could detect the baker's heartbeat.

She dropped the hand and stood up, searching her mind for an excuse to leave, but no one else needed her. This was the only place she was supposed to be now.

Griselde kindly saved her. "What time is it?"

Duck found the mechanical clock on the opposite wall. "Just past six."

"Zounds! It's getting late." Griselde started stacking the remnants of their feast in her arms. "Time to start winding down. Yes, I know it seems early, but come three in the morning, you'll be happy that you got rest."

The baker refused Duck's help with the dishes, instead nudging her off toward the stairs. "Get to sleep. You'll be working twice as hard tomorrow."

Upstairs, Duck used the chute above the cellar, took off her apron and whites, and lay on her bed.

She had never slept on a linen before.

Duck rolled over and stared out the window. If she bunched herself up toward the head of the bed, she could just see the top of the cathedral—the big ugly gargoyle silhouetted against the sky.

I should go to sleep, she kept thinking, but her mind did not want to settle. It was wound up tighter than a fishing net, and her thoughts seemed caught within—

Gnat and his scheming.

The Red Swords, skulking around Odierne.

Ash and the other Crowns, waiting for their bread, which Duck was supposed to supply.

Finally, she curled up on her other side, the cathedral behind her, and let sleep find her.

Tomorrow morning, the real work would start.

Journeyman

"So. You're the new apprentice."

The journeyman who had handled the trays of rolls and buns on market day now looked at Duck with an expression of pure disdain.

Duck didn't even bother trying to answer; he made her so nervous, she knew she'd be stammering until kingdom come.

The man was lean, with a boyish face, as though he were not fully grown yet, despite being several years into adulthood. His skin was a rich brown, and his eyes were deeply vigilant.

Duck had drifted through the night in a light, unsatisfactory slumber, worried that she'd be late on the first day of the job, but she'd finally fallen into a good, deep sleep when she'd heard someone downstairs. Frantic, she'd jumped into her uniform, come into the kitchen, and found not the baker but this stranger, prepping the yeast in bowls along the counters.

Now he poured a miller's bag of flour into a large mixing tub, glaring at her with suspicion. "Exactly how old are you supposed to be?" The way he phrased it made Duck freeze. Had he already figured out that her apprenticeship was a scam?

He tossed the empty flour sack onto a chair, whipping it past Duck with extra speed. "Do you even talk?"

"Eight," she squawked.

"For the love of Saint Odile!" he said in exasperation to Griselde as she strolled into the kitchen, wiping her hands on her apron. "I thought you were going to find someone who would actually help this season. This is a mere child."

"This," Griselde said, crossing the room to clutch Duck's shoulders, "is Duck. Duck, meet Petrus, my journeyman. He was once an apprentice, just like you." There was force in those words, Duck could hear—a request for manners, a plea for sympathy.

"I was once an apprentice," Petrus echoed, "but at least I was larger than an oatcake."

"Ignore him," the baker cheerfully told Duck, and then said to Petrus, "You may have been as long as a string bean when you were a lad, but you barely had a nose, and you don't have much more muscle now as an adult, so I would hold my tongue when it comes to criticisms of the physical form if I were you."

Petrus scowled. "I just don't like the way you open your doors to any mangy scruff that needs a home—" he started, but the baker snapped her fingers.

"Enough. This isn't scruff. This is Duck. And you will treat her with the same respect that I treat you. Understand?" She said all of this with a smile, but there was something formidable in the way she held her jaw.

Petrus mumbled a reluctant agreement, then stalked off to the storeroom.

Duck hovered where she was, afraid to move, until she heard Master Griselde whisper, "Don't pay any attention to him when he's in a mood like that. He's got a baby who won't let him sleep—wild-spirited, that Hugo is, which is just what Petrus needs to teach him some patience. He usually takes it out on the dough, which is good for the bread—but if he tries to bully you again, come find me."

But Duck knew she would never tell Griselde when Petrus picked on her again. No one liked a rat.

Besides, Duck was used to being badgered, especially by an authority figure.

At least he wasn't calling her Garbage.

She already knew she needed to be careful around Griselde, but she had to be doubly careful around Petrus—he had the air of a constable about him, always watching for even the slightest whiff of trouble.

Master Griselde saw many things, but Petrus would see even more. Duck would need to stay on his good side.

She studied the journeyman again when he came back into the kitchen. He lifted another sack of flour with minimal strain, a movement that had obviously been practiced many times over the years. He tossed the empty sack on the chair with the other one, then reached for a spoon and made a crater in the flour into which he poured a bowl of wet, foaming yeast.

There was something about how he worked, Duck noticed, that was . . . graceful. Equal parts habit and pride.

He'd rehearsed everything until it was total reflex—now he could putter around the kitchen with the yeast and the salt and the peel, king of the bakery.

Perhaps it was jealousy that had him so sour at her. Perhaps Petrus hated that there was someone else here to soak up Griselde's attention. Well, the last thing Duck wanted was to step on any toes. She was not here to be Griselde's pet. She was here only as a funnel—bread and coin went through her to the Crowns.

She was here for nothing more.

"Are you waiting for written instructions?" Petrus noticed Duck watching him. "Make yourself useful, Duck. Get moving." He'd used her name, but he'd also used the same tone Gnat did when he called her Garbage.

"I don't—" Duck started, but Petrus gave her a look of pure venom, so she scampered around to the other side of the oven to hide and think.

She could fill the water tubs, she decided. That was one of those endless chores that always needed doing. She carried buckets in from the outside barrels, then found a rag and cleaned up a bit of flour that had sprinkled onto the countertop.

"What is this?" Petrus pointed at the stack of empty flour sacks that Duck had moved onto the floor in order to wipe off the counter.

"Are you trying to kill her?" he snapped, nodding in Griselde's direction.

Duck shook her head, baffled, but Petrus flung the sacks into her hands so hard, she nearly tumbled backward.

"She can't see, nitwit," Petrus growled. "If the flour sacks fall onto the floor, she could trip over them and fly straight into an oven." He ended his lecture by thumping her on the head. "Think!"

Duck flooded with shame. At his command, she walked the empty flour sacks out to the back porch, then fetched ingredients, cleaned spills, and stirred water into flour until her arms ached, trying to get everything right, trying to stay out of Petrus's way, but feeling very much like she was one slipup away from ruining this whole scam.

Duck's first full day as a baker was finally over.

She lay flat on her back in her bed, her body sore, reviewing the day's hardest work.

First she'd helped Petrus make dough for the trenchers, the long, flat loaves that were the cheapest ones the bakehouse sold, the perfect bread for soaking in stew. People bought them in bulk, then let them grow stale for three or four days—that way they could be used as plates and spoons.

Duck made the mistake of asking if this particular batch would be saved for market day—five days from now—and Petrus snorted.

"We can try that, if you've got an extra hundred coronets lying around for the penalty." He continued to mold the loaves with his hands, muttering, "Save them for market day, honestly. Listen here—there are laws about bread—"

"No less than thirty," Griselde Baker piped in.

"And if we don't follow them, we get fined like a law office," Petrus went on. "We can't bake anything any sooner than midnight the night before we sell it—and that's not just for market day; that's any day."

"But you sell so much," Duck said, aghast. "It must take hours to bake them all! Surely there's another way—"

"Oh, if there was a loophole, we'd have found it." Griselde chuckled. "Such strict regulations come from the guilds, who get them straight from the queen of Avilogne herself: All breads must be baked fresh that same morning. Standards for sizes and flavors and quality of ingredients must be upheld. Every region has its own rules. Even prices are set in stone. Bread is the staple of life, after all. Makes sense that they'd monitor it more closely than sin."

So baking bread was much more than flopping dough into ovens—and Duck's eyes were opened to the realities of this trade more than once that first day.

Such as when the baker showed her the difference between yeasted and unleavened loaves. The unleavened loaves were thick, impossibly wet masses that had to be thrown into the oven the second they were shaped so they would crisp up, get a nice hard crust on them, and keep their forms.

But the yeasted loaves . . .

Those were monstrous blobs.

The very concept of yeast had Duck's head spinning—little granules of something that was living? You fed it sugar and warm water, and then it grew? And you put it inside your bread, and it grew even more?

And then you ate it?

Duck had never heard such a wild thing in all her days.

"You like cheese, don't you?" Petrus quipped, but Duck needed further explaining before she understood his point—apparently cheese was alive, too.

And worms in apples, and maggots in meat, and mold on cake—was there any food in the world that was just . . . food?

Petrus mixed the yeast into the flour, then covered it with a towel and told Duck not to touch it under any circumstances. Within a few hours, the dough had tripled in size! Petrus poked his finger into it, and it shrank back, then rose up again as if it had a will of its own.

"Now we shape the loaves," Griselde Baker informed Duck, using a pastry scraper to get all the sticky dough out of the bowl, "and leave them in a patch of sun so they can have a second rise. That way they hold their shapes in the oven."

The only thing that cut through Duck's wariness as she stared at the moving, living dough, soaking in the sunlight like a drowsy cat, was the thought of the end product—fluffy, lovely bread.

Worth the strange path through bubbling yeast, absolutely.

After mixing, rising, shaping, rising again, and baking, they had nearly ten dozen trencher loaves cooling on the racks.

"Let's take a break before we open shop," Griselde announced, and spread out a meal of cold smoked ham, half a loaf of horse bread (wheat dough containing beans and peas), and mugs of tea.

Petrus went home to eat with his wife and son, cutting through the backyard.

The baker settled into a chair at the table and inhaled her tea, letting the steam waft into her face—and then a knock came at the door.

Griselde groaned. "Good gracious me! Ah, well, this is why I have an apprentice, I suppose. Duck, go open that. If it's the miller, give him the empty sacks and tell him a hearty thanks from me."

But when Duck opened the door, she found three farmers on the porch, all of them sunburned beneath their brimmed hats. They each held a five-pound burlap sack in their arms.

"Uh . . . one moment," Duck stammered, then reluctantly fetched the baker, feeling guilty and useless, but Griselde didn't seem to mind.

"A bit early today, aren't we, boys?" Griselde held the door open as the farmers stepped into the bakery.

"A bit hungry, you mean," said one of the men as they congregated in the entryway, away from the heat of the ovens.

"It's harvest season," another one added. "Sun don't go down until late."

"Well, then, let's get you on your way. Your usual, Josse?" Griselde waited for an affirmative answer before wrapping up five of the cooled trenchers, trading them for Josse's sack of flour.

"Same for me," said another farmer. All three relinquished their flour sacks to Duck, who, at the baker's instruction, carried them into the storeroom.

The last man asked for only three trenchers, then reluctantly said, "You wouldn't happen to have anything . . . special I could trade you for, do you? Maybe some sweet buns? Only it's my little girl's birthday today. I'm happy to bring you another sack of flour to make up for the price, or even a cartful of potatoes—"

"Don't be ridiculous." Griselde felt for the handle of the nearest cupboard, then opened it and pulled out a small, round, white thing. "There. A delicious almond and honey cake. Cateline still likes unicorns, doesn't she?"

The farmer did a double take. So did Duck—the cake Griselde had produced was covered in a thin layer of goopy white sugary cream, and she'd also shaped horned beasts out of marzipan that danced across the top.

"Unbelievable," the farmer said, nearly in tears. "You never forget a thing, do you?"

"I could never forget the sight of you and your wife showing off your precious bundle, wrapped in her blankets. That tiny pink face!" Griselde folded her arms, as prim as someone her size could be. "You tell Cateline that Griselde Baker says happy birthday."

The farmers left with grins on their faces, one of them already breaking one of his loaves in half. Another one tried to slip Griselde a penny, which she turned down with a sneer. "Don't insult me." But when she shut the door behind them, she was smiling.

"You just witnessed a bit of a workaround, you see," she informed Duck. "Technically, we're communal property—this entire bakehouse belongs to all of Odierne. So if folks want to come in with their own flour and use our ovens to make their own bread, the guilds say we have to let them. The problem is, no one but us knows how to make a decent loaf of bread." She slapped the back of the largest oven affectionately, then rubbed it as if it were sore from all its hard work. "So instead, if a villager wants to bring me a sack of grain with the idea that they would bake themselves some trenchers if they knew how, and I whip it up for them instead . . .

well, do you see? Then I don't have people messing around with my ovens, and they're not out more than a bit of flour."

Duck did see. It was an under-the-table, sneaky kind of deal—loaves of ready-made bread in exchange for flour, which went right into the storeroom for the baker to use that week. A barter instead of dealing in cold hard cash.

Very clever. Gnat himself would have been proud.

"As for the cake," the baker went on, "that's my own vice. I just love them. Making them. Baking them. Selling them. Eating them. There's nothing better in the world than a nice slice of something sweet, don't you think?"

Duck had to decide quickly whether or not to lie. Instead of saying anything, she gave the baker a noncommittal shrug.

Griselde made a face like a cat whose tail had just been stomped on. "Haven't you ever had cake?" she demanded, and when Duck shook her head, she gasped. "Never had cake? Oh, my dear, dear Duck!" She held her hands to her heart, pressing deep into that barrel chest of hers. "We'll have to remedy that at once! I believe I have enough sugar—"

But Petrus came in just then, smelling faintly of sour milk.

Griselde put a finger to her lips and whispered, "Petrus doesn't approve of the way I bend the rules. Let's not tell him about the unicorn cake." She arranged her face in a professional smile, but there was a faint twinkle in her opaque eyes.

The baker thought she had a secret. A secret with Duck.

An odd feeling swelled in Duck's chest, but she flushed it out with the thought of the Crowns, Gnat in particular, asking her to spill everything she knew about the baker.

Duck couldn't have any secrets with Griselde. Duck was here to keep her own secrets.

"How is little Hugo?" Griselde asked.

To Duck's surprise, Petrus lit up. "He's in such a mood today! Babbling and kicking like an egg dancer—" Seeing that Duck was still in the room, Petrus darkened. "He's well enough. I'll open the shop now, yes? Let's get those loaves moved."

He sauntered off to the counter, and Griselde leaned over to Duck.

"It's been years since I took on an apprentice," she said, "because my last one turned out to be a thief."

Duck's insides went cold and slippery.

"He stole money, bread, tools to resell." Griselde shook her head, rolling her eyes. "Hardly an international crisis, if you ask me—but it put Petrus on high alert. He isn't . . . keen to hire anyone new. Not after what happened last time. But don't mind him, like I said—only he's very protective of me and of our establishment. He's protective of his own job. Give him some time to warm up to you. I know he will."

Could the baker hear the way Duck's heart pummeled her rib cage? Surely it was as loud as a stick against a barrel. But regardless, Duck felt compelled to ask one tiny question as she glanced down at her toes: "What made you change your mind?"

Griselde inhaled, and Duck could see she was about to laugh, say something lighthearted, make a joke—but instead, she froze. She'd been smiling, but now her mouth hung open, her eyes going even hazier than usual.

Another knock at the door shook Griselde out of her trance.

"The work summons," she boomed in her usual warm tone, and headed back down the hall to the porch, leaving Duck to wonder what she had been thinking, asking questions like that.

She should know better than to go off script. From now on, she would only ask questions about flour measurements, yeast protocols, and mixing techniques.

Nothing that might cause the baker to go quiet like that again. Nothing that might cause a ripple.

Duck definitely couldn't afford to cause ripples now that she knew what the last of Griselde's apprentices had been—a thief.

She hoped she was long gone before Griselde Baker figured out that she was housing another one. She did not want to see the disappointment and the betrayal in those milky blue eyes.

Market Day

Duck was sacked out in her bed at three o'clock in the morning when Petrus stuck his head through her doorway and said in a gravelly, sleep-choked voice, "Wake up already. Time to make bread."

Roosters snoozed. Dawn bells wouldn't ring for another three hours. It was black outside, dark as a grave, all fog curls and cold thatched roofs. Duck shivered as she crawled out of bed and dressed in her uniform.

It had been a long first week, but she'd survived.

Every day, they worked from sunup to midday, making trenchers and table breads both for the villagers who purchased them from the storefront window and for the people who came a-rapping on the back door. Griselde traded bread for sacks of flour or occasionally—and technically illegally—a fistful of garden carrots or a dozen eggs.

"Come along," Griselde had said to Duck only yesterday, "it's time for a primer on kneading. Have you got strong hands?"

"I . . . I don't know."

"You will soon. Trust me." The baker had shown Duck, with her own powerful hands, how to fold the dough over on itself again and again, stretching it, lengthening it, toughening it.

As she came down the stairs, Duck took inventory of the things that hurt. Her fingers hurt from clenching the spoons as she measured yeast. Her palms and forearms hurt from kneading the dough. Her neck and shoulders hurt from stirring, her back hurt from lifting, and she had sneezed probably a hundred times this week, her pipes clogged with flour and semolina—which meant that her lungs, throat, nose, and eyes hurt, too.

Griselde had been right: it was easy to fall asleep with the sun still up when you were bone tired.

Duck had managed to bamboozle her way through the first week of a false apprenticeship, and today, she would experience her first market day on this side of the counter.

Not only did Duck have to help Griselde and Petrus run the actual bakery, but she also had to feed the Crowns. Had to slip them free bread and loose coins, cover it all up properly, and not get caught.

Easy as that.

If she failed, the Crowns would starve.

Or, more accurately, they'd be relegated to the scraps of the streets—and Duck? She would *be* a scrap on the streets. Gnat would yank her from the bakehouse, boot her out of the Crowns, and she'd be fending for herself, a lonesome duckling, hiding in alleys, begging for bread crusts, and hoping the Swords didn't sniff her out.

If she got caught, it wouldn't matter how charmed Griselde was by her new apprentice—Petrus would drag Duck out of the bakehouse by the ears and lock her in the stocks himself.

Duck rolled up her sleeves and tied her apron, ordering herself to stop shaking. It was only a bit of bread and a few spare pennies.

Other Crowns had stolen far grander things; if she couldn't pull this off, she didn't deserve to be a Crown. Simple as that.

"Are we ready?" Griselde asked, her breath reeking of barley tea.

She was having a good sight day today. Days like this came and went, Duck was learning. Some days left the baker in a murky brown world, and navigating it made her understandably grumpy. But other days, there was very little difference between what Griselde saw and what Duck saw. The only reminder of Griselde's altered experience came when she mistook a red cloth for a green one.

"Help me with the pastries," Griselde instructed Duck. "I want everything orderly and glistening in that morning sunshine."

They'd been baking for hours, and not just a couple varieties of grain bread, but their whole selection—white and wheat, rye and barley, crusts of the palest tan and crusts that were brown as char. Loaves of all shapes—long baguettes, rounded cobs, twists and curls, fat and fine-floured, textured with seeds, smooth as a friar's bald head.

But they'd also baked other things, things that were not as simple as mere loaves: hot cross buns, pillowy soft rolls, morning pastries sprinkled with cinnamon, tarts and puddings . . . Duck's head spun trying to keep it all straight.

Compared to the work of the weekdays, which had been a mild summer breeze, market day baking was a whirlwind hurricane.

Every inch of counter space was covered in baskets overflowing with loaves and trays lined with sticky masses.

Griselde was an enigma; she planted herself in one place so as to be maximally effective at rolling and stretching and shaping all the different doughs, and yet she was everywhere at once.

Duck tried to be helpful by fetching the baker things she might require, but mostly Duck felt like she was in the way.

Underfoot.

Petrus was not in the way. He and the baker had their own rhythm, a symbiotic one, born of years working and dancing around each other in this very kitchen. They anticipated each other's needs and completed tasks not one after the other but together. They did all this without even speaking—at least, not speaking instructions. Griselde loved to talk, loved to fill every silence with a story.

And her stories were always entertaining and funny. If Duck hadn't been a Crown, if Duck were truly a random orphan placed in this apprenticeship with Master Griselde, well . . . she'd have considered herself very lucky indeed.

Lucky to dream that someday, she might be as known by Griselde as Petrus was.

Just before prime bells rang, Griselde placed boiled eggs on a slice of rye for Duck. "Nibble that down," she said, "and then we'll open shop. You'll handle the baskets. Loaves are six a penny. Gallon loaves, two. Anyone gives you trouble, send them right to me."

Duck stared down at the baskets. So many varieties—and now that they were all together, they started to look the same.

"They'll let you know what they want." Griselde winked and then, without further ado, unfurled the shutters.

Time to sell.

Daylight poured into the kitchen, illuminating the dust on the flour and the ground spices that still hovered in the air. The ovens glowed, their mouths flaming like bonfires.

A crowd had already gathered, and they all looked hungry as they pressed themselves to the counter.

"Good morrow!" Griselde called out. "Come, make your orders while it's still hot!"

People shouted at Duck from all angles, singing out names of breads and pastries. She tried to focus on just one word at a time, tried to select the orders and pass them to the right customers, but it was too much.

"Three cockets, I said!" a fishwife with an impatient purple face shouted. "Do your ears even work?"

"Bite your tongue, Master Polly," came the booming voice of Griselde, her reassuring hand falling on Duck's shoulder. "I won't have you harassing my new employee—and I'll remind you how flustered you and William were on your first market day. Why, I called for a herring, and you handed me an eel!" The baker passed the fishwife her order and stayed beside Duck until she left.

"How about I put you in charge of the strongbox?" Griselde Baker said. "Do you know how to count change?"

Duck's heart thumped.

She made herself nod, but inside, she was all aflutter. Yes, she could count change—but did Griselde Baker realize that she'd just handed over the care of her cash to a thief?

Not just any thief—a Crown?

Duck had planned to find a reason to stand near the strongbox and wait for Griselde and Petrus to be distracted, then plunge her hand in and swipe a coin—but this was much better.

Gnat himself had never had such a lucky break.

As Griselde fended off the clamor of hungry customers, Duck positioned herself at the strongbox—and caught sight of Petrus, who swiftly moved through the crowd and back to the counter with flashing eyes. "You're giving her the money?"

"She's doing you a favor," Griselde defended. "We both know you hate dealing with the strongbox." Duck could detect the undercurrent in her tone: *Don't question me, and don't question what I choose to do with my own apprentice.*

But Petrus did not look very grateful.

Duck took in a deep breath, staring at the stacks and stacks of coins before her. She couldn't let the journeyman's wary eyes stop her from doing what Gnat had sent her to do, even though her lungs felt squeezed with nerves.

When someone handed her a pile of pennies to pay for a dozen oatcakes, Duck's fingers slid one coin free from the stack and dropped it into her apron, smooth as cider.

When another someone needed change after purchasing five morning buns, Duck counted out a little extra from the strongbox and pocketed it, unnoticed.

And when some dirty-cheeked, smirking boy passed her a shiny penny, saying, "All the bread I can get for that, please," she kept her cool.

Frog Eyes.

Even under the ridiculous wrappings of a moldy old brown robe, Duck would know that scrunchy face and croaky voice anywhere.

Behind him, wearing a faded farmer's wrap, Le Chou was trying very hard to pretend that he didn't know the baker's new apprentice personally, and he was doing a poor job of it. He kept grinning at Duck, then forcing himself to look away with a start, then slithering his eyes back over to her, guilt in his smile.

Duck wanted to cry.

She grabbed six trenchers and, along with the penny and the rest of the coins she'd stored in her apron, passed them into Frog Eyes's hands.

Then she waited.

She held her breath.

She counted to ten.

She glanced at Petrus, who was out in the square with a tray of baguettes, and at Griselde Baker, who was pushing an extra hot cross bun into the hands of a haggard-looking mother.

"Come back again," Duck said.

Frog Eyes tucked the coins into his robe and saluted her. "Oh, we will. Without a doubt, we will."

Then he and Le Chou slunk away from the counter. At the edge of the crowd, they were joined by a third figure in a monk's robe—one who held his right arm tight against his body and walked backward so he could watch Duck until they disappeared from the square.

Gnat.

Duck wished she could have seen Ash today—though maybe

it was for the best that he hadn't come. It would have been too hard not to leap over the counter to hug him.

But she'd done it.

She'd stolen bread and coin for the Crowns—the whole reason Gnat had stationed her at the bakehouse—and so they'd be able to eat this week.

The Red Swords couldn't accuse them of picking pockets or swiping goods.

And Duck would do it all again next week. Every week until Gnat decided she'd be more useful somewhere else.

The bakery stayed open until they were out of loaves, then out of prepared dough, then out of flour altogether, and then the whole town decided it was finally satisfied.

Griselde and Duck cleaned the kitchen and put equipment away. Petrus went home to his family. They wouldn't see him again until Tuesday.

Duck retreated to her room and collapsed on her mattress of hay, where she lay, too exhausted to move, too achy to sleep.

Griselde had done the final tally and announced the sums: a hundred coronets in her strongbox. If she missed the few extra coins Duck had skimmed off the top, she made no indication, and so the nerves that had rushed through Duck since this morning finally settled.

Duck recited that figure again in her mind. A hundred coronets. She'd never seen so much money.

It really did pile up, she'd learned, if there was enough of it. She'd always thought that was a myth—but Griselde had dumped the cash out on the kitchen table, a tiny mountain of wealth. Even though some of the money went to the guild for dues and to Petrus for his salary and back into the bakehouse for ingredients and supplies, it shone like possibility.

Like security.

Duck picked bits of dried dough from under her nails and the ends of her hair.

She had not expected to be this tired.

Bread was so soft, so warm. It shouldn't take so much work to make.

Long days on her feet, pouring, spinning, stirring, kneading, punching, and otherwise throttling the combination of flour and yeast and water until it was stretchy, scalding her eyebrows every time she pushed raw loaves into the oven's chasm, reaching with the peel, her wrists aching—and this was just the first week.

She found the rooftop of the abandoned cathedral, found the hulking gargoyle staring off into the setting sun, and stared at him as though he could see her.

What had Frog Eyes and Le Chou thought today when they'd seen her?

Did they miss her as much as she missed them?

Were the Crowns talking about her now? With gratitude?

Did they know how much it hurt to be away from them for this long? Did they know how much Duck wished she could be back in that cathedral, sitting around the busted-up nave, sharing the remnants of a marbled cob?

"Duck?" Griselde called through the door along with a friendly knock.

Duck scrambled off the bed and stood just as the door opened.

"Oh, I'm sorry, dear, did I wake you?" Griselde had changed out of her usual whites and into a smart blue tunic and deep charcoal trousers.

Duck swallowed a yawn and shook her head. She was tired, yes, but too antsy to sleep. Too many bread recipes in her mind. Too many kneading techniques and types of grain to remember. Plus, all her hours belonged to the baker now—even the nighttime ones.

Griselde fiddled with the edge of her tunic. "I was only seeing if you wanted . . . if you wanted to . . . do something."

"Of course." Duck braced herself for a request to lift a heavy bag of flour, to deliver correspondence to the guild headquarters, or to do something even more taxing.

"Bless you." Griselde chuckled. "Strictly speaking, it isn't apprentice work, so you're absolutely within your rights to say no. But I thought maybe you'd like to do something fun . . . with me."

Duck said nothing.

"You know, fun?" Griselde teased. "You've heard of it, haven't you? I thought we could celebrate your first successful market day. Only if you want to. I'll understand perfectly if you decide to stay home." The baker was trying so hard to relay to Duck that this was not required, that Duck could say no—but the longing in Griselde's cloudy eyes gave away the truth.

The baker was really, really hoping Duck would say yes.

And Duck, whose very skeleton was so tired, who knew it was a miracle that she was upright, felt a whisper of intrigue. Fun? Celebrate? What did the baker have up her billowed sleeves?

An apprentice was obligated to do anything and everything her employer asked of her—but Duck was only thinking of the evening's possibilities when she said timidly, "All right."

"Yes?" Griselde confirmed, then clapped her hands, the meat of her forearms rippling. "Get your shoes on, then. I'll fetch my cane. Oh, and make sure you leave any valuables here. Not so much as a penny in your pockets—where we're going, you want to have as few reasons for people to pay attention to you as possible."

And Duck, who knew those kinds of places very well, changed out of her smudged uniform and into her second set of clean clothes, noting, without entirely meaning to, that Griselde did not lock the bakery doors when they left.

Tournament

"Tell me when you see the sign for the Cheap Wife," Griselde told Duck as they moseyed down the street, going quick as they could for a mostly blind baker and a mostly small child.

Duck did not want to tell the baker that she could not read. She knew only a few letters—but she didn't want to admit that out loud. It didn't matter for her job; plenty of beginning apprentices didn't know a *b* from a bee. But she didn't want to reveal anything about herself that the baker wouldn't like. It was a strange feeling—why should she care what Griselde thought of her? As long as Duck was a competent enough apprentice and flew under both Griselde's and Petrus's noses, nothing else mattered.

With a sniff to gather her pluck, Duck murmured, "Perhaps you can tell me what color the sign is instead?"

"Oh, I see." Griselde put a hand on Duck's shoulder. "It's nothing to be ashamed of, my dear. You know, Petrus wasn't a well-versed reader when he started at the bakehouse. He knew just a handful of words he'd plucked from scripture—he was for the church, believe it or not. Wanted to become a monk, devote his life to God, but then he decided his true calling was bread, not Bibles." Griselde chuckled. "I like to think it worked out for God in the end."

No wonder Petrus had such a suspicious air about him—he was churchgoing folk. Crowns, in general, did not trust clergymen or anyone adjacent—people who would rat you out to the constables and people who would rat you out to God were one and the same. All the more reason to stay out of Petrus's way.

"Part of my duties as your master is to ensure you learn your letters," Griselde Baker said. "We'll get you started with a proper tutor this week— ah, I think we've made it. Yes, the smell of rubbish ale and unwashed men—we're here."

They'd stopped down near the southern docks of the Sarluire in front of a rather clandestine entrance, which led into a poorly thatched building, its whitewash stained with soot.

Duck prepared herself to enter a dark, flickering tavern where she'd be forgotten in a corner with the spittoon while Griselde guzzled spirits and socialized. Not exactly her idea of fun, but she was Griselde's apprentice and therefore at her beck and call.

"Stick with me," Griselde warned Duck, bringing her cane closer to her body, "and keep your hands where people can see them."

Inside, the Cheap Wife was stuffy and loud, with lambent candles illuminating the crowded tables and the rushes thrown on the floor to cover the sour slicks of either booze or previously ingested booze. People leaned over the counter to shout their orders to the barkeep, who scrambled to keep up with the hordes of thirsty customers.

But the baker pushed Duck past all of this, weaving among chairs and drinking games and arm-wrestling matches, through a back door, which opened up into—

A stadium.

A square field of dirt, surrounded on four sides by raked seating. It was open to the sky but invisible from the street—the only way to get to this stadium was to go through the Cheap Wife . . . which essentially guaranteed that all the spectators would be slightly tipsy when they took their seats.

In the ring below, a parade of horses trotted through the dirt, their riders wearing various colorful tunics beneath their plated armor. Duck spotted a cache of weapons leaning against the far wall, blunt swords and axes and lances. All around the stadium, spectators were waving the colors of their favorite knights— oranges, reds, greens, purples.

A tournament!

"So, where shall we sit?" Griselde asked, but Duck was gob-smacked. She never would have guessed that the baker was leading her someplace like this!

"On . . . a bench?" Duck offered when she realized Griselde was waiting for her reply.

Griselde threw her head back and laughed. "You're too easy, Duck. Too easy."

She led Duck all the way to the northernmost side of the stadium and plopped down right in the very first row. There were a couple of interesting characters sharing their bench—a hiccup-ping friar who nipped from a flask when he thought no one was looking, a toothless jester, an old woman who resembled a witch in both hair and face—and Griselde greeted them all.

"I've never been to a tournament before," Duck confessed, though she supposed her wide-eyed expression likely gave that away.

"This isn't exactly a *real* tournament," Griselde said as she pulled a cornflower-blue handkerchief from her tunic and began waving it like a banner. "This is really more of a pre-tournament, you might say. A practice. The real tournament season begins next week—this is just a bit of frippery."

Frippery! This was anything but. Duck was close enough to see the stubble on the jaw of the knight in purple. She could see the braids decorating his gray horse's mane. Track marks in the ring, dirt mounds from the horses' gallops, scuffs where someone had fallen from their ride—no, this wasn't frippery. This was the most serious, wonderful thing Duck had ever been a part of.

And they were right in the front row! Duck scooted forward so her arms dangled over the wall—she could reach out and grab a handful of horse tail if she wanted.

Wait until Gnat heard about this, she thought, and a delicious hit of vengeance warmed her chest.

Wait until they all heard about what quiet little Garbage got to see.

"Is this all right, then?" Griselde Baker asked discreetly, her arm pressing up against Duck's.

"Yes!" Duck blurted out, then arched around, studying the baker. "But . . . what about . . . ?" She stared at Griselde's spilled-milk eyes for about two seconds longer than she should have, then glanced away.

The baker stretched back in her seat. "Maybe some blind saps prefer to stay inside a dark house all day and watch the shadows, but not this one. I enjoy the tournaments for the same reasons you do—the sounds, the blurs, the movement, the thrill—whoa, look alive!" Griselde grinned as a thunder of applause rippled through the stadium. Trumpets blared. The riders charged their horses forward in the dirt, their stomps making everything shake.

Griselde lifted her arm, showing Duck the hairs that had risen, standing in rank like wiry soldiers. "You don't have to be able to see to feel that." She then dropped her head back and let out the most earsplitting whoop Duck had ever heard: "Huzzah!"

The spectators around them chorused with her, and the knights lined up in the ring, triumphant.

People chanted slogans—some church-appropriate, some dirty as sin. They threw peanuts and held up flags. Ladies threw ribbons to their favorite competitors. Men threw flowers down to the green knight, who held her silver helmet under one arm while twisting back her brilliant blond hair.

"The Green Dragon!" Duck gasped.

Griselde Baker nodded. "She's good—very good. A real rising star. You're a fan?"

Duck watched the Green Dragon greet her adoring fans and thought of Fingers, awestruck at the hot fair, itching for an autograph.

"I . . . know someone who is," she said.

If Griselde Baker had any other questions, she kept them to herself.

A herald in a black surcoat and white hose walked to the center of the ring and introduced each rider, pausing while the crowds cheered for their favorites. He explained the rules, and then the knights split off to their respective corners, waiting for their turns at the joust.

Griselde hollered, making her blue handkerchief dance. Duck glanced around the stadium. There were only a few others holding up blue banners, and so Duck, feeling bold, tapped the baker on the shoulder.

"Why blue?" she asked. The blue knight, by Duck's assessment, was the shortest, the stockiest, and the slowest—the least likely to win by far.

Griselde let out another tremendous yawp, then answered, "It's the last color I have left."

Duck frowned.

"Every other color faded to a tea-stained brown long ago," Griselde explained. "But blue stays." She tugged on the hem of her blue tunic and winked at Duck, who looked back out at the knights in the square, trying to imagine such a murky world.

"What about you?" Griselde nudged Duck. "Who will you root for?"

There were so many colors and knights to choose from—but Duck's eyes kept going right to a villainous-looking man in a hooded plum tunic.

His tassels were silver, his horse white as ice. There was

something sinister about him, his shifty eyes framed by thistly eyebrows, and the chain mail on his armor made him look like a dragon transformed. Duck couldn't help but smile as she pointed and said, "Him. Purple."

The baker clicked her tongue. "Ahhhh. Sir Hugh the Horrible, is it?"

"Undefeated," piped up the witch with the frizzy hair.

"So far." Griselde's words carried the spirit of playfulness. "But let's see what Blue makes of him."

"Rigby the Pygmy?" The witch chortled, showing her seed-brown teeth. "You couldn't pick a less worthy opponent."

"Perhaps," Griselde fired back. "Perhaps I just like an underdog."

And then the drums rolled, the trumpets sounded, and the audience settled.

The tournament was about to begin.

It was, without a doubt, the most fun Duck had ever had.

Red beat orange, green beat white, pink stripes beat black checkers, and then green beat red in a last-minute upset that threw both riders to the ground. The two knights, green and red, drew their swords.

This, Duck thought, her grin so wide her teeth dried out, was sport.

Purple, on the other hand, absolutely slaughtered yellow, slaughtered black checkers, and slaughtered gold—metaphorically, of course, because no one was really running their opponents through with sword or lance.

But Hugh the Horrible acted as if he were killing for real,

strutting around with his elbows bent, his chest as wide as he could make it, his weapon at the ready at all times.

And the audience absolutely loved to hate him—they booed and hissed when he beat the Green Dragon, but he just waltzed around the edge of the arena, pumping his arms as if to say, *Let's hear it! Let's hear how much you despise me!*

He thrived on it—and Duck thought it was pure delight to root for someone so obviously evil.

The baker bought Duck a candied apple, and as the tournament continued, she munched contently . . . until it was down to the last round.

The sun had set, the lanterns were lit, and in the corners of the ring, the two opponents prepared for the final fight.

Purple versus blue.

"Well, what do you think about that?" Griselde smirked at the witch.

"I think Hugh will have Rigby stuffed and use him for target practice," sneered the witch.

Griselde rubbed her hands together. "Well, Duck, what do you suppose we put a wager on this?"

Duck, full of sugar and punchy from the exhaustion of the long week, the market day, and now cheering her lungs out for two straight hours, didn't even pause before she said, "What terms?"

Griselde's eyebrows shot up with amusement. "If purple wins, you get a penny."

Duck's jaw dropped. A whole penny for doing nothing except rooting for the most obvious winner? That meant an extra penny to pass to the Crowns next market day.

"And if blue wins," Griselde said, and her eyes suddenly slipped far away, and her voice grew so soft Duck had to lean in to hear her, "you have to accompany me to another tournament sometime."

Duck frowned, even though she was relieved that the baker wouldn't expect a penny from her if purple lost. "That . . . doesn't seem like much of a prize for you."

But the baker pressed her lips together, solemn as a law clerk. "It is." She extended her huge hand, and Duck shook it.

Blue and purple fought. The audience pressed forward collectively—Duck was up against the wall, close enough to smell the tang of the metal armor, the sweat on the horses' rears, the kicked-up dust as the two knights sped toward each other, their lances at their sides—

And in a swift move, Rigby the Pygmy and Hugh the Horrible knocked each other off their steeds, each rolling into the dirt.

"They both survive the fall!" the herald shrieked. "To the swords!"

Rigby the Pygmy only came up to Hugh the Horrible's shoulders—and Hugh looked absolutely furious as he yanked his sword from his belt.

"Rigby's in for it now," the witch said with a rude cackle.

Duck was going to win. The blue knight scrambled to find his sword and, in a fit of panic, grabbed a massive ax from the armory wall—a weapon that was nearly as tall as Rigby himself.

Hugh the Horrible smiled wickedly, charging toward his opponent with all the ferocity of a rhino—

But Griselde erupted in an exhilarated "Come on, Rigby!"

Duck looked at her, then repeated, as loud as her tiny voice could go, "Come on, Rigby!"

The others on the bench, the friar and the jester and the witch, stared at them, flabbergasted.

"Come on, Rigby!" Griselde shouted again, more in the crowd's direction than into the ring, and then Duck joined in, and they sang it out together: "Come on, Rigby!"

Crooked smiles appeared all around them. "Come on, Rigby!" the friar shouted.

Then the crowd, somewhat sincere but mostly amused, chanted with them: "Come on, Rigby!"

Out in the ring, Rigby the Pygmy stopped mid-slash, bewildered. He stared blankly at the crowd; this was probably the first time he'd ever heard an audience chant his name, Duck realized.

She shouted even louder.

She didn't know she could shout so loud.

Hugh the Horrible, however, looked positively poisonous— and in the split second that the blue knight was distracted, the purple knight struck.

He swiped at Rigby the Pygmy, and like a pitched ball, the blue knight went flying, his own weapon falling to the ground with a clatter.

Purple had won.

The crowd collectively *awwe*d, then regained their bearings and cheered for their champion, wildly, without hesitation, even though he was clearly something of a scoundrel. Even Duck screamed until her throat was raw.

And then the tournament was over.

The knights removed their armor and rubbed their aching limbs. The horses were whisked away to be tended to, and Hugh the Horrible lingered near the audience, inking his signet ring and stamping it onto the hands and faces of anyone who wanted an autograph.

The witch folded her arms. "How do you like your underdog now?"

It was a gentle enough ribbing, but Griselde didn't take the bait. "Some things never change," she said confidently, "until one day, they do."

When they got back to the bakery, the exhaustion of the day hit Duck like a concrete brick.

She turned to Master Griselde on the back porch, wanting to say thank you before she fell asleep standing up, but Griselde spoke first.

"Thank you for coming." The baker sounded almost shy. "I used to go to all the jousts with my Symon before he passed. I dragged Petrus a few times, but he doesn't care for the violence—and anyway, he's got Raina and Hugo now, so he's much too busy to take an old woman to see the worst knights in Avilogne bash each other to bits. So thank you. It was lovely to have your company." She paused, her hand on the doorknob. "I always thought I'd take my own children someday. I wanted them, you know. So did my Symon. 'A boy for you, a girl for me, and a spare, just in case,' he'd say."

A strange feeling crept over Duck.

A cold dread prickling her skin.

The baker had a funny look on her face. As if she were close-up and faraway at the same time. "That was the plan, but you can't always plan for such things, can you?"

Duck's heart thumped. *Danger*, it called. *Danger, danger, danger.*

"You know this all too well, don't you? Losing your own parents so young." Griselde breathed in. "Would you like—?" she started.

And Duck, knowing it was rude to interrupt her employer, cut in anyway: "I'm tired."

Griselde Baker blinked, her eyes refocusing. "Of course you are. Go right along to bed, now, and sleep as long as you'd like. Tomorrow's Sunday—day of rest. The bakehouse will keep. And Duck, there's plenty of other places we could go. There's a greyhound race Monday afternoon—money's on a pup named Nosewise to take it all."

Duck said nothing. Her pulse spiked, sharp as the tip of a lance.

"Yes, let's think it over," Griselde finally said, "and see what Monday brings. Oh, before I forget." She reached into her pocket and held out a single shining penny. "Hard won, if you ask me. Promise me you'll spend it on something utterly delightful."

Duck took the penny, then went straight up to her room without looking back.

Curled up on her mattress, the noises of the tournament rang in her ears—the rattle of armor, the clinking of swords, the rush of movement against a blur of color as if she, too, were dependent on clouded eyes.

But the sound she could not shake, not even by the arrival of the slivered moon, was the baker's unfinished question.

"Would you like . . . ?"

What had she been about to ask?

Would you like a buttered roll for a bedtime snack?

Would you like a cup of warm milk to help you sleep?

But maybe Griselde Baker had been about to ask something else. Something far more dangerous.

I've always wanted a child, the baker had told Duck, so maybe she was going to ask: *Would you like a mother?*

As the baker's apprentice, Duck would give Griselde anything she required—a scoop of flour, a pastry cutter, a wedge of salt, hard labor in the form of lifting and pounding and slapping and reaching into hot ovens and dragging thirty-pound sacks of leavening and handling every market day sale—

But she would not give Griselde this.

Duck did not need a mother. Duck was a Crown.

And Crowns were the children of nobody.

Tabula Rasa

True to her word, Griselde Baker set Duck up with reading and writing lessons—not with her, for the baker was, in her own words, "far too impatient to sit and draw lines on a chalkboard, even with the likes of you for company."

Nor did she employ Petrus to teach Duck her letters, for which Duck was tremendously thankful—he'd recently given her a firm tongue lashing for accidentally killing a batch of yeast. She'd fed it water that was too hot and scalded the weird little growths to death.

"That's all right," Griselde had reassured Duck as she scraped the dead dough into the compost bucket. "It's happened to the best of us once or twice."

Baking was notoriously difficult, the baker reminded Duck almost daily, and every step in the bread-making process required delicate balance between two opposites. The water for yeast could not be too hot or too cold. Not kneading the dough enough would mean the bread had no spine; kneading the dough too much would turn the bread into wood. Duck had almost let herself be comforted.

But when the baker's back was turned, Petrus had glared at Duck with poisonous barbs for eyes. "Money," he'd hissed. "Flour costs money. The time it takes to make a new batch of yeast costs money. Do you have extra money, Duck?"

Duck had shaken her head, her gaze on the floor.

"Then I suggest you be extra careful from now on."

Yes, it was a relief that Duck would not be spending any more time than necessary with the journeyman. Instead, Griselde farmed out Duck's education to the local notary, who lived two streets over in the law district, and to Duck's surprise, she took to learning her letters like, well . . . like a duck took to water.

Master Nichol Frobertus was a wiry old man with a pair of coin-size spectacles that hooked over his springy ears, and he was never not squinting; he glanced at everything around him with ancient suspicion, his forehead collapsed in permanent wrinkles.

And from the moment Duck entered his office, he was nothing but patient.

"So, this is the baker's newest protégé."

He leaned over his pulpit and examined her, his mouth serious, the yellow tassels on his robe and cap dangling—but his watery old eyes twinkled amicably.

Duck squeaked out an answer in the affirmative, then peered at the room around her.

She, made of one-fourth street dirt and three-fourths stolen food scraps, felt like standing in this office was sacrilege—it was towering with books, shelves reaching the ceiling and overflowing with gold-flecked spines and tomes that looked older than the notary himself. Where there weren't books, there were parchments stacked and covered in scribbled ink, and where there weren't parchments, there was a small amount of walkable floor. Everything smelled like antique oak, rich velvet, and expensive ale.

And everywhere Duck looked, there were knickknacks and artifacts that could likely feed the Crowns until Epiphany, were she to swipe something . . .

"You call yourself Duck? Is that your Christian name?"

Duck ripped her eyes away from a tiny volume on the corner of Master Frobertus's desk, which would just fit into her pocket. "I'm . . . not sure."

"You're a foundling, correct?" Master Frobertus peered down at the paperwork Griselde Baker had sent with Duck. "Well, good. Not good for you, of course," he scrambled to clarify. "It's better for me to have a completely blank slate. Tabula rasa, you know?"

Duck did not know, so she just stood there, her hands clasped, ignoring the stare of the marble bust of a young man on a pillar behind the notary's pulpit.

"What I mean is," Master Frobertus said, coming around from behind the pulpit, revealing himself to be a shockingly shriveled specimen, almost bent in half by the stoop of his ancient back, "many children pick up bad habits or falsehoods drilled into them by their well-meaning families. But you come to me with a completely unfilled head. I don't have to help you unlearn anything vile. We'll save time."

He moved painfully slowly, shuffling along from his pulpit to a desk the size of a coffin. It took him a good minute to lower himself into his chair, and, once settled there, he looked as if he might remain in this very position until the Last Judgment.

"Now," he said as soon as he'd convinced Duck to take the seat opposite him, her feet dangling from her chair, "show me which letters you already know."

The session was not as excruciating as Duck had expected, but she was rusty—she had to admit her ignorance when she could not pick out a single letter correctly.

But the notary was never rude. He praised her every small success, and by the end of the hour, Duck was able to identify all twenty-six letters, which made her prouder than a peacock—and Master Frobertus seemed rather smug as well.

"Either you're a wing-dinging natural with your syllabary," he fizzed, his glasses falling askew in his excitement, "or I'm an even better teacher than I thought!"

And Duck immediately wished that she could bottle up this compliment and play it again later when she needed it—and that the Crowns could have heard him.

She wished the Crowns could hear how smart she was.

"You'll come back on the morrow, then," he instructed her when they'd finished, "and we'll see what shape your penmanship is in."

Very poor shape, as it turned out; she'd never held a quill before and made trembling squiggles on the parchment for a while before she could persuade her fingers to make an *a*.

But she soon got better.

Under the careful, wizened tutelage of Master Frobertus, on Tuesdays, Wednesdays, and Thursdays after the chores at the bakehouse were done, Duck came to his office and absorbed his lessons the way clapbread soaked up molasses.

After only a couple of weeks, she started to see letters everywhere—on the signs of the various shops around the market square, stamped onto the flour sacks delivered to Griselde, scrawled on the mail that arrived for the baker. Even Griselde's own seal, branded into the tops of her bread loaves: GB. When Petrus was on the other side of the kitchen and Griselde was otherwise occupied, Duck practiced sounding them out, tracing them with her fingers, imagining them tacked onto the beginnings of other words like *goose* and *gravy* and *bacon*.

Her whole world was letters. *H* for *horse*, *d* for *dog*, *n* for *knead* and *knot* and *Gnat*.

She heard the letters when Griselde sang her boisterous songs near the ovens; she picked out the sounds when Petrus bragged about Hugo's latest infant tricks; she listened for the moments when her words stuck together like underproofed rolls when the Crowns sneaked up to the counter and placed their orders on market day.

It felt good, to fill up her brain with new knowledge. When the baker sent her off to bed after a long day's work, Duck could feel all that information in her head, sloshing around like water in a jug.

The next time Griselde decided to take Duck to a tournament, she'd be able to read the sign for the Cheap Wife, no problem.

"Any questions?" Master Frobertus always asked at the ends of their lessons, and Duck always shook her head and meant it; the notary's explanations were clear, his orders thorough and gentle. She could have listened to him drone on about proper inking practices and common spelling variations for hours.

One Thursday, Duck finished a session and opened the door to leave. The contrast of the notary's dimly lit office and the bright sunshine of the late summer afternoon made her squint—and when she stepped off the porch, she bumped right into Griselde Baker.

"Out you come, and in I go!" the baker thundered, reaching down to steady Duck by the shoulders.

"I'm sorry," Duck chirped. "I didn't see you there."

"How did she fare today?" Griselde directed this question to Master Frobertus, who, upon hearing the baker's voice, had ambled to the door to greet her.

"She's much brighter than your last one was," the notary asserted, and Duck immediately warmed. She had not been sent here to practice letters or learn the reading and spelling of words, but it turned out she was more than just a thief. Maybe there was an academic within her as well.

"I told you so." Master Griselde folded her arms. "Think she'll do as well with numbers?"

"I should think." Master Frobertus scratched his chin. "By next year, you'll be able to pass all the accounts to her, I'd say."

"Wonderful! A triumph!" Griselde clapped her hands. "I so weary of the little things. Now, here. For your trouble." She pressed a parcel of steaming bread, wrapped in muslin, into the old man's hands.

"She isn't any trouble at all," the notary said. "Not a lick." But he held the loaf up to his nose and breathed in deeply all the same.

Duck chased a pigeon down the road while the grown-ups caught up on neighborhood gossip, and when Master Frobertus finally landed a thin-lipped kiss on Griselde's mitt of a hand, Duck made her way to the baker's side—not to escort her, exactly, since Griselde's steps were confident enough to lead her around Odierne unaccompanied. But if Duck was asked to navigate, she would do it.

"He's very pleased with your progress," Griselde said, "and so am I."

Duck inhaled, long and slow, filling her lungs—and her smile couldn't be stopped.

"You're an excellent listener, he says, and always very practiced," the baker went on. "However, he did say he caught you reading and that you denied it."

A thorn pricked Duck's insides. "I . . ." she started. Quite suddenly, and without any warning, Duck had seen the letters *b-a-t* on a parchment in the notary's office, and, sounding them out, found herself muttering the complete word under her breath as if it were a spell:

Bat. Bat. Bat.

She peered up at Master Griselde with guilt shining in her eyes. The baker, however, gave a giggle and nudged her apprentice playfully.

"You rascal," the baker said with a wink. "Now that the truth is out, there'll be no more resting on your laurels at the bakehouse. From now on, you'll be in charge of reading every label, every invoice, every order." She sighed in amusement, and then: "I certainly understand that there are reasons to keep your true capabilities under wraps—new skills mean new responsibilities, after all. But perhaps you might show off to Master Frobertus next week? He does love to see proof of his handiwork, and, well,

I plumb enjoy it when he brags about you." She glanced down at Duck, and her cloudy eyes were like torches, gleaming with pride—

And Duck could not endure it.

She skipped ahead a little, pretending to be burning off excess energy after her long lesson, but she was actually slightly frantic.

Two adults knew she was smarter than she was pretending to be.

Duck needed to be careful, or else both Master Frobertus and Master Griselde might notice other things about her.

Things Duck didn't want them to notice.

And Duck was trying very hard not to notice how glorious it felt when Griselde praised her.

It felt like sunshine, and she could not endure it.

I n all of my summers, I have never seen such a thing.

Three tiny, fluffy nestlings in the crack of my left claw. They have ground the shells of their eggs to dust beneath their scaly feet. The baby birds have two modes: mouth or eyes. Hungry or staring.

I wonder if they can see things that I cannot. I wonder what a worm tastes like.

Several times a day, the mother bird flies off to find them grubs to eat, and in those moments, the babies are in my care.

"Hey! Come back here!" I called the first time she soared away from my toe. "I never agreed to any bird-sitting!"

She is gone for longer and longer stretches as the summer days march on, and I am left alone with the nestlings.

The three birds stare up at me, unblinking. Their feathers are pure fuzz, nothing like the sleek gray feathers they will have when they get older.

"What are you looking at?" I growl.

The birds bob their heads, and one of them lets out a single chirp. Something inside me flutters. Such a small, small sound, that chirp.

"What about you two?" I address the other nestlings, all round black eyes and pointy beaks. "What do you have to say for yourselves?"

One of the birds stretches its skinny neck, as if trying to make itself taller. "No need to hurry time," I tell it. "You'll be grown soon enough."

Stretch. A good name for this bird—if someone were to care enough to name it.

The third bird seems unable to wait for its mother to return with its food; it tears a twig away from the nest to munch on. "Yes, I know you're hungry," I say. "Your mother will be back soon, and then you'll feast. Be patient."

Chirp. Stretch. Munch.

I have tried to evict the mother bird more times than I can count. I have tried to kick out my foot so the nest flies out of my toe, eggshells and all. I want them gone.

But I also know exactly what I could call these nestlings, if they were to stay.

"Listen to him, cooing over his babies!" Harpy jeers. "The old devil's gone soft!"

"Eat a rock!" I shout back. "Do us all a favor!"

If watching these nestlings makes me soft, then I am cotton. I am feather. I am fluff. I was made to watch.

"Grow," I tell them. "Grow tall. Grow strong."

And grow they do. The nestlings shed their down. They nip at their sleek new pinfeathers. Their heads and bodies get bigger, and their eyes do not; they lose that wide, staring sense about them, but there is something wonderful about the way they look out at the city now.

Seasoned. Their first summer. A miracle.

And then one day, when the mother bird leaves to get their food, she does not return. The nestlings and I watch the skies, but even when the clouds drift and the afternoon deepens, she does not come back.

"Do not worry," I tell the birds. "There are plenty of things that crawl along our stones. You will be well fed." But something in my stones is unsettled, hollowed out.

Tonight, for the first time, I can sense a chill in the air, the end of summer approaching. One of these mornings, I will wake up and find frost on my horns, and the woods beyond the fields will be flame-colored. Another autumn, and our cathedral is still here.

And the next morning, when I wake up, Chirp is not in the nest.

Chirp is standing on the ledge, leaping off the edge that faces the roof. Its wings flutter, barely stirring the air, and it spirals down to the stones with a small thud.

"A noble attempt," I tell it.

It tries again, this time hovering in the air for a moment, catching the wind with its wings before falling.

Still, with every thud of baby bird on stone, I am crackly with pride . . .

Until Chirp, finally getting the hang of it, turns its beak to face the long, far drop off the ledge.

"N-no," I stammer. "No, Chirp—"

But it is gone.

Three flaps of its wings, and it glides down through the air, steering beautifully away from the cathedral, off to somewhere else.

Somewhere else.

My insides tighten. I feel heavy, as though I were just cut out of the mountain yesterday.

"May you be plucked and boiled by nightfall!" I shout into the air, then turn with a chortle to the other nestlings. "What a fool, don't you think—Stretch?"

Stretch has already practiced on the ledge like Chirp and now stretches its neck out with glee, fluttering alone into the sky.

"Stretch!" I call. "Come back here, you featherhead!"

But Stretch does not come back.

The mother bird, gone. Chirp and Stretch, gone. Our cathedral's financiers, gone. The mother and baby, all those years ago, gone.

Even with the summer sun bleaching the top of my head with its heat, there's a new chill in my stone.

"Well?" I growl at Munch, who eyes the ledge where the other birds disappeared. "You have wings. Use them. Go already."

If I could kick out my foot, I would. If I could shake the nest loose from inside my toe, I would. If I could turn away from the sight of Munch making its own flight away from our cathedral, I would—

But I watch. I watch the last of the nestlings leave.

Serves me right for letting that mother bird build her nest here. Serves me right for giving them names. Our cathedral does not have a name. Things without names get forgotten.

And so I forget their names.

I forget the stale nest in my toe. I forget the gentle nuzzle of their downy feathers against my stone. I forget the street children living beneath us. I forget that they might be hungry, might be weary of the heat, might be lonely.

The next time a bird tries to land in my mouth, I'll roar its feathers clean off. And I'll laugh by myself.

Always by myself.

Another summer, come and gone. No more remarkable than any other. Just another summer. And autumn approaches.

May we be stone at the bottom of the river by the time the next summer rolls around.

Midnight Visitors

In the middle of the night, Duck woke up.

She was still tired, the sorest parts of her singing out like gonged bells. She'd been at the bakehouse for weeks, and she'd expected her muscles to be used to it, but by the time dinner rolled around every evening, her arms and legs were wet noodles and her brain was no more useful than a bowl of lukewarm mush.

Groggily, she lifted her head off her pillow at a sound at her window—

And looked directly into a pair of wide, laughing eyes.

"Wake up, sleepyhead," Ash said.

Duck immediately threw back her covers, scrambling to wrap her arms around his neck.

"What are you doing here?" she whispered as fiercely as she could. She wanted to pinch him, she'd missed him so much—the familiar scent of her beloved Ash filled her with new energy, that sweet dirt under his chin and behind his ears, the bite of days-old, half-rotted fruit on his breath, too much fresh air on his scalp.

"We just came to see how you're getting along." Ash looked to the window just as Gnat dropped into the room, quiet as a pouncing cat, his right arm up against his body.

"Cock-a-doodle-do," Gnat said, his eyes narrowed, his mouth already smirking. "So. This is where you live now." He considered the beams in the ceiling, the varnished walls, the stale old trenchers covered in birdlime on the floor to kill off bedbugs.

Duck fussed with the edge of her nightshirt, trying to predict his assessment.

Did he think the room was ritzy and that Duck was now a snob just for living here? Well, if he did, she argued ferociously to herself, he was the one who had arranged for her to be here in the first place—

Or was he turning his nose up at the splinters on the windowsill, the faint stink of sour pee that constantly drifted up the chute outside her door, the bits of hay poking out of the bed linens like spines? He could hardly blame Griselde for such inconveniences, Duck argued in her mind. She was only a baker, not some wealthy blacksmith—

Holy bones, she thought. *Which is it, a palace of a bakehouse or a sorry shack?* Was it rubbing off on Duck, or did she seem unworthy of it?

And which was Duck more afraid of: Gnat thinking she was a snoot or Gnat thinking she didn't belong where she was?

Ash sat on the bed beside Duck, making the frame squeak. "How's it going? Are you a master of dough yet?"

Duck shrugged, watching Gnat pace along the floorboards, inspecting the tarnished old horseshoes that hung on the wall in a sort of attempt at decoration. "It's only been a month. I—I could probably make a decent cob, if I had the right stuff."

"Well done!" Ash thumped her on the leg. "You're a domestic hero!"

"You should see the ovens that are down there," Duck went on, feverish with Ash's approval. "They're huge! You could make a loaf the size of—"

"Of a duck," Gnat provided.

Duck shrank down like old dough. "Much bigger," she whispered, then sat on her hands.

"You're doing it, Duck." Ash's grin glowed in the dark. "You passed us enough coins this week that we were able to buy milk and cheese and have a proper feast with the bread—oh, cripes, I almost forgot to give you this!" He reached into his pocket and pulled out a cube of something white and gooey and covered with lint—a bit of cheese that was so smelly, Duck could almost taste it.

Duck took it gratefully, but Gnat stepped forward and snatched it from her hands.

"She doesn't need our grub." Gnat popped the cheese into his mouth, lint and all. "She's getting hand-fed by the baker now. She's probably had ten feasts this week alone." He chewed, staring at Duck, and swallowed with a sigh of delight.

Duck peered back at Ash, who was looking at her differently now. Like she had taken a bite of a turkey leg right in front of him and flung the bones in his direction.

Yes, Duck had already eaten cheese twice this week, but the cheese Ash had saved for her was symbolic cheese. That cheese was supposed to be hers.

Hers as a Crown.

Just as she was gathering the courage to say exactly this to Gnat, he spoke instead.

"Good job this month, Garbage. You managed to slip us bread and coin, and you haven't gotten yourself kicked out of the bakery yet. It's far better than I thought you'd do."

Duck's face grew hot in the dark room. "Thank you?"

"Just keep on doing what you're doing," Gnat said.

Duck bit her lip, then glanced again at Ash.

Ash turned to Gnat. "For how long, do you think?"

Something in Duck's chest loosened.

Good.

So Ash still knew her.

She'd been worried that he wouldn't recognize her at all—and not just because she was covered in globs of dough and dust.

But Ash still knew what she was saying without Duck having to speak at all.

"Well, that all depends . . ." Gnat began pacing the perimeter of the room, which made Duck nervous; she wished he would sit down or hold still. Griselde was asleep downstairs, but her room was directly below Duck's—any scuffles or scrapes could wake the baker up.

Plus, the sight of Gnat shuffling around, touching the walls and the door frame and the furniture as if they were his own . . . it made Duck feel supremely strange.

He stood next to the armoire in the corner, guffawing at what was on its surface. "Well, I'll be!" Gnat slapped his knee with his left hand. "Duck went and got herself educated!"

Duck burned as she dashed to the armoire, reaching out to wipe a hand across the flour she'd sprinkled there. She didn't want to bother Master Griselde for a pen and parchment, so she'd been tracing her finger in the flour, writing out her letters, practicing small words in her shaky, unsure print.

Gnat blocked her from ruining her latest attempts: *bred, yeest, duk.*

Duk.

The exhilaration of writing her own name was gone now, replaced by shame as Gnat whooped with recklessly unquiet laughter.

"Our Garbage, a writer!" he said. "Next thing we know, she'll be passing out our bread in a velvet cape and crown—"

A sound downstairs made them all freeze. Duck held her breath, searching for exactly what she would say if Griselde Baker pushed open the door and found these two unwashed boys under her roof.

No one came up the stairs. The bakehouse was silent again, except for the gentle hum of the ovens licking their coals, but inside Duck, a storm of shame and soreness rolled and roared.

Shame that Gnat had caught her practicing her letters, shame that she'd been so motivated by the baker's acclamations that she'd wanted to impress her further, shame that she ever cared about fitting in here.

Soreness about the fact that when Ash and Gnat left, she wouldn't be able to go with them.

She wouldn't be able to go back home.

"Gnat . . . how much longer?" She would not cry. She would not cry.

"Until further notice. Or until you mess it up, whichever comes first." Gnat peered out the window at the street below. "Time to go."

"Things aren't the same without you around," Ash quickly said, his hand on Duck's shoulder in a comrade's grip. "The rest of the Crowns send their love—oh, and Drippy requests morning buns next Saturday, if you can swing it."

"If I can swing it," Duck agreed. Her chest brimmed with memories of the other Crowns, the memories of their voices, the giddy games they played.

She would not cry.

"I guess we'll see you around." Ash slid out the window.

"Yes. Market day," Duck replied, even though he was already gone. Six days. Six days, and then she could see them again.

Gnat paused at the window, turning so his right arm was outside and his left arm was inside. "Keep up the good work. What a handy little duckling you've turned out to be." And then out the window he went.

Duck watched them run in the shadows of the square, then vanish down an alley.

When she flung herself back onto her bed, she balled up her hands and pressed them to her eyes, breathing in and out until she was certain the tears were gone. It had been so good to see their faces, to see Ash, his kind smile . . .

And Gnat, too. Duck had missed him—she'd missed his curtness, his authority, the way he prowled the perimeter of every area he entered, something that had always comforted her. She missed being under his thumb every day . . . because that was how she knew she was a Crown. There was no place she'd rather be than on the receiving end of one of Gnat's commands—

Suddenly, she sat up, her eyes flying open.

Gnat hadn't been aimlessly pacing this room.

He'd been casing the place, getting a feeling for the layout of the bakery, the distance from the windows to the doors, the shapes of the rooms and their relations to one another.

Duck's stomach twisted as she lay back down.

Why would Gnat be trying to bust into the bakery?

Wasn't it enough to have Duck there, working from the inside?

It shouldn't have surprised her to know that Gnat didn't trust her to handle this scam on her own . . . but she was surprised by how much it bothered her.

Or maybe that sinking feeling was because it felt like Gnat was casing a place that now belonged, partly, to Duck?

Yeasted Cakes

Sundays were the hardest.

Sundays, Duck lay on her bed, staring out the window, or busied herself with small chores when the baker wasn't looking. Griselde Baker believed the Sabbath should be saved for lounging, mostly in the forms of card games, telling bawdy stories, and feasting, but Duck spent her Sundays either missing the Crowns or trying to forget how much she missed the Crowns.

On Mondays, Duck woke, ready to work.

Work kept her mind busy.

All week, she hauled flour and mixed yeast and shoved dough in and out of ovens. She practiced her letters and went to Master Frobertus's office for her lessons. She helped with inventory.

And on Saturdays, Duck was up hours before the sun to prepare for the market day rush. She got all jittery and pleased when the Crowns came up to the counter and buzzed with exhilaration when she pressed coins and bread into their hands. She sank with a certain disappointment when the Crowns said, "Right, thanks," and vanished into the crowd.

She knew they couldn't exactly linger to chat. She knew they wouldn't slip a note between her fingers when she gave them their spoils; Gnat was the only one of them who could write, and she didn't think he was sympathetic to her homesickness. But still. Every time they left without so much as a glance up at her face, she felt like she'd become a stranger.

One Monday, after Petrus had stopped by to borrow a bit of licorice root for poor Hugo, who was teething and miserable, Duck went outside to refill the water barrels.

She paused on the back porch, leaning against the door, very much in the manner that Gnat liked to lean.

It was chilly now in the evenings, the seasons beginning to turn. Soon the trees in the forest outside Odierne would turn golden, the air smoky. And Duck had given a month of her life over to the baker—a month away from the Crowns.

If she'd known that Gnat would keep her at the bakery for this long, would she still have agreed to come?

She couldn't say, but it was a frightening thing to consider— both how quickly time was passing and how much more of it Duck might lose before Gnat yanked her out of here.

When Duck went back inside, Griselde was cracking three eggs into a bowl, separating the yolks from the whites.

"Special order today," Griselde informed Duck. She whisked the egg whites, her muscular forearm handling the strain as if she were merely swatting a fly. "We are making you an anniversary cake."

Duck's heart pitter-pattered. "Me?"

"You've been in my employment for exactly one month," said the baker gleefully as she poured a generous helping of honey into the bowl. "And you still haven't had a proper sweet."

Duck watched Griselde grind cloves, cinnamon, and a cardamom pod into dust beneath her pestle. She'd had sweets—she'd sampled the biscuits; she'd tasted the morning buns. But she knew Griselde wouldn't be satisfied until Duck took a bite of cake.

She wanted to hide under the counter when she remembered that only two days ago, she'd swiped three pennies from Griselde's strongbox and passed them along to Spinner, along with six hot cross buns, two trenchers, and a fancy garlic loaf that she knew would give the Crowns terrible breath but was too scrumptious not to share. And now the baker wanted to celebrate? It was too much. Duck could taste the guilt in the back of her throat like bile.

"But—" she started.

"I'm the boss, and I insist you help me make a cake for us to gobble up this afternoon." Griselde reached out her hand, and Duck, biting back some words that were far too honest to be sweet, passed the baker her wooden spoon and stepped up to her place at the counter.

For the next hour, Duck and Griselde worked on a concoction all their own. The baker showed Duck how one could beat egg whites until they were fluffy as castles made of clouds, giving air and lift to the batter without sacrificing texture. She insisted they use sugar, which was expensive, and demonstrated to Duck how one could grind it up and mix it with butter and cream, making a thick, candied frosting that melted quickly in the kitchen's heat but was delicious in any form.

The cake they built was multilayered, and Griselde promised it would be taller than Duck once it was all stacked.

When they'd tipped the cakes out of their tins and put them near the windows to cool, they supped on vegetables, fowl, and tea.

"We'll bring a few slices over to Petrus and Raina," the baker said, propping her feet up on a chair as she reached for pickled cauliflower. "Technically, this is a non-guild bake. Illegal. So we'll want to eat the evidence as quickly as possible."

Duck balked as she nibbled her meat. "They're so strict."

"Oh, yes. A friend of mine was fined ten coronets just because his bran was a slightly different content from what he'd advertised. He wasn't being fishy; he's just a simpleton who mixed up his own recipes." She chuckled, slapping her belly. "They've got their reasons for their rules; that I understand. People care deeply about their bread. But they certainly weren't this strict when I was starting out."

Duck tore off a chunk of horse bread, then made herself pause and chew it carefully. A whole month of living at the bakehouse, and she still wasn't used to eating as much food as she wanted; sometimes she had to refrain from gobbling all the baker's offerings. Sometimes she had to remind herself that they weren't going to run out.

"Back then, they were much laxer about certifications, too, so I apprenticed at none other than my mother's," Griselde went on. "We lived outside the city—my father was a miller, which meant we had plenty of grain. By five years old, I could tell the difference between millet and barley just by smelling them. Yes, everything I learned about kitchens, ovens, bread, I learned at my mother's feet."

Duck tucked a strand of hair behind her ear. Hearing the baker talk about her mother made her all cozy inside, as if she had fallen into her mug of tea.

"She was good," Griselde went on. "Good with breads, yes, but she could open up the larder, see what ingredients she had, and whip up something delicious and hearty without so much as a recipe. That was . . ." The baker exhaled out her nose, lost in memory. "That's a kind of magic. That's the measure of a true master."

Duck glanced at the spongy, sugary cakes that were cooling on the windowsill. Griselde had made those without a recipe.

"She taught me everything I know about baking, just as her mother had taught her," Griselde went on. "And my Symon was able to fill me in on anything I'd missed." She drank the last of her tea. "I do wish they were both still around. To meet you, if for nothing else."

Duck's skin prickled. Was it the gasping heat of the ovens? Or a warning signal from within, some Crown's instinct whispering, *Be careful. Tread lightly. Danger?*

"What about you, dear?" Griselde patted Duck cheerfully on the wrist. "Did you ever know anything of your mother? Or your father, come to that?"

The last slice of the trencher was clutched in Duck's hand; she froze with it halfway to her mouth, scattering crumbs into her lap.

What should she say?

Before she could answer, a familiar scent hit her nose.

Rosemary.

That scent always found her.

"No. I never met her. Or my father. I—I don't know anything about them." The goose bumps on her arms began to settle. "The . . . uh, orphanage. That's where I've always been. That's all I've ever known."

Until you, she did not add.

The baker took in a deep breath. "You poor, poor dear."

"No." Duck spoke without thinking. "They took good care of me—at the orphanage. The best they could. The best they knew how." No fabrication required; this was among the more honest things Duck had ever said.

"Isn't that what we're all doing?" Griselde crossed her arms, her eyes fading to a spot on the wall. "The best we know how? Ah, well. What I wouldn't give for you to know your mother, Duck—if only so you yourself could know where you came from. But I also know this: whether you come from a long line of bakers or you're the first of your kind, you have to start somewhere."

The cakes were cooled and ready to be decorated.

Griselde Baker moved them to the counter, inhaling their honeyed aroma with closed eyes. "Hand us the frosting, will you? I'm not sure I can resist it much longer."

Duck found what she thought was the creamed butter and sugar—but when Griselde removed the tea towel covering the bowl, they found a bubbling, gurgling mass of uncooked dough.

"Whoopsie daisy! This little beauty's been waiting a while, hasn't it?" She leaned down to take a whiff and whistled. "That is rank!" They could hear the air in the dough, left to rise in the corner and forgotten, as it hissed and expanded—it was practically breathing.

"All right, you monster. Into the bin you go." Griselde held up the bowl and passed Duck the business end of a spoon. "Help me out, will you, Duck?"

Duck intended to wedge the spoon into the dough and pry it loose from the bowl, but as soon as she touched the surface, there was a horrendous pop.

The dough blew up.

Little bits of damp flour went everywhere—all over the counters, the sides of the oven, the floor, the ceiling, and all over Duck and the baker.

Duck stared in horror. This was it. She was about to be fired for sure—never had this kitchen seen such a mess. It would take hours to clean up! She tried to brush the dough off her arms, but it was sticky, awful little globs clinging to her hairs and her apron. Any second now, Griselde Baker would order her to leave, and Duck would have to crawl back to the Crowns and explain to Gnat what had happened.

The baker had her back to Duck, hunched over, and wasn't making any noise at all, just short puffs of breath as she took in air, her entire body quaking like a great volcano about to erupt.

"I'm sorry," Duck whispered. "I'm so, so sorry—"

But Griselde turned around, the dough coating her hair and face like tacky snow . . . and she was bright red from laughing so hard. "Overproofed . . . is . . . an understatement!" she choked out.

She reached out a hand and placed it on Duck's shoulder, steadying herself.

Steadying herself on Duck.

Duck tried to stand as sturdy as possible, but she was suddenly buoyant enough to float up to the ceiling. Griselde wasn't going to fire her—not for this. Worry gave way to relief, and she herself broke loose with a snort of a giggle.

And then the two of them toppled over, falling into the smears of gooey dough on the floorboards, laughing and laughing.

"I'm—so—sorry," Duck managed to repeat, wiping her eyes. "I didn't mean to!" Despite the hilarity of the situation, she was genuinely alarmed by the mess she'd made—not to mention the cost of the wasted ingredients.

If Petrus were here, he would have sent Duck out the door by now.

"Of course you didn't!" Griselde pulled herself up to standing, smearing a particularly large glob of dough off her forehead and throwing it into the bin. "But it was a handy little experiment, wasn't it? Now we know to never, ever touch the dough if it's . . ."

"Breathing?" Duck suggested, and the ridiculousness of this had them both barreling over again.

"We'll never again have to wonder what our spoons are capable of in the face of such dough," Griselde said. "Now, I believe our cakes are still waiting to be frosted—shall we?"

Ignoring the dough disaster, Griselde found her way back to the cakes, and with sure hands, smoothed the frosting between the layers, then stacked the thing up, up, almost higher than she could reach.

"Come on, place the last layer for me." The baker patted the counter, and Duck obediently climbed up and set the final cake in place, like crowning an angel with a halo.

"Glorious," Griselde marveled. "Absolutely glorious, don't you think?"

Duck hopped back down. "I've never seen anything like it." The cake was simple, except for being as tall as a horse's hindquarters. The individual crystals of sugar in the frosting sparkled like stars in the early evening light.

"Well." Griselde put her fists on her hips. "It's one thing if it looks delicious—but it's the taste that counts, isn't it?" Her hand reached out, asking for something, and without a word exchanged, Duck fetched it for her.

A fork.

"Do us the honors, will you?" The baker nodded at the cake.

With Griselde's blessing, Duck dug into the cake willy-nilly, right in the center, without ceremony.

It tasted even better than she'd expected.

AUTUMN

Another autumn. And this one louder than any other.

Those damn east-side chickens wake in the chilly dawn and start their scrabbling. The laundresses sing off-key as they scrub their linens under gray clouds. The Glorious Sisters of Mercy chime their benedictions as they pluck apples from trees and boil tomatoes for winter jams.

The sky tastes of charcoal. Like something is burning in the clouds.

Autumn brings everyone outside—bustling around in the golden light for one last gasp of sunshine before the snow keeps everyone inside by the hearth. The good thing about the cold and dead of winter? It brings the quiet.

But for now, I endure the clatter of carts on the cobblestones, the shouts of sheep farmers selling their wool for capes and scarves, the hauling and chopping of wood.

The street children in our cathedral leap like goats from the worm-eaten pews, the altar, the piles of broken stone slabs—but they are not loud enough to drown out the songs of the Sisters of Mercy.

Usually the hags next door sing only until afternoon prayers, and then they quietly make their suppers and read scriptures until lights-out. But as soon as the river shines a rusty silver in the sunset, the abbey music starts again. A second session of songs from the Hideous Sisters of No Mercy.

"Enough!" I cry. "No more singing! No more!"

The sisters' voices carry down the cloistered hallways where the breeze, a coconspirator, brings their noise right to my ledge.

"Would that my maker had poured concrete in my ears!" I bark. "This is outrageous!"

"At least their music blocks out the worst of your gassy fanfares!" Harpy snaps from across the rooftop. "Are you trying to out-fart every gargoyle in the city?"

In response, I make my nastiest grimace and let out a bugle song of my own in her direction, which shuts her up for a moment.

If only I could fly down to the abbey. I would glide through their gates and surprise the sisters, serenading them with a growling melody. I would scare them out of belting forth another hymn ever again.

"It is evening!" I cry. "This is supposed to be my quiet time! Are they going to keep up this racket all night?"

Night is not for hearing nuns praise the saints and sing about all the things I cannot bring myself to care about anymore. The sisters have the daytime, when the bustle of the streets muffles their odious music.

Day is for watching Odierne walk past our stones as if they cannot see us anymore. Night is for stars and for listening to the city breathe.

Day is for being forgotten. Night is for forgetting.

"If they are not going to stop, then I will just have to join them." I clear my throat, preparing to belt out my favorite version of "Be Thou My Vision," which includes far more references to butts than the original.

"They're holding a vigil," Goathead speaks up in defense of the sisters. "There's a fire in the great forest outside of Odierne—can't you smell it?"

My chest is full of rude lyrics, but I inhale. Yes, I can smell it. Now that they have pointed out the fire, I can see it, too. A dark thickness hanging over the city streets, smoke making everything hazy, an orange glow to the north.

No matter to me. We all have our problems.

"Music makes my stone itch!" I shout. "I want quiet!"

"Then shut your ugly mouth!" Harpy shouts back.

I wonder what it was like to be the side of a mountain, before I was chiseled free and given horns and claws and teeth. And ears.

I wonder if mountains and quarries and rocks truly appreciate how good they have it. No blusterous abbey choirs, no pestering, itchy bird's nest rotting away in your claws, no ache of panic when a fire devours the nearby forest and there is nothing for a rocky gargoyle atop an unfinished cathedral rooftop to do.

No lingering memories of a night when the river overflowed with rain, enough to drown every pigeon in the city, a night when the watchmen's buttons shone like cat eyes in the dark.

No memories of seeing mother and baby fall into the water, the splash so quiet, it almost didn't happen. No memories of your stone clenching, your heart startling out a cry. Being unable to move when you longed to help, to protect—

A mountain cannot move, after all. It knows this and has made its peace. All a mountain can do is watch. And I was once a mountain.

"Perhaps instead of griping about the disruption to your evening, you might offer up a prayer of your own." Harpy narrows her eyes at me, then closes them, emitting a nasally supplication.

I listen for a moment. The nuns' music scrapes like a stonemason's chisel inside me. And then I chortle, trying to laugh away the dull feeling in the center of my stone.

"Do you really think God will listen to you?" I call to the eastside gargoyles. It's a reasonable equation to me—we are too far off the ground, but not quite high enough to reach heaven. Our cathedral has a structure but no name. Why would God remember a cathedral with no name?

"Do you really think your prayers can make it past this smoke?"

We are stuck between worlds. The seasons cycle, cold and warm and cold again. The river freezes, the wind blows leaves from their branches, and still we crouch, never changing.

"Pray all you want. God cannot hear us."

I whisper my final point to myself, always to myself: *No one heeds the prayers of the ugly.*

I should know.

I remember the fire.

I remember the heat—it was the first thing I ever felt. Before I even had eyes to open, I could feel the heat—

And hear my maker, her voice steady as she lifted her hands

to my horns, a mere apprentice, but she worked as if she'd been working stone for decades. "My master said I could make you in any form I liked," she whispered to me, "and so I'm making you the biggest gargoyle of them all."

When she made my eyes, I could see the dancing orange glow of the ovens and the other pieces for our cathedral that had already been shaped and were being fired, their clay hardening: accents for the pillars, flourishes for the walls. Harpy, Goathead, and the others were made by the master sculptor, a man who had created gargoyles for many cathedrals in Avilogne.

But he passed his last project to his apprentice, and she is the one who made me.

I wish I could remember her face. All I remember are her hands, her words, the way she held her breath when she hammered her chisel into me, as if it were cutting away at her own form, too. How gentle she was with her hammer and chisel. How carefully she shaped my snout, my fangs, as though she were shaping an angel for the queen's courtyard and not a monster for a rooftop.

"Yes, you're a frightening one." I remember the feel of my maker's gaze on me, the satisfaction in her smile. "You will keep them all safe."

A gargoyle's job is to protect. I am not a proper gargoyle.

As I watch the north woods burn, the rush of Odierne's watchmen to hurl barrels of water at the flames, the fire sparking, and below me, the dirty-cheeked street children staring at the blaze, I am reminded of the fires in my maker's workroom. I am reminded of my maker.

I wonder what she would think if she saw me now, just a

crumbling heap of rocks atop an abandoned cathedral. Unable to guard. Unable to protect.

I cannot do anything . . . except speak. And sing.

In the blackest hour of the night, when the east-side gargoyles are snoring and the watchmen are digging a trench around the trees to keep the fire from eating the fields, I issue a note. A warble. A hum. A song of my own.

I did not think my voice could sound this soft. It is no louder than the *shush-shush*ing of the Sarluire, which streams along, unknowing. The river could put out the fire, if only it could cut its own path through the land. The river, keeping the forest safe. So much it could do, if only it could move.

"Please," I whisper, and it does not sound like a song, but like a prayer. "Please."

I cannot protect, but I can pray.

Above, clouds crackle with thunder. The autumn sky splits open, and the wind blows clouds over Odierne.

For a minute, I think it's going to happen—it's going to rain. My prayer, bringing the rain to put out the fire. I can smell it, even above the smoke. That damp cotton and earth smell. The rain. My prayer. A miracle. It is almost enough to make me believe. It is almost enough to make me hope again, the way I used to, that the cardinals will come back, that they will bring a bishop and a master mason, that they will begin to build—

No.

The clouds dissolve as quickly as they arrived, and not a single drop of rain falls. The forest fire burns, and my prayer becomes a song becomes a croak on my tongue.

God will not put out the fire. The cardinals will not finish our cathedral. It's been ninety-nine years. Far too long since anyone has glanced at our stones and seen something worth salvaging.

We are already forgotten.

The watchmen rush past us, trying to drown the fire with their barrels of water. The river is right there, and it does nothing. It, like me, can do nothing.

Around dawn, the men set a fire wall, and by the time morning breaks, crisp and bright, the trees are no longer burning. Smoke still rises, the horizon as blurred as a chimney.

"Oh, thank heavens!" Goathead cries when he sees the wreckage. "They put it out. It's a miracle!"

They are too busy celebrating; they do not hear my grumbles. The trees are twisted by the fire. The fields are charred black. This is no miracle.

"See, ugly? See what happens when you bow your head and pray?" Harpy tut-tuts in my direction, and the east-side gargoyles devolve into their usual scuttlebutt.

Let them gossip. For once I am in agreement with Harpy—see what happens when you bow your head and pray? Nothing.

Nothing has changed. A fire is put out, yes, but then you are left with acre after acre of scalded forest and ashy earth.

Ugly does nothing. Prayer does nothing. Music is grating to the ear when you want silence. And hope burns fast, leaving nothing but ash.

Another autumn, and it ends in ash. If only the fire had burned us down, too.

Suspicions

On the first day of September, Duck was in the storeroom preparing for a flour delivery when she heard Petrus say from the back porch in a flat tone, "They're gone."

"Shut the door!" Griselde barked from the kitchen. "You're letting all the heat out!"

Petrus did not close the door, so the baker sent Duck to investigate.

Autumn had come in the night.

Yesterday had been a heady summer day, the smell of warm ale and freshly trimmed sunflowers in the air, the light full and opportune. People had stood in patches of sunshine, soaking up the rays while they had the chance.

But this morning, Duck had woken up with a chilly nose. People were bundling up to go outside, wearing scarves and mittens. There was frost on the bakery's wrought iron sign.

And now, as Petrus stared at the rug on the back porch, where he'd gone to meet the miller, his breath came out in fat white clouds.

The miller stood there in the chill, overladen, several pounds of various flours sinking lower and lower in his arms, but Petrus was unmoving, looking down at the rug as if something was terribly, terribly wrong.

"They're gone," Petrus repeated.

Duck rubbed her arms to keep them warm, scanning the porch steps beyond him—and then she realized what was missing.

A pair of oversize leather boots.

They'd been sitting on the porch for as long as Duck had been here, perhaps longer—they'd been parked there so long, in fact, that they'd left behind dusty outlines on the rug.

"What's going on?" Griselde came out the back door, wiping her hands on her apron. "Has Jon Miller shown up?"

"Here, madam," the miller croaked out, and the baker rushed off the porch to collect the flour.

"My goodness, man, give it here, lest you snap a knee!" Griselde hefted all the bags into her thick arms without so much as a grunt.

"Your boots are missing," Petrus said as soon as the miller left. He searched around the porch, as if the boots were merely hiding from him in the shadows. "They were here yesterday. They were here this morning, in fact—I nearly tripped over them when I came in."

"Who cares? Look at this pandemain flour—it's like snow!" Griselde opened the sack of thrice-sifted white flour and ran her hand through it.

Petrus was not deterred. "Those were top-notch boots."

"They're misplaced," Griselde argued. "Perhaps I wore them somewhere and forgot."

"They didn't run away by themselves," Petrus said.

"Check the front door," Griselde suggested cheerily, and she and Duck put the flours away and straightened the storeroom while Petrus searched the bakehouse. He checked the front door, the back door again, the yard, the kitchen, the counting room, every drawer and cupboard, and, with the baker's blessing, her own bedroom.

"I can't understand it," Petrus said. "Where could they be? I checked everywhere . . . except *your* room."

When Duck realized Petrus was looking at her, a nip went through her.

Griselde clicked her tongue. "Now, now, Petrus—what are you insinuating?"

"I should think it's obvious. The apprentice quarters are the only ones that haven't been searched. Statement of fact." Petrus narrowed his eyes slightly as he spoke—and Duck could hear, in the way he said "the apprentice quarters" instead of "Duck's bedroom" that he absolutely thought he'd find the boots in her room.

To Duck's surprise, Griselde did not protest but pressed her lips together thoughtfully before waving a hand toward the stairs. "All right, Petrus. Go and have your look."

Petrus marched up to Duck's room, a smug smile in the corner of his mouth, and Duck held her breath.

Why on earth was she so nervous? She hadn't taken the boots. He would come out empty-handed. He would admit the boots must be misplaced, hiding somewhere unusual, and then the three of them would carry on with their day. Maybe he'd even apologize to her—anything was possible. Still, her heart skipped like a frog across a pond.

Petrus emerged bootless, but before Duck could exhale with relief, he held out something in the palm of his hand, his grin satisfied. "Care to explain this?"

Duck stared down at a shiny silver penny, the butt-shaped divot looking back up at her.

It was the penny from the hot fair all those weeks ago. She'd kept it stashed under her mattress in case of . . . well, she wasn't sure. Emergencies. Or until Gnat and the Crowns needed it.

Either way, it didn't look good. Duck's face burned red; she couldn't stop it in time.

Petrus saw her reaction and widened his grin.

"Those boots were broken-in leather." He circled her slowly like a cat about to pounce. "They'd have been an easy sell to any dirty pawnbroker who peddles in stolen goods."

"I didn't." Duck shook as she whispered it. She had not taken the boots. She did not know what had happened to them. But she couldn't explain the money, not in a way that would satisfy the journeyman.

To Petrus, the penny was as good as evidence.

"Now, hang on a minute." Griselde plucked the coin from Petrus's palm, then positioned herself between him and Duck. "She says she didn't take the boots."

"She says that, yes!" Petrus exploded. "But that doesn't mean—"

"I've lost things plenty of times," Griselde went on. "Just because the boots are missing doesn't mean they won't turn up—remember the bellows? Remember the hammer? Remember when I misplaced an entire barrel of oat bran? Remember how I'm blind?" She chortled as she said this last piece. "There's a dozen places the boots could be, Petrus, just like there's a dozen places Duck could have gotten that money."

"A dozen compartments in your strongbox, maybe," Petrus muttered.

"Stand down." Even though Griselde's eyes were cloudy, she fixed them right on Petrus until he softened.

"All right," he said at last. "Fine." But Duck could see he wasn't convinced.

Griselde passed the penny back into Duck's hands.

Duck, trembling, waited for the baker to ask her exactly where the money had come from and tried desperately to come up with a proper fib—

"You keep this someplace safe." The baker closed Duck's fingers around the coin. "Seems like things are disappearing around here."

Griselde Baker went back to the ovens, and Duck started up the stairs to her room, coin clutched tightly in her palm. But Petrus's voice came from behind her, low and strong: "A penny for a pair of boots as fine as that? You should have held out for more."

With a squeak in her voice, Duck faced him and gasped, "I didn't take the boots, I swear it!"

"You swear it," Petrus echoed with a laugh.

"I brought this penny with me," Duck continued. "The—the orphanage thought I should have a bit for spending, just in case—"

"You must think I'm dense as dough." Petrus leaned up the stairs, boring holes into her with his eyes. "I know you. I know your kind. And I know why you're here. She might be blind, but she's not alone. I'm here, too."

Duck felt as if he could see her very ribs. How much did Petrus know? And how?

Or did Duck just have the stink of the streets on her, no matter how many baths she took, no matter how many loaves of bread she baked?

"I'm watching you," Petrus said. "Every coin you handle, everything you touch in this bakery—you remember that I'm watching, always. I won't let anyone take from Griselde again. She gives far too much already."

The tournament. The anniversary cake. All the extra food, the feasts, the looks of pride and adoration when Duck kneaded dough, even if she sprinkled too much salt in the batter or undermixed. Griselde acted as if Duck could do no wrong, even when Duck did nothing right. The baker couldn't help it. She gave it all to Duck—far, far too much, and so it was without restraint that Duck whispered, "I know."

If Petrus heard her last words, he made no show of it. And then Griselde called for his help in the kitchen, and Duck scurried the rest of the way up the stairs and dropped her penny into a spare stocking before rejoining them at the counter, where the three of them set to work making the day's trenchers.

Duck kept an eye out for the boots, but she knew that there was nothing she could do to clear her name.

Petrus knew her for what she was.

A thief.

Hours later, once the kitchen was closed for the day and everything was scrubbed clean, Duck carried the rubbish bin out the back door.

The surrounding buildings were turning black against the lavender sunset. Moths flew toward the glow of Griselde's lamplight, visible through the cracks in the door.

And standing in the yard, yowling like it was the lead in a church choir, was a dirty, incredibly persistent gray cat.

The creature was long-eared, crooked-tailed, and yellow-eyed. It stared at her from the rim of the well as if it had been expecting her, then leaped down into the yard and trotted to her side, where it rubbed up against her legs, meowing and crying.

Duck immediately recognized it—this was the cat that roamed around the yard of the cathedral. Frog Eyes and Spinner had tried to tame it into staying with them, but the cat did not want to be a Crown. It seemed utterly incapable of the kind of loyalty a pet required.

But it cried at Duck's feet as if it knew her—as if it recognized her—and Duck wondered, panic in her throat, if this beast would somehow out her as a Crown.

"Shoo." Duck nudged it away with her feet, but the cat stuck to her like cotton. "Shoo. Go away, I said. Get out of here."

"Is that damn cat back again?" Griselde poked her head out the door.

The cat, upon seeing the baker, ditched Duck's legs and made a beeline for Griselde, arching its back, meowing pathetically—a gesture that made Duck exhale in relief.

"Hello, you old rascal." Griselde bent over, scratching the cat's head. "I've been wondering when you'd be coming around again." To Duck, she explained, "This cat finds his way back to my yard every fall without fail. God knows where he spends his summer months—hopefully somewhere warm and breezy. But as soon as it gets cold, he comes here for his milk—and so his milk we shall get. Duck? Fetch him a dish, will you?"

Duck poured a shallow saucer of cream, feeling both amused by and leery of this cat, who had made a mark of the easiest shopkeeper in Odierne.

"Ah, you gave him the good stuff." Griselde had been stroking the mangy thing under the chin; he leaped from her arms to dip his pink tongue into the milk, his tail slowly calming itself as he slaked his hunger. "With a bribe like that, I can't imagine he'll be skipping away anytime soon." And then, after a moment: "We should name him."

Duck balked. "But he's a stray."

"He is a cat with many homes," Griselde defended, "and we are lucky enough to be one of them. So he ought to have a proper title. Any thoughts?"

The cat finished the milk, then cleaned his paws thoroughly. Once he was satisfied, he pawed at Griselde, mewing until she scratched his ears.

Something about the way he held himself, something about how he was capable of being pesky and affectionate at the same time . . . well, the cat reminded Duck of someone.

"Ash," she suggested.

"Ash," Griselde repeated. "All that's left after the fire. Ash and dust." She frowned, glancing down at the gray-streaked creature. "Ash it is, then. You are hereby christened."

The cat, for his part, did not seem to object.

Duck had to force her mind away from a particularly rowdy

and considerate street orphan or else risk bursting into tears, so she offered her fingers to the cat.

Ash—the feline, not the human—sniffed at them nonchalantly, and then obliged her by licking them.

It only wanted to get at the salt on her skin, she knew—but to Duck, it was almost affection, and this cat was almost Ash.

Let the baker give you all her milk, if she wants, Duck said silently to the cat. *Let her house and feed not one but two thieves.*

"Duck?" Griselde cut through Duck's meditations. "Don't let Petrus get to you." She sat on the porch, taking up the entire step, the outlines of the missing boots still visible on the rug. "Like I said, he's only protective of me, especially after our last apprentice. He's determined never to let anyone take advantage of me again, which I do appreciate—but he forgets that we don't have to worry about such things with you."

Duck didn't know what to say.

She dodged a flea that flung itself from Ash the cat's back, tracking it onto the porch, her mind racing—anything to avoid the naked trust on Griselde's face.

"However, I don't think it would be wise to try any of your tricks on Petrus." Griselde Baker took something out of her apron pocket and flipped it at Duck. "I'm not sure how you would explain this away."

All the blood rushed out of Duck's face as she caught it.

The wooden coin.

The same wooden coin Duck had used to trick the baker out of an entire coronet that first market day in Odierne.

Here it was, back in Duck's hands.

Then . . . the baker knew.

She knew who Duck was.

She knew what Duck had done.

The jig was up, then. Duck probably had only a few minutes to escape back to the streets before Griselde called for the constables.

She held her breath, watching the baker very, very carefully as she slowly took a step backward . . .

Griselde's eyes were focused on the line of sunlight along the fence, which was growing thinner and thinner with every minute that passed. Soon the entire yard would be in shadow—but the baker did not look distressed.

Not by the impending coldness of a fall night, not by the darkness, and not by what she'd just said to Duck.

She did not look like she was about to have the orphan apprentice scoundrel arrested for robbery.

She looked . . . happy.

Ash the cat made himself comfortable in the baker's lap. "Duck, I don't care where you come from. I don't give a rat's ratty behind who you were before you walked in the door. Now that you're here, I want you to stay. For as long as you'll let me feed you and clothe you and give you work, I want you to stay."

Duck's heart pounded so hard, she feared it might explode.

Only ten steps to the fence, she calculated, and then a quick scamper up and over. She could run to the cathedral and warn the Crowns—they might still have time to leave Odierne before nightfall.

"I do want to hear about it when you're ready to tell me. I want to hear about the orphanage, and how you fared, and who on

earth taught you how to swap out real coins for dummies like that."
Griselde tilted her head so her eyes were level with Duck's; if not
for the fading light, Duck might have seen herself reflected in the
misty lenses. "But if you're not ready, I'll wait. I'll wait for as long
as you need me to wait."

With that, Griselde patted the cat's head one last time, then
lifted herself off the porch and sauntered back into the bakery. "It
smells like rain tonight, doesn't it?" she called before the door shut
behind her, but Duck was still too shocked to speak.

Griselde knew about the wooden coin. She knew that Duck
had tricked her out of a coronet.

But Duck's nerves were tempered by one simple fact: Griselde
didn't seem to know about the Crowns.

She didn't know that the "orphanage" Duck kept referring
to was actually a scummy group of strange children who would
swiftly make off with every loaf in the bakehouse if given half a
chance, and without so much as a teaspoon of remorse.

She didn't know that the Crowns had planted Duck here
specifically to weed the bakery of bread and coins.

She didn't know that every Saturday, Duck passed loaves from
the basket and pennies from the strongbox into the hands of the
Crowns.

Duck wasn't compromised. She didn't need to run away. Not
yet. She could stay.

The sky darkened with the woolen clouds of autumn's first
storm, and Duck's fingertips and nose were bitten red with chill,
but she couldn't go back inside. Not yet.

I don't care where you come from.

That's what the baker had said.

And Duck had almost believed her.

Duck had almost believed that if she told Griselde Baker who she really was, Griselde would smile and give her an encouraging squeeze of the shoulder and say, "Well, that's all in the past now, isn't it? You're here now, and you're Duck, and that's quite enough for me."

It sounded exactly like something Griselde would say—but of course the baker wouldn't, not really. The baker would whistle for Constable Deveraux the minute Duck confessed. "Well, look what we have here, Constable!" Duck could imagine Master Griselde saying in her deep, booming voice. "A little thief! And doesn't her neck look just the right size for the stocks?"

No, Duck would not tell Griselde who she really was.

She would not tell Griselde who she had been before she walked in the bakery door, and she would not tell Griselde who she continued to be as she slept in the apprentice quarters and kneaded dough and poured cream for the cat.

She would protect the Crowns from the law with her life—and likewise, she would protect the baker from the truth.

But she knew she had to tell Gnat what had happened.

Gnat needed to hear that the baker knew about the wooden coin. He'd know what to do.

Maybe, if Duck was lucky, he'd pull her from the apprenticeship and bring her back home.

D o you know, pray, how a cathedral is built? It is a very complicated process to build something made of hopes.

If you walked past such a construction site, you might see the mortar maker inspecting a seam between two stone blocks, his master nodding with approval, and you may think this is all it is—one block after another until the whole building is finished.

But every completed cathedral is a stone-made miracle. A miracle.

All cathedrals start as dreams. Not one person's dream but the collective dreams of many. It is a heavy thing to share, a dream. Person after person, some important, some insignificant, and they all must be willing to die for this dream.

A person who builds a cathedral knows that they will probably not be alive by the time it's completed. To find someone willing to live with this kind of eternal thinking? Nearly impossible. But there are some.

The bishop who laid ground for our cathedral all those years ago was a man already in the hard winter of his life. Yet he still dug in his shovel, making the first ceremonial hole for our foundation, knowing he would not be alive when our doors finally opened.

He died four years after he dug that first hole.

Where one man drops his shovel, another man picks it up again; the bishop's sprightly young son inherited his father's dream and oversaw the cathedral's construction until his own death.

Sometimes I wonder if humans would prefer to be made of stone.

Once the plans are in place, hundreds of laborers are sent all over the continent. They cut timber and sail it back in ships made of the same timber, carved into boats and smoothed and salt-eaten by water. Our own cathedral's logs came from the trees of Telgary, those weathered beams. They used to whisper to me late at night when we were a young construction. I could hear the rustle of wind through phantom leaves, the groan of something ancient stretching its roots.

Our cathedral was once a tree. But I don't hear them anymore. Stone outlives even wood.

The laborers cut limestone from a quarry to shape into our walls, our arches, our roof. The blacksmiths used tools to make new tools to replace the old tools.

Every stone was marked—not with the master quarryman's ordinary seal, but with a sacred seal, one created for this cathedral alone. A cathedral's stones belong to everyone. But those seals have now been rubbed out by time, worn down by dust.

Our cathedral was once a mountain.

The master quarryman died before he saw all the stones set into place. The blacksmith and his journeyman both died before they saw their handiwork finished.

A cathedral takes many lifetimes to complete. Many seasons. A few more seasons, and it will have been a century.

In the winters, the stonework was covered with straw and dung to prevent frost from cracking the mortar. In the summers, the timber was coated in pitch to keep it from splitting and rotting. Building a cathedral is a delicate balance—you must think as big as God can, but you must also remember the tiniest mouse-size details.

It's putting up walls, dropping keystones into arches, sanding the pews. It's watching the children in your neighborhood grow into men and have babies of their own, all before your window-panes are finished cooling. It's a thousand things to finish and only a forever in which to complete them.

We were never finished. And we were never given a name.

A cathedral takes a lifetime to build—and it is good to wait, good to hold still, to listen, to watch. It is good to be part of something that is bigger than you are.

But to wait for almost a hundred years? To watch when a mother and her baby leap into the river below, able to do nothing? Not protect, not stand guard, nothing but watch?

I would give all of my stone teeth, my claws, all my gravel if I could go back to that night. Even if it meant I had to live those years over again. I would stand up here and wait for a thousand more years if it meant I could go back and save them.

A proper gargoyle.

Sunday Morning Services

Duck was allowed to sleep in on the Sabbath—encouraged, even, to catch up on the rest she had missed during the busy week.

But on this particular Sunday, she was already up and dressed by the time Griselde ambled out of her bedroom, still in her night-dress and stocking cap, her face bleary with dreaming.

"Morning." Duck pulled a chair out from the table for her employer. "Tea?"

"What time is it?" Griselde yawned, scratching her belly as she sat.

"Prime bells rang about an hour ago." Duck poured the baker a mug of tea and passed her a slice of bread, which she'd coated with a generous spread of butter—the baker's favorite.

"What the devil's gotten into you?" Griselde grunted, but she gave Duck a groggy smile as she lifted her tea.

"Nothing. Just thought you might—might be hungry when you woke." Duck lingered at the table, her fingers fiddling with a stray thread on the runner.

Griselde set down her mug and laced her great hands together. "All right," she said. "Let's hear it. I know a bribe when I drink one."

"I . . ." Duck pretended to be utterly clueless, but Griselde shot her an expression of such disdain, she quickly stammered out the lie she'd been rehearsing all morning. "Church," she breathed. "I— I wish to worship."

Griselde Baker tipped her head back, searching for just the right angle of light to properly see Duck's face. "Truly? But you haven't been to a single service since you arrived."

"I know," Duck rushed. "But today is a holiday." She'd prepared the lie the night before, practiced it a little on her way downstairs, but even she was surprised by how smoothly it rolled out of her mouth.

"A holiday." Griselde folded her arms. "My stars. I had no idea."

"A special holiday." Duck held herself steady. "A feast day, one we celebrated in the orphanage. The Feast of . . ."

The Crowns popped into her head one at a time, those grubby faces. Frog Eyes, Spinner, Le Chou—

"The Feast of the Cabbage," she blurted out. "And I've never missed it, never once in my life. So can I go?"

Griselde Baker shrugged. "Fine by me. Go right ahead and feast on all the cabbage your little belly can hold." She sipped her tea, then asked, "Would you like me to go with you?"

Duck didn't move.

What could she possibly say?

She'd been banking on the one thing she knew about Master Griselde without any doubt: the baker loathed church services and would do all sorts of things to avoid going when invited.

"No, thanks!" she'd called to Petrus when he'd bid her join his family at the Feast of Saint Odile. "If you get to the church and God Himself is seated in the congregation, you can send for me then!"

If Griselde accompanied Duck to church, then she'd see there was no cabbage, no feast—and then the baker would know Duck had lied.

"Apologies." Griselde chuckled before Duck had a chance to answer. "I thought if anyone could persuade me to step foot in a church, it would be you . . . but no. I haven't been in a church since my Symon died, and I'm not about to today, not even for the Feast of the Cabbage. You'll have to indulge by yourself."

Duck sat and ate her own bread, nearly jumping out of her skin, but triumphant. She'd done it.

The baker had fallen for her lie.

"Do you need anything for the offering?" Griselde asked. "Penny? Bread? I may have a little ale tucked away somewhere, though I can't promise it'll be good enough for God."

A coin? A bit of bread? A nip of ale, perfect for warming the belly on a chilly autumn day?

And Griselde Baker was offering it all freely? Imagine the look on Gnat's face if Duck waltzed into the cathedral bearing gifts—how clever she would be in his eyes, how enterprising, how dependable.

The ultimate Crown.

But Griselde bit into her slice of bread with a hearty "Mmmm! That first bite. It never gets old, does it?" and Duck decided not to take the baker's alms. Bread, so much bread Griselde had already provided to the Crowns without knowing how philanthropic she'd been, and to Duck, it suddenly seemed unwise to press her luck.

"Take your time," were Griselde's final words before Duck walked out of the room. "It's the day of rest, after all. Take the long way home if you like." She turned back to her tea, smacking her lips as if it were the most delicious cup she'd ever savored and not, as Duck suspected, a weak brew concocted by an eight-year-old who was barely tall enough to reach the kettle.

Duck slipped out the door, telling herself all the while to slow down on the cobblestones, slow down, there was no need to run, no need to think the baker was on to her fib, no need to hurry—

Until she reached the abandoned cathedral, the stone blocks still crooked, the mortar still bunched up and bumpy, the beams still splintered with dampness.

And then she stood very still in the stretched morning light.

Her hands were in her pockets—the stance of a stranger.

She pulled them out and tried to remember how it felt to think of the cathedral as home, and then she went inside.

There was no sign of them, nothing but the crown symbol etched into the wall. Duck's stomach clenched at the possibilities—they hadn't left, had they? Gnat would have come and told her if they'd had to move their base . . . wouldn't he?

If not him, then Ash—wouldn't he?

"Hello?" Duck called out, uncertain, then chewed her bottom lip.

A pair of eyes popped up over the nearest pew. "Who is it?"

She couldn't instantly tell who was talking—it was either Frog Eyes with a growl or Drippy with impossibly clear sinuses.

"It's me, Duck," she answered.

"Duck who?" said a familiar voice. "There are a lot of ducks in the world, aren't there?"

Gnat. He was tucked somewhere in the nave, out of sight— if Duck listened hard, she could hear the rest of them breathing, some of them trying not to snicker from their hiding places.

Duck flushed. It kind of felt like they were laughing at her. "Come on," she said. "You only know one Duck. It's me."

"Yes, but are you the same Duck? How do we know the baker hasn't reformed you?" Gnat stepped out from behind the altar, inspecting her head to toe. His left hand clutched his knotted rope. "How do we know she hasn't renamed you Tiffany von Sugarfoot? She's already had you deloused and de-fleaed and brushed until you sparkle."

Inside her pockets, Duck's hands clenched. "I've still got plenty of fleas," she said quietly.

A figure sprinted across the cathedral and flung himself at Duck, lifting her up and spinning her around. "You're here!" Ash cried. He set her down suddenly, frantically searching her face. "What's wrong? What happened? Did that baker hurt you? Are we found out? Are the constables on their way now?"

"No, no." Duck said this to all the Crowns, who were emerging from their nooks and crannies to greet her—holy bones, she was so happy to see them, her chest felt like it was going to spill over. They were still as smudged as ever, but they looked exceptionally well fed, which pleased her. "Everything's fine."

"I'll say!" Ash tugged a crust of bread from his pocket—Duck instantly recognized it as yesterday's specialty loaf, a swirled rye with sesame seeds. He took a ravenous bite and chewed at her, grinning. "Such a bounty, and it's all thanks to you!"

"All right, pipe down." Gnat grabbed Drippy, who was prancing around Duck in celebration, by his tunic. "We don't want to send her back to the bakehouse with a swollen head." He whipped the rope in Duck's direction suddenly, the knot undoing itself, and then the rope was just a rope; when Duck flinched, Gnat smirked. "By the by, what are you doing here? The great Griselde Baker let you off your leash so you could have a stroll?"

Duck wiggled her toes inside her shoes. The wooden coin. She was here to tell Gnat that the baker knew about the wooden coin.

But it twisted her up inside to hear Gnat talk about the baker like this, as though she were keeping Duck prisoner there.

"I came here to tell you something. Yesterday, the baker—"

The sight of something tucked behind the altar made her pause.

Slouching soft leather, the brown mostly eaten away by dust.

The baker's boots.

"You—you took them." Duck walked away from Gnat and picked up the boots. The Crowns hadn't cut them up for foot wrappings or ripped off the buckles to gamble with. Good.

"Stole them," Gnat corrected. "So what?" He picked his nose with his left hand, looking at her askance. "Why are you so worked up about it?"

"Because," Duck blurted, her breath hot, "the journeyman thinks I stole them!" *And probably Griselde does, too,* Duck realized, a pit growing in her stomach. Even though the baker had instructed Petrus to back off, Duck hadn't exactly been exonerated. Petrus's accusations hung like a cloud over her head, and when Duck came back to the bakery, it would still be there . . . unless she could fix it.

She eyed the boots in her hands, and Gnat snorted.

"Don't even think about it," he said. "Those boots are ours now."

"If I don't clear my name, that journeyman's going to accuse me of thieving every time something goes missing," Duck pointed out. "And then the baker might fire me—"

"That baker's wrapped around your finger." Gnat kept digging in his nose for something grand. "You could rush back in there and pour dirt and water in her bed, and she'd beam while you made mud pies. She adores you. It's perfect."

Something warm radiated from Duck's very center . . . followed by a splash of cold as she reflected on Gnat's words.

How was Gnat so sure of the baker's devotion toward her impostor apprentice? The clamor of market days didn't allow for more than the affectionate barking of orders. Then a thought struck her:

Had Gnat been eavesdropping last night when the baker and Duck were talking on the back porch?

"She'll even let you get away with passing her a wooden coin, and she'll welcome you into her home and her strongbox all the same." Gnat wiped his finger on his pants, and Duck blinked, the shock of this truth plunging her into even chillier temperatures. So he *had* been spying on her.

"While she's busy fawning over everything you do and say," he went on, "we get fed. So you just keep on milking her for all she's worth. Unless you'd rather return these so you can get an extra pat on the head?" He jutted his chin at the boots. "Maybe she'll even adopt you, and then you'll be Little Master Baker—"

"Don't be mean, Gnat." Ash draped his arm around Duck; it was heavy on her shoulders. "Duck's one of us."

"Then let's see her act like it."

All the Crowns stopped skipping around and pressed in closer. Duck could feel their eyes, curious, hopeful, maybe even a little anxious—but she looked only at Ash, who shrugged.

Not a shrug of indecision or a shrug of carelessness.

A shrug that indicated it was entirely up to Duck.

She started to put the boots in Gnat's hand . . . but then held them back. "You can't have them."

Gnat chuckled, tugging them from her grip. "Why, Garbage, you certainly have changed. I don't think you've ever said this many words to any of us in your life."

Without another word himself, he strolled away toward the cathedral's entrance, the scuff of his hardened bare feet echoing in the vaulting.

"He's off to pawn them," Ash told Duck, as if she were still five years old, needing everything explained to her.

With a shock of irritation, she moved away from his side.

"I know." Of course Gnat was going to pawn them—what else would a Crown do with such fine boots? Wear them? Clomp around Odierne with them on his feet so every constable he passed could see the stolen property for himself?

Duck was one of them still, through and through. And to prove it, she marched after Gnat, following him out of the cathedral and toward the pawnbroker, where she'd help him haggle for a decent price. Those boots were too nice to sell for mere pennies.

Duck was a Crown.

She was.

But when she remembered what Gnat had said—how Griselde was so fond of her that she could do no wrong—the feeling inside her felt like a yeasted loaf, rising up and out of a pan she'd outgrown.

Overproofed. Messy.

WINTER

nother winter. The world, white. Icicles dangle from my fangs. Below me, the river is a silver zigzag.

Every word out of the east-side chickens' mouths creates a little cloud as they yap in the frigid air, and every pigeon is wearing an extra layer of feathers as insulation against the cold.

Down in the city, every person walks the snow-sprinkled streets with a bounce and a grin, and every door is freckled with holly berries. The smell of piping-hot ham and spiced wassail is everywhere, and no matter the hour, someone in some godforsaken corner of some building is singing a jolly carol for Christmastide.

And it makes me want to hurl.

"I heard the tanner got the laundress three yards of the most beautiful silk for Christmas," Goathead discloses to the others in a snickering tone that does not betide holiday cheer.

"And what'd he get his wife?" Harpy presses.

"Pregnant again!" comes the reply, and they all cackle.

"Wait until you see what I give you, you great clucks," I call across the roof. "Here is a hint: It's not the north wind; it's better out than in—"

"We'd love to give you the gift of a big push," Harpy snaps back. "Now keep quiet, ugly. No one likes you."

Quiet—the one thing I wish for every year but never get.

Soon it is Christmas Eve. A heavy snow falls all night, blanketing my horns and head. It chokes my throat and piles into my ears, and for this one glorious evening, everything is perfectly and completely still. Silent.

We gargoyles are coated in the stuff, and the snow hides the cathedral so perfectly that if someone were to look up at our stones, they might not notice us at all. So this is what it would look like if Odierne did not have us. So this is what it would feel like to be wholly forgotten.

I am so cold, I cannot tell if it is everything I ever hoped it would be. I cannot tell if I have broken a little inside or if that is just the frost splitting another one of my claws.

I cannot tell if I am broken a little inside.

Feasts and Frolics

Christmas.

First, the celebration of Winter's Tides, marked with a dry month—no spirits, no rich foods, so as to crush your personal demons and keep your temptations at bay.

Griselde had held out until a few hours before the fast ended with a blessing and a feast; Duck had awoken to the smell of grease over fire and found the baker nibbling on a burnt sausage.

"There comes a time in every woman's life, Duck," the baker said, lifting her chin unapologetically, "when she must make her own rites based on the needs of her own soul—and the needs of her own stomach."

Duck suspected such a revelation would not be approved by a bishop, but she accepted a sausage from Griselde as a pledge to keep quiet.

Winter in Odierne was a wonder. Bonfires blazed on street corners, and the river was frozen white against the stark black of leafless trees. In the distance, the hills beyond the city walls were snowcapped and glowed blue in the afternoons, and lush evergreen boughs decorated every doorway and shop front.

After a month of abstaining, the good people of Odierne were starved for something delicious and filling, and so the lines outside the bakery were longer than the days themselves.

They baked simple loaves with hearty grains and ale, and they sold from dawn until they were out of flour. People handed the baker gifts along with their coin: slow-roasted chestnuts, spiced wine, mushrooms picked in summer's floods and dried through fall.

"Such bounty we do not deserve!" Griselde thundered when a farmer gave her a scarf his wife had knitted with their own sheep's wool; Duck tried not to giggle when the scarf barely wrapped around the baker's thick neck.

The heat from the ovens wafted out of the bakehouse, beckoning passersby to come and warm themselves. Duck found it strange to be sweating buckets as she kneaded dough while outside, men's beards were frosted and women shivered in their surcoats.

Griselde handed out orange rolls and mugs of hot cider, laughing with the customers who lingered, many of whom were neighbors and friends she'd known for years.

"Won't you join us for backgammon, then?" the barber pleaded. "Next Thursday—Samson's roasting a pig, special."

"Sure, if you don't mind a big fat cheater sharing your board." Griselde tossed an extra hot cross bun into the man's basket. "You tell Samson a happy Christmas from me, and I'll see you next week."

To Duck, she whispered in a too-loud voice, "I'll be staying for one round only—his backgammon nights always devolve into much more . . . lewd games." She shook her head at an awkward memory. "Like Mould My Bread, a sport that is meant to showcase proper kneading techniques but is about something else entirely."

On Christmas Eve, the bakery's last customers of the evening were a trio of children, all of them wearing thick, unkempt furs.

Duck locked eyes with a familiar pair of hazel peepers—Ash.

"Got any trenchers left?" he asked.

Joy washed over Duck, even though the coat Ash wore smelled so rank, it made her eyes water. The furs had doubtless been swiped from clotheslines or closets or from someone recently buried.

At least they wouldn't freeze to death, Duck told herself as she passed the last of the trenchers into Ash's waiting arms. Griselde was chatting with another customer; Petrus was scrubbing the counters.

"Here you go," she said, sliding an extra penny into Ash's palm. "Enjoy. And happy Christmas Eve."

"Happy Christmas Eve," Ash echoed, and then the Crowns shuffled off just as the heavens let down a soft rain, pelting the roof of the bakery with gentle plinks like holiday bells.

They shuffled off together. All of them . . .

And as quickly as her cheer had flourished at the sight of them, Duck's heart now fell into her stomach with a plop.

Every Christmas, the Crowns would catch and pluck a pigeon, then roast it on a spit and eat it with their fingers. They would find a mystery play to sneak into, watch some fat old monks recite lines in bad wigs, and the Crowns would heckle until they were kicked out, and then they'd swipe some honey sticks and wassail if they could find them, and all huddle up and sleep, preferably somewhere they could see the stars.

But this Christmas, Duck would be sleeping beneath ceiling beams. It was unlikely the baker would serve her pigeon or subject her to anything remotely biblical.

It would be an entirely different kind of Christmas, and what should have been a holiday of pure, wild fun would be, for Duck, just another night away from the Crowns.

Duck woke on Christmas morning to find it was snowing. It made her room frigid as an ice cave, but it was worth it to witness the fattest flakes she'd ever seen drifting down in spirals.

She jumped out of bed and hurried downstairs, filled her bed warmer with fresh embers, then bundled back up in one of the spare blankets, bleary-eyed and cozy, watching the world outside her window magically turn white.

The scent of the Christmas feast finally lured her downstairs. On the table was a glorious spread of pies—mince and pork and beyond—as well as roasted partridge, almonds, cheeses, game hens, potatoes sprinkled with saffron, fish, and the Yule boar. All of it was lit with real beeswax candles, stretching high, bathing the kitchen in a golden glow.

"Our dear Duck!" Griselde pulled her head out of an oven, a tray of tree-shaped gingerbread in her hands, a look of triumph on her face. "A merry Christmas to you!"

"And a merry one to you," Duck returned, staring around the bakehouse. It had been transformed—sprigs of holly tucked in every loose brick, red ribbons trimmed in gold dangling from the rafters.

"Petrus and Raina will be here in a minute to eat," Griselde said, "but I don't think I can wait another second." She wiped her greasy hands on her apron, then felt around on the counters until she found a parcel, wrapped in a simple brown cloth, which she thrust into Duck's arms.

Duck fumbled with it; it was lighter than it looked. "What is this for?" she asked blankly.

"What do you mean? It's Christmas, isn't it?" Griselde chortled. "Now, hurry up and open it. I've been waiting to see the look on your face for weeks now."

Duck opened the parcel and forgot how to breathe for a moment.

It was a figurine of Rigby the Pygmy, the diminutive knight Duck had seen at the tournament, carved of wood and painted to a shine. Wrapped around it was a silk banner, blue as Rigby's tunic, the silhouette of a knight on a horse stitched in black thread.

"For your room." Griselde held the banner up to demonstrate how it would hang neatly on a wall. "I thought you might like to display a winner's colors," she added with a teasing wink. "What do you think?"

Duck's heart suddenly felt too big for her chest. She kept opening her mouth, hoping the right words would come out, but instead her breath grew hot and the corners of her eyes stung.

"Thank you," she whispered. "I've never gotten a present before."

"Never? Well! A merry Christmas to you. May you put it to good use." Griselde stepped forward and planted a sloppy kiss on Duck's forehead.

Then she rushed back to the oven to tend to another batch of gingerbread, and Duck stood there, holding her gift, feeling as if a hole had been punched straight through her.

Petrus, Raina, and little Hugo arrived, and the morning dissolved into feasting and frolicking. During "feasting," Duck was ordered to shovel as much food and drink into her as she could possibly fit, and during "frolicking," Griselde sang out her favorite Yuletide hymns, which did not exactly match the church's official versions word for word.

The more wine she took in, the more ridiculous the lyrics became.

"The boar's head, I understand," she sang out during dessert, lifting up her glass in the direction of the piping-hot pig on the table, *"is chief service in all this land. Wheresoever it may be found . . ."* She held out this note, long and low, drawing closer and closer to Duck, until their noses were nearly touching, and then belted out the last line: *"Servitur cum sinapio!"*

Then she broke into belly laughs, and Duck, confused, looked to Petrus for clarification.

"'It is served with mustard,'" he translated with an affable eye roll. "Apparently it rhymes in Traditional Avilognian."

"Pipers!" Griselde suddenly cried, darting outside the bakehouse without so much as a surcoat.

Duck, feeling plenty warm from her own sip of wine, followed along into the cold, stuffing a slice of fruitcake into her pocket.

The pipers marched through the square, their music at once jolly and sad in that way that Christmas songs tend to be. Griselde traipsed right alongside them, singing when she knew the words, humming when she didn't, the great puffs of air escaping her mouth as fat as clouds.

Other familiar faces joined the parade as it wove through the streets of Odierne, and up and down the streets they marched until the sun began its descent and the horizon gleamed like a brass instrument.

Duck's fingertips were frozen, her cheeks were like panes of frosted glass, and her teeth were cold from grinning so hard, but she felt as if she could stroll in the baker's company with the pipers forever—

Until she turned her head, pulling out her fruitcake for a nibble, and spotted the cathedral, alive and aglow.

Shadows danced around a fire, the unmistakable noises of celebration and laughter wafting out through the gaps between the stones.

Duck halted, the fruitcake halfway to her mouth.

The rest of the piping parade went on without her, Griselde Baker leading them on a final loop away from the square, but Duck stayed put.

There, in the blue twilight, was a party.

A Christmas party for the Crowns.

A Christmas party without Duck.

Duck inched a bit closer, unsure if she wanted to see but unable to resist. She could pick out the unrestrained chuckles of Le Chou; the high, airy voice of Fingers singing; the chiding, authoritative orders of Gnat chiming in every once in a while.

He called out to no one in particular, "Turn the bird, will you? It's charring."

"Thought you liked it charred," said Frog Eyes, but he spun the spit anyway.

Ah, Duck thought as she saw what they were roasting, her stomach in knots.

Not a pigeon.

They'd procured a goose. Maybe they'd chased it down themselves and wrung its neck; maybe they'd used the coins Duck had been sliding them to buy it honest.

Good, Duck tried to tell herself, *very good that they will not be hungry tonight*—and yet she felt like she'd been pinched.

Christmas without Duck.

Ash danced near the unfinished wall of the cathedral, grinning and chattering as he swigged from a bottle of wassail.

They'd gotten wassail.

Duck pleaded silently for Ash to look up, look outside at the figure standing in the snow.

But he never did.

She was a Crown.

And yet they were celebrating without her.

But wait a minute, a voice within her cut in. *Just wait a minute.*

Weren't you feasting and frolicking without them, too? You ate your way through several pies and a boar without a single Crown there to share it with.

And that fruitcake in your pocket is for you to eat, not them.

Feeling odd, feeling too full to eat another bite but also hollowed out, Duck trudged to the spot where the cathedral wall crumbled into a ledge and set her fruitcake on the stones.

She did not wait for them to discover her small offering but turned away from the music, away from the light, and headed for home—no, not home. Home was here, at the cathedral, because home was wherever the Crowns were.

The bakery was a sort of strange coin-and-bread trap that Duck needed to tend to day and night. It wasn't home, no matter how warm, how cozy, how safe it felt.

Her steps were heavy in the white snow.

The bakehouse was dark when Duck came in. Drips of beeswax from the candles had dried on the table, and the remnants of the food lay out, pies picked over, bones chewed clean.

Duck was certain she'd managed to sneak back in undetected, but Griselde's voice rang out from the shadows of her bedroom. "Ah, there's our Duck."

Peering into the open doorway, Duck spotted the baker in a rocking chair, creaking before a fire that had eaten its logs down to embers. A nearly empty bottle was in her hand.

"You were gone for a while."

Duck had not thought up a decent lie on her way back; she'd been too distracted by the image of all the Crowns circling their bonfire, the gap where Duck would have stood closed.

"I'm glad you got some fresh air." Griselde rocked the chair back and forth, back and forth. "Good feast tonight. And good company." She drained the last of her wine, then let the bottle drop onto the floor. "Did you know those pipers thought you were my daughter?" She looked in Duck's direction and laughed, both sharply and joylessly. "My daughter. Can you imagine?"

Duck suddenly didn't know where to put her hands.

Duck was not the baker's daughter.

Duck was a Crown.

"Duck?" Griselde reached out her hand. Her pale eyes were swollen—not as if she'd been crying, but as if she were very, very tired. "It's dark in here."

The fire was almost completely out now, giving off nothing more than a star's glow. It was chilly in here, the bakery's usual heat leaching out of the slightly ajar window.

And dark, so very dark.

Duck navigated her way across the room and latched the window. She let the baker find her hand and clasp it.

Crowns were good at the dark.

And Duck was a Crown.

Duck tugged Griselde, intending to lead her to bed, but the baker did not move.

"I have no daughter," Griselde said without a hint of Christmas jolliness, "and you have no mother."

Her grip on Duck's hand was tight as a child's. Duck had no words.

Not the wrong ones, not the right ones.

And even if she had the right words, would she say them now? Now, to fill up this space between the baker and herself, which was already shrinking with every breath—

"Ah, well." Duck could make out Griselde's smile in the dim light. "We both seem to be doing just fine for ourselves, wouldn't you say?"

Duck couldn't tell if she was supposed to answer this or not, but then the baker started snoring, her head tilted back against the chair, her teeth gleaming, and Duck let go of her hand.

It was still snowing outside. The shutters on the baker's bedroom window were bolted closed, but even with the ovens blazing, it would be a chilly night.

Duck took the quilt from Griselde's bed and draped it over the baker, tugging it up to her chin.

She left her there in the rocking chair and backed out of the room, feeling as though she had just been shown a bit of Christmas mercy. The conversation had ended unnaturally early, and furthermore, the baker likely wouldn't remember it in the morning. Duck was grateful on both counts. Griselde's hand remained outstretched, as if still reaching for Duck.

Offering Duck a spot beside her, even in sleep.

All the gargoyles on the abandoned cathedral overlooking the Sarluire in the market district of Odierne are asleep on Christmas night except one.

Which means that all the gargoyles will miss the most rapturous, otherworldly show of stars that the heavens have ever displayed—except one.

The snow has melted off our rooftop, leaving a sheen of crystal ice on our stones. Overhead, the clouds have blown clear, leaving a sky as thick as velvet, blue and purple swirling into black, speckles of light piercing through the darkness. Dazzling.

Every night for ninety-nine years, it has been me and the stars. All the gargoyles asleep, except for one—

"Is the sky always this bright?" A familiar croak, coming from the east side of the cathedral.

Harpy is awake, groggy, blinking as she tilts her head back and looks up. All the gargoyles, except for two.

"Look at all that mess." She clicks her tongue, and I am about to reprimand her for her irreverence—how many times has she scolded me for my hymnal interpretations or my gaseous offerings to the daily gossip, and yet she'd disrupt this heavenly glory?—but a streak of light catches my eye.

The glow of stars, like they have their own souls, and the way the darkness sometimes collapses on itself, as though the night is made of billowing fabric or a black upside-down sea. There is nothing to watch and everything to watch. There could be anything up there.

Yes, a mess. A glorious mess.

"All that up there, and we are here. We are still here," Harpy says, and her voice is softer than I have ever heard it. "We are still here, and it is a miracle."

She cannot see my eyes, but I glare at her all the same.

"We are not here," I growl. "We have never been here. We are nothing. We might as well be snow and air."

Down below the cathedral, carolers march along the street. I wait for them to pause their music, to glance up at us, to notice how beautifully our icy stones sparkle in the moonlight. But the singing goes on uninterrupted.

"They don't even look at us," I tell Harpy. "We're just here to block out the sun, and your big fat rump does most of that work."

Harpy is silent for a moment, and I wonder if she has fallen back asleep.

"Can't even be nice on Christmas," she finally mutters. "Worthless and ugly." And then she snores loudly to spite me, and I stare back up at the sky.

Ugly on Christmas. Ugly and useless all year long.

And this year is now drawing to a close. Another year coming soon, and I plan to be just as ugly, just as foul, just as sore.

Another year coming soon, and without even looking, I know it will all be the same. Watching and waiting by myself. Always by myself.

Another winter, and I wish the snow would just freeze our stones and crackle us into shards of ice.

Reassurances

Winter did not leave.

Duck always forgot that Christmas did not take the cold with it. Winter's presence felt like a great hole that everyone had fallen into. The morning air was frigid, biting at one's extremities; the afternoon sun was far too weak to thaw bones or melt away frost. The nights would have been miserable, too, if not for the ovens, constantly blazing.

On a particularly teeth-chattering morning, Griselde opened the shop windows and found people piled up, sleeping against the residual warmth of the bricks.

"Let them sleep," Griselde said when Petrus threatened to call for the watch. "Actually, no—wake them up, and let's get hot tea and rolls going, shall we?" When Petrus gave her a pained look, she scoffed. "If someone freezes to death in front of our counter, it's going to be very bad for business, wouldn't you agree?"

Duck twisted tea bags and watched for familiar faces as she

distributed mugs, but she didn't see a single Crown among the piles of cold-wearied grown-ups.

She wasn't sure if she should feel relieved by this or sore.

She still felt sore when she thought of Christmas night, the Crowns jigging around the nave with nary a Duck in sight, the greasy stink of the goose, the flicker and snap of the fire.

Christmas without Duck—

But what did you expect? she tried to reason whenever she found herself dwelling on this particular hurt. *For them to sit around on Christmas night, silent and bored, their toes turning blue from cold? For all laughing, singing, and stories to halt until you were back in their midst?*

Yes, a darker part of her thought. Yes, she wanted them to miss her as much as she missed them.

The only times she'd seen them since Christmas were market days. Up the Crowns would march in pairs, wearing shoddy disguises, and they would take their vittles without fanfare.

Duck was always overjoyed to see them, and then after they left she would have to stand next to the ovens in order to fight off the icy feeling in her chest when they addressed her like a stranger.

She was right where Gnat wanted her, she tried to remind herself. And so she kept her head down, pocketed coins from the strongbox to slide into their palms, and chose the largest trenchers to pass to the Crowns on market day.

Enlightenment came with the turn of the year, and Griselde hosted another feast, this time for several other bakers in the guild. Their shops were scattered throughout the region, yet they all saddled horses and came to Odierne, bearing miraculous hostess gifts: wreaths made of sweet dough, candied galettes, loaves dipped in wassail and dotted with currants.

"Watch out!" Griselde warned Duck when she opened the door to let them in. "This is the finest group of ruffians you'll ever meet!"

They didn't look much like ruffians to Duck; they looked like mild-mannered, solemn, committed breadmakers, some of them still bearing streaks of flour on their cheeks. But they all had the same twinkle in their eyes as Griselde, which made Duck wonder if they, too, would one day see their vision blur, their irises go cloudy, the color leached from their worlds, just like Griselde.

Perhaps it was the price one paid to make bread.

Duck greeted them as politely as she could and took her seat next to Griselde's at the table. She watched them feast on game hens and fruit and listened to their hilarious tales of bread gone wrong.

A real brotherhood, she observed as Griselde and her guests splashed back wine and sang raucous baking chants. When they broke bread, they broke it together.

Duck ought to have felt welcome in such a warm fellowship, but instead she sipped her small dram of wine feeling, even surrounded by loud voices and raised glasses, more alone than ever.

Duck could not sneak off to the cathedral in January because it was inspection month. Every week, leaders from the guild showed up at Griselde's gate, as well as an assortment of royal scribes and lawyers, who were to be "considered proxies for Her Majesty the Queen and treated as such," as they informed Griselde.

"Well, then, I'll go ahead and line the chamber pots with velvet," Griselde retorted with a jolly smirk.

Despite the baker's snide comments, the bakehouse passed all their inspections without a single fine—due in large part to Petrus, who had spent every waking moment either scrubbing and tidying or commanding Duck to do odd chores like measuring grains with a magnifying glass.

Yes, even the grains had to adhere to a standard average.

But Petrus's doggedness paid off. The bakery received its stamped, sealed papers from the guild. Griselde could sell her bread for at least another half a year, and Duck—

Duck looked up and another month had passed.

Another month given to the baker.

Another month away from the Crowns.

One Monday in February, Griselde had a headache and took to her bed to nap it away. Petrus helped Duck clean the ovens, then went home, and Duck brought some empty flour sacks to the back porch—

And found Ash hiding in the hedges.

"Duck!" he whispered loudly. "Duck, it's me! Hello!" He shivered in the chill, his nose red with cold, but his eyes were brilliant with joy.

Warmth poured into Duck's chest, and before she could stop it, a huge, toothy grin stretched her mouth.

There was the face Duck had looked up at almost every day of her life, and to see him now, after so long, made the moment warp and wiggle in a strange way.

As if it had been twenty years since she'd seen him, and also as if no time had passed at all.

Duck dropped the flour sacks in a pile for the miller. "Wait there!" she commanded Ash in a hushed voice as she peered behind her at the bakehouse.

Griselde's window was closed. Duck tiptoed closer and put her ear to the shutter—yes, the baker was conked out, in a deep sleep.

She glanced at the opposite end of the yard, beyond the fence to Petrus's house. All his upstairs windows were open, Raina letting the light sweep through the halls, but Duck knew that even if Petrus looked down into the baker's yard, the hedges would be obscured by the fence.

And so Duck let herself cross the long yard, rushing along the crust of old snow, brimming with elation until she was standing in the bushes with Ash—

But by the time she got there, her chest was a tangled, thorny mess. Ash let out a quiet whoop and picked her up in a monstrous hug, swinging her around, but Duck kept her arms stiff as boards, pinned to her sides.

"What's the matter with you?" Ash set her down and frowned. "You look sick—did you eat raw potatoes again?"

"No." Duck took in a breath, momentarily distracted by the memory of bygone days when the Crowns had to choose between the gurgles of an empty stomach and the gurgles of a stomach that had just been fed an uncooked tuber.

Griselde had served Duck potatoes cooked three different ways just this week alone.

"How come you haven't been to see me?" Duck managed to say without her voice breaking. "It's been forever."

Ash folded his arms. "I could say the same thing to you! Where have you been? We miss you!"

Those were it. The magic words Duck needed to hear in order for the pond within her to thaw.

It had all been a misunderstanding.

She'd been waiting for the Crowns.

The Crowns had been waiting for her.

All that brooding for nothing.

"It was inspections," she blurted out. "All of January, we were getting ready for these inspections—did you know a baker can be fined if they don't grind their grains to the right consistency? Or if their loaves are more than one one-hundredth of an ounce lighter than they advertise? I swear, they're stricter than a priest at the Feast of Divine Mercy." She shook her head, exasperated, then realized, with a light chuckle, that she was mimicking Griselde to a tee.

"It's all with the best intentions, of course," Duck went on. "If you don't have strict regulations, then some bakers will try to find shortcuts, ways to cheat their customers. They'll fill their dough with sawdust. That's what they were doing in Telgary until their guild tightened the laws—" Then she stopped. "What is it?"

The corner of Ash's mouth tugged up in a surprised smirk, and his eyes were teasing. "Wow, Duck, you sound like a real grown-up."

Duck said nothing. Above her, in the branches of the oak tree that grew in the corner of the yard, a pair of pigeons trilled and cooed, then took off together, the flap of their wings sounding like the pages of a book rustling.

It wasn't necessarily a bad thing, to sound like a grown-up, Duck thought. Surely Ash hadn't meant it as an insult.

But it felt as if Ash was pointing out how much Duck had changed.

"The rest of the Crowns say hi," Ash said, plucking a blackened leaf from the bush to shred in his fingers. "Drippy had a cold last week, but he's doing much better. Spinner's been holding these wall ball tournaments; she's undefeated . . . so far. Oh! And Frog Eyes wanted me to tell you that Ringer had babies!"

Duck chewed her bottom lip, thinking hard.

"You know, the worm he got at the hot fair?" Ash prompted. "So now we've got all these wriggly baby worms on our hands. What's wrong, Duck? You—you don't seem yourself."

A lump swelled in Duck's throat. She had to concentrate so her eyes wouldn't spill over. No, she didn't seem herself. The old Duck would have remembered that Drippy got a cold every February without fail, and she would have helped the gang scrape together some stuffed eggs, Drippy's favorite, in order to cheer him up. She never would have forgotten about Frog Eyes's precious pet, no matter how squirmy. She would have found it unbearable to go so long without seeing them, because to be without the Crowns was to be without a part of herself, a rib or a finger.

She'd missed them the first night she was away. She'd missed them the second night. But somewhere between the third night and now, the old Duck had . . . gone.

She'd been replaced by this apron-wearing, flour-streaked version of Duck who thought about proper yeasting techniques and whose forearms were bulging from all that kneading.

"Hey." Ash crooked a finger under Duck's chin, lifting her face until she was staring into his steady eyes. "It's still me. And you're still you."

Happiness fizzed deep in Duck's bones. At least this hadn't changed.

Ash could still look right at her and know.

Know what she was thinking, know what she was saying.

They didn't need words, she and Ash.

They were beyond them. Now more than ever.

But Duck still wanted to use them. She still wanted to tell Ash everything, about how much it had hurt to see the Crowns on Christmas, about how strange it was to be in this bakehouse day after day, like being trapped in a cage and yet also free in a way she'd never felt before, both at the same time—

But the sound of shutters clattering open made Duck straighten. Ash dropped down to the ground, ready to crawl out of the hedges on all fours if necessary.

"Duck? Is that you out there?" Griselde's face was still drowsy as she stood at her window.

"Yes!" Duck called, her insides fluttering. "Just . . . just talking to Ash!" She said it before she had time to truly think, but one could argue it was the truth. After all, Ash the cat could be skulking around the yard like he did most afternoons, fruitlessly hunting pigeons.

Griselde chuckled. "That rascal's back, is he? Tell him I've got a few sardines lying around if he's interested."

"All right." Duck forced herself to exhale; beside her, Ash tugged on Duck's tunic and whispered, an insatiable gleam in his eye, "Sardines?"

"The headache's gone," Griselde went on, "so I'm off to see Master Cooper about my barrel repairs. I'll be home in time for supper. Is there anything you need?"

"No!" Duck prayed to every saint she knew of that Ash the cat didn't choose this moment to come sauntering into the yard. How on earth would she explain such a thing to Griselde?

"All right, then, I'm off!" Griselde said. "My, what a glorious day! Good on you for getting some sun! And Duck, maybe tonight we'll break out the jacks and play a little—I'm feeling lucky!"

Duck waited until the baker moved away from the window, then said to Ash, "You should go."

Ash got to his feet, not bothering to brush the dirt off his knees, then blinked at Duck. "Holy bones, Gnat wasn't kidding! You've got that baker eating right out of the palm of your hand! Listen to how she fawns over you!"

Maybe this should have pleased Duck, but instead, a flame of annoyance curled within her. Why did everyone assume she was masterfully manipulating the baker?

Maybe the baker just liked Duck.

Maybe Duck was actually likable, once everyone stopped underestimating her and acting like she was too quiet to bother listening to.

"Aw, Duck, I didn't mean it like that." Ash nudged her, and that singular motion was almost enough to transport her back to that moment on the roof right after she'd made her first lift.

Almost.

"You should go," she repeated, somewhat snappishly. "I don't want you to get caught here."

"Come on," Ash persisted. "I can stay awhile longer. We can hunt for skipping stones. Or play jump the shadow."

When Duck looked at Ash, ready to tell him no and insist that he leave before he said something else to inflame her, there was a curious furrow in his brow.

His mouth was smiling, but his eyes were glazed with melancholy.

He missed her, Duck realized, more than he would let himself say.

"You really have grown," Ash repeated, "but you still look like yourself. Same round face, same serious eyes. Still my little duckling."

His little duckling. But this time, instead of feeling comforted by the thought of brave young Ash wading into the river to rescue baby Duck, whom he would keep under his wing for the rest of their days, an uneasy feeling settled in her middle.

There were so many holes in the story. How had she never noticed before? In Ash's version, there was a cry in the darkness, and then a bundle in the river, and then a baby in his arms . . . but how had she gotten there in the first place?

Where were her parents? Her mother?

Had anyone gone looking for her?

Were they still looking?

Duck had always thought it was such a grand story of how she'd been chosen, but now as she listened, she couldn't hear it as anything but a bunch of unanswered questions.

"And now, here you are, getting us our bread, slipping us coins, keeping us in a manner to which we have grown quite accustomed—the luckiest Duck we ever did fish," Ash said proudly.

How strange, Duck thought, to wonder about a piece of yourself that you'd never even known was missing.

"Ash?" she started tentatively, but before she could say anything else, the baker leaned over the gate.

"Yoo-hoo, Duck!" Griselde shouted. "I'm afraid my eyes aren't in much of a cooperating mood today, and with the snowmelt, that canal sounds mighty full. Raging. Would you mind being an old bird's escort around town for a few hours?"

"I've got to go," Duck whispered to Ash after she'd answered the baker. "After we leave, count to fifty, then crawl out the back way—don't stand up until you're back in the square, understand?" She paused, then added, "See if Gnat'll let you be the one who comes next market day."

"I miss you, too." Ash's mouth split into a wide smile, but he grabbed Duck's arm. "Duck . . . do you think you could get those sardines for me? I wouldn't want them to spoil."

Duck grinned. "I'll go through the house and leave them on the front windowsill. Take them quickly and don't let anyone see you."

He held up his hands defensively. "I'm a Crown. I know the rule: Don't get noticed."

Duck nodded, but a pang of homesickness twinged beneath her ribs. She missed the Crowns. She missed the rules. She even missed Gnat's lectures, his sternness, the way he sometimes glared at every Crown as if he were minding a herd of guileless sheep in a field of sleeping wolves—all of it. She missed all of it.

"Does Gnat ever say . . . how much longer?" Duck suppressed a sob, gesturing around her, and Ash shrugged.

"He seems pretty happy to keep you here awhile—we're living the high and fat life, thanks to you." He plunked a kiss on her forehead. "You clever thing, you." Then he tucked himself beneath the hedge, patiently waiting until the coast was clear so he could collect his sardines and scamper back home.

Home.

Duck turned back around at the door, and she couldn't see him among the leafless skeletons of the bushes.

Like he was already gone.

A storm of emotions welled up in her throat.

How could the Crowns stand it without her? Wasn't there a Duck-size hole in their group every day that she was at the bakery instead of the cathedral?

For every day that she stayed here, stealing and lying until her lungs were black, she could feel such holes being carved out of her, one for every Crown.

And yet if Gnat came for her tomorrow . . .

Would it be as easy as that to go with him?

Would it be easy to walk away from the bakery in order to go back home?

Or would Duck feel, with every step, a Griselde-size hole cut right out of her middle?

SPRING

A Cake for Bacon

Duck blinked and it was spring.

One minute her head was down as she scraped out the ovens, scrubbed the dishes, flipped dough out of bowls, and the next, trees were in full green. Dark mornings at the bakery were suddenly made much cheerier with the accompaniment of birdsong. Butterflies flew past the open storefront, glittering in the sunlight.

Duck inhaled and smelled the dandelions and the cowslips and the forsythia from the wild hills beyond Odierne, all of them mixing with the warm scent of hardening crust.

Griselde Baker, too, reveled in the shift of the seasons. "I do enjoy a good winter feast," she said, "but I am always happy to see the sun return."

Such a beautiful, colorful world, Duck thought, taking in the geraniums in window boxes and the boughs of Saint Justine's lilac hanging over every door. Such a shame that Griselde could only see the blues.

At her lesson with Master Frobertus, she read a full page from the Book of Kells without stumbling over a single word. He was so pleased by her recitation, he was practically frothing at the mouth. "If you ever want to abandon the baking life and come work as a notary's apprentice, I'd be happy to have you."

"I didn't know notaries took apprentices." Duck had never seen anyone else in Master Frobertus's dusty old office except a few clerks, all of them as wizened and puckered as he was.

"We don't," he said with a smug wink, and Duck had to glance down at the book to keep from blushing.

So now there were two doors open to her: one to a bakery and one to a notary.

Doors she had no intention of walking through.

But Duck couldn't stop replaying that conversation in her head. It was nice to hear that she was good for something other than palming coins.

Gnat wanted Duck to be a siphon.

Master Frobertus and Griselde Baker both thought she could be more.

One bright morning, Petrus went to assist the local bishop with a minor home repair, leaving Griselde and Duck to handle the baking by themselves. "You go ahead," Griselde had insisted. "Help the bishop. We may need him to vouch for us at the pearly gates someday."

Duck mixed up the trenchers, the barley loaves, and the horse bread as easily as if she'd done it a thousand times already—which, she realized as she counted back the seasons, she may well have.

She did not kill the yeast. She did not overknead the dough. She shaped the blobs of dough on the trays so they would bake straight and fat and pushed them into the oven without breaking a sweat.

Her very temperature had changed. She was now able to tolerate the great heat of the ovens without getting flushed. At night, she could kick off all her covers, and she never woke up with the shakes.

The evening chills of spring were actually refreshing to her; her life as a Crown had weathered her against the cold, and now her life as a baker's apprentice had hardened her against the heat. Soon she would be like one of those old gargoyles: crackly skin made of stone, able to thrive in all manner of climate.

All the regular loaves were either in the oven or cooling, so all that was left on the list was a special order.

A honey cake.

It was going to a farmer, John Bacon, who had helped Griselde seal off a hole in her storeroom through which the mice had been relentlessly attacking her grain sacks.

The baker had gone into her counting room to tabulate this week's earnings. This used to terrify Duck, who would yank her hair out with nerves, hoping that the baker didn't notice that a certain number of coins had been taken from the strongbox.

But she knew by now that the baker's grip on math was . . . less than masterful, and that her record-keeping was somewhat slippery. Perhaps Gnat had already known this, Duck sometimes thought. Perhaps he had witnessed the ways in which Griselde Baker rounded up, tallied up, always assuming an obnoxiously optimistic way of viewing everything, including income.

Perhaps Gnat had known, months before Duck did, how perfect this was going to be—she wouldn't put it past him.

Gnat always thought of everything.

Griselde seemed happily lost in her columns of numbers, and since Duck had seen the baker make honey cakes numerous times now, she decided to go ahead and give it a try.

A good apprentice tried to make life easier for their master, after all.

Every cake needed the following building blocks: flour for structure, yeast for leavening, something sweet for flavor, like honey or beet juice or, if you could afford it, sugar. It also needed salt for contrast, fat for richness, and a binder—eggs or milk or something moist.

Butter.

Griselde was a firm believer in butter.

The larder had all these things, but Duck's eyes went right to something else.

A basket of spring's first peaches, fresh from the market.

Her mouth watered.

Peaches in a cake would be delicious, wouldn't they?

And there—a bowl of strawberries, ripened red, waiting to be mashed into something worthy.

Her nose hunted down the last ingredient: rosemary.

It always found her.

She inhaled again.

Peaches, strawberries, and rosemary.

A perfectly springy, refreshing cake.

Two layers.

She measured flour, added warm water and sugar to a bowl with a few other things, then set it in the sun to work its rising magic.

She mashed the peaches and strawberries into a paste and added honey—would she need additional eggs? she wondered. Or would the fruit and honey be enough of a binder to keep the cake together?

She paused, thinking deeply, then opted for a bit of milk to keep everything clumped and moist. She decided she wanted a cake-like texture, yes—but she wanted it to melt in the mouth, a representation of how it felt to bite into a juicy peach.

She used a knife to chop the rosemary into fine bits, then sprinkled them into the mixture, the oils making her fingertips smell piney.

Finally, she poured the batter into the cake tins, and just as she turned to put them in the oven, there was the baker, standing in the doorway of the kitchen, taking up all the space and blocking out the sunlight—and it startled Duck so much, the cake tins nearly jumped out of her hands.

"Whoa, there!" Griselde reached out to steady Duck. "That would have been a real mess! But what's all this?"

"I—I'm sorry!" Duck said. "I was just trying to help!"

Griselde dipped a finger into the batter, bringing it to her mouth. "Is this . . . peaches?"

Duck was silent.

"And strawberry . . . and what is that, mint?" Griselde tipped her head back as she let the taste soak into her tongue.

"Rosemary." Duck's heart pummeled against her chest. Why had she ever thought these flavors would work together? What a waste of perfectly good ingredients! Now she had surely found the baker's breaking point.

"That," Griselde said, a grin spreading across her face, "is brilliant!"

Duck's insides flooded with warmth. "Really?"

"It's delicious!" Griselde took another swipe just to be sure. "Sweet, but not cloying. The strawberries add that tartness, and the rosemary is so fragrant and cuts through all of it so it's not so sugary—and did you use yeast, then?"

Duck shook her head. "Yogurt. And powder. That way the cake won't expand too quickly and lose all its—"

"All its air!" The baker slapped her knee joyfully. "Well, I'll be! Look who's developed her very first recipe! You keep this up, you'll be making guild-ready masterpieces in no time!"

Duck carried the tins to the oven, grateful to the blast of heat for covering up her blush.

The peach-and-strawberry cake was baked, cooled, and passed off to John Bacon (who took one whiff of the parcel and practically swooned), and Duck had just finished washing the last of the tins when she felt the baker's eyes on her.

"Turn around," Griselde instructed.

Hesitating slightly, Duck spun around once, and when she stopped, the baker's face was twisted up in a scowl. "Well, you've gone and done it."

"Done what?" Duck glanced down at herself, at the state of her clothes. Yes, her apron was stained, but that was the point of an apron, wasn't it?

"You've gone and grown." The baker broke into a smile. "Shot up like a weed. I thought as much. Come over here, and I'll show you."

Duck took a step toward the baker. Griselde ran her massive hands along Duck's arm and wrist, pinching the spot where the hem of her sleeve stopped short. "See? Look at how small this is on you now!"

Yes, Duck had noticed that her clothing had grown short in the sleeves and snug at the armpits, but the baker had been generous enough to buy this set. The last thing Duck wanted was to appear ungrateful. "I'm sorry," she whispered, and the baker chuckled.

"No need to apologize for doing just what nature wants you to do," the baker said. "You're a good three inches taller, thanks to all the bread you've been eating. Nothing to be ashamed of. But we should probably get you something new to wear. Something that fits, don't you think?"

Griselde extended her hand. "Come along. To the tailor's with you. Might as well get yourself measured so she can start snipping and sewing now. No, not a word of protest out of you! As your master, it's my sacred duty to clothe, shoe, and house you, and I won't go back on the vows of my guild."

Duck, having no other option, took off her apron and let Griselde Baker lead her out into the sunshine.

Master Katrina, the tailor, measured parts of Duck's body that she had never even considered: the distance between her shoulder blades, the circumference of her elbows, the space between her nose and her navel.

If Duck didn't move fast enough for her, the tailor simply grabbed her like a rag doll and pushed her arms and legs into position. "She certainly has grown," she assessed. "Her bones are practically longer than her skin. She won't stop, you know. You buy her new clothes now, she's just going to shoot out of them by fall."

"Then we'll come back in the fall." Griselde watched the proceedings from a cushioned chair. "I want her to be comfortable now."

The tailor wrenched Duck into a particularly twisted position and measured her neck, but Duck was too distracted to be bothered. Would she still be at the bakehouse in the fall? Most apprenticeships lasted five to seven years—was that Gnat's plan? To keep Duck there indefinitely, shelling out pennies and bread?

Duck waited to feel panicked or disappointed, but instead she felt . . . peaceful.

Excited, even.

Fall would mean ginger cakes. Cloves and pumpkin and nutmeg.

Duck had still been so green last fall, she hadn't had a chance to make anything with those spices.

"You yourself have not been measured for new clothes in many years, Master Baker." Katrina Tailor snapped her measuring tape at Griselde in a vaguely threatening manner.

"No need," Griselde chortled. "Just roll a barrel on down here and measure that. Same dimensions."

"Will you take a new set, then, if I trim them?" the tailor pressed. "A lady should look her finest."

"And a baker should be well ventilated." Griselde lifted her arm, showcasing the split in her tunic. "I'll look at my wardrobe after Easter. In the meantime, fix her up today, and her alone."

As Duck walked back down the street with Griselde at her side, she dragged a long stick in the canal. The water was clearer than she'd ever seen it, shining a mirror at the blue spring sky.

Her new clothes would arrive at the bakery within the week, and Duck could hardly wait to put them on; she still remembered how it had felt to get dressed on that first day of her apprenticeship, the softness of the tunic, freshly laundered . . . And this week she'd get to put on clothes that had never been worn by anyone else before.

Truly a luxury.

What would Griselde do with her old ones? she wondered. Would she hang on to them for her next apprentice?

Or should Duck try to pass them on to someone else who could use them?

One of the Crowns, maybe?

Duck's stick hit the bricks of the canal bridge, and she looked up.

And then her stomach flopped.

The laundry was in view, and the sandy bank that fizzled into the worst stretch of the Sarluire, and then, looming above them like a castle tower, was the abandoned cathedral.

"Uh," Duck started, her breathing suddenly shallow and prickly, "we are very far from the square! We must be lost—"

"We are not lost, little Duck." Griselde's footsteps never faltered. "It's a good day for my eyes. Nice and clear. I can even make out your face today." She peered at Duck just then, and her cloudy eyes were almost as blue as the water.

This is it, Duck thought, clenching her fists. *She's found me out. She's brought me to the cathedral to meet my doom with the rest of the Crowns. Constable Deveraux will probably show up any second to herd us all to prison—*

"Duck? Are you coming?"

While Duck had been panicking, Griselde Baker had walked right past the old cathedral. She now stood in front of the abbey, waiting at its iron gates while a plump nun fiddled with the lock.

"We have another errand to run," the baker said. "A special errand." She flexed her hands with jubilance and nodded at the sister with a restrained smirk.

Duck managed not to look again at the unfinished cathedral until she was inside the abbey gates. Then, pretending to scratch her back, she arched her head around to glance at the structure once more. She thought she could make out a single face poking through a gap in the stones of the southern wall, but she couldn't tell who it was, or if it was a person at all. Perhaps it was only a trick of the light.

She couldn't see that far.

The Garden

Inside the abbey, the sister led Griselde and Duck through the cloisters. Duck stayed right behind the baker like a puppy, but Griselde seemed to have forgotten that her apprentice was even there; she was chattering away with the nun, who was called Sister Ernestine, as if they were very old friends.

"And how is business?" Sister Ernestine asked.

"Business is good!" Griselde stayed near the far side of the cloister hall as they strolled, nearest to the colonnades, so every few steps, her face was illuminated by sunlight and then went dark again. "Booming, in fact—oh, hello, Sister Daphne, Sister Ursula, lovely day, wouldn't you say?" She waved in greeting to two other sisters they passed. "People need their bread. People need to eat. We'll always have customers!" She chuckled—a very irreverent sound for this space, Duck thought. "And how is . . . God?"

"Ever benevolent," Sister Ernestine answered without skipping a beat. "Ever a mystery. Every once in a while, I come to terms with the knowledge that I will never truly be as good as He wants me to be."

"You, Sister Ernestine?" Griselde Baker spat out a noise that reminded Duck of a disgruntled sheep. "If you are not good, then I must be one good fall away from the devil's scaly-knuckled clutches—oh, hello, Sister Margret, Sister Emma."

Sister Ernestine laughed. "Sister Baker, you have such a way with words. The pictures you paint!" She slowed as they reached the end of the cloister, where the hallways opened up to the sunny gardens. "But in truth, I do sometimes fear that there is not enough good in this world to keep up with the rising scourge of evildoing. Why, only yesterday, the constable was here to pick up comfrey and lady's mantle for a man who was attacked outside his shop."

Griselde gawked. "Took him for his coin, I suppose? The bastards."

"Indeed," the nun said. "And stripped him of his coat, and took his shoes as well." She shook her head, crossing herself. "All they found of the perpetrator was a single red glove, lying in the gutter beneath the poor man."

Goose bumps erupted on Duck's skin.

The Red Swords.

It had to be.

Jacques and his boys had taken down the merchant and left their trademark red glove behind, claiming both the crime and the territory.

A warning to other gangs: *This is our city.*

"I'd like to track the crooks down and show them how I can knead." Griselde wrenched the air with both her hands, as if twisting the neck of a Red Sword. "Justice is godly, is it not?"

"God favors mercy," Sister Ernestine replied diplomatically. "But I myself saw the bruises on the merchant's face, and I believe the only proper, godly vindication would be for every thief in the city to be rounded up and introduced to the thumbscrews."

The invocation of such a miserable fate—and in Sister Ernestine's sprightly, birdlike voice, no less—was too much. Duck stumbled over her own foot, making an *oof* sound that echoed in the cloister.

Griselde Baker turned her head, her eyes widening when she saw Duck. "Forgive me! Sister Ernestine, meet my newest kitchen helper. Duck, this is Sister Ernestine, a very dear friend."

"Good day." The nun bowed her head, then stood back up and locked eyes with Duck, and Duck was taken aback—Sister Ernestine's face was as soft and round as pie, but her eyes glinted wise and dark and were so sharp as to be almost pointy as they perused her. "Sister Baker is very fond of you, I hear."

"With good reason." Griselde Baker patted Duck fondly on the head. "She's a right hard little worker, this one. Smart as a button, too."

Duck shyly tucked her chin down and stared at the dirt floor, hundreds of mounds and shuffles showing the pathways of footsteps that had come before her. There was something in Sister Ernestine's eyes that seemed . . . if not familiar, then recognizable, at least. Or perhaps it was just that inquisitive, almost intrusive gleam that compelled Duck to avoid her gaze.

"Well, any friend of Sister Baker is a friend of ours." Sister Ernestine spread her arms wide as they reached the open archway that led to the abbey garden.

Duck took in the heavenly mix of scents: fresh wild grass, daisies, dried dandelions pressed into spiced tea, lemons, milk thistle, the damp scent of the wattle fences, all of it.

"Pick your fill." Sister Ernestine handed Griselde Baker a basket. "There is plenty of mercy to be had for all of us."

"Oh, no." Griselde pressed the basket right into Duck's hands. "This is for you. You've got the nose for herbs, and the taste for them, too. From now on, this is your charge."

Across the garden, another sister was heaping dirt-crusted carrots into the arms of some equally dirty peasant children. A man was exchanging a sack of what looked like rags for a bundle of cabbages.

A communal garden, Duck guessed, and Sister Ernestine confirmed it.

"You come and take what you need," she said, "and you bring something in return. Or you take with the understanding that you will pay in some other way as soon as you are able."

"You would not believe how many morning buns these sisters can eat," Griselde Baker added with a wink. "So you take all the herbs you want."

Duck held the basket close to her body.

She was nervous for a moment—she was not trained for this, she wanted to protest! She only knew rosemary, and only because she seemed to have some instinct for it and had therefore grown fond of it—but then she glanced at the plants around her.

Rosemary. She could sense it . . . and also thyme, when she searched with her nose, and the peppery scent of chives.

"Come." Sister Ernestine kindly took Duck's arm. "Let me show you around."

Nose first, Duck let the sister walk her up and down the rows, cataloging the plants as they were pointed out to her:

Sage-green shrubs with spikes of purple flowers: lavender.

Button-like yellow flowers growing in clusters: tansy.

The big, woody, showy flowers on long thorned stems were wild roses, in all shades and varieties of pink.

And these strange white bulbs half buried in the dirt, green stalks sprouting up like grass?

Duck knelt and examined them like a curious bird. Fennel.

"Excellent digestive aid," Sister Ernestine narrated. "Also excellent cooked in oil with garlic."

Duck plucked a few bulbs. She was pretty sure the baker used fennel in her horse bread.

In a raised bed, Duck found more sprouts of green, but she couldn't figure out which one was which. The one with the long, flat pale-green leaves—was this sage or basil?

What about the curly green stalks? Parsley or chamomile?

Sister Ernestine had wandered over to the stew pond, where Griselde had broken apart one of her seed loaves and passed it to the rest of the sisters.

How would Griselde do it? Duck asked herself. The baker could not rely on her sight to identify the plants, after all.

Kneeling down in the dirt, Duck bent over so the leaves were right under her nose.

She took a deep whiff.

Deeply aromatic, almost sweet, almost savory . . . that was basil.

Grassy, but not unpleasant. Pungent . . . parsley.

She plucked a bunch of each, along with sage and thyme.

She moved into the medicinals—milk thistle, chamomile—and then the root vegetables and the savories, the onions and the garlic.

When the abbey bells signaled that it was time for afternoon prayers, Griselde put a hand on Duck's shoulder.

"All right," the baker said. "It's almost bedtime for us."

The sun had not yet started its descent behind the horizon, but Griselde's words summoned a fatigue, which settled over Duck. She'd been up since four, worked her shift in the kitchen, then had gone to the tailor. So even though she was reluctant to leave the garden, she straightened and brushed the soil from her whites. A bee circled her head once, then flew off to the honeysuckle.

"Goodbye, sisters!" Griselde Baker called out. "Don't worry about the bread—there's plenty more where that came from!"

When the iron gates shut behind them, Duck surveyed the cathedral. No difference except that the late-afternoon light, sheer and pink, angled sideways on the stones, making them gleam.

It almost made them look new, Duck thought. It almost made you forget the building was slowly collapsing on itself.

Even with all that light, she still did not see any Crowns—no faces staring at her, nothing but the gargoyles, lined up along the ledges of the roof, watching over their city.

"From now on," Griselde Baker said, tucking her basket under her arm and starting along the canal, "you're in charge of fetching the herbs. Every Thursday, once you're finished with Master Frobertus, you'll come here. Sister Ernestine will let you in, and you'll fill the basket. I'll send you with bread to distribute. Does that sound all right?"

"Yes." Duck didn't have to think twice before answering; she had loved the garden instantly and fiercely, and there were still so many plants to smell. But more than that, she'd just been ordered to keep close proximity to the Crowns. Every week, she'd have a chance to visit the cathedral—perhaps to sneak them some extra trenchers or simply to drop by on her way home from the garden. Anticipation thrummed within her; she skipped to catch up with the baker, just to relieve a bit of that zest and energy.

"Sister Ernestine keeps a beautiful garden," Griselde said. "The abbey is lucky that she took up the veil."

"She knows a lot about herbs." It felt aspirational to say this—Duck hoped someday someone would be able to say that about her.

"Ernestine has always been excellent with aromatics," Griselde told Duck. "Before she took her vows, she was my best customer, always coming up with new flavor ideas, new combinations for us to try."

"Before? She wasn't always a—?" Duck stopped herself, realizing how silly she sounded. Of course nuns were not born in their habits. But it was odd to imagine Sister Ernestine as anything other than a Glorious Sister of Mercy, just as it was odd to think about Griselde Baker as a child, dressed in anything but her baker's whites.

Griselde patted Duck's shoulder. "Isn't it strange to think of who we all were before we became who we are? Sister Ernestine had quite the path that led her here—as we all do, I'm sure." She walked along for a moment before leaning over to add, "However winding your path has been, I'm glad it crossed with mine."

Onward to the bakery they went. Duck pulled out a special sprig from the basket—rosemary—and sniffed at it all the way home.

Handshakes

"Juicy tomatoes, a few heads of lettuce, and enough carrots to give your skin a nice orange glow." Sister Ernestine rattled off a list of everything within the basket she was pressing into Duck's hands, in addition to the one Duck had brought from the baker's and already filled with herbs.

"We have too much food this week and not enough people to share it," the sister went on. "God favored us with this harvest; the last thing we want is to let it rot on the vines."

"But . . ." Duck glanced down at the two baskets in her hands. She knew for a fact that the baker's storeroom was already bulging with fruits and vegetables. (Griselde had bartered a cartload of produce off a farmer for his weekly bread.) Most of this would go bad before they had a chance to eat it.

Sister Ernestine instantly interpreted her hesitancy. "Ah, you and Sister Baker are also blessed with more than you can use? Well, perhaps you know of someone else who can use it." She tilted her face up to the bright sky. "What a bountiful spring He has given us."

Duck studied the way the sun bounced off the bright-red tomatoes. "I do know a family," she said slowly, her heart prancing merrily. "Very hungry. Very . . . smelly. They would certainly appreciate the food."

"Duck, you are truly the Lord's servant." Sister Ernestine crossed herself and kissed her thumb, and Duck awkwardly followed suit.

She departed from the abbey, but this time, instead of heading straight back to the bakery, she made a detour to the cathedral.

She'd come to the abbey every week this month, picking the usual herbs, sampling new ones, listening to the sisters as they explained how the elderberry bushes had been grafted from a mother plant that lived on the grounds of the count's castle or when they pointed out the variety of birds that landed in the trees.

"We need a birdbath," Sister Margret said decidedly. "That rapscallion of a cat who chased all the birds must have found a new place to menace. We haven't seen him in weeks."

Ash the cat, Duck thought with a rueful chuckle.

But she didn't see the cat or the human as she went up the cathedral steps.

It was quiet. The rush of the Sarluire echoed through the empty chambers of the cathedral; the few pigeons she could see in the eaves were nestled together, sleeping.

But there was evidence of the Crowns everywhere:

A few wooden cups scattered here and there. Scraps of cloth— bits of the banners from the hot fair, saved in pockets and used as handkerchiefs. Discarded orange peels sprinkled on the altar.

A single shoe wrapping—an extra? Or was there a Crown running around with only one foot garnished in leather?

Duck squatted over the firepit, stretching out a hand over the embers. Still warm. So they'd been there recently. Scampered off just before Duck arrived.

Outside, the clock tower was about to chime for afternoon prayers. Duck would be expected home soon. The baker wanted to try a new cake recipe for supper—beets this time, which Duck thought would go very well with soaked dates and cinnamon.

She peered around at the mess again. Not everything here was run-down or worn out, proof that the Crowns had been using their new stream of income to buy straight from merchants.

No swiping. Not anymore. As decreed by the Red Swords.

On one hand, she was thrilled to see that the Crowns were living so large. Someone had bought themselves a comb and matching brocade sheath—proof that the Crowns' scant hygiene had been due to a lack of money all along? Someone else had bought a brand-new set of pegs and crosses, the knights scattered along a pew.

Yes, it was excellent to see the Crowns finally having the things they'd always desired, the things they deserved . . .

But surely none of these things compared to Duck. Surely every Crown would volunteer to sell these things immediately and go back to foraging for tubers if it meant Duck would be back with them . . . right?

Duck set down the basket of produce on the altar. They couldn't miss it there. But as soon as they realized she'd brought them a bonus supply of colorful eats, they'd miss *her* . . . right?

She would write them a note, she decided. She found a sharp

piece of brick and turned to the wall where Ash had scratched the crown all those months ago.

Duck would jot a quick note to let them know that she'd missed them, and then—

But wait.

She thought of that night at the bakery when Gnat and Ash had sneaked through her window and found her practiced letters in the flour on top of her armoire.

She thought of how Gnat had made fun of her.

Duck's letters were far steadier now, and Master Frobertus himself said the angle of her script was a notary's highest aspiration.

But Gnat had acted like Duck reading and writing was akin to a poodle learning to walk on its hind legs.

Gnat was the only Crown who could read, anyway.

Leaving a written note on the wall might remind the Crowns of just how different their lives were from Duck's right now. It would certainly remind her.

She dropped the rock and picked up her basket of herbs, then turned to go—

But spotted something familiar in the corner of the nave.

A pair of tongs, long and black iron.

Duck recognized them immediately; these were the same tongs that Griselde Baker used to reach into the backs of the ovens and rearrange the coals.

Or at least she *had* used them, until whenever Gnat had crept into the bakery and stolen them off the wall.

A peculiar impatience consumed her. She'd told Gnat already not to swipe things from the bakery.

If Griselde found out that Duck and the Crowns were scamming her out of bread and coin and the occasional pawned tool, she'd call for the constables.

And then the Crowns would all go to jail.

Duck hid the tongs up her sleeve. They were heavy, and she couldn't exactly bend her elbow when she swung her arm. But if she hurried, she could replace them on the wall before Griselde or Petrus noticed they were missing.

Duck raced down the steps of the cathedral and scurried past the tannery and the laundry, the sun beating down on the back of her neck. She did not keep to the shadows; in her baker's whites, she could move out in the open without fear. In her baker's whites, she looked like she belonged to someone—

A movement caught Duck's eye.

Down a dead-end alley, a flash of red.

An outstretched hand.

A red glove.

Duck's throat clenched.

She backed up and flattened herself against the wall of the tannery.

Red Swords.

And so close to the cathedral—had the Crowns finally been surrounded? Her heart squeezed with terror, thinking of her beloved Ash, Frog Eyes, and the rest. Where were they? Someplace safe?

Or had the Swords already found them?

Duck allowed herself to peer around the corner of the wall, watching for signals that the Crowns were caught.

There was Jacques, the Jackal of Avilogne—Duck could never forget the sight of the scar on his cheek or that lightning-white hair.

But he did not look quite so vicious now. He was smiling, even.

And then his red glove reached out to shake hands with someone—

Duck leaned farther, her one unobscured eye squinting, then widening in shock.

She couldn't see the person's face—but she didn't need to.

The other person did not extend his right hand, which he held close to his side, but his left.

It was Gnat.

Duck blinked, trying to make sense of what she was witnessing.

Gnat, meeting with the Swords?

But why?

Had the Swords cornered Gnat, and he was still trying to talk his way out of it?

Duck prepared to fly to his aid—

But then Gnat chuckled, and the truth hit Duck with unmissable force. The handshake. The scheming smiles. The casual postures of all involved.

Gnat wasn't in trouble.

He was in *cahoots*.

Gnat spoke then, loud enough for Duck to hear: "How do I find you when it's done?"

"You don't find us," Jacques answered curtly. "We'll find you."

Duck managed to slip from the alley just in time, crouching behind a row of barnacle-covered barrels as the Red Swords emerged and vanished into the streets of Odierne.

273

Gnat headed straight for the cathedral. He jogged up the steps, seeming pleased with himself, and Duck counted to one thousand before she let herself back on the street.

Her thoughts raced.

What on earth was Gnat doing?

No Crown shook hands with a red glove unless he was readying a knife with the other—but Gnat only had one working hand to get him through this world, and he'd offered it to the Jackal himself.

Duck had that feeling again, the same one she'd had on the rooftop of the cathedral hours before the hot fair, a penny in her hand: Gnat was up to something.

Something bigger than Duck knew—and her gut told her the Crowns didn't know, either.

And last time, Gnat's scheme had brought the Crowns right into the Red Swords' hands . . . and it had landed Duck in the bakery, doling out their livelihood one market day at a time.

For some reason, Duck didn't think they'd be so lucky this time.

"Duck?" Griselde Baker waved a hand in front of Duck's face, startling her out of her daze. "Is the stew too hot?"

"Oh." Duck obediently dipped a spoon into her bowl and took a bite of her now-tepid dinner. "It's fine, thanks."

Griselde clicked her tongue, then pushed her own bowl away. "Something's eating at you. And you certainly don't have to talk about it—there's nothing in the apprentice vows that requires you to spill your guts to your master—but I am a good listener."

It was a quiet enough meal. Raina had brought over a share of their eggs, since they were currently making Hugo break out in a rash, and Griselde had boiled them and split them and nestled them into their chicken stew.

Now the yolk looked up at Duck, a knowing yellow eye, and she thought of all she had seen that she could tell.

The cathedral, empty of Crowns.

The Red Swords, tucked in a nearby alley.

Gnat with the Red Swords, shaking hands over a secret.

She had borne this knowledge since this afternoon, and she still did not know what to do with it.

Should she run back to the cathedral as soon as she could find an excuse to leave? Should she tell the Crowns what she'd seen?

Should she confront Gnat first? Give him a chance to explain? Was there even a chance that this could be a misunderstanding? A good thing for the Crowns? A blessing?

Or should she do nothing?

Since Gnat had placed her here, did that mean she was no longer allowed to tangle herself in the day-to-day goings-on of the Crowns?

Did that mean that she was no longer—?

"If you knew a secret about someone, would you tell it?" Duck asked.

The baker frowned. "Now, you and I both know that there must be a big piece missing from that question. Of course you don't share someone's secret, not unless you have good reason to."

"But what would be a good reason?" Duck pressed.

"If someone's in danger," Griselde answered at once. "If someone's going to be hurt."

Duck stirred her spoon around in her stew but did not take

another bite. The Crowns might be in danger. The Crowns might be hurt.

But Duck had a secret of her own, and she knew that if Griselde Baker ever found out the truth about her apprentice, she'd be hurt. Sometimes holding on to a secret was the only way to keep someone safe.

So it wasn't as simple as measuring flour.

"I don't know what to do," she said in a small voice.

Griselde gave her a kind, consoling pat on the shoulder. "I don't know what you should do, either," she said, "but I do know that almost everything is improved by a good night's sleep."

That night, Duck looked at herself in the mirror above her washbasin. Dark circles hollowed out her eye sockets, and her skin was all ruddy from the heat of the ovens.

She was taller. Maybe mirrors didn't show such things, but Duck could tell. Her face was fuller, too. And her eyes . . . deep in her eyes, a new glow, a wisdom, even.

She shook her head, her hands against her cheeks, pressing them like dough.

A Crown shaking hands with a Red Sword—Duck never thought she'd see such a sight.

But she never thought she'd see herself looking like this.

She looked tired, but also . . . happy.

Or if not happy, fulfilled.

Like a plow horse that had been worked to its limit.

Some things never change, Griselde Baker had said that night at the tournament all those months ago.

Until one day, they do.

Easter

"A question for you," Griselde Baker said one day when Duck was filling a basin with water to soak some dirty tins. "Do you have any special plans for Easter?"

Duck tried not to think about the Crowns' single Easter tradition of stealing a cured ham from the first nobleman that crossed their path—this would be the first year she'd miss it.

"No," she told the baker. "Just another Sunday for me."

"Sister Ernestine is hosting a planting party in the abbey gardens," Griselde said. "She's asking everyone who can spare a hand or two to come till and seed the ground for fall harvest. Since Petrus will be at Mass and you and I will be waiting at home for the sin wagon to collect us, I thought we might go."

"Sounds wonderful," Duck replied, and she meant it.

Playing in the dirt and tugging up weeds seemed like the perfect way to spend a holiday.

But Sister Ernestine's quiet, intimate planting party turned into something more akin to a spring festival—when Duck and

Griselde arrived at the abbey gates, they were shocked to see dozens and dozens of folks digging and dancing and feasting.

The garden had never looked more beautiful, Duck thought. Pastel streamers and silky ribbons hung from the cloisters, and the newly blooming apple trees made the air sweet enough to taste.

A ring of dancers wove through the grass beyond the vegetable patches; Master Frobertus, who seemed too frail to be holding hands and grape-vining with the rest of them, nevertheless nodded at Griselde Baker and Duck, grin stretching from wrinkled ear to wrinkled ear.

"Hello, you two!" he called, spinning a young lass around his hunched old frame. "Enjoying the sunshine?"

"Taking to it like beavers to mud!" Griselde answered. "On your left!"

A dancer twirled into the notary; he dizzied himself trying to keep up with her and nearly tumbled into the dirt.

"Huzzah!" he cheered, then spun back into the fray.

Griselde chuckled. "Spring does her best to make young chicks out of all of us, I suppose."

The Glorious Sisters were bending wildflowers into halos for women and children to wear, and many men were lacing dandelions into their beards. There was planting happening, but also tippling of drinks, strumming of lutes, and swatting of balls against wickets in the grass—and that's exactly where they found Sister Ernestine, pumping her mallet in the air triumphantly as her ball hit a wicket, then quickly resuming a more reverent stance.

"My dear sister," Griselde boomed, "what a marvelous party

you've thrown! I had no idea there were so many amateur gardeners in Odierne."

Sister Ernestine bowed her head. "Some like to plant, some like to dance, some like to eat, and some like to do all three. Please, enjoy yourselves. Later, we'll blow and paint eggs, and I believe several people are clamoring to raise a Maypole."

"In God's house?" Master Griselde pressed her hand to her chest, pretending to be appalled.

"If it means our collection basket is full and our garden is planted, God will allow it," Sister Ernestine retorted. "Besides, this is more His yard than His house."

The sister then joyfully shooed the two of them away and returned to her ball game, and Griselde and Duck wandered through the grass.

"Well? What shall we do first?" the baker asked.

Duck was about to tell Griselde that she was anxious to try her hand at planting—but then she saw it.

Over in a clump of choristers singing out springtime hymns, there was a hand.

Reaching for a woman's belt, swiping a purse by the strings.

Duck recognized that grimy hand.

Frog Eyes.

Crowns.

They were here.

"Oh! Father Hicks is selling ale!" Griselde Baker pointed to a table near the walls of the abbey. "Let's go sample a pint, shall we? Looks like it's for a good cause."

Duck was alert as a rabbit downfield of a fox, but she let the baker lead her to the drinks.

All proceeds of the ale went directly to feeding the hungry, but it also provided enough social lubrication that even Constable Deveraux was sporting some ribbons on his uniform.

Griselde said hello, and the constable greeted Duck by name.

"My goodness, you've grown!" he said between sips of his overflowing cup. "Soon you'll be looking our Griselde right in the eye!"

"And what a sight to behold!" Griselde clinked her cup with his, then drank.

Duck thought of the first day she'd gone to the bakehouse to swipe loaves from Griselde. She'd seen the baker pass a bundle of sweet buns to the constable, no money exchanged, and at the time, Duck would have sworn she'd witnessed a bribe.

But after months of working as Griselde's apprentice, Duck now knew that Constable Deveraux's wife got terribly sick during her monthly bleedings and that the only thing that cheered her up was her favorite treat. Griselde Baker's sweet orange buns were not a bribe for special treatment from the constable, but rather another opportunity for the baker to brighten up Odierne with her goods.

Not an extortion.

Simply Griselde being Griselde.

Duck was about to ask how Lady Deveraux was faring, but as soon as she opened her mouth, she spotted him.

Across the garden.

Behind the knobby trunk of the apricot tree, staring right at her.

Gnat.

Ash stood beside him, munching on a turkey leg he'd likely grabbed from an unsupervised plate. He lit up when he saw Duck.

But the smirk on Gnat's face sent a chill down Duck's spine, even on this warm spring day.

She still hadn't told any of the Crowns about what she'd seen that day. She still hadn't told Gnat.

Fear jolted through her. Would the Red Swords crash the planting party, too? She darted her eyes around the crowd, scanning for a flash of red gloves or lightning-white hair, but she did not see any jackals.

When she glanced back at the tree, Gnat and Ash were gone.

Master Griselde and Duck had come to the planting party bearing refreshments: a stock of lavender cakes, which were a new concoction developed by Duck herself, with the baker's approval. Small enough to hold in your palm, round and squat, filled with equal parts vanilla, lavender, honey, and Duck's now-signature rosemary, Griselde said they were the very essence of the season.

They lay them out on a table now. As people bit into the fragrant cakes, swooning and licking their lips between murmurs of contentment, Duck busied herself by brushing the crumbs off the table, trying to keep from beaming.

It was strangely satisfying, to hear from the people who were eating her food. The tailor who had fitted Duck for her new clothes ate her lavender cake in one chomp, then nodded and looked Duck up and down, as if admiring her own handiwork.

"These are delicious," she told Griselde. "Now you can retire and let her take over, yes?"

Griselde laughed. "Let's wait until she's big enough to see over the counters, shall we? At the rate she's growing, that'll be very soon."

Light filled Duck's chest as the baker showered her with compliments, but then she looked across the table—

Drippy and Spinner, both of them shoveling lavender cakes into their mouths, one after another. When they noticed Duck, they gave her sugar-sprinkled grins, then dashed back into the hordes of people, Spinner grabbing one last cake before she ran.

Duck stared after them, a knot of worry tying itself in her middle.

They shouldn't be here, among so many people, where they could so easily be caught.

But she wasn't sure what bothered her more: the idea that they were recklessly running and swiping and giggling, or the dark longing to be one of them.

Duck peered across the garden at the stew pond—and locked eyes with Gnat. He stood, his right arm loose, his left arm trailing down his baggy tunic sleeve and into his pocket.

She held his gaze till someone walked in front of her, and then Gnat was gone.

Duck knew he wasn't really gone, though. He'd wait a few minutes, then pop back up in the crowd again, watching her like a ghost come to taunt her, and a kernel of tenacity hardened within her. It was time to talk to Gnat—time to see if she could persuade him to spill his schemes. She couldn't avoid thinking about Gnat's hand and a red glove, clasped in some sort of transactional arrangement, for much longer.

"I need to—go," Duck stammered to her employer. "Go . . . uh . . ."

"Go to siege?" The baker winked, then pointed to the abbey. "Privy's just off the gate, there. And after you're finished, I'd like you to wander around and have fun. That's not a suggestion. That is a direct order coming from your master." Griselde cheerfully smacked a coronet into Duck's palm. "I see Master Bell is selling her trinkets and toys, just underneath the willow tree there. Oh, and Sister Margret embroidered some lovely capes—come fall, those might be nice to don."

"But—" Duck started, the coin burning her hand.

"Go on!" Griselde barked with a grin. "Go buy something utterly frivolous. In the name of spring."

Duck made not for the privies, but for the pond at the far end of the garden, though when she got there, she found she was no longer small enough to crouch behind the reeds. She'd grown, and she would have to wait for Gnat to approach her here, out in the open, where anyone could see her.

Marks

Wildwort.

Sister Ernestine had just taught Duck about it last week—it grew along the banks of ponds and other bodies of still water, vivid green leaves in perfect coin-shaped circles.

"If you pick it, dry it out, and crumble it into your tea," the sister had explained, "it'll do nothing except ruin what was probably a very nice cup of tea, but it'll help with inflammation in dog and cat paws."

Duck pushed the leaves down into the mossy water, watching them expand as they were submerged, almost as if they were breathing.

A shadow engulfed Duck and the wildwort; she knew it was Gnat even before he spoke.

"I can't remember if ducks sink or float," he said snidely. "Shall we find out?"

Duck whipped her head up, dropping the wildwort. Gnat and the rest of the Crowns stood all in a row, a formidable line that would have pinned Duck against the water with no escape—but Duck was one of them. She was one of them, and so she tried to think of it more as a seven-on-one conversation.

Standing so close to them, she realized that they'd all grown, too. Spinner and Fingers both looked like they'd been stretched on the rack, and Le Chou seemed more muscular than husky.

Even Ash had grown; if Duck squinted, she could almost see a bit of stubble growing on his face.

"What are you all doing here?" she asked. "I thought we weren't allowed to pick pockets—"

"How dare you." Gnat picked at his teeth with a twig. "This is a planting party. A community event. All of God's children are welcome here."

"You aren't . . ." Duck trailed off, her cheeks flushing red. She'd almost said it.

But Gnat smirked knowingly. "Oh, yes. I realize we're not part of the community in the same way you are. I've never seen such a social butterfly! Why, I believe you've greeted at least ten people by name: a bunch of nuns, a tailor, some sort of lawyer—and who was that person you spoke to near the ale? Was that a constable?"

The rest of the Crowns tittered.

Duck felt an old, instinctive fear arise at the mention of the law. But this was different. This was Constable Deveraux. Duck knew him. She knew his children. She knew he was curious about the ovens. She knew he hated when it rained.

"You're pretty chummy with him," Gnat went on. "Maybe he'll introduce you to the sheriff—"

"I'm not chummy with him." Duck's nostrils flared as her

breathing deepened. "He's just a customer! And I pick herbs from this garden with the sisters, and they're nice to me because they're nuns, so I'm nice back. And the notary is . . ."

She trailed off, noticing the way the Crowns were looking at her.

Their arms, folded. Their jaws, firm.

They were all staring at her as if they didn't know her.

"Nice duds," Spinner commented, and Duck swallowed, peering down at her clothes. They seemed almost blindingly white now. She hadn't noticed before.

Duck nearly sank into the mud. She was in her baker's whites, and her hair was now long enough that her braid stayed tucked behind her shoulders.

But she was still the same old Duck . . . wasn't she?

"Those cakes you made?" Gnat said. "They're pretty decent. You're turning into quite the baker."

Something twisted within Duck, and her mouth grew bitter. She thought of Gnat shaking hands with the Jackal. She thought of the way he'd walked back to the cathedral afterward, a bounce in his step, as though he'd gotten away with stealing the entire Avilogne palace without a single golden brick to indict him.

"We're not supposed to pick pockets," she repeated.

Gnat snorted. "Things change. Cry about it."

Yes, Duck knew things changed. She knew this better than any other Crown. Everything in her life had changed: where she slept, how she spent her afternoons, the calluses on her palms, the number of times she bathed per month, the company she kept. It was a miracle she was not amorphous at this point, a mere liquid to be poured into any shape, any container.

Any version of herself.

"Don't swipe anything else, all right?" Duck pushed her hair off her forehead. "You'll cause suspicion—"

"And then what, you'll turn us in? Get your precious baker to call for your buddy the constable?" Gnat raised his eyebrow, as if daring her to answer honestly.

"I would never turn you in." She gritted her teeth so hard, her ears ached. "I'm robbing the baker every week so *you* can eat! And I'm a Crown!"

"Maybe you've been seduced by bread." From this angle, Gnat's eyelashes were so blond, they were almost invisible. "One can hardly blame you. It's irresistible. But you're right. We should get out of here. We've seen enough." After a moment of considering her, he added, "I liked you better when you didn't talk."

Duck stared down at her shoes, now soaked in pond water.

The Crowns trailed off one by one, and she could feel them looking at her with curiosity, as if she were an entirely new specimen to them.

Only Ash lingered.

He kicked at the reeds lining the pond, and when she finally met his eyes, they were apologetic. "He brags about you, you know. All the time. About how clever it was for him to put you there in the first place. How great it is that you haven't scrubbed out yet. How much you're bringing in every month."

"So he's applauding his own cleverness." There was a time when

Duck would have given her own foot to have Gnat be proud of her. But the praise now seemed false, hollow, misdirected.

"The Crowns are thriving," Ash argued, "and it's thanks to you. And Gnat knows that."

"Ash?" Duck said in a small voice. "We—we can't do this forever."

"What do you mean?"

"You think we can keep doing this without getting caught? They'll hang us for real—in a few years, you and Gnat'll be old enough to get the rope." Duck's heart pattered; she didn't like to imagine Ash in irons.

"What are you talking about?" Ash jostled her by the shoulders. "I think that bakery's clogging up your brains with butter. We'll always be Crowns, or we'll die with dignity—to our graves be swift, remember?"

Duck remembered.

And she remembered that Crowns were supposed to stick together, to always share their spoils, and to never, ever keep secrets.

"Ash," Duck breathed. "It's Gnat. I think he's—"

"Ash!" Gnat hissed from beyond a flowering azalea, a cup of ale in his left hand. "Are you coming? Or should we get you a veil and habit and call you Sister Sweetbottom?"

"I've gotta go." Ash cupped Duck's arm, right in the spot that always got sore after putting away the ten-pound flour bags. "Keep your nose clean, all right? Just keep doing what you're doing." His words made Duck feel like the Sarluire on a stormy day, all waves and ruckus and roar.

For how long, Ash? Duck wanted to shout. *How long am I supposed to live in two worlds? Split in half like a cleaved loaf, one foot in two camps that are miles and miles apart?*

Only after Ash left did Duck let herself whisper what she almost said to him: *I think Gnat is planning something. Something big. I think Gnat has a scheme, and I'm worried it's a bad one. Gnat's always plotting, and I know he's our leader, but I don't think he always has the Crowns' best interests at heart.*

I think Gnat is keeping secrets from us.

I know Gnat is keeping secrets from me.

Ash said Gnat thought she was doing a good job. A part of her clung to that, clung to this puny praise the way a pigeon clings to air.

And another part of her knew it was just that, just air—just more praise to convince her to stay quiet, stay little, stay in her place and never be anything more than a tool.

And it was only after Ash left that Duck reached into her tunic, feeling for the coronet Griselde had given her, and found only pocket.

Her coin was gone.

Her pocket picked.

Someone had swiped from *her*.

She went red first, and then as pale as the whites she wore.

To the Crowns, she was only a tool and a mark now.

And to Duck, Gnat was starting to look a lot like a sword.

*S*pring. My very first.

My first spring atop the roof.

The masons set me on my ledge. I am not fixed, not yet attached to the stonework, so I cannot drain the water from our rooftop when it rains. But I am high enough that I can watch.

Below me, the river sparkles, calm and blue and full. The last of the ice melted only this morning. Townsfolk march their fishing poles down to the canal bridges, ready to try their luck in the teeming waters.

The fields beyond the Sarluire stretch brilliant yellow all the way to the verdant green trees on the horizon; the lion's-tooth is in bloom. Soon the farmers will walk through with their sickles and cut down the stalks, then press the flowers into oil and sell the greens in Odierne's markets.

I breathe in the fleshy, pollinated scent of the lion's-tooth. It mixes with the gritty, sunburned smell of the freshly smeared mortar on our stones. This is the smell of springtime.

The fields, yellow. The trees, green. The sky, heaven's blue. These are the colors of springtime.

All around our cathedral, the laborers bustle and bend to build walls, make arches, finish floors. The people of Odierne clutch their hats as they tilt back their heads to look at us, look at our height, the way we reach up into the clouds.

Just you wait, I want to tell them. *Just you wait until our last stone is placed. Just you wait until our doors open.*

I hold perfectly still when I feel eyes on me, and puff my chest out with pride and widen my grimace. See how ferocious this gargoyle is? See how sharp my fangs, how strong my horns? No demon, no spirit, no ruffian or army could stand a chance against such a monster.

Everyone comes out of Odierne's city gates to celebrate the end of the icy days with a festival. They raise a Maypole and dance around it in the grass, braiding its streamers, and I wait for them to glance up at us, glance up at their half-finished cathedral.

It is spring here on the roof, too.

And I am not the only one here, I recall. Other gargoyles have been placed on the opposite ledge; they stare out over the city of Odierne. Five of them, five grotesques made by the master sculptor.

"Welcome," I told them when they arrived this morning. "Welcome to the cathedral."

"The cathedral what?" said one of them, who fixed me with a sharp glare. "The what cathedral? The cathedral of what?"

"We don't have a name," I told her. "Not yet. Not until we are finished."

She said nothing else—not to me—but I've heard whispering on the east side of the roof all day.

They are made of a different stone from me. Shaped by different hands. But we were all made from the same mountain. We are all here for the same purpose.

We are all here to keep watch.

Springtime, and the breeze brings me the smells from the abbey garden next door: basil, lavender, thyme. The sisters are diligent as they water and weed and prune, a promise of great harvests to come. Their gardens will feed the hungry, and our cathedral will shelter the afflicted. I want it to always feel like springtime inside our doors.

From the east, I hear whispers. My stone itches as I realize the other gargoyles are looking at me as they talk among themselves.

I am not alone on the roof, but I am by myself.

Another spring. My tenth.

Another spring. My twentieth.

Another spring. I pretend I have lost track, but I know it is my thirty-fourth, and that means we are thirty-four years closer to being finished.

Another year of hearing the east-side gargoyles yap all day about everything under the sun, another year of seeing the villagers drag out the Maypole and douse themselves in ale. Another commemoration, and they have forgotten all about us.

Harpy laughs, and it is so shrill, it is a knife in my ear.

"Hush!" I growl. "I'm trying to hear the music."

"Hush yourself, ugly," she retorts. "Your voice is worse than a badger with a cold."

Ugly. My master made me ugly for a reason: to scare away anything that might harm our parishioners. Ugly is a shield. Ugly protects.

But I do not want to glance down at myself in the puddles of rain on my ledge that serve as mirrors.

Ugly is no insult. But I do not want to look.

Another spring. My fiftieth.

Half a century they have been building our cathedral now, and the seasons of labor match up with the seasons themselves.

There are weeks in the summer when the laborers are here for every moment of sunlight. They come singing to their stations at dawn and leave only when the shadows are too long for them to see the gaps between the stones.

There are weeks in the fall when the chill is enough to make joints stiffen and fingertips ache, when the sunlight is dulled by gray clouds and the carpenters move slowly in the biting wind.

In the winter, when the world is frozen and still, there is no one here at all except pigeons.

Springtime means new blocks from the stonecutters, timber deliveries to be measured and trimmed, domes and pillars to be commissioned. It is a burst of production, a hundred measured steps forward—

But this year, my fiftieth spring, it just sounds like noise.

I prefer the quiet.

Those east-side gargoyles never shut up, no matter the season. They don't talk to me unless it's to insult me or because I insulted them. That busybody Harpy sticks her beak in the business of every person who crosses her field of vision; she loves gossip the way the birds love grubs.

Me, I prefer to conserve my words. I must be ready to protect.

As soon as they wipe the last of the dust from our stones and hinge open the doors, I must be ready to—

Not just another spring, after all.

I do not know what flowers are growing in the fields. I do not know what villagers are dancing in the grass. The sky may be blue, bluer than it has been in all my fifty years, but I do not notice it. Not today.

The gargoyles on the other side of the roof are as silent as I am, all our stone ears straining to hear what the cardinals are saying below.

"What did they say?" Goathead says. "What's going on?"

"Quiet!" I bark. But then I hear, and hope flickers within me and dies like a late star.

"I can't understand them," Harpy whines. "What is it?"

"The money," I say, teeth in my throat. "The money is gone."

I do not hear every detail, but I hear enough.

"The relic," I tell the other gargoyles. "They are talking about the relic."

"What's a relic?" wonders Goathead, and I scoff at his ignorance. I suppose relics have never come up in all their gossiping.

"A relic," I say, "is something sacred. Something from the Bible, or a prop that once belonged to a prophet. Or the body part of a saint. Something that takes a holy story and makes it real." And ours was a relic that brought in plenty of coin for our cathedral's funds: the Cross of Saint Odile.

It was said to be the crucifix of the rosary she prayed with for two weeks straight, night and day, until she collapsed in the Sarluire in the distant hills. It was said that the water carried her to

Odierne, and the rosary kept her buoyed, kept her from drowning. It was said that the crucifix contained a sliver from the Holy Cross itself.

It was said to be a miracle.

And so it was said, as the cardinals took the Cross of Saint Odile on a tour of Avilogne—a penny to see it, a penny to pray over it, and every one of those pennies went into the fund for our walls, our roof, our bell-less belfries.

But I hear the cardinals now, and the truth sinks me lower than the Sarluire.

The relic was a sham. False. It had never been blessed. It had never been authenticated. It was not canonized—it was just a random sliver of wood.

And now the funding is gone. The construction halted.

We spend the rest of our spring watching the labor slowly cease. The cardinals stop visiting to see how the walls are coming along. The bishop doesn't show up to look at the foundation. The carpenters, the stonecutters, the masons, the glassmakers all arrive one last time, and then they never come again.

If every relic bought by a bishop were real, then John the Baptist would have grown and lost more than a dozen heads. The Holy Baby would have lost ten sets of milk teeth on every continent. The apostles would have dunked their feet into hundreds of washbasins with enough droplets of water to make an ocean, and a whole tree could be made from all the splinters of the true cross that had been recovered over the years.

All that work, all those years, all those springs—

And no one has come for us.

Every spring for fifty years now, I have remembered our last spring as a cathedral in progress.

Fifty years now without hope. Without purpose.

I think of the false relic, how it made liars of the cardinals. How it made a liar out of me.

"I am a gargoyle," I used to say with pride, "and it is my duty to keep watch. I will watch over everyone in the city. I will keep them safe."

A hundred springs, and I will sit up here for a hundred more. A hundred springs, and every time I close my eyes, I see her face— the face of my maker. How she would crumble if she knew I had failed.

I see the faces of the mother and the baby, sinking below the surface of the Sarluire, her hair like a red flame in the water.

I see my own stone claws, clutching my ledge. The night I was a mountain, unmoving. Useless as a rock.

And I will sit here for another hundred years, until, like a mountain, I crumble.

Every spring the same. Every day the same.

And so this morning, when Harpy breathes in and croons, "Ah, smell that lilac this morning! What a glorious spring!" I feel my stone flare hot.

I am mineral and flame. I burst out laughing, even though it costs me a breath that I don't think I can spare. "Is it, now? Is it glorious? More glorious than that spring day our cardinals walked away? More glorious than the first spring with no new stone? No new ribbing? More glorious than—"

I pause. Something is stuck in my throat.

I cough and hack it up: a pebble. A pebble, dislodged from my own stone.

I spit it out; it bounces down the wall of the cathedral and lands on the ground with a *plink*. A part of me, loose.

It's happening. I am turning to gravel as we speak. It should fill me with dread. I am coming apart—becoming dust. But instead, all I can do is chuckle.

"What?" Harpy screeches. "What's so funny?"

My laugh makes my whole self shake, and another chunk of me falls down into the water—a piece of my claw, where the bird's nest is musty and old.

After all these years, it's finally happening.

"We are finally falling apart," I say. We are finally crumbling— and all I can do is watch. Watch and wait, the gargoyle's curse.

Some things never change—until one day, they do.

"Don't be ridiculous!" Harpy bursts out. "They won't tear us down; they've only had a hiccup in funding! They'll be back to finish us. You've got loose gravel for brains!" Her voice is shrill, but it trumpets with the sharpness of panic. She doesn't believe a word she is saying.

Perhaps if this were another spring, our first spring on the roof together, I could comfort her—

But I was not made to comfort.

I wonder what would happen if a gargoyle tried to cry. I wonder if rainwater would leak out of our stony eyes.

Harpy sounds close enough to it; I can feel her clinging to her tattered hope, holding on to it the way the river grips its banks.

But it is over. A hundred years since our first stone blocks were set in the dirt, and a hundred years of waiting. We will never be completed.

A pigeon chooses this terrible moment to flap toward me, looking for a safe place to land, and I growl. I growl so loud, it rattles off the tops of the buildings all around us. I growl so loud, the laundress next door drops her basket and the fruit on the trees in the abbey garden quivers.

The east-side gargoyles go quiet, and the sky darkens, almost as if the spring sun itself is cowering.

The bird flies away in a frenzy, her heart pitter-pattering away inside her chest.

And down below our cathedral, one of the Glorious Sisters of Mercy is in the garden, and she glances up at our roof. The first time someone has looked at us in so many years, but it's too late.

"You are too late!" I thunder. "You want to stare at the ugly monster? Look all you want while you still have a chance—we'll be dust soon enough!"

Above, the sky is heavenly blue. Below, the Sarluire streams cold.

The east-side gargoyles do not whisper. After a hundred years, they have run out of things to say.

And now it is finally quiet. Quiet enough that I can hear the clouds move. Quiet enough that I can hear the hiss of candles' wicks in the windows of Odierne as day becomes night. Quiet enough that I can hear water dripping off a distant roof, mocking me. I am not a waterspout.

And now I know that I will never be.

A gargoyle is not made to house nests, to court birds, to sing, or to pray. A gargoyle is for spitting water and protecting its cathedral and nothing else.

I am no waterspout, and I have no cathedral to protect.

I have a pile of stones, some unfinished walls, a nave full of grimy child thieves, and a rooftop with the worst view in Odierne. I have a broken claw and an empty toe. I have a headache that squeezes my stone like a vise and a hunger that cannot be thwarted. I have dislodged enough pebbles today to know that the end is coming soon.

There is something eating away at my insides, something dull and many-legged, something that aches.

And I cannot stop seeing the mother and the baby, leaping off my roof and into the water.

She came to the cathedral for sanctuary, but I could not protect them.

I should have protected them. I should have growled at the constable, snarled and grimaced. I should have dived into the water after them.

But I am not a proper gargoyle—and I never will be.

Our dusty stone blocks will be split up, our timber sent to other construction sites to raise up new walls. Some of the stones will go along the edges of the canal when it inevitably floods. Some will go to build additions to parish churches, to make fireplaces in orphanages, to line village greens. The humblest of building materials, though they were once set aside to be a part of something truly great. A miracle.

Some of the stones will go back to the quarry where they came from. Pulled from a mountain, shaped and polished, sent down the river to be slathered in mortar and stand for a hundred years, and then back they will go, back out into the wild.

After all these years, and our cathedral will be sectioned off. Split apart.

I do not know what will happen to us gargoyles. Perhaps if I had not been worn down for one hundred years, I might hope to be taken somewhere I could still see the stars. But I don't have it in me to hope.

Gargoyles do not hope. Gargoyles protect.

No more whispers on the roof. No more east-side gossiping, no more wind howling through our stones.

It is almost too quiet—

But when the Glorious Sisters of Mercy ring out their voices proudly in chorus, the sound of it makes me quiver with rage.

"Stop!" I cry out. "Stop, stop singing!"

Every note they hit is joyful, faithful, and I can only think of the baby's coos, its whimpers. I am crumbling, crumbling, when I think of those sounds again.

I try to sing out over the Sisters' hateful hymn with my own dirty words, but my chest spasms. Just as well. What can I do? I am only a gargoyle.

A gargoyle, alone in a world that has forgotten me.

Alone. Always by myself.

Soon I will be dust.

I wish I had saved them. Of all the things I wish for, I wish I could go back to that night and move.

I wish I could hurl my stone body off the roof, down into the river.

I wonder what happens if a gargoyle cries. I wonder if tears can leak from stone even when there is no rain.

I gasp out a sob, and I have my answer.

SUMMER

Suspicion, Again

A few weeks after Easter, Griselde Baker was called to a guild meeting in Perpinnet. She'd be gone for several days . . . which meant the bakery would be left in the care of her journeyman and her apprentice.

"Now, technically, Petrus is in charge," Griselde said as she set her bag into a waiting cart, "but you're the only one who knows where the extra sugar is."

"Down in the cupboard beneath the tins," Duck recited, but she couldn't keep the glumness out of her voice. She had a sinking sense of dread whenever she thought about being alone with Petrus.

He still looked at her sideways, and she was still a thief.

"I'll be back Saturday if I have to pull the wagon myself." Griselde patted the rump of the gray mare that would be towing her to Perpinnet as if to say, *No pressure*, and climbed into the cart, her cane in hand. "Now, I made Petrus promise not to push you around, but perhaps you should voluntarily stay out of his way." To her journeyman, she called, "Remember, we're legally contracted to keep our apprentice alive."

"Indeed." From the doorway, Petrus scowled at Duck as if he'd just been asked to care for a cockroach.

When the handler cracked his whip and the horse jolted forward, the journeyman spun on his heel and went back inside. Duck lingered, watching the baker travel down the streets of Odierne until she was nothing more than a dot, indistinguishable from any other person strolling the city.

It felt colder all of a sudden. Duck glanced up, expecting to see the gray clouds of an impending storm rolling through the sky, but it was sunny.

She rubbed the chill from her arms and headed back into the bakery.

Petrus was examining the daily task list, frowning, and Duck tucked herself at the table, sifting the flour for this week's sweet cakes.

"What on earth does she mean?" Petrus scratched his head, looking utterly confounded. "Can you tell what this says?" He held out the list, and Duck leaned closer.

"Trenchers for Farmer Chewins," she read.

"Huh. She must have written this in a rush."

Duck hunched over a little as she made her confession: "Um, I wrote that."

"You?" Petrus narrowed his eyes as he inspected the list again. "You wrote this bird scratch?"

Duck sank back in her chair.

She'd been working hard at her letters. Master Frobertus said she was getting better with the pen, but Petrus was right: the writing was shaky and messy and—

"I mean, it's decent enough for someone of your age and status. You're a mere child, after all," Petrus said after a moment. It was the closest he'd ever come to complimenting her.

"I am learning," she replied quietly.

"You are." Petrus straightened, clearing his throat. "I'll handle the wheat loaves and the miller if you'll do the trenchers."

Duck nodded, and the two of them set to work.

Petrus was usually a quiet worker, much more so than Griselde, but he seemed to forget that Duck was in the kitchen, and he started to hum.

He hummed "The Song of Roland" and "Foy Porter," then started in on some *pastourelle* about a knight and a common woman, turned into a rabbit by a witch's spell—it was familiar to Duck, but she hadn't heard it in years.

"By your joy, I am gladdened," he warbled as he kneaded the dough, *"if only . . . if only . . ."* He paused and searched the vents above, as if the rest of the lyrics were written there.

"If only toward me you were more human," Duck finished in a tiny voice.

Petrus spun around, a grin on his face. "That's it!" he cried, and sang the line again in his own airy tenor. He pushed the tins in to bake, then reached into a drawer for the chisel to chip out a bit of charred dough that had hardened near the mouth of the oven—

And then he stopped.

"Duck?" He peered around him, looking at all the counters.

"The chisel is gone." He opened the drawer again. "And I know it was here yesterday, because I used it. And I put it right back in this drawer." He turned and looked at Duck, hardness in his eyes.

Her heart dropped into her stomach—but before she could mumble out an alibi, Petrus sighed and straightened.

"Let's look together," he said. "You check the kitchen. I'll go search the storeroom. Maybe Griselde . . ." He trailed off, giving Duck an almost rueful glance as he vanished down the hall. They both knew it wasn't likely that he'd find it in there.

Duck opened every drawer, searched every cupboard. She got on her hands and knees and scanned the floorboards, checking every corner, every crevice—and all the while, her pulse hammered faster and faster.

The chisel was gone. Duck definitely hadn't taken it.

And Griselde wasn't here to help her fend off Petrus, who would undoubtedly call the constable.

"It's not in the storeroom. Or on the porch." Petrus laced his tone with an added optimism, but his brows were already knitted together as he strolled back into the kitchen. "Did you find it?"

Duck swallowed. "No."

It was quiet. "No?" Petrus repeated, troubled.

"I'm sorry," Duck murmured. "I—I don't know where it went."

"Oh, I think I have an idea." Petrus folded his arms, his jaw clenched. "And I have some ideas about how much it's worth. Shall I check your mattress for spare coins again?"

"N-no," Duck stammered. "I mean, yes. You can check my mattress. But I didn't take the chisel." Let him turn her whole bedroom upside down—he wouldn't find so much as a loose penny.

She'd given all her pennies to Le Chou last market day.

Petrus leaned against the counter, away from her—but it still felt like he was looming over her. As though he already knew what she was and was just waiting for her to say it. "Then where is it?"

Perhaps last summer, Duck would have stayed silent. Last year, Duck would have just stared at her feet and let Petrus accuse her.

But she and Petrus had just started getting along.

Even without Griselde here to play peacemaker or command Petrus to be nice to Duck as if it were one of his official tasks as journeyman.

Working with Petrus today had even been . . . fun.

Last year, Duck would have only cared about not getting caught.

But things change.

"All right," she said, her legs trembling. "I don't know where the chisel is." She took in a long, deep breath. "But . . . I think I can get it back."

It was the most terrifying thing she'd ever said out loud. She set a hand on the table to steady herself.

Petrus said nothing for the longest time. He stared at her, and Duck stared at the floor, and inside the ovens, the flames licked and crackled.

"All right," he finally said. "Go get the chisel. Bring it back." No promises that she would be absolved if she could retrieve it. No promises to let this whole incident go, to forget it had ever happened—

But right before Duck left, Petrus ran his fingers through his hair and sighed. "Duck, I . . . I know I've been hard on you. For good reason—our last apprentice . . . he took advantage of Griselde, and it—it devastated her. I won't let anyone else hurt her like that. Never again."

Duck bit her lip.

"But Griselde adores you," Petrus went on. "She loves you like you're her own—" He broke off and clenched his fists, a burst of frustration. "Just . . . you'd better make this right. For her. Or else . . . don't even bother to come back."

As if Duck needed to hear that.

She scampered out of the bakery with single-minded purpose.

It was too late to clear her name. And she supposed Petrus would never again trust her—not as an apprentice, and not as a human beloved by his master, of whom he was so protective.

But after what had happened in the garden at Easter, when Gnat had picked her pocket as if she were a common mark, Duck was fuming.

Gnat had wanted her to be a funnel for bread and coin so the Crowns could stay in Odierne and survive.

But this was turning into something else entirely.

Duck marched, blazing hot, into the cathedral. She'd stomped all the way from the bakery, every step—but it hadn't done much to alleviate her anger.

Here Duck was, trying her hardest not to get caught, even though the baker knew she had a seedy past and Petrus now had confirmation that his suspicions were justified—and Gnat was still sneaking into the bakery to swipe these pathetic little tools and sell them for pennies?

Was he trying to get her caught?

She came up the stairs and into the nave, pausing to wipe the sweat from her forehead. She was burning up. Fired up.

Ready to do something no other Crown had ever done: demand that Gnat give her answers.

But no Crown had ever poured yeast into flour or shoveled dough into ovens before, either.

"Duck!" Le Chou leaped up from where he was playing pegs and crosses with Spinner and Frog Eyes; his clumsiness knocked over their board, sending the knights rolling across the stones.

The other two Crowns stared at Duck like she was an apparition. "What are you doing here?" Spinner asked.

Duck ignored the accusatory tone in Spinner's voice. "I live here," she retorted. "Where's Gnat?"

By now, the other Crowns had heard the commotion and come running.

When Ash saw Duck, his face went pale. "What is it? What happened?" He jumped over a bench, fell, scraped and bloodied his knee, but was still at Duck's side in a matter of moments.

"Gnat," she said. "Where is he?"

Without waiting for Ash's response, she charged through the cathedral like a bloodhound, watching for a slanted shadow, the swing of a rope in a hand. She started up the masons' stairs, but Ash called her name.

"He isn't here," Ash said. "He went out to run an errand. He left right after noon bells."

Duck paused halfway up the steps. She glanced down at the rest of the Crowns—all those faces staring up at her, all variations of confusion.

Spinner seemed insulted that Duck had disrupted their good time.

Le Chou and Drippy looked genuinely shocked that Duck, whom they'd always known to be quiet and small, had this kind of a spine.

Fingers looked worried, and the way Frog Eyes held his mouth in a line meant he was leery, trying to decide if Duck could be fought off with mere words or if he'd need to throw some punches.

And Ash, his heart beaming out of him like sunshine, was looking at her as though she were made of glass, about to shatter, and he only wanted to catch her.

Duck wanted to grab them all by the shoulders and shake them, shouting, *What about this is so hard to understand? You think I've never been able to speak before? You think it's okay that Gnat parked me at the bakery for forever, hoping I'd never come out, never come back, never say a thing?*

"Right," she said instead, a lethargy sinking into her limbs. "Well, I have to talk to him now. Right now. So . . . see you around."

She dragged herself down the stairs and left the cathedral, vaguely aware that Ash was hopping along behind her, calling, "Wait, Duck! Wait!"

Duck did not want to wait.

Duck had waited every week, making bread in that sweltering kitchen, for the Crowns to show up on market day and give her thin-lipped smiles—or sometimes ignore her outright, except to take the bread and coins from her hands.

She was a Crown, damn it all. She was part of this family.

She was tired of feeling like she'd been the one who had left.

She'd gone to the bakery *because* of the Crowns, *for* the Crowns. She wanted answers.

And Gnat had them.

Away from the cathedral Duck scampered, away from the market district, away from the shops.

Away from the Sarluire, which rushed past the cathedral and curved along the city walls and streamed behind the bakery.

Away from even Ash, whose footsteps echoed behind her.

Just south of the market square, past the abbey and the abandoned cathedral, was a scattering of run-down businesses and churches so tiny, they seated only a single pew full of parishioners. Farther south, and you hit the bridges and the docks, the places where fishing boats found their moorings and the porches of the smokehouse were kissed by the Sarluire's ripples during the spring floods.

Northern Odierne was for the farmers and artisans, the people who sold grain and saddles and could craft you a yoke, and the hedge witches who sold seed, and beyond that, the Count de Chatoyant's manor and private chapel, with its steeple that glittered above all the other churches in Odierne.

Right where the houses started to change from thatched-roof rustic one-stories to the elaborate, wood-carved, painted and tiled rooftops of the rich, Duck found the pawnshop.

And leaning against the counter, his right arm tucked safely against him, was Gnat.

He saw Duck and Ash coming and didn't have time to hide the surprise in his eyes before Duck spotted it, but quick as a wink, he twisted his mouth into a smirk and crowed, "Well, well, well."

"Give it back." Duck extended a hand. "Right now." The pawnbroker glanced at Duck, then at Gnat, and then tucked himself behind his curtain, leaving them to sort out their quarrel.

"I don't know what you're talking—"

"Don't, Gnat. Don't deny it." Duck thrust her hand forward until her fingertips almost touched his chest; Gnat sneered at her but made no movement. "I know you took the chisel. Now give it back."

Gnat paused and looked at Ash, who came a-puffing up between them. "You're about a minute too late," he told Duck, and opened his hand, showing a pair of pennies in his palm.

It was gone. He'd pawned the chisel, and soon it would be resold at a markup.

"If you ask me, he overpaid," Gnat pretended to whisper, nodding in the direction of the pawnbroker's curtain.

"Buy it back," Duck demanded through gritted teeth. "Right now."

"No." Gnat rubbed his thumb against one of the coins until it shone. "Tell your baker you dropped it down the well. She'll buy you ten chisels if you ask her to."

Duck waited to feel upbraided, scolded back into line by a leader who had always fended for the Crowns as a whole, one many-limbed, many-headed organism that needed bread and coin and little else.

She waited to feel that old obedience settle over her like a yoke.

But vexation surged within her. The Crowns were getting enough from the bakehouse—free loaves and buns, coins to pocket—and it was Duck who was working for it. Duck who was delivering, week after week.

It was Duck's neck on the line.

She smacked the pennies out of Gnat's hand, letting them scatter on the cobblestones. Ash hurried to pick them up, but Gnat rolled his eyes.

"Aw, don't get your tunic twisted," he said. "That's why we put you there, isn't it? You're there to play the part of the dutiful apprentice so we can take what we need to survive—oh, wait a minute. I get it." Gnat cackled as if he'd just seen someone fall head-first into a barrel of eels. "You've gone soft for old Griselde Baker."

Duck could feel her pulse in her temples. She tried to think of something to say, the perfect retort, anything that would convince Gnat that this was not true—

But the longer Duck stood in silence, the louder Gnat hooted.

"You're in love with her! I knew it!" He slapped his leg. "That's why you came charging down here to bark at me about the chisel. This is too much! And you know what's the funniest part?" Gnat leaned closer; he could no longer loom over her. She'd grown tall enough to meet his eyes. "There's no way that baker would love you back if she knew what you really are."

Duck folded her arms. Her throat felt tight and scratchy, and her stomach ached.

This was her big chance.

Her moment to say it.

"Gnat," she started, her head searing, "I know. I know . . . what you did."

She was dizzy all of a sudden. She wished she could sit down, but she didn't want Gnat to think he'd won. She hated the idea that this was a competition at all.

"What?" Gnat said, and it was almost a snarl. "What did I do?"

Duck glanced helplessly at Ash—Ash, who could always tell what Duck meant to say without her speaking a word.

Ash, who could always read her moods and be her words. But he shook his head now, frowning. "I don't . . . What is it?"

Duck felt like she'd been dropped down a drain and forgotten.

"That baker only likes you as a pet," Gnat went on. "Once she learns you're still just a thief from the streets, she'll kick you out. Once she finds out how much you've taken from her, she'll be happy to see you go."

"I'm not from the streets. I'm from the river." Duck couldn't explain why she needed to say this, let alone why she needed to say it through gritted teeth. But Gnat didn't know how Griselde looked at Duck, even with her imperfect eyes. The baker knew that Duck was imperfect, and it didn't matter to her. It didn't matter to Griselde where Duck had been before she'd shown up on her porch.

All that mattered to Griselde was that Duck was part of the bakehouse now, part of the team.

Part of the family.

But Duck wanted Gnat to remember that she was different. She was not like the rest of them; she had a story. She had a beginning before she was a Crown.

He'd always treated her like she was the odd Crown out, but right now she couldn't be prouder to wear that like a badge.

"No, you're not from *the* river. You're from *this* river," Gnat fired back, his eyes burning.

"What are you saying?" Duck asked, glancing at Ash, who was utterly confused.

Gnat turned to Ash now, too. "Doesn't this city seem familiar to you?" Gnat waved his hand at the streets around them, and Ash suddenly choked.

"This is it, Duck! This is the place where we found you! This very river!"

Duck held her breath.

A baby in a river, the rain pouring down.

"You mean . . . you found me here? In Odierne?" Duck directed her question to Gnat, but Ash answered in an excited rush.

"Right over by the cathedral, where the water dips down into the sand!" Ash cried. "Holy bones, I don't believe it! I forgot about the cathedral—in my mind, the walls were much bigger, but maybe they've crumbled since then—"

"You knew." Duck glared at Gnat, her jaw set. "You knew all along that this was where you found me, and you didn't tell me—"

"Because it doesn't matter." Gnat stood as tall as he could; if this had been last year, he'd be towering over her. But things had changed. Heights had changed. "It doesn't matter where you're from, remember? Are you a Crown, or aren't you?"

Yes, she was a Crown, Duck wanted to shout. And as a Crown, she had the right to know what Gnat was up to.

It was time. Time to tell Gnat what she'd seen.

"Gnat," Duck tried again. "I know—I know what you did." Her words, again, slippery as fish within her brain, her throat raw.

The Red Swords. You saw him with the Swords. Say it, she commanded herself.

But Gnat was already walking away. "So you caught me," he called back, raising his left hand in surrender. "You win. I won't take any more trinkets from your beloved baker, all right? Count on it—but Garbage, I won't have you getting in my way. Change is coming, so get ready."

Not the chisel, Duck wanted to call. *I know what you did with the Swords*. Her head spun, so she didn't see where Gnat went next, but she could hear the jingle of the pennies as he carried them off, back into Odierne along with the rest of his secrets.

"Duck? Are you all right?" Ash's grin was cluelessly bright. "Shall we go throw stones in the river? Or go for a swim in the river—*your* river?"

Ash wanted to play, to celebrate, no doubt buoyed by the new additions to the story of Duck's origins.

But Duck shook her head, her eyelids heavy.

She was not at all in the mood to think about the past. She wanted to know about the future, the future only, but she had no answers.

She stumbled out of the pawnbroker's, feeling her skin crawl with flushes and chills, leaving Ash behind without a word. He called after her, but his voice soon grew blurry and faint in her ears.

Duck kept her head down the entire way back to the bakery.

Inside, she went right to the kitchen, prepared to face her fate.

Petrus spun around at the counter, a scowl on his face. "And where have you been? You left this place such a mess—oh." He stopped, peering at her with concern. "You don't . . . you don't look like yourself."

Duck felt like she was going to combust and freeze to death, both at the same time. Her teeth chattered, but her forehead dripped with sweat. "I'm sorry," she whispered as she climbed up the stairs on all fours. "I couldn't get the chisel back. I'm so tired, I'm so sorry. I just . . . need to sleep."

She trembled and lay her head on the top stair. This was close enough to her bed; she could rest her eyes here, away from the light of the oven.

Petrus hovered above her, placing a hand on her head as if he thought maybe she was faking—but he pulled it back with a hiss. "Duck, you're on fire."

"The ovens," she murmured, "make it . . . warm in here."

This very river.

This very cathedral, this very city.

Gnat knew.

He knew all along that this was the place where they'd found her. She'd slipped through the city gates right behind him and the rest of the Crowns, and he'd known this was not an arrival for her, but a return—and he hadn't told her.

Once you were a Crown, it wasn't supposed to matter . . . but how could it not?

The Sarluire had brought baby Duck to the very spot where a ragtag group of street kids were passing by, scrounging for food— was it God who had orchestrated this? Or fate?

Duck didn't know, and she was still grateful as she had always been that Ash had plucked her from the water. But what if the river had carried her a little farther downstream, nearer to the market square?

What if the baker had been the one to hear the squawks and cries of a baby in the water? What if Griselde had been the one to wade out, pick up Duck, dry her off?

What would Duck be like now if the Sarluire had delivered her to the bakery instead of into the grimy hands of the Crowns?

Duck was suddenly aware that she was being carried; she opened one eye and saw the bottom of Petrus's chin, his Adam's apple bobbing with worry as he brought her to the bedroom downstairs.

"I'm fetching a doctor," he said. "Hold on, Duck. We'll get you right again. Hold on."

What if Duck had never been Duck?

Who else could she have been?

Sickbed

Duck opened her eyes.

The ceiling above her was low, the window beside her open to a pleasant early-summer morning.

Not her own room. Not her own bed.

She rubbed her eyes and pushed herself up against the pillow. Her ears rushed, but her head was no longer dizzy.

She was in Griselde Baker's bedroom. The bed was propped up on blocks, which made Duck feel like she was a long way from the floor, and the quilts were heavy and cozy. In the corner of the room, tilted back in her rocking chair, the baker herself dozed, a bearlike snore emerging from her nose and throat.

Duck tried to get out of bed quietly, but the second her foot hit the floor, the boards squeaked.

Griselde Baker's eyes snapped open. "Duck!" she bumbled. "You're awake! That's wonderful!" She crossed the room and felt Duck's forehead. "And your fever's gone. Thank the Lord— you were burning up so hot, we could have flipped you over and cooked the baguettes on your back!" There was nervous relief in the baker's laugh.

Duck glanced down at herself, noticing she was no longer in her whites but wearing one of the baker's massive tunics; it hung on her like an unbelted robe.

"The doctor insisted we change your clothes every day," Griselde explained, "and the bedding as well. And the laundress couldn't keep up, so . . ." She gestured to a small pile of old bedding and worn tunics, and an alarm sounded inside Duck.

"How long was I—?" She had the swollen, cotton-stuffed feeling of having slept for longer than was necessary, but when she tried to account for the time, she couldn't.

"It's Monday," Griselde replied cheerfully. "You've been sleeping on and off for nearly a week. The doctor suspects you got grocer's fever, an awful strain. He hasn't seen such a bad case in years, you poor dear."

Monday.

Griselde had left for Perpinnet last Wednesday, the same day Duck had chased Gnat down and confronted him at the pawnshop.

Her gut twisted. She'd been sick in bed for five whole days?

"Petrus said you went out for a delivery, then came back and practically collapsed on the floor," the baker went on. "He sent for me immediately—luckily, we'd paused just outside of Chatoyant to water the horses."

A delivery.

So Petrus hadn't told Griselde about the chisel.

He'd . . . protected her.

And Duck had lost their chisel to the pawnshop—no, to Gnat.

Gnat . . . Again, Duck's stomach hollowed itself out. Five days, sick in bed? Then she'd missed a Saturday.

Market day.

She hadn't been there to pass the Crowns their bread and coin.

And after the row she'd had with Gnat, she knew he probably thought she'd blown them off. On purpose.

"I . . . I have to go." Duck took a step and wobbled on weak legs.

Griselde tut-tutted. "The doctor says you should take it easy for a few more days. Grocer's fever has a long recovery time. We'll handle the baking and the cleaning and the selling. Your job is just to rest."

Duck's mind raced. She had to get to the Crowns. Right away. She had to explain that she hadn't snubbed them—

"Now, you had quite a lot of people very worried." Griselde's voice was as radiant as the hearth. "You have fans, Duck, and they all sent their tokens of love and wishes for swift healing." She gestured to a table in the corner, and Duck's heart skipped.

There was a whole hoard of baskets and flowers and fruit. Griselde explained that Master Frobertus, the Glorious Sisters of Mercy, the tailor, Constable Deveraux, and a few of their regular back-door farmers had all come to check on Duck or sent baskets of goodies when they'd heard she was unwell.

Duck's smile grew watery as she looked at the bounty—and then melted into a frown.

"Did anyone else . . . inquire about me?" she asked, her voice much, much smaller than it had been in months.

The baker cocked her head. "Too many to count. You've got a good number of people who care about you," she said with gruff affection.

But something in Duck's core hardened.

Five whole days she'd been sick.

She'd missed a market day, and yet none of the Crowns had come to see if she was all right.

Surely they'd been worried about her when the shop had unfurled its shutters and Duck was nowhere to be seen. Even if they thought she'd stiffed them, surely they would've sent someone to check on their youngest member. If they really cared.

Duck shivered at the cold reality that none of the Crowns had come for her.

The baker frowned. "Was that a chill? All right, get back into bed this instant. Cover up your feet. The doctor said it'll be another couple of days before you're completely out of the woods."

Griselde scooped up Duck as easily as if she were a sack of flour and plopped her back into bed.

"Master Frobertus sent these." Griselde handed Duck a few fat leather-bound tomes. "Light reading, he called them. Watch out for that green one—I flipped through the pages and spotted a few more butts than you'd expect in a holy book."

Duck stifled a laugh, and when she glanced up at the baker, Griselde wore a strained smile.

"I'm very glad you are on the mend. Very, very glad."

Duck did not look away immediately, but locked eyes with her employer. The baker who had taken such scrupulous care of her. Griselde looked away first, bustling into the kitchen to fetch her patient some tea, and Duck leaned back, too tired to attempt standing up again.

But her mind was alive and racing.

Did the Crowns really think she would cut them off like that, without warning? Without so much as a goodbye?

She wanted to cry with ire and to cry with heartbreak—the Crowns were her family. How could they think she would just let them go?

As soon as she was well enough to walk, she'd march down to the cathedral and confront them—but in the meantime, these books were a heavy comfort on her legs, reminders that there were people who cared about her in a way that weighed as much as rocks.

Saturday.

Market day.

Duck was well enough to stand at the counter and handle the strongbox, and as the bakery opened, she smoothed her apron with fretful fingers. What would she do when she saw the Crowns?

She'd considered writing a note of explanation, slipping it into their hands with the bread, but only Gnat would be able to read it, and she wasn't sure she could trust him to pass on the message.

She had to find some way to tell them that she had been sick. She had to find some way to make sure they knew she hadn't abandoned them on purpose—

But the Crowns didn't show up.

Duck stood at the counter all day, craning her neck, staring out into the square until every loaf was gone and Griselde and Petrus had swept the kitchen clean.

No Crowns.

"I think we should celebrate," Griselde said as she wiped the counter. "You've finally recovered! Maybe we'll make a pie."

Duck was only half listening.

While she'd been staring out at the square, feeling sorry for herself, she'd caught sight of someone moving along beneath the awnings of the shops.

Jacques, red glove on his hand.

"Boysenberry, maybe?" Griselde's voice only vaguely registered in Duck's mind; she was tracking the rest of the Swords, following behind Jacques, and then she couldn't catch her breath.

It was like seeing a pack of wolves marching through a city in broad daylight—the Red Swords, who normally stuck to the shadows, strolling along the streets as if they were harmless puppies.

Getting bolder.

What an ominous sight, to witness that red glove during daytime hours . . . and the Crowns were out there somewhere, vulnerable.

Suddenly, it was very clear what Duck needed to do.

Either Gnat knew what the Red Swords were up to now . . . or he'd be able to find out. For the sake of the rest of the Crowns, Duck knew it was time.

Time to confront Gnat. Time to confess what she knew.

"We have all those blueberries from Josse and Ellie"—Griselde was still talking—"and I've got more than enough butter to whip up a crust—"

"I need to go," Duck cut her off. "I need to leave. There's something I have to do."

Griselde blinked, her gaze on the sky behind Duck.

"I would tell you what it's about if I could," Duck added, "but I can't. All I can say is that it's very important."

Behind them, Petrus loomed from the kitchen, wiping a bowl with a towel.

Duck felt something crumple in her chest. If she left now to help the Crowns, did it mean she was choosing to leave Griselde and Petrus behind?

What if the Crowns needed more help than she could give in a single afternoon? Would she ever walk through the doors of the bakehouse again? Her future was murky all of a sudden, but she swallowed down such dramatics. The Crowns needed her. So she would go. It was as simple as that.

"I promise I'll be back by dark," Duck added to reassure herself. "Please."

Petrus stepped forward until he was within view of Griselde. He peered at Duck and seemed to be calculating something. Duck held his eyes until he looked to the baker, who nodded.

"We trust you, Duck," Griselde replied. "If we can be of any assistance —"

"You can't," Duck blurted out. "I have to do this by myself."

"Well, if you change your mind, send up a flare, and we'll come running. Oh, and take this." Griselde wrapped up some rolls in a tea towel. "Just in case. It's always a good idea to have a bit of bread on hand."

Duck left at once.

Not only was she finally going to confront Gnat about his secret meeting with Jacques, but she was also going to warn the Crowns about Jacques and his crew, skulking around the neighborhood.

Gnat may be chummy with the Red Swords, but Duck couldn't allow the rest of them to be vulnerable.

With the Jackal of Avilogne out prowling the streets of Odierne, the Crowns were as good as sitting ducks—and Duck wasn't about to abandon them.

Even if they'd abandoned her.

Confrontations

Inside the cathedral, Duck announced herself without hesitation. "It's me," she called, "your long-lost Duck! I come bearing bread, and no, I didn't bring any constables or watchmen with me!"

"That sounds like something a snitch would say." Gnat was leaning against a pillar in the unfinished nave, tying knots in his rope.

He did not look rattled to see her. His face was neutral, his mouth smirking—but his eyes were the color of secrets.

The other Crowns, if they were there, were nowhere to be seen. Good.

Duck wanted to talk to Gnat alone.

"I don't believe you had an appointment with us today." Gnat slid the rope around itself and tugged.

Duck was getting better at steeling herself against his barbs; the work at the bakery had given her all sorts of new calluses. "I didn't think I needed an appointment to come home."

Gnat snorted, then took a seat in the nearest pew and started cleaning his toenails with a twig. "Then make yourself at home."

As Duck gingerly leaned against the incomplete altar, Gnat scanned her up and down. "You look like a math lesson."

A comment on her new set of clean, starched baker's whites. Duck dodged the insult as best she could. "I needed new clothes; I've grown three inches since last year."

"Yes, well, now that you have your wonderful benefactor to keep you in fresh duds, why not?" Gnat's jab hit her in the chest.

"You mean *our* benefactor," she pushed back. "And you don't look like you're using any of the coins I've passed you—holes in your tunic, hair as greasy as tar, no shoes . . . unless the money's been going somewhere else?"

There.

She'd opened the door to the conversation she'd been wanting to have for weeks now.

Gnat raised his eyebrows slightly as he dug with his twig, but Duck charged on.

"I saw you with them," she said, her heart going rat-a-tat. "I saw you with the Swords. You shook hands with Jacques. I don't know what you're up to, but—"

"That's right." Gnat peered right into her eyes, and a jolt ran down her spine. "You *don't* know what I'm up to. You're always at least two steps behind, Garbage, so I suggest you stop trying to chase me. You'll never catch up."

Duck was so weary of this back-and-forth, this cat-and-mouse game she'd never agreed to play. "Please, Gnat. Please, tell me what's happening. I'm still a Crown, aren't I? I deserve to know."

"You are a Crown," Gnat said after a moment. But he used the same tone someone might use to say that technically, an apple was a flower, since it had started out its life as a blossom. A tenuous argument at best. "And as a Crown, I'll expect complete and utter fealty from you when it happens."

Duck's insides dropped like a blob of underproofed dough. "When what happens?"

But just then, the jolly, grubby hubbub of the rest of the Crowns echoed through the ribbed vaults, and Duck's dread flattened itself, at least for a moment.

They came cackling up the steps, Le Chou doing some goofy dance, Drippy explaining something excitedly to Frog Eyes, Spinner and Fingers passing a golden-skinned fruit between them, and Ash . . . Ash strolled into the nave, hands in his pockets, whistling without a care in the world.

Duck wished she could be that light, that untroubled. She whispered fiercely to Gnat, "When *what* happens?" but did not brace herself for the truth. She knew he wouldn't give her a simple answer.

"Hey, Crowns! Look who came for a visit!" Gnat opened his arm wide, gesturing to Duck, who stood there, frozen, as the Crowns noticed her and grew silent. She felt like she'd shown up to a party that she wasn't supposed to know about.

"What's going on?" Ash instantly rushed to Duck's side. "Duck?"

"We thought you'd left!" Frog Eyes burst out. "We came to the bakery last week, but the only one behind the counter was that mean journeyman —"

"You forgot to get us our bread!" Drippy cut in with an aggrieved sniffle.

"Where were you?" Ash asked so only she could hear.

"She's here now," Gnat interrupted, hopping up onto the altar, "and she's arrived just in time. Crowns, take your seats—we're going to have a little meeting as soon as our special guests arrive."

Duck's stomach barely had time to turn before she spotted the shadows on the ground.

Silhouettes. People.

"Your guests are here," said Jacques from where he stood on the masons' stairs, and then it was pandemonium.

"It's the Swords!" Frog Eyes cried. "Scatter!"

Crowns ran everywhere, taking cover in the nave. Some of them hid beneath the old tattered tapestries, some climbed into urns, some simply bolted for the porch, escaping out the doors that weren't there.

Duck, for her part, stayed right where she was.

Ash tugged on her arm, urging her to join him beneath a pew. "Come on! We'll wait until they're distracted, and then we'll crawl out of here."

But Duck, to her surprise, held steady. The Red Swords didn't strike the same fear into her bones as they used to—perhaps her work with blazing-hot ovens, swarms of demanding customers, and the constant panic that her employers would discover she was a liar and a thief had toughened her against such melodramatic villains.

Besides, today the Red Swords were here by invitation—Gnat's invitation. Surely even the Swords would exhibit some restraint in the event of such a privilege.

Gnat put his fingers in his mouth and screeched a shrill whistle. "Take a seat," he repeated, and, shaking, the Crowns obeyed, filing into a single pew.

"Do they fetch and roll over, too?" Jacques quipped. He led his men down the stairs, and Duck marveled at their numbers—more weight than she thought that roof could have possibly held, and yet they kept coming and coming and coming.

"Hey," Gnat said, "show some respect—"

"Relax." Jacques held out his hands—Duck knew every Crown's eyes went right to that red glove. "You're very well organized for a bunch of kids. If we didn't think that, we never would have answered your call in the first place."

Duck gawked at Gnat with round, searching eyes. Beside her, Ash was doing the same, but his mouth was closed, his jaw rigid with the pain of betrayal.

What have you done? Duck thought as she watched her leader, but Gnat had never been able to read her silences, not the way Ash could. And what's more, he'd never wanted to.

"Crowns," Gnat began, "we're about to enter a new phase of our career. Jacques here and I have been having some very interesting discussions of late. Apparently, the word's out about Odierne. Lots of other gangs are eyeing this place, wanting it for their own; luckily, the Red Swords have managed to scare all of them off."

The Crowns tittered. Ash furrowed his eyebrows. "Uh, are you forgetting that you tried to scare *us* off?"

"It's not too late," Le Chou muttered, staring at the closest Red Sword, who held a baton in his hand and twirled it in a not-so-subtle fashion.

Jacques puffed out his chest importantly. "Things change, don't they? We've decided that you can stay."

The rest of the Crowns cheered; Duck alone did not.

There was something missing.

Something big. A key ingredient.

"In exchange for what?" she called out, and the cathedral grew as quiet as a prayer.

Jacques the Jackal studied her thoughtfully, his lake-water eyes cold. From his place on the altar, Gnat narrowed his eyes at her, too, almost as if he were trying to decide if he'd defend her when the Jackal sprung for her throat or if he'd shrug and let her be torn apart.

"Ah. You must be the one who's been holed up in that bakery," Jacques finally said. "Gnat told me all about you." No one, not even a flea, could have missed the jeering in his words.

Duck lifted her chin, preparing to hear it—the truth about what Gnat really thought of her.

She hated that she still cared to know.

"He says you're the one we should be thanking, since you're the one who's making all of this possible." Jacques suddenly clapped his hands, the slap of his bare palm against the red leather of his glove ominous.

But Duck couldn't be swayed by this odd flattery. A knife of nerves buried itself beneath her ribs. "Making all of what possible? What are you going to do?" she asked—not of Jacques, but of Gnat, who leaped off the altar like a cat and tucked his rope back into his pocket.

"Listen up, Crowns. For the past year, we've been getting our grub and coin in small doses. But now it's time to go for the whole hog. We're going to bust in and take it all."

Jacques let Gnat do all the explaining. He and the Red Swords stood quietly, legs slightly apart, hands by their sides, all rehearsed and polished and completely out of place against the crumbling backdrop of this old cathedral. They definitely did not fit in with the raggle-taggle assortment of Crowns.

Gnat announced that he wanted to break into the bakery and empty the strongbox, and he wanted to do it tonight. Today was market day, after all, and Gnat knew exactly how much money would be in there. He knew because Duck had told him: the baker got more than a hundred coronets every market day, slightly more in the summertime because people were desperate to get out of their stuffy homes and walk through the square, and no one could resist the scents wafting out of Griselde's bakery.

"The best part? We can make a nice clean entry, thanks to our little plant here." Gnat held Duck's shoulders, showing her off; Duck thought his fingertips would leave bruises. "That means we can break in tonight, take all the cash, then come back next month and do it again, and no one will be the wiser—"

Duck pulled away. "We won't get away with it. Petrus—the journeyman—has pegged me as a thief since the day I arrived. He knows the chisel was stolen, and the boots. He thinks I did it, so if you do this, he'll point his finger at me, and then—"

"And then your precious Griselde will tell him he's wrong again, and she'll snuggle you tighter and buy you a puppy." Gnat's nostrils flared. "Come on, Duck. Think of all that money, just sitting there in her strongbox. Think of what you could buy for your

Crowns. We could live like kings. We could live as well as you've been living."

Duck's heart pounded through her whole body. She could feel him tugging her strings, manipulating her like a doll . . . but it was working. She did want the Crowns to have everything they wanted, everything they deserved. She did want to deliver that to them, just as she'd been doing for the last year of her life.

"What about them?" She nodded at Jacques and the Swords, and Gnat ran a hand through his hair with a chuckle.

He was nervous, Duck realized. If this went south, the Red Swords would eat him up, and Gnat was depending on her to make it all work.

"The Red Swords have kindly agreed to let us stay in Odierne and allow us to do what we need to do in order to eat," Gnat said, "in exchange for . . . a portion."

Duck didn't so much as blink. "How much?"

"Twenty-five percent," Gnat said, and Duck balked.

"Twenty-five percent? We're risking our necks, breaking into the bakery, and they're taking a quarter of the cash—"

"The twenty-five percent is for you." Jacques came the rest of the way down the masons' stairs, stopping in front of Duck, and she had to hold her breath to keep from shaking.

As Jacques bent over her, Duck could see the scar on his cheek—could see that it was not just one long slash, but many tiny cuts. She wondered exactly what he'd had to escape from . . . and she wondered what had happened to the other person.

Left for dead, likely.

"Gnat," Jacques said, although his eyes were still fixed on Duck. "Do we have a problem?"

A problem.

Duck was used to being called many things.

"A problem" would be just another one of her many charming nicknames.

Gnat locked his left arm through hers. "Give us just a moment, please."

He steered her away from the Swords, away from the Crowns, past the open wall where the stone blocks were stacked only as high as her nose, up the masons' stairs to the roof, where they could both see the Sarluire flowing, blue and crystalline.

"Are you going to throw me off?" It was the first time Duck had ever made a joke to Gnat. She felt like she had nothing else to lose now.

Gnat crossed to the ledge and leaned his back against the largest gargoyle, the one with the horns, then stared out at Odierne, at everything that stretched before them. "It's funny, isn't it? How much this place has come to feel like home?" He motioned for her to come closer, to take in the view.

Duck stayed where she was. All those rooftops and roads were familiar to her now; she didn't need to look too hard. There were the notary's offices, and beyond, the miller who brought Griselde her flour, and the tailor, and the cooper who fixed up Griselde's water barrels, and the bishop, who loved Griselde's cinnamon bread almost more than he loved God Himself.

Even the abbey's garden, right next to the cathedral—it had

once seemed strange to Duck, but now she could walk up and down the rows and know exactly where every plant was.

She could find rosemary even before it found her.

"They've come to know this city," Gnat went on. "They've come to love it. I don't want to rip them out of here and make them learn a whole new city. Not again. I don't want to do that for a long, long time."

Something inside Duck welled up. She thought about how good it had felt when they'd arrived at the cathedral. She thought about how much it had felt like home.

A home for the rest of the Crowns—but Duck had been relegated to the bakery. A lovely place, yes, and Griselde was joyful and kind and warm as bread . . . but it wasn't the same.

Not the same at all.

Not home without the Crowns.

"Duck." Gnat was staring at her, his eyes wide and fearful like she'd never seen them before. "Please. We have to do this. If we don't . . . everything's going to fall apart." He pressed his lips together, and he looked so young. Soft. Defenseless.

Like a child.

If she said yes, the Red Swords would bleed Griselde until she had nothing; they would hit her over and over until she was dry.

They'd use Duck as the funnel, and then she, too, would be squeezed and tossed aside.

But what else could Duck do?

What else could the *Crowns* do?

They were completely at the mercy of the Red Swords. If Duck refused to do her part for this job, Jacques would sweep them clean out of Odierne, and the Crowns would have to start over somewhere else. A new city, new marks, new scams—they'd have to make a whole new home, and that was only if they survived the wrath of the Swords.

"All you have to do," Gnat went on, "is go back to the bakery. Turn on your bedroom lamp as soon as the baker is asleep—as soon as it's safe. Then you unlock the door and let us in. We'll take care of the rest."

But if Duck did this, if she ushered the Crowns into the bakery and let them "take care of the rest," they'd snap up everything. All of Griselde's equipment, utensils, tools, anything that was worth its iron in pennies—things the baker had inherited from her own mother would be pawned and resold and scattered through the underground market of Avilognian goods, lost forever. They'd take every last cent in the strongbox. They'd take all they could carry and more, and then they'd do it again.

Griselde Baker without a way to make bread—Duck couldn't bear to think of it.

She scrambled for a loophole, for some way out of this mess that even Gnat hadn't calculated. If Duck went to Constable Deveraux right now and turned herself in as a thief, she'd be marched off in cuffs. The Crowns would lose their easy access to the bakehouse. Without their helper on the inside, their plot to simply stroll in and gather goods and coins as if the bakery were the hot fair would be foiled—and Griselde would be safe.

But Griselde would know.

If Duck told the constable who she was, what she was, then Griselde would know the truth about her at last.

And the Red Swords would never forget it if she ruined their big swipe. As long as the Crowns were in Avilogne, the Jackal would make them pay. The Crowns would be on the run forever.

"Do it for them." Gnat's voice floated from behind her, right into her ear. "If you don't do it for me, do it for them. For your family."

Your family.

And that was all Duck needed to hear.

"All right." She trembled, pushing away thoughts of Griselde, and tugged off her apron, draping it over her shoulder. "All right, I'll do it. But, Gnat?"

Facing him, she pressed a finger right into his chest. She could look him directly in the eye now, after all those months of eating bread and sleeping on a mattress and working hard. Her muscles were pretty thick, too—she was certain that if she pushed him, he would feel it.

"Do not mess this up," she said. "This is the Jackal of Avilogne—"

"And tonight, he's on our side." Gnat pushed Duck's finger out of the way and straightened his tunic. "So don't *you* mess it up. I know you're an inside cat now, but we need you to think like a Crown."

Shadows

When Duck got back to the bakery, it was late.

Far later than she'd promised to return—but she couldn't worry about that now. Coming home after dark was a small sin compared to what Duck would be doing later tonight.

The air smelled like wet ryegrass, earthy and pungent. Above, the clouds were swollen and dim; speckles of rain hit Duck on the tip of her nose and the back of her bowed head.

She opened the gate as quietly as she could. Ash the cat mewled in the yard until she tossed him one of the old fish tails from the scrap bucket, and then she paused in the storeroom to take a breath.

Gnat and the Red Swords were coming. She'd told them to come. There was no stopping them now.

Into the bakery Duck tiptoed. It was dark, and Griselde had not left any candles burning.

The baker would already be snoozing. In a few hours, the storm would stop, the dawn bells would ring, and people would start filling up the churches for the Sabbath.

Duck scooted through the kitchen. It was so dark, she should have banged her toes on every single chair leg, but she'd spent a year dancing around this kitchen now. She knew every corner of the countertop. She knew every uneven spot on the floor.

She could have made it to the stairs with her eyes closed—but even without the light, Duck could see a shape at the table.

She paused and held her breath, her heart thumping, imagining the possibilities—Gnat? The Red Swords? Had they beaten her here and found a way inside?

Then Griselde Baker's voice croaked, "It's all right. Only me."

"Oh." Duck was not comforted; her pulse still hammered in her throat. "Hello."

"Light a rush, will you?"

Duck fumbled to get the candle on the table lit, then balked when she saw the baker in the flame's glow.

Griselde was crying.

Her eyes were red-rimmed and puffy, and tiny tearstains dotted the front of her apron, but she chuckled as she wiped her cheeks.

"I wondered if I'd see you again tonight." The baker lifted a mug and sipped; even from her spot across the room, Duck could smell the sourness of ale, and she knew this was not Griselde's first drink of the night.

"Forgive me for not warning you before you found me completely sauced, but I always drink myself into a stupor on this night. Much easier to fall asleep. Much easier to avoid sad dreams." Griselde drained her ale, then swayed a bit in her seat, eyes closed. "There's one day a year that I dread more than any other. And it seems to have come around again, despite my protestations." She bent her head low, and when she looked back up, she looked so lost, so afraid. "Today's the anniversary of the day I lost my Symon."

Duck felt like the breath had been knocked out of her.

"Yesterday, it had been six years since he passed, and today, it's seven. Next year, it'll be eight, and then one day, I'll have had more years without him than I had with him, and I—"

Griselde's voice broke, but she did not put her head down. She stared straight ahead, searching the flickering light.

"I can't believe how quickly you get used to things. I remember thinking I wouldn't be able to breathe without him. But here I am, filling my lungs, like I've done a thousand times since he passed."

Duck was aware of her own lungs, seized, frozen. The thrum of the rain against the windows reminded her that there was a world beyond this room, beyond this table, though in this moment, it was hard to imagine there was anything else but this sorrow.

"You know something funny?" Griselde suddenly turned to Duck. "The day after Symon—" Here she paused, unable to say the word; Duck didn't blame her. It was a word that had always felt haunted. "Somehow I found a way to fall asleep that night, and when I woke up the next morning, I went out for a walk around town, just to give my feet something to do. I'd barely left the square when I walked past a shoe in the road. Can you believe it? A single shoe, worn-down leather, just staring up at me as if it was lost. Where its match was, I don't know—but it felt like a sign. My Symon would have said a single shoe is good luck, that it means a new beginning, a step in a new direction."

The baker grinned at the memory. "And so, while the anniversary of my Symon's passing is absolutely wretched, I know that the day after this awful day, something wonderful will cross my path. I can always count on it." She paused. "Do you know what crossed my path last year? The day after the most terrible day of the year?"

Duck didn't need to hear it. She could see it in the baker's face. They had moved beyond needing words now.

She blinked rapidly before her eyes spilled over with tears. Her vision blurred; she couldn't tell if the baker was smiling or frowning when she said, "It's been a difficult seven years, Duck. It's been so hard without him. My Symon was . . . he was my everything. My person, my family. But having you in my life . . . it's made me remember what it is to have someone to wake up for."

If the Crowns hadn't walked past the Sarluire at the exact moment baby Duck had cried.

If baby Duck had floated past the cathedral to the banks behind the bakery.

If Griselde Baker had been the one to fish her out—

"My stars, it's getting late." Griselde stood up, wiping her face with her apron. "We'd better get to sleep, Duck, or tomorrow we'll be the undead living among the bread." She chuckled at her own rhyme, then placed a hand on Duck's shoulder. "Oh, I wanted to ask you—the tournament season starts soon. Would you like to go watch one of the warm-ups again? With me?"

That hand.

Huge and strong and soft at the same time.

Always reaching out. Always open.

"Yes," Duck said quickly. "Of course." Anything to shoo Griselde out of here, to make that hand go away.

That hand, that weight.

The baker leaning on Duck, steadying herself on the last wonderful thing to cross her path.

A weight that was far too heavy for Duck to bear.

Griselde refilled her mug with ale one last time, then ambled off toward her room. "Make sure to blow the light out before you turn in, will you?" And then she shut her door, and Duck was left alone in the kitchen.

A sour feeling crept into her stomach.

If the baker had found Duck as a baby, and raised her here, and taught her everything she knew about bread, just as Griselde's mother had taught her—

But that wasn't what had happened.

The Crowns had found Duck first.

And so the Crowns were Duck's family.

Duck extinguished the rushlight and glanced around the bakery one last time. The mouths of the ovens glowed orange; they did not seem as huge as they once had. She'd cleaned them out so often, she knew every inch, every stone.

Tomorrow, the baker would be expecting something wonderful.

Instead, she'd wake up and find that her strongbox had been emptied, her home burgled, her livelihood gone.

Clenching her eyes shut for a moment, Duck made a wish in the darkness.

Then she went upstairs.

Outside, the clouds had broken, letting the moon shine through the rain on the streets of Odierne, washing everything in a silver mist that seemed like it belonged more to fairies than to a city in the country region of Chatoyant.

A sudden wave of protectiveness flooded Duck as she knelt beside the windowsill with her lamp—not just for the bakery, but for Odierne. She didn't want to leave. Ever.

She'd never been in one place for this long, but the unthinkable had happened. She'd grown roots.

She struck a light and set the candle in its metal holder, then curled her feet beneath her, watching as the glow of the lamp filled the window, highlighting the rivulets of water as they wept down the pane.

She did nothing except breathe in and out, listening for the sound of Griselde's snoring, which came after a few minutes, as predictable as summer.

If she looked above the tops of the houses and shops around her, she could see the roof of the cathedral, the gargoyles bathed in drizzle and moonlight, one single star agleam even as the clouds blew back into place, thickening over the city once again.

The baker was drunkenly slumbering, dead to the world, and would hear nothing. The Crown instincts within Duck knew it was the perfect night for a break-in.

She looked down at the river and saw the sprinkling of ripples as the light rain became a torrent.

She looked down at the cobbled roads and saw shadows in the rain, darting back and forth between the buildings, peering up at Duck's window, and knew they were waiting.

Waiting for the go-ahead to make the day after this anniversary of Symon's death as terrible as the last one had been wonderful.

Break and Enter

A jiggle.

A scratch.

A whisper.

They were here.

It was still raining. The moon was gone once again, making the night so dark, Duck could barely see her hand in front of her face—which was how she knew it was them.

Crowns were good at the dark.

She grabbed her lamp and stumbled down the stairs.

Someone was working the back door. Duck flung it open, and there, looking smug as a pig and wet as a field mouse, was Gnat.

"Oh, good," he said, pushing his way into the bakery. "I was about to kick down the door."

The rest of the Crowns filed in, hair dripping, faces shining at her in the blue dark. Frog Eyes smoothed his eyebrows with spit as he entered the bakery as if it were the queen's palace. How long had it been since any of them were inside a place with both floors and a finished roof?

Behind them, the rain-soaked Red Swords loomed on the porch, the hungry gleam in Jacques's eyes making Duck's skin crawl.

"Wait here." She was breathless, her heart jittery. "I'll go and get the strongbox."

Jacques swept right past her, pushing her back into the open door. "We'll look around ourselves, if you don't mind. And even if you do."

And then, like a herd of soldiers, the Red Swords poured into the bakery, making Gnat and the Crowns look like sheepish children accompanying their parents on their first trip to the pub.

All of a sudden, the dreadfulness of this whole plan hit Duck's gut like a thrown brick. How could she have ever thought this was the right thing to do?

Duck tugged Ash's drenched sleeve, bringing him into the storeroom. "We have to get them out of here! These are Swords—we don't know what they're capable of!"

Ash scratched the back of his head, peering warily over his shoulder at Jacques. "I don't know, Duck. I think you need to just . . . let them do this." He squeezed her arm, and a rush of anguish made Duck tear up. Last year, she would have been reassured by his touch, by his words. But right now, even though they were in the same room, it felt like they were worlds apart.

"Trust Gnat," Ash finished. "He's always taken care of us."

He emerged from the storeroom and followed the rest of the group down the hall. At the entrance to the kitchen, Gnat met Duck's eyes, giving her a look so full of venom, she felt the sting of it in her chest—but she was not the quiet little duckling Gnat thought he knew. Not anymore.

She shuffled down the hall to Gnat and grabbed him by the crook of his left elbow. "Gnat," she pleaded, her voice low. "What if—what if we strike up another deal with them? What if we offer them bread? All the bread they can carry? All the bread they can eat?"

Gnat grinned, water seeping down his forehead from his soggy hair. "Good Lord. That baker sure has made an impression on you."

Duck gritted her teeth. "I just don't want to steal from her. Not like this."

"Whether we steal her strongbox or a cupboard full of bread, it's stealing." He leaned in, close enough that their noses were almost touching. "You're still a dirty thief, through and through."

"We shouldn't be doing this!" Duck felt braver just saying it out loud, as if all her meat and guts had been replaced with something stronger. "We've taken enough from her already!"

Gnat tried to peer at her down the length of his nose, but Duck was nearly his height exactly, tall enough to level him with her eyes. "You think you're better than us now that you're an inside cat?" he sneered.

"What? No—"

"You're not. It doesn't matter that you're sleeping on a pillow and consorting with constables and that your new mommy the baker wipes your face clean every night. You'll always only be garbage." With one final glare, he pushed past her, and Duck, her blood boiling, followed the Crowns into the kitchen as silently as she could, though her heart pounded like drums in her ears.

It smelled like a stable in here, all wet hay and horses—there were ten times as many people standing in the kitchen as usual, and the ovens blasted their heat, making everyone sweat.

The Swords were opening drawers and cupboards, rummaging through Griselde Baker's things like a horde of raiding ants, hushed and polished as professionals. Duck tried to be reassured by this. If she could get them to quietly swipe the strongbox and leave before the baker woke up, it would look like she had had nothing to do with this. And if she couldn't . . .

Every once in a while, a Red Sword would find something he liked, something valuable, and pocket it: a hammer, a strip of leather, a wedge of cheese.

A knot of guilt tied itself inside of Duck, almost choking her. If Griselde came out of her room right now and saw what was happening, and saw that Duck was here, a part of it—

But Griselde Baker wouldn't wake up. She was passed out, snoozing through ale dreams. They could set off a cannon in the kitchen, incite a clatter that would wake up Saint Odile, and Griselde wouldn't stir.

Duck could get away with this. If she wanted to, she could absolutely get away with this.

Spinner found the jug of ale, unplugged it, and took a possessive swig. Le Chou pocketed a spoon, trying to look tough as he pilfered right alongside the Swords, like a piglet sharing a trough with a wolf.

Duck could be in her bed tomorrow morning, wake up with the dawn, pretend to be shocked when the baker discovered the aftermath of the robbery.

"All right." Jacques pushed a drawer closed and turned to Gnat, the glow of the ovens casting golden jack-o'-lantern shadows on his features. "Enough rubbish. Where's the strongbox?"

Gnat looked to Duck.

Duck's eyes welled with angry tears. She'd stood here frozen while they'd pillaged the kitchen—all of Master Griselde's things, all her tools, the items she used every day, things she'd held on to since before Symon passed . . . Griselde Baker's little corner of the world, picked over and pocketed by a bunch of scoundrels.

"Well?" Gnat prompted, his eyes impatient.

She had to do *something*. She had to at least try. She'd already let the beasts in, let them scavenge.

Her stomach flip-flopped. "I just remembered! Her banker has it for the night," she fibbed. "It's official guild policy. Sorry. Quarterly accounting. But I can offer you some trenchers for your trouble—"

"Liar." Gnat stepped toward her. "That strongbox never leaves the bakehouse. Griselde sends her journeyman to the bank with the coins in a little white sack every other Thursday. Now, tell me where it is."

Gnat, Gnat, always watching. Duck should have known he'd have the baker's routine memorized. He probably didn't need her to show him to the strongbox at all; he no doubt knew exactly where the baker kept it. Duck could vanish up the stairs, hide in her bedroom, and pull the covers over her head. She could let the Crowns and the Red Swords swipe all they wanted from the baker while she settled into sleep, then awaken tomorrow morning as if this were just a bad dream.

Yes, he'd be able to find it—but he wanted her to do it.

He wanted Duck to choose.

The Crowns or the baker.

Jacques strolled around the oven and clamped Gnat's skinny neck in a red leather glove. "Is there a problem?"

Gnat writhed, trying to stay upright. A fire gleamed in his eyes as he spat, "Dammit, Duck! Are you a Crown or aren't you?"

"Duck," Ash pleaded, coming up behind her. "Just get the strongbox." And then, after a moment, "Since we're already here."

She looked at Ash, and after rummaging for a moment, she felt it—their connection, still strong as twine, even after a year of living apart—and she knew that he understood.

We're already here. The Swords are already in the bakery. The glove is already gripping Gnat's neck. You already said you would do this.

Duck already *had* done this.

She was a Crown, yes. And she was more.

She was a baker's apprentice. She was here to serve Griselde and protect the integrity of the bread.

And Duck did not need Ash to speak for her anymore.

She could speak for herself.

She pushed past Jacques to grab a pot and lid from the counter; she held them a foot apart in her hands, her body tense with pluck. "Get out now, or I'll wake her up. I'll do it."

Jacques narrowed his eyes, irritated. "You're bluffing. You wouldn't dare—you and all your pathetic cohorts will be rounded up and shackled. It's summertime. Prime gallows season." The

Jackal of Avilogne grinned; clearly he thought he had her between his teeth.

All around her, the Crowns bristled, their quarrels on the tips of their tongues. Gnat glared at her, Jacques's fingers tightening around his neck.

But Duck remained calm, pot and lid in hand, smiling as she lifted her chin to meet Jacques's furious regard.

Let Gnat throw a fit. Let the Swords thrash around until they found the strongbox—it was almost an inevitability now. Only a matter of time before Jacques got his hands on it.

But when Duck thought back over the events of the night, she wanted to remember this—

She wanted to remember herself here, standing between Griselde's rightful money and the thieves who would take it from her.

And she wanted the Crowns to remember her not just as the quiet little duckling they'd pulled out of the river but as someone who loved them enough to brave pulling a scam on the Red Swords.

A Crown, through and through.

"I'll do it," she repeated evenly. "You take one coin out of that strongbox, and I'll bang every pot in this kitchen. I'll shout myself hoarse, and when she wakes up, I won't run."

There—that last bit did the trick. Jacques tried to mask his reaction, but Duck caught the way his breath snagged in his throat.

Duck would make such a ruckus, the baker would stumble out of her bed, head spinning. And while the rest of the Crowns and the Red Swords raced out the door, scurrying off to hide in the dark pockets of the city, Duck would stay.

"I won't run. I'll stay. And confess," Duck went on, heart fluttering with nerves, "and I'll be arrested. And then you'll be cut off. You won't be able to swipe from this place ever again. And you'll have every watchman and constable in Avilogne on your tail. I'll make sure of that."

Duck would stay.

Instead of pretending she'd been asleep the whole night, she'd wait right here, and she'd tell Griselde Baker she'd done it: She'd let a band of rowdy thieves into the bakehouse. She'd let them rifle through her drawers.

She'd stay, and Griselde Baker would call for Constable Deveraux.

But the Crowns could get away. They could find somewhere else to live, set up a new scam. Start over.

Yes, the Red Swords would probably chase after them in out-raged vengeance, but at least the Crowns would have a chance.

"Duck . . ." Ash spoke her name in barely a whisper; when Duck stole a peek at him, he was gawking at her in speechless puzzlement.

The Jackal of Avilogne was perplexed as well, but only for half a moment. He shoved Gnat down to the floor and stepped over him, a mere pile of trembling limbs, and then that same red glove pinched around the back of Duck's own neck.

"You'll just have to come with us, then." Jacques shuffled Duck toward the counting room. "Good thing you're pocket-size."

"Duck!" Ash cried, diving forward; she could hear the other

Swords blockading the rest of the Crowns. In a panic, she dropped the pot and lid, letting them crash to the ground with a ricocheting noise, but it quieted soon enough, and no sleepy-eyed Griselde emerged to investigate.

Once Jacques and Duck reached the counting room, it was over pretty quickly.

The Swords lit a candle. They found the strongbox. They found the key and wrenched the strongbox open. They took all the cash, every coin.

Duck watched numbly from her front-row seat, Jacques's hand digging into her spine.

All that tough talking and threat-making . . . it was all for nothing.

A whole year at the bakery, and it was all for nothing.

Griselde would wake up the next morning, and Duck would be gone. Snatched by the Red Swords and squirreled away, never again to feed sugar to yeast or handle the crisp crust of a fresh baguette.

"So," Gnat said to Jacques, "when do we get our red gloves?"

Jacques didn't bother looking up from his pile of coins. "What gloves?"

"We're honorary Swords now, right?"

The words made Duck's insides tangle. No more Crowns?

Jacques flashed a jackal's smile. "I'm afraid we can't allow just anyone into the Red Swords. Only the best and brightest get to wear the glove. This should have been a simple operation, but you let your gang turn it into a long, dragged-out drama." Here he nodded at Duck. "You kids are reckless. Far too reckless to ever join our ranks."

Gnat breathed in through his nose, and his fist clenched. "We had a deal—"

"And the deal changed as soon as you became liabilities." Jacques nodded at the other Swords, who started closing in on the Crowns, surrounding them. "You have until sunset tomorrow to leave Odierne." When Gnat started to protest, Jacques pulled out a blade, letting a glint of hazy moonlight reflect off its edge. "If you aren't gone by then," said the Jackal of Avilogne, "I'll finish you myself."

Thunder peeled outside, rolling through the yard like a church bell.

We never should have come to Odierne, Duck thought, unable to look away from the knife, inches from Gnat's throat. *We should have found somewhere else to settle. We should have taken our chances in Perpinnet or pressed on to some other place.*

But then you never would have met Griselde, a tiny voice inside her whispered. *You never would have learned how to make bread, or how to read, or how to garden. You never would have seen a real jousting tournament or celebrated a real Christmas.*

You never would have come back to the place where Ash found you, the very spot where the river curled behind the cathedral.

The very spot where you found your family—

And now you're about to lose them again.

Both of your families.

Another crash of thunder sounded outside.

Duck wouldn't let the Red Swords scare her away from the things she'd come to love.

She wouldn't let them take her away from home.

Jacques had his red glove around her neck—

But Duck was no longer the tiny, wimpy youngest Crown. She had shot up three inches in the past year, she had muscles from hauling sacks of grain, and she had an unwavering courage from pushing dough in and out of fire.

She twisted forward with all her strength, releasing herself from Jacques's grip, and seized a nearby candle, disregarding the dripping wax that scalded her fingers; she'd learned to handle the heat after working with those ovens all year. She turned and thrust the candle's flame at Jacques. "Get out," she snarled, "or else—"

The back door creaked open.

Jacques and the Red Swords held still; the Crowns in the hallway were motionless.

In the middle of the counting room, Duck waited, petrified.

"Duck?" Petrus called over the sound of the storm as he entered the bakery. "Is that you?"

Fight

At her side, Gnat thumped her on the shoulder; when she turned to him, he mouthed, "Answer him."

But to what purpose?

To stall Petrus so the Red Swords and the Crowns could escape undetected?

To alert Petrus to the robbery that was currently taking place?

To warn Petrus to let them flee or else he'd get hurt?

"Duck?" Petrus called again, and Duck tracked the sound of his footsteps past the storeroom and down the hall, toward the kitchen. "I saw a lit candle—are you up? Raina made you a posy. Gillyflowers. They're supposed to help with your sniffles . . ."

He trailed off when he entered the kitchen and spotted the Crowns, clustered around the entrance to the counting room, and found Duck, still holding the candle, her eyes wide as stars.

"What's going on?" Petrus said, rain dripping from his tunic.

The Red Swords held statue-still, but the flame of Duck's single candle was enough to illuminate every one of their faces. Jacques tightened his grip on the blade in his red glove.

When Petrus looked at Duck, calculating, configuring, the fury in his expression was undeniable. She could feel it flooding from him—every assumption he'd ever had about her, every judgment he'd decided was too harsh, every time he'd been suspicious but had backed off for Griselde's sake—all of it, rushing back to his mind.

He had his proof now. Here it was in the form of a dozen unwashed kids, pockets full of bakery tools, the strongbox lid still open, the key lying on the desk.

"I'm sorry," Duck blurted out. "I'm—"

"Master Griselde!" The volume at which Petrus bellowed this warning was astonishing. Duck instinctively hunched over, her shoulders shrugging up as if she could use them to cover her ears. "Wake up! We're being robbed!"

That word jumped out at Duck—*we're*.

When Petrus said it, he glowered right at her, his eyebrows scrunched down, all of his teeth showing, and she understood what he meant. She wasn't part of the *we*.

Not anymore.

Say something, Duck commanded herself.

Open your mouth. Speak. Explain yourself—offer excuses, apologies, promises to make it right.

But her mouth, even though she flung it open so the right words could spill out, was useless to her.

"It's not what you think—" she stammered.

Petrus scoffed. "Really?" He threw the posy onto the floor, where it broke apart, the petals scattering. "It looks like you brought your whole pack of rat friends in here to take us for all we're worth. I always knew you were nothing but vermin."

Duck trembled, but Ash sang out from the hallway, "Hey, she's not vermin."

"Vermin. Liar. Thief." Petrus spat out each word as if it were a bite of too-hard, poorly yeasted crust.

Duck's face crumpled, her nose running hot. "I'll get them out," she whimpered. "I'll get her money back, and then I'll go—but please, just don't tell her."

She'd dig into their pockets herself if she had to, every last Sword; she would get that money back for Griselde.

But the Jackal of Avilogne held up his knife and, with a slashing motion, lunged at Duck.

Someone tugged Duck back and out of the blade's path. She was thrown sideways, the candle's flame doused with the motion, and when she straightened again, the Crowns and Red Swords were in the kitchen, and Jacques was swinging his knife at Petrus.

"Petrus! No!" Duck scrambled into the fray, yanking Jacques's knife arm back, ready to sink her teeth into him if she had to—

Two Red Swords pulled her away from their leader.

The other Crowns joined in the fray. Frog Eyes and Fingers kicked and slapped the Swords who held Duck; Drippy, Spinner, and Le Chou tried to down the largest of the Red Swords, a hulking lad who had picked up one of the bakery stools and was using it to corner them against the closed shutters.

And Ash . . .

Ash was swinging at both Petrus and Jacques, dodging the knife, and Duck was unsure who he was trying to fight and why.

"You won't . . . get away with this!" Petrus shouted as he dipped away from the blade.

Panting, Jacques grinned. "We already have." He sliced his knife down, aiming right for Petrus's chest.

"No!" Duck shouted. She kicked both legs at once—how was the baker still sleeping through all this ruckus?—and freed herself from the Red Swords who held her. She rushed at Jacques and tackled him.

His knife missed Petrus by an inch but cut right through a rope that held a string of pots, pans, and cauldrons above the ovens.

The noise was deafening—a clatter of cookware landing on the floor.

The rope itself landed on the counter, draping right across the open mouth of an oven.

Duck watched it happen—

The fire licked the rope at first, as if giving it a taste test, and then the rope was engulfed in flames.

"Fire!" she shrieked, pointing at the oven.

The fire had already traveled across the rope to the opposite counter, where baskets and sacks of ingredients were lined up against the brick walls.

A new heat radiated from the kitchen, and smoke began to billow as the fire ate up whatever it could find—towels and rags, burlap, wooden mixing bowls that had, only hours earlier, been used by Duck and the baker to make the rye loaves.

Duck's throat closed up. She coughed, trying to peer through the smoke. Most of the Crowns and the Red Swords had abandoned their fight, running for the door. Ash made his way to the windows, throwing them open, which helped with the smoke, but the fire spread outside the bakery, up to the thatched roof, and then Duck knew they were in trouble.

Griselde Baker had warned her—entire bakeries, blocks of homes, could be devoured in minutes by a single greedy fire. Even in the rain—a storm was no match for the appetite of a fire.

They had to stop it before it ate everything.

A row of barrels holding water were bunched together in one corner of the kitchen; Duck coughed as she rushed to them, struggling with the gnarled ropes that held their lids in place.

Her fingers were no match for the knots. She fumbled, her eyes stinging from the smoke, but it was useless—

"Here." A single hand reached for the knot, and Duck didn't have to look up to know who it belonged to.

Gnat.

Gnat had come to help her.

She couldn't afford to dwell on this right now—they had to save the bakery before it was completely lost to the fire.

"Hurry!" she sputtered. "We're running out of time!"

"That's helpful, truly helpful!" Gnat shouted back at her, but he somehow unleashed one of the barrels, took off its lid, and the two of them lifted it, hurling the water at the fire.

"Another!" Duck commanded as soon as the water landed, the fire hissing. "Get another one!"

"It won't be enough!" Gnat coughed, lifting his left arm to breathe through his sleeve. "We can't stop it!"

"Yes, we can!" Duck's eyes spilled over with tears—the peppery air was too much for them. They closed, and even when Duck tried to force them open, they refused. *So be it*, she thought. *I'll do this without seeing.*

Her hands found the knot holding the second barrel's lid in place; she fumbled with it, the heat from the fire close enough to feel on her cheeks and down one side of her body.

One moment, Gnat was coughing beside her; the next, he had shuffled off into the smoke, and Duck was alone with the barrels.

"Duck!" someone shouted. "Leave it! Get out!"

"No!" she shouted back. She wouldn't let Griselde's bakery be ruined like this—she couldn't let it happen, not after everything else she'd ruined tonight. "Come on, knot," she murmured, feeling it with her hands, trying to find a way to loosen the ropes, trying, trying, but to no avail—

"Duck, you have to get out of here!" Petrus grabbed her around her middle, taking her away from the barrels. She cracked a leaky eye open, watching the floor move beneath her as she was carried across the bakery—

"Wait! Griselde!" Duck thrashed. "She isn't out yet!"

"You have to get yourself out, Duck!" Petrus carted her to the door, but as soon as she felt the sprinkle of rain on her outstretched hands, Duck let out a screech and squirmed so hard, he had no choice but to drop her.

"You can't go back in there!" Petrus called as Duck got to her feet. "What are you doing, Duck? You'll die!"

"I have to save her!" Duck held her breath and, with her vision blurred by the smoke, raced back through the kitchen and charged into Griselde's bedroom.

The baker was coughing in her bed, and Duck could see by the puffiness of Griselde's face and the disoriented murmuring coming out of her mouth that Griselde was just now waking from a drunken sleep so intense, it would make the dead jealous.

"Griselde!" Duck pushed at the baker's window, but it was stuck, its wooden frame swollen by the stormy air. "We've got to get out of here!"

Griselde rolled out of bed, still drowsy. "It's late. Or early. Kind of the same thing."

"Listen." Duck gave up on the window and grabbed Griselde's hands. "There's a fire in the kitchen—"

"Fire," Griselde repeated, and she was suddenly awake. Her eyes searched the ceiling, frantic, and her grip on Duck tightened. She sniffed the air, and a shudder ran through her, sobering her. "A fire, Duck—"

"We need to get out of here," Duck said, tugging the baker toward her bedroom door. "We'll have to slide past the flames and make a run for the back door—"

"Griselde! Duck!" A slick and wet Petrus appeared in the hallway, his voice hoarse and raw. "Come on, let's go! This way!"

But then there was a crash. A beam fell from the kitchen ceiling, the scorched thatched roof caving in. With it came a deluge of trapped rainwater, splattering on the floor, hissing as the heat licked it up.

Petrus was blocked from them, the hallway sealed off with flames.

Duck and Griselde managed to dodge the beam just in time— but now there was nowhere to go. Kitchen on fire, front door ablaze, back door and hallway full of flames, and the downstairs window stuck.

Nowhere to go but up the stairs—

And so they ran up.

Into Duck's bedroom they scampered, but the fire—the fire followed them.

Fire blazing below, fire blazing above them now, too, and all around them. Duck knew they had only moments to escape before the fire blazed right through them.

Duck glanced out the window. It was a long drop to the black, snaking Sarluire below, the rain peppering the surface of the water, texturizing it, reminding Duck of the way their white grain loaves got all dimply in the ovens.

"Duck?" Griselde reached her hands out, and Duck took them again. "I need you to—I can't see it. The smoke—I can't see."

"It's all right." It always startled Duck how soft the baker's hands were, like rounded dough. "We're going to have to jump."

Duck ducked her head out the window, peering again at the great drop that awaited them. Some of the Crowns spotted her and ran to the river's edge, shouting encouragements. She scanned their heads, counting to make sure everyone had made it out alive—and an urgent relief warmed her chest when she saw that Petrus, too, was safe.

"Out the window," Griselde said. It wasn't a question, but Duck understood that the baker was having trouble visualizing what they needed to do. How terrifying this whole ordeal must be without proper sight.

"It's a long way down, but we'll land in the water," Duck said. "We should be fine."

"I trust you." Griselde squeezed Duck's hand, and inside Duck, something broke.

The thunder boomed overhead, and another section of the roof snapped, collapsing, water and fire. Duck grabbed Griselde just in time, ushering her to the window.

The two of them climbed through the frame, Crowns and other bystanders at the river's edge, yelling indecipherable instructions to them through the tempest—

And then they were plummeting.

Under and Out

Duck couldn't see.

The water was dark. Above the water, the night was dark.

Every time her head bobbed up to the surface, she heard blasts of noise: Wind rushing past her ears. Thunder belching. Rain dropping.

People shouting—

Then water rushing around her, water rushing over her, something splashing.

The fire . . . its orange glow still burned in her eyes. The thatched roof in flames.

As the river tugged her away, she could still smell it, the scent of charred wood and scalded oil.

She searched around in the water for the baker; she choked out her name. The only response was the river, rushing into her mouth, tasting of mud, cooling her burnt throat.

But no matter how much she cried out for the baker, she was alone.

"Duck!" she thought she heard someone call through the drizzle; the water disoriented her, so she couldn't tell where it was coming from or who had said it. It sounded like—like—

The river curved her away from the shore suddenly. It tugged her down, and this time, no matter how much she kicked, she did not resurface.

Then it was quiet.

Duck was surprised by how peaceful it was, here at the bottom of the river.

Here at the end of it all.

She'd always feared death, feared the violence of it. As a child of the streets, she'd heard stories . . . but now that she was here, she understood: when you died, you just got very, very quiet.

You floated backward, you glanced up at cathedrals, whether real or imagined, and you marveled at all you had seen and done.

Duck had lived grandly. She'd slept in trees and jumped off barns and eaten stolen apples on rooftops. Such a life might have seemed grimy and maddening to some . . . but it hadn't been. Not to her.

It had been glorious.

She'd had the Crowns . . .

And she'd had Griselde.

And Griselde had given her the world.

Her eyes fluttered open, and through the river, through the rain, she saw the cathedral—dilapidated beams, white stones against the gray of the smoky sky.

The very place where she'd started—the very place where Ash had pulled her out of the water as a baby.

Her beginning. And now this would be her end.

The river would keep her this time.

Ash had given her another chance.

A chance to live.

And the baker, too, had given Duck another chance—a chance to be loved.

And now there were no more chances.

Duck surrendered, lolling in the current, ready to be taken farther downriver, all the way to the sea, perhaps, and then on to the sky. Wherever she was meant to head next . . .

If she could do it again, she thought, she would have tried to have it all. She would have fought harder.

She would have stopped them from coming into the bakery. She would have stopped the Swords from even coming into the cathedral. She would have told the baker what was happening as soon as she'd come home tonight, even if it meant the constable dragged Duck away while Griselde watched.

But she would have told the baker other things, too. Things that it was now too late to say.

If Duck had another chance, she would say them—

But there comes a time, Duck knew, when the lights must be snuffed. The door to this life must be closed, and onward a person must go, off to heaven or hell or wherever one might end up.

She had fought fire and water.

And now she was done.

INTERLUDE

Someone is in the water. A child.

Nine years ago, on a stormy night just like this, a mother and a baby fell into the river. On that night, I watched them both wash away.

Nine years ago, I watched. My claws, my wings, my whole self, made of stone, unable to move.

A hundred years I have watched, watched and waited—and I will not wait another minute.

I am done with waiting.

Nine years.

It takes me nine years—a hundred years, all told—but at last, I do it. I leap from my ledge. Into the rain.

All of Odierne is dashing to the bakehouse to fight the fire, but I am for the river, made brilliant orange by the flames. My tiny stone wings unfurl from my back. I sail down the height of our cathedral, the air rushing past my face, making my gravelly eyes sting.

I recall the spring day when I was carted from my maker's

workroom and brought to the foundation. I recall the four masons who carried me up, up the stairs and the scaffolding to the roof. I recall when they positioned me on my ledge, faced me west, and I took in my first view of the fields, the river, the horizon.

This is what flashes through my mind as I hurtle down—all my years, one after another.

The rattle of crooked wheels as I was carted to the cathedral. The sound of my maker's voice as she shaped me with her hands, her convictions. The laborers as I was chiseled from the mountain—I am a mountain again—

All of my years, and this is how they end.

This is the last thought I have while there is still wind in my face; this is how it will end. I may plunge straight down into the water and never emerge; I may miss the river altogether and crash into the ground, breaking into pieces—

But if I do not at least try, I will shatter. I was made for this. Made to protect.

I'm diving, diving for the water, and the river is coming up fast—

I go under with a tremendous splash. The water is much colder than I was expecting, but it feels good on my hot stone.

I am heavy, so I move quickly, reaching my claws around the girl. She doesn't resist, limp in my arms—too late.

Please, don't let me be too late.

The river has never seemed this violent from my spot on my roof, but now that I am down here, I see that to cross the river at all is to fight. What look like ripples from atop my cathedral are actually waves, water pushing me down.

But I am strong. I am a gargoyle.

I was made to protect.

Please, please, please.

The girl flops as I push her to the shore, and I whisper, over and over, *Please. Please don't let me be too late.*

I let the water do the rest. The river presses her up against the bank, where there will soon be people rushing to pluck her from the ripples. There is nothing else for me to do.

From my place in the shallows, I wait and I watch and I whisper. *Please, please, please.*

I was made to protect—and I was made to pray. *Please—*

She sputters first, rolls to her side. Her eyes blink open, find the sky. She coughs and coughs. Coughs up water, coughs up smoke.

She is still limp, but she is moving. She is breathing.

She is saved.

The silhouettes of the Sisters of Glorious Mercy rush to the water's edge, and I let myself be swept away by the river.

My wings struggle to keep me afloat. I am too heavy. After all, I am made of stone. I turn and see the fire, still ablaze, and without even thinking, I utter another prayer.

I pray for more rain. I pray for it to put out the fire before it can spread to other buildings. I pray for the loss to be manageable and for the recovery to be swift.

The storm intensifies at once, the rain slapping the surface of the river, but I am too far gone to see if the fire is doused.

I can only trust that, fire or no fire, God knows what is best.

⌗   ⌗   ⌗

As I sink to the bottom of the river, my head tilts back, letting me see the Odierne skyline that I have been a part of for so many years.

There is our cathedral, situated between the abbey and the laundry, in the market district of our fair town. I imagine the space it will leave when it is dismantled.

I ache to know it will go. I suppose I have kept a kernel of hope, hidden away in my stones all these years. It hurts to let this hope die. But I also know that they will build something else here, something great.

Odierne will go on without us.

At least there will always be stars.

As if waiting for me to think this, the cathedral suddenly shifts. It moves.

At first I think it is the water, warping my view, but then the cathedral trembles. Stones crack. The foundation shakes.

The first stone block hits the ground, and it is explosive—the loudest sound in the world, even from beneath the waves, and my heart cracks.

The pillars tremble like legs too weak to hold their own weight.

Think of darkness. Think of how darkness would sound if it had a voice. Think of the noise of rocks being chewed, the lick of fire, the crack of stone splitting from a fall. That is what my soul sounds like right now.

A cry. Lonesome, twisted, agonized.

The black water swirls around me, and I watch the horizon fall sideways. The cathedral, tumbling down, and down I go, too, to the very bottom.

Lower than low, water and earth and heaven above me.

Far above, through the current, I see the sky. I was once part of the sky.

I sink.

When I settle on the bed of the Sarluire, it is dark. I cannot see the stars from here. I cannot even see the sky. I am alone in the river.

I am by myself. Always by myself.

But I have done it. I have protected. A proper gargoyle at last.

It ends not in dust, but in waves and water.

Aftermath

Flames licking.

Smoke coursing out into the night.

Fire roaring, ash flying up.

Ash.

Ash's face aglow, Ash's voice calling her name—

Duck opened her eyes.

She was flat on her back, somewhere new. Her hair stank like charred bread.

Dark ceiling above her.

White sheet on a simple cot beneath her.

Duck swallowed, and her eyes watered from the pain; it felt like she'd inhaled a chimney. She coughed, and the pain surged worse.

Beside the cot, a pitcher and cup waited on a table; Duck hobbled out of the bed and poured herself a drink. When she'd guzzled down three cups of water, temporarily quenching the fire in her lungs, she glanced around her.

A cot, a table, a pitcher, and a chair. An imprint on the sheet, the soot from her skin dirtying it in the shape of her body.

And a window.

Duck glanced outside, her head pounding at the brightness of the day.

A garden.

Patches of roses, neatly trimmed honeysuckle, rows of herbs and root vegetables.

Instantly, she knew where she was—she should have recognized the half wall that lined the hallway or the pointed arch over the door.

She was in the abbey.

How?

Her mind tried to wrap around what had happened.

The last thing she remembered was the rush of water, the river pulling her under—

She was very cold, and then she was no longer cold—no longer anything, really, and then . . . she was dead. Or asleep, or something akin to both.

But apparently, she was none of those things—she was alive.

She was alive.

A Sister of Mercy passed her room and, seeing Duck on her feet, paused. "Look who's awake."

Duck turned from the window but said nothing.

"How are you feeling?" the sister asked.

Duck took a quick inventory. Sore throat and chest, like a flue that hadn't been cleaned out in ages. Stinging eyes, aching muscles, and a pit in her stomach that threatened to tug her into darkness—and also a strange hurt on her forearms that she couldn't explain. She pushed up the sleeves of her nightdress and found bandages from her wrists to her elbows, tight and greasy with a minty-smelling salve.

"You were very fortunate." The sister nodded at Duck's wounds. "Sister Ernestine was shocked that the burns weren't deeper."

Burns . . . Duck had vague memories of the fire licking at her, memories of pain.

"She'll be around within the hour to change your wrappings. In the meantime, someone would like to see you," the sister said, and as she bowed and departed, another person peered into Duck's room, and the look on his face was enough to set water to boil.

"Well, you did it." Petrus spoke with nettling sarcasm. "Well done. Truly outstanding achievements—you must be so proud."

Duck kept her eyes on a beetle squeezing through a crack in the wall—she tracked it as it moved across the floor on a diagonal path.

"Burned the bakery to a crisp, destroying hundreds of coronets' worth of inventory, supplies, and tools," Petrus started. "Not to mention costing us all our lungs, our hair, and our skin—we're lucky we weren't cooked to a crisp!"

We. Petrus had said *we.*

Petrus and Griselde.

Not Duck—but her guts suddenly squeezed in alarm.

Did that mean—?

Was the baker—?

"And the worst part?" Petrus fumed, his arm muscles straining as if he were barely resisting the urge to throttle Duck. "Griselde let you into her bakery. She let you into her home. She bought you clothes, took you to tournaments, gave you everything she had. She trusted you—*I* trusted you, damn it!" He slammed a fist against the door frame, sending the beetle scurrying beneath the cot.

The baker. Was the baker—?

Had the baker made it out of the fire? Or was she—?

"I should call the constables. I should report you and let them haul you off to the dungeons. That's what thieves deserve. And arsonists, too."

And . . . murderers?

Duck swallowed, her throat pained. Had Griselde made it out of the river? Or was Duck responsible for the loss of Odierne's greatest dough puncher?

"I should be happy to see you arrested and hanged. But I won't." Petrus sniffed, straightening, as if he'd just made up his mind about something. "I won't, because Griselde wouldn't want me to. Griselde would no doubt want me to forgive you, even. But that I won't do. God will forgive you long before I do."

With every word, Duck's stomach wrung itself tighter.

Griselde would no doubt want me to forgive you.

Does that mean Griselde was gone?

Was the baker—?

Was she—?

"Griselde," Duck finally rasped. She had never felt so small in all her life.

Petrus glared at her. Duck could see all manner of thoughts rising up within him, and it gutted her. Not just the anger—the confusion. It was the confusion that undid her.

He had accepted Duck. He had trusted her—not only with the bakery, but with a spot in their strange, cobbled-together family—and Duck had ruined it.

He owed her nothing, absolutely nothing. He could turn on his heel and leave now and never say a word to her again. But instead, he looked beyond Duck, nodding at the window.

Far off, on the other side of the garden, Griselde Baker limped past the radishes, her grin jolly and wide despite an ankle so heavily bandaged, it was three times its usual size. She used her cane to steady herself, but other than that, she looked like the same old Griselde—wearing her baker's whites, her rusty gray hair piled in a tiny knot on top of her head, her pink skin blotchy in the sunshine.

She was all right.

Thank the saints.

Petrus, as if reading her mind, scoffed. "She survived the fall, yes. And your nasty crew of cutpurses. But I'm not sure she'll survive you."

Cutpurses.

Thieves.

The Crowns—their faces suddenly popped into Duck's mind like apples in a barrel of water.

She rushed toward the door, the quick motion sending a shockwave of pain up her legs and back, but it wasn't enough to stop her.

"Where do you think you're going?" Petrus blocked the exit, but Duck was too fast—she dipped under his arm and out the door.

"Duck!" A Sister of Mercy tried to catch her as she ran down the hall. "Please get back into bed! You're injured! You need rest!"

No, what Duck needed was to get to the cathedral, right now. Of course, they wouldn't be there, not with the Red Swords loose in the streets, but maybe there would be a note, a sign, a clue about where she could find them, because she had to make sure that the Crowns—

She had to make sure that the Crowns had survived Duck, too.

Across the garden she flew, every step lighting her up with pain, and out the gates, aware that several nuns were chasing her, bound to catch her, since she was slowing with the strain of running on scorched feet and breathing with lungs full of smoke—

But they didn't need to stop her.

She came to a screeching halt all on her own.

Gasping for her next breath through a scalded throat, Duck closed her eyes. She rubbed the grime out of them, then looked again.

The cathedral.

The unfinished cathedral that the Crowns had called home—

It was gone.

Remnants of the cathedral were piled beside the river—broken stones and splintered beams—but it was leveled.

No longer could you skip up the porch or climb the downed pillars in the nave. No longer could you roll yourself up in a moldy old tapestry or sleep beneath a pew. No longer could you stand atop the roof, place your hand on a gargoyle's head, and stare out at the horizon.

Gone, all gone.

Clouds of dust from its destruction still hung in the air . . .

or were those the billows of smoke from the bakery fire, lingering above the city?

And where were the Crowns?

Their hideout was gone. Were they safe? Were they tucked away somewhere, hacking and coughing, binding their own burns?

Or were they—?

Duck heard footsteps behind her. The Sisters of Mercy, giving her a berth of space as she stared at the rubble, the river behind it still flowing, still coursing as if nothing had changed.

And then someone touched her shoulder.

"So. There's our little daredevil."

Every last crumb within Duck wanted to turn and throw herself into the baker's voluminous embrace, to sob her guilt and sorrow into the baker's white tunic. To demand the comfort that she knew the baker would give freely, lovingly, even after everything Duck had done to her.

Instead, she shrugged off the hand. She should flee, she should hunt down the Crowns, wherever they were, and she should—

"Please, Duck. Don't leave me."

Duck's breath caught in her throat. Everything was quiet, quiet enough that she could hear the beat of her own heart, every thump full of regret, full of despair, full of hope.

Even after everything Duck had done to her, Griselde still wanted her.

She wanted Duck to stay—

And that's what did it.

That was what finally broke Duck.

She clenched her eyes shut, her chest heaving as she wept, and Griselde cooed as she pulled the thief into her arms.

And it was just as comforting as Duck knew it would be.

Like a warm loaf of freshly baked bread.

The baker rocked Duck, patting her on the back, making shushing noises into her smoky hair. "There, now," she boomed. "Let's get it all out now, shall we? And then we can move on to more practical things, like tweaking your new bread recipe. I believe you had the ovens a bit too hot."

Duck issued a wet, snotty laugh, then immediately pulled back from the baker and gawked. "You—you still want me to be your apprentice?"

"Oh, Duck." Griselde took Duck's chin in her hand and leaned forward, close enough that Duck could see the opulent blue of the baker's eyes beneath the clouded lenses. "I want you by my side in any way I can have you."

Blue.

Blue stays.

Griselde inspected Duck through those milky blue eyes, searching, searching, and Duck couldn't stand it another second. She dropped to her knees, hands folded together as if in prayer. "I'll pay you back," she whispered, her head bowed low, nose in the dirt. "Every penny. It'll take me some time, but if I work around the clock, even on feast days—"

"Nonsense." Griselde shifted her feet, wincing a bit when she stepped on the one that was bandaged. "I think you owe me an explanation, first and foremost." She paused, then held out her hand. "Walk with me?"

Duck peered at that hand. A fat red wound streaked across the palm; the baker had cut her hand on something, perhaps on the windowsill as they'd leaped or on a rock in the river. But even with the cut, the hand was still soft, still doughy.

Still strong.

Duck took the hand.

Griselde and Duck did laps around the garden, bumblebees and Sisters of Mercy buzzing around the plants, tending to the flowers. While they walked, Duck did something she had not done enough of in her life—she spoke.

She told Griselde everything: all about her life as a Crown, how they had come to Odierne and settled in the old cathedral, how the Crowns had been threatened by the Red Swords, how Gnat had schemed to put one of them into the bakery as an apprentice, how Duck had slipped them bread and coins every market day.

"Approximately how much have you given them, do you think?" Griselde cut in. Even though her eyes were especially cloudy today, staring beyond Duck at the nothingness of the sky, Duck had a hard time meeting her gaze.

She mumbled a figure, and the shock on Griselde's face was there, then gone in a flash.

"My stars," the baker said with a sigh, but offered no further comment. Duck couldn't tell if she was impressed or horrified.

"And then there was a plot to rob your strongbox, and I ... I ..." She popped a dandelion's head off its stem and picked at the yellow petals until her fingers were stained. "I let them in."

She didn't bother defending herself—the way she'd changed her mind once the bakehouse was swarming with Swords, how she'd wrestled with Jacques, how she'd tried to douse the flames.

None of that mattered. She was the one who had let them in. She was the one who had opened the door to everything that followed:

Jacques, pulling out his blade.

The awful moment when Petrus had walked in, when he saw Duck, saw what she was doing, saw what she was.

And then the fire.

"Well, the good news is, the bakery is completely ruined." Griselde didn't hesitate to give this report.

Duck was instantly sickened. "Oh, Griselde! I'm so sorr—"

"Good news, I said! Complete structural damage! Not even the bones can be saved!" Griselde Baker chuckled. "Now we can rebuild! You have to tear things down in order to start again, don't you? This is an opportunity in disguise!"

"But without the bakery, how will people eat?" Duck worried.

"Master Maria will be glad for the business," Griselde said. "Marvelous baker. She's up in Julion, so it'll be a bit of a walk for most folks, but they'll do it. People will do anything to get their bread."

All of Griselde Baker's customers, sent off to another baker. "Won't the guild fine you?"

Griselde shrugged. "Nothing I can't talk my way out of—don't you fret." A bee flew between them, and then the baker said, "They got away."

Duck sucked in a breath. "Who did? The Crowns? Or the Swords?"

"Not sure." Griselde picked a bit of soot from under her

fingernail, flicking it into the grass. "The little ones were all safe, last I saw. They scattered before I could introduce myself. That tall, lanky one? The boy with the stork legs? He asked about you—but I didn't know. I didn't know yet if you'd made it."

Ash.

Ash had asked about her—and it cut a hole right through her to think that the others hadn't asked. Hadn't *cared*. They thought she'd betrayed them. They thought she'd chosen the baker over the Crowns.

But that was wrong.

She'd tried to choose both—and she'd lost it all.

"How did you make it out?" Griselde asked after a moment. "That current was mighty strong. If I hadn't been swept right past the tannery and managed to grab on to their gutter, I'd be somewhere in Perpinnet by now, feeding their eels."

Duck recounted the details of the night—the river's strength, the moment she'd surrendered to its pull . . . and the strange sensation that she'd been lifted up through the water—but she couldn't explain beyond that. "I'm . . . not sure," she told Griselde. "I must have washed ashore somehow."

"Lucky Duck," Griselde commented with a smile.

Not quite luck, Duck thought.

She'd fallen into the Sarluire twice and lived to tell the tale, but it wasn't luck that had saved her.

Both times, someone had pulled her out.

Ash . . . and her mystery protector, whoever it was.

"Those other ones, the older boys," Griselde said. "The Swords, was it?"

"Yes." Duck felt her muscles tense at the very thought of the Red Swords.

"Well, they got away, too, just before the watch arrived. Scattered like cockroaches. And looks like they managed to swipe my strongbox. Every last penny."

Duck's eyes fell. She searched the ground beneath her for something to say, the right thing to say—something more meaningful than another *sorry*—but Griselde nudged her.

"I don't want to talk about this anymore, you hear? The insurance will keep us afloat until we can rebuild, plus there are some old guild secrets, some loopholes and fine print I can utilize to get us back on our feet. We'll be just fine. The important thing is that you're safe and well—a scratch here or there, to be sure, but nothing time won't heal."

But Duck knew there would be no healing her heart.

She'd had a family, and she'd lost them.

She'd had a new home with a baker who adored her, and she'd lost that, too. She was lucky—Griselde was still here, still wanted her—but the truth was plain.

Duck had burned it all down.

"Now, Sister Ernestine has kindly made room for us here at the abbey," Griselde said as she took a seat on the marble bench near the stew pond. "I'll file paperwork with the guild in the next few days, and we'll get a sense of how long it'll be until a new bakehouse is up and running. In the meantime, we'll just consider this a nice holiday from bread . . . Duck?"

Duck was listening, but plans of her own were spinning through her head as she looked down into the green water.

She would stay on with the baker as her apprentice for as long as Griselde would have her—not only for the sheer thrill of the work, work she felt devoted to as if it were a sacred calling, but also because she was determined to pay the baker back what Duck had cost her. Griselde wanted to wave a hand and forgive it, but Duck could not forgive herself so easily, not without making things right.

What would she do about Petrus, besides stay out of his way as best she could? She didn't expect it would be possible to rebuild what she had lost with him, but she wished there were a way to tell him that she grieved it, grieved that loss, and grieved the loss of what the three of them had had in the kitchen. A rhythm, a system, a sense of belonging.

What would she do about the Swords? Holy bones, she had no idea. The thought of Jacques the Jackal prowling around Odierne, waiting for a vulnerable Duck to be alone . . . it sent her up in sweats.

And the Crowns.

What about the Crowns?

They couldn't stay in Odierne. No, they were known thieves now, and arsonists, and the Red Swords were surely hunting them down like mice—

And it was all Duck's fault. Duck's fault they'd lost their home, Duck's fault their deal with the Swords had soured, Duck's fault they were now without bread or coin, just a bag of old tricks for a city that now knew to stitch its pockets closed and tighten its grip on its purse.

Looking down at her arms, she considered her bandages, wrapped around her sore wounds. Nothing magical about a bandage or a salve, but they allowed for healing.

That's what Duck needed to do now—find the Crowns and start the healing.

An apology.

A possible goodbye.

A bandage.

"I have to find them," she croaked. "I have to find the Crowns. They might—might not want to be found. But I have to try. I know you may not understand—"

"They're family. And I understand family." Griselde, bless her, pushed herself up to standing. "Where do we start?"

Ruins

Every time Duck breathed in, she coughed.

Every time she coughed, her lungs hurt.

And every time her lungs hurt, her eyes watered soot, so she approached the cathedral ruins with black tears streaking down her cheeks.

Sister Ernestine said that time was the best balm for her wounds and that she should keep her throat lubricated, her body rested, and her mind calm, and one day, she would wake up and discover that she no longer felt like a newborn dragon, clumsily breathing fire.

Duck couldn't think that far ahead. She could barely imagine what would happen right now, as she walked with Griselde to the cathedral grounds. They'd already checked the Crowns' usual haunts: beneath the canal bridges, down every shadowy alley, in hay bales and barn lofts.

For three days, they'd walked the streets of Odierne, and now Duck had steered them back to the piles of stones that used to be the Crowns' home. They were probably already gone, Duck had thought several times during the search; they had probably already fled Odierne, getting ahead of the Swords. Maybe they weren't in Avilogne at all anymore—but Duck wouldn't stop until she'd combed every cobblestone and peeked in every shop, scanning for clues.

"This was where you were all camping out?" Griselde Baker ran a hand along the former southern wall, frowning when the wall suddenly dropped off, her fingers now touching air. "A bit drafty, wasn't it?"

Duck, however, was solemn as she stepped over the uneven stones. It was strange, seeing the gap in Odierne's cityscape where this cathedral had once towered; even though it had been crumbling and ancient, the street felt emptier now, as if it had truly suffered a loss.

The rain that had fallen off and on since the night of the fire puddled in the mud beneath the cracked foundation. The whole place smelled of mildew and something foul from the tannery up the road.

Behind the churchyard, the Sarluire was calm, its water pushing past the banks with a gentle lull.

And absolutely no one was there.

"Well, they don't seem to be here." Griselde limped slowly around the busted-up pieces of the floor, her cane poking at the sharpest stones. "Duck? Any other ideas?"

"I don't know." Duck looked beyond the remnants of the cathedral, out at the river and, beyond it, the unknown forest. It was devastating to think that they might have left without so much as a goodbye, but, painfully, she understood why.

Something caught her eye.

Scratched into the only bit of standing wall, there was the bottom half of the pronged crown that Ash had drawn on their first day in Odierne.

How joyous that moment had been, how triumphant; Duck really had thought that this cathedral would be their forever home. She really had thought they'd be in Odierne until kingdom come— or at least until they ran out of pockets to pick.

They always scratched out their crown when they left.

Always.

Duck risked half a smile.

They were still here.

They had to be.

"Our fingers be nimble!" Duck suddenly burst out in her gravelly voice.

Griselde lifted her eyebrows.

"To our graves, be swift!" Duck got louder with every word. "And on every head a crown!"

No unwashed heads popped up from behind the piles of demolished wood and rock—but Duck could hear something rustling.

Movement somewhere near the roof, which was now in chunks on the banks of the Sarluire.

Perhaps just the wind.

Perhaps just Ash the cat, sniffing for rats.

But something deep inside of her, some forgotten instinct, told her to be patient.

"It's me!" she rasped. "Duck! Your Duck, the same one you pulled out of this very river. The same one you babied and raised and fed. The same one who has been feeding you for the past year, so the least you could do is talk to me!" She surprised even herself with how boisterous she sounded, but her anger was a wonderful amplifier, as it turned out.

It wasn't fair for them to ignore her, wasn't fair that she was being treated like an outsider. Gnat was the one who had put her in the bakery—she hadn't even wanted to go! She'd wanted to stay behind, let some other Crown risk their neck with Griselde, but she'd done it.

She'd done it so they could eat.

Yes, she'd wrecked their scheme with the Swords, and yes, she'd cost them a strongbox and a home, but who had taught her to treat the bonds of family like iron chains? Who had taught her such loyalty? Who had taught her to put the good of the group above all else?

She'd learned this devotion from them. The Crowns. Gnat. He'd instilled that in every one of them, a law to triumph over every other law.

The Crowns were her family. But Griselde was family, too.

Duck had much to apologize for. But she wouldn't apologize for protecting her family.

A head poked out from behind a mound of toppled stone slabs. Ash.

Another head, another Crown, and then they all climbed out from their hiding places—Fingers, Le Chou, Drippy, Frog Eyes, Spinner, and Ash, and they approached slowly—

Until Drippy cried out in his congested voice, pointing with a stubby finger, "She brought the baker! Run!"

And run they did—but before they could get very far, Duck lifted up the basket she'd brought with her. The abbey's single oven was no match for what Griselde usually worked with, but she and Duck had been able to whip up some loaves.

Some crusty, delicious-smelling rosemary and olive oil loaves that were still steaming beneath the towels.

She didn't need to say another word; the scent of warm yeasted bread hit the Crowns, spun their heels, and practically forced them to march back to Duck's side, their stomachs seizing control of their legs.

"What is that?" Frog Eyes inhaled deeply through his nose, then sighed, as if the scent alone could fill his empty tummy.

Duck smiled. "Rosemary," she said, "the best smell in the world." She passed the first loaf to Ash.

Her eyes found his, which were full of questions, full of uncertainty. Duck saw all those things bubbling up and out of him, and she tried to give him a look in return.

A look of hope.

"How do we know this isn't poisoned?" Spinner said, refusing to reach into the basket when it was offered to her.

"Or a bribe?" Frog Eyes folded his arms defiantly.

"Oh, please." Griselde Baker chuckled. "My bread and coin have been keeping you alive for a good year now. I think we're well past bribes."

"No strings attached," Duck insisted. "Just bread."

Ash tore his loaf in half, breathing in the intoxicatingly cozy smell. "Forgive us for being a bit . . . careful," he told the baker. "You could have us arrested."

"That I could." Griselde glanced at each of the Crowns with her cloudy-day eyes. "The sheriff would likely make examples of you. A public hearing. Prison forever."

"Or the gallows," Drippy put in with a shudder.

"But I won't." The baker lifted up her chin, and some of her whiskers caught the eastern sunlight. "I won't punish people who are doing the best they can. But I can't abide people who let good bread go to waste, so eat. Eat!"

Ash took a bite of his loaf and groaned, "Oh, sweet saints, that is good!"

That was convincing enough for the rest of the Crowns. They lunged for the basket, every hand grabbing and groping, every mouth stuffed with crust. A few eyes still glanced up at Griselde with suspicion, but the bread had done its work.

Duck took stock of them while they ate, assessing them for damages. They were all absolutely dingy with soot, their clothing full of charred holes where the fire had bitten them. But they were all okay. They were all *here*.

All except . . .

Duck's gut twisted when she realized who was missing. "Where's Gnat?"

They all slowed their chewing, looking at each other.

"Haven't seen him," Frog Eyes finally said, gulping down a chunk of bread.

"Since when?" Duck pressed. If the Red Swords had found him, Duck knew, they would not show him any mercy.

"Swords got snagged by the constable," Ash reassured her. "The watch stuck them in a wagon bound for Perpinnet. They're wanted there for grand larceny and fish theft. Stole from the count's private pond."

Duck couldn't resist a grin. "Fish theft?"

"The great Jackal of Avilogne, downed by a bunch of whiting," Ash added, and with the relief of the Red Swords being locked away in a Perpinnet prison by now, they laughed loosely, freely . . . until Duck sobered and asked again, "So, nothing from Gnat?"

Ash met her eyes and shook his head.

The Crowns had seen him scurry away from the burning bakery, but now, three days later, they hadn't heard a peep. Guilt and worry flooded Duck like twin rivers; Gnat had asked her to help him secure this deal with the Swords, and Duck had crushed it for him.

"We've looked all over," Ash said, his cheek bulging with bread. "No sign of him. But I'm sure he's all right. You know Gnat. He's the best of all of us."

Yes, Duck knew Gnat. And she also knew that if Gnat didn't want to be found, they would never be able to track him down.

A shock, right in her chest. Duck could barely stand it—the Crowns with no Gnat?

Without Gnat, they were just a group of runny-nosed kids scratching for bones. But Gnat without the Crowns . . .

Gnat without the Crowns was the cleverest mind in all of Avilogne.

But he was, at the end of the day, still just a kid.

"We have to find him," Duck said to the baker. "We have to make sure he's all right. But it won't be easy. We'll have to be sneaky. We'll have to bait him."

"More bread?" Griselde Baker lifted up the now-empty basket, and Duck shook her head.

Something else. But she didn't know what.

The Crowns finished their crusts and licked their grimy fingers, then stretched themselves out on the rubble to digest. Duck thought of a hundred moments just like this one that she'd shared with the Crowns—that post-feast, post-swipe delight, the road already calling.

But things were different now. Duck knew how it felt to grow roots—a different kind of delight.

"What happens now?" she asked. "Where will you go?"

The Crowns looked at one another, and Ash shrugged.

"Well, since we don't have to worry about the Swords anymore, I suppose . . ." He trailed off, glancing up at Griselde, and Duck understood. He didn't want to say out loud in front of the baker that the Crowns would go right back to the way they'd always done things.

Picking pockets.

Swiping coins.

Scrounging and pinching and rustling, day after day.

"I thought maybe," Duck said slowly, "you might like to come stay with us." She looked to the baker, who nodded once in confirmation. "After all, the cathedral's gone—"

"It's not gone," argued Fingers, patting the ruined wall she sat upon. "It's just . . . shuffled a bit."

"But you can't stay here. This pile of bricks will be cleared up by the end of summer," Duck said. "There'll be people poking around here day and night."

"Well, then, we'll head out to the canals," Frog Eyes said. "There's plenty of bridges—"

"True, but most of those are already claimed by vagrants and pigeons," Duck pointed out. "And it's a terrible place to be during spring floods."

"Then we'll go to the forest," Drippy said.

"It's the queen's forest," Duck argued. "You'll be tossed into the dungeons if you're caught with so much as a mushroom!"

"We won't get caught—we're Crowns!" Frog Eyes shouted. "And if we do, to the grave with us, and make it swift!" A few others echoed him, fists in the air.

Duck pushed her hair off her forehead, exasperated. "I'm only trying to help—"

"You're trying to make inside cats of us," Spinner said, "but we'll never do it! We're Crowns!"

"I'm a Crown," Duck snapped, "and for the past year, I've managed to swipe enough dough to keep you all fat and happy, and I did it while sleeping on a mattress, wearing clean clothes, and using a fork. Are you going to tell me I'm less of a Crown than you?"

There was silence while the Crowns mulled this over, and then Ash spoke out. "We'll be fine, Duck. We don't want any more trouble. All we want is for things to go back to normal. Back how they used to be."

A cough rolled out of Duck, and the sudden gasp of pain was a sharp reminder that things would never be the same again. *She* would never be the same again.

She would sleep in a bed and work with her hands to earn

her bread now. And maybe the Crowns couldn't fathom life as inside cats, but whether they wanted it or not, some things had changed.

Duck surveyed the Crowns, this time taking stock of their tired eyes, their bruises, the way they barely held themselves up, their very bones exhausted. One thing would never change—she would never abandon them. They were her family.

Gnat was gone, but Duck was here.

And Duck was going to make sure they got their bread.

"Listen," she said, "the bakery won't be up and running for a long time. Master Griselde and I will be staying with the Glorious Sisters of Mercy, right over there." She pointed at the abbey. "There are plenty of cots, and there's enough food to keep even you lot full. I'll ask Sister Ernestine to leave the gates unlocked. If you decide you want a nice safe place to sleep, come inside. If not, well . . . I'll leave some breakfast here tomorrow morning."

That was all she could do.

If she tried to put collars and leashes around them, they'd buck and scare and run away.

She nodded warmly at Ash, and then she and the baker walked away. Duck felt the eyes of the Crowns on her back with every step.

"Well done," Griselde said when they were out of earshot. "Very, very well done."

"They're not following me," Duck muttered, glancing over her shoulder as the cathedral ruins faded from view. "I wanted them to follow me."

"You gave them the choice," Griselde said, "which is all you can do. It's what I did for you."

Duck sighed as they reached the abbey. "I hope they make the right one."

"But that's just it, Duck," Griselde Baker said as Sister Margret unlocked the gate. "There is no right choice. There's just this way and that way, and it's up to every person to decide for themselves which turn to make. Ah, smell that? Sister Ernestine's roasting beets! I'd bet my life on it!"

The baker headed down the cloistered hallway toward the kitchen, and Duck went in the opposite direction, to her room, where she watered her scalded throat and changed her bandages.

Then she wandered around the garden and up into the stone tower, the highest room in the abbey, where she stared out the round window that looked out onto the street until it was too dark to see.

Dinner was set.

All the sisters were at the table, Sister Ernestine at the head, Griselde Baker opposite her. Duck had her eye on the chicken, on a juicy-looking drumstick smeared with lemon and thyme, when all of a sudden there was a creak.

The sound of the gate opening, and a shudder as it closed.

Footsteps, falling softly through the cloisters.

Someone tripped in the shadows, and a whisper: "Get up, you oaf!"

"But look! Strawberries!"

Duck's eyes grew wide.

That was Le Chou, unmistakable in his fondness for strawberries.

"Come on, muttonhead, Duck said there'd be food! Real food! Can't you smell it?"

The footsteps grew closer.

Inside the dining room, it was quiet as a tomb. Sister Ernestine cocked her head, angling her ear toward the disturbance outside in the garden.

Griselde Baker looked at Duck, who was frozen, the smallest one at the table.

Every sister watched in dismay as a pair of hands reached through the window, past the curtains, and seized the bowl of mashed turnips.

The bowl hovered. It was pulled out the window, and then a voice said, "Ugh, turnips! Forget those; get the bird! The bird!"

The turnips were put back.

The platter of chicken was lifted instead and disappeared through the window.

And the footsteps faded as the Crowns raced through the garden with their stolen bird, off to find some hidden place to eat.

Duck met Griselde's eyes, and the two of them shook with laughter, even as Sister Ernestine clapped her hands together in a call for prayer.

So the Crowns had arrived at the abbey. Maybe they would even be persuaded to come out in the daylight, meet the sisters, sit at the dinner table . . . or maybe they would only ever swipe their grub from the open windows like thieves.

Either way, Duck knew she'd be able to sleep easier tonight knowing they were safe and well fed.

But somewhere out in the city, Gnat either was lying low, waiting for the right incentive to emerge from his nook, or was long gone.

No mere bribe of bread or bird would work to lure Gnat out into the open—but Duck had something else in mind.

To Catch a Gnat

Asking Gnat a question was always a game of chance.

Some days he was in an honest mood, and he'd tell you exactly what you wanted to know, no sugarcoating: yes, there were enough bites of pie left for everyone to have one; no, the constables in Perpinnet did not have access to underground tunnels that let them chase after criminals without pushing through crowds; yes, the women in Telgary wore trousers, and yes, they carried quivers of arrows on their backs, and yes, they could easily beat up any Crown if provoked.

If you asked Gnat a question about himself, however, he almost always spoke in riddles.

Many a Crown had asked him about his disabled arm, and many a Crown had asked him about his origins, and many a Crown had walked away, defeated.

Gnat had even convinced the rest of the Crowns that their own origins should be considered inconsequential, the kind of debris

. . . . .

that washed down a drain and into a river, where it streamed away to the sea.

Once you were a Crown, it didn't matter what you had been before.

Once you were a Crown, you were supposed to have no past, no future—only what was currently in your hand, and then you were supposed to eat it.

But Ash loved to talk about fishing Duck out of the Sarluire as a baby. Gnat always seemed to hate this, the recitation of Duck's origin story, and for a long time, Duck thought it was because he hated her—or because he was jealous.

Jealous because she knew where she'd come from and he did not.

But she had a hunch that the truth was something else entirely, and Griselde encouraged her to chase it.

First, she went to Master Frobertus. The notary's offices were filled with archives of Odierne's dealings—all the business licenses, building permits, town events, and legal proceedings, as well as the christenings, baptisms, confirmations, marriages, and deaths—stretching back nearly eighty years. Master Frobertus himself had been keeping records for most of that time, and he was only too glad to help Duck with her search.

"I don't suppose you have his surname," Master Frobertus wheezed as he climbed back down the ladder, bringing with him a stack of papers from the shelves. "Or even the parents' occupations? That could help."

"No, sorry," Duck said. "We have nothing." Nothing except a rough guess at his age and the state of his right arm, which might be something Gnat had been born with or might have resulted from an injury when he was young—Gnat had never said.

Master Frobertus helped her decipher some of the shakier scripts. Some of the records were written on such old parchment, the ink was already fading from age.

Duck tried not to cough on the records, and sipped her water dutifully, and took notes, and considered timelines, and then—

And then Duck got lucky.

A single line written on a scrap of paper, tucked into the back of a file that perhaps no one else would have looked at for a hundred years.

And then she had it.

A way to lure Gnat out into the light.

"I think I know where he is," Duck said when she explained it to the baker. "And I think I know what he wants."

"Wants and needs, my dear," Griselde Baker retorted with a finger wag, "are very different things."

"Not when you're a Crown," came Duck's reply.

Even after preparing for the worst, Duck was beside herself when she saw the state of the bakery.

Most everything was burnt. Everything that wasn't burnt was wet.

Huge piles of ashes were scattered throughout the kitchen. The remaining beams in the ceiling were barely intact, scorched black. The ovens were cold, and without their emanating heat, they reminded Duck of the sad, toothless mouths of great monsters. But while the kitchen was a flame-eaten disaster, the storeroom and the office were smoke-damaged, a weird state to be sure. On first sight, one might think that these rooms were unscathed, but after one attempt to breathe, it became clear that these areas would need to be ventilated before they could be inhabited again.

Very well ventilated.

Torn down and rebuilt. That kind of ventilation.

Clouds of flour hung in the air, and the overwhelming stench of the river's sulfuric low tide was almost strong enough to cover up the bitter scent of scalded yeast.

It was uninhabitable—and that's why Duck knew that Gnat would be here.

The bakery was the site of an inquiry, of constables asking questions about the fire, of masons and carpenters poking around, planning their reconstruction—and so Gnat would be tucked away in here somewhere, hidden in plain sight.

This kind of liminal space, which no longer belonged to the public or to an individual owner, was just the kind of place Gnat had always directed the Crowns to haunt.

So Duck crept around the bakery. Griselde had opted to wait outside, respecting the Crowns' privacy, and had warned her to be cautious, and Duck in turn had warned the Crowns to be cautious, but she could feel all of them, of one mind as they walked from room to room—what if he wasn't here?

What if he refused to come out?

They had to at least try. The Crowns were a family, and together, they'd come to fetch their own.

"Gnat?" Duck called as she peered into empty barrels, into cupboards, behind the baker's desk in the counting room. "I know you're here, Gnat."

"We just want to talk to you," Ash added. "Please."

"Then I promise we'll leave you alone forever." Duck went upstairs, checked the bedrooms, made her way around the perimeter outside, looking for Gnat's footprints in the piles of ashes . . .

Nothing.

Her worries doubled and tripled in size.

"Maybe he didn't make it," she murmured as she joined the Crowns at the bottom of the stairs. "Maybe the fire hurt him too much to get very far. Maybe he's rotting away in some jailhouse. Maybe he's already gone—"

"I was wondering when you'd show up."

Gnat's voice was as raw as Duck's was from breathing in smoke and heat, yet he was still able to sound like a stern shepherd commanding his flock. Duck peered up at him as he hopped down through a hole in the roof and marveled at how, even when he looked like he'd been sleeping in a fireplace, he had such power.

"We've been looking everywhere for you." Duck didn't bother to hide the tearful frustration in her words; she was so grateful to see him alive and in one piece, and yet the urge to whack him square in the jaw was overwhelming.

Gnat shrugged one shoulder. "Odierne's crawling with watchmen now. Not good for business."

He faced her directly, and the red, oozing burns on his shoulder and round, plum-swollen shiner puffing up his left eye made Duck's stomach twist. "Gnat, I . . . Are you all right?"

Ash put a hand on her back, steadying her.

"What does it matter to you?" Gnat said dully. "Looks like you got everything you wanted."

With all the Crowns gathered around her, and the baker just outside, keeping watch—Duck knew it must have been quite a shock for Gnat to look down the stairs and see them all together, still intact even without their fearless leader (no doubt he'd always assumed they'd crumble without him). But Duck's pity was burned away by a glimmer of rage.

"What about me?" Duck fired back. "Do you want to ask if I'm all right? Did you even check to make sure I was alive before you ran away?"

She waited for a flash of defensiveness on Gnat's face, or regret, something to let her know that he'd thought about her at least once in the past few days since the night of the fire.

But Gnat's expression remained gloriously neutral. "I figured most garbage floats."

So he wanted to taunt her. Exchange words with the newly verbose Duck, a real battle of banter. But Duck knew she would never be able to match him wit for wit, especially not after the week she'd had.

She suddenly felt exhausted. She looked at him, at the way he leaned against the banister, holding his right arm extra tenderly. The cold of winter always made it ache. Had the blazing heat of a fire done the same?

He'd never ask for help. He'd never admit he was in need of bandages, salves, healing, and Duck suspected he'd slip out of Odierne as soon as he was well enough, on to find a new city to haunt alone. And the Crowns?

They'd be nothing more than another origin story. Something to forget as quickly as possible. But Duck was hoping she had a good reason for him to stick around.

"Gnat," she said, "I have something for you." With nerves prickling, she reached into her pocket and pulled out a bit of parchment, crookedly folded.

"What is it?" Gnat eyed it through his purpling slit.

"It's . . . an answer." Duck betrayed nothing as she held it out to him, but it didn't surprise her when he refused to reach for it. "It's . . . about your mother."

A ripple of shock went through the Crowns, but Gnat remained unfazed.

"Why in hell would you think I care?" he said.

"Because"—Duck paused and took in a deep breath—"this is the real reason you wanted to come back to Odierne. And this is why you didn't want to leave when the Swords tried to push us out. It's why you're *still* here, even after everything."

It all fit together. The Crowns had already been to Odierne once before, nine years ago, when they'd pulled baby Duck out of the river. They never visited the same city twice, and yet last year, when the Crowns had picked every pocket in Perpinnet and needed a new place to play out, Gnat had led them back here.

Why else but to search for something he'd lost?

"We came to Odierne because it's flush with bread and coin," Gnat countered, but Duck knew this was only a half truth. Gnat had made a beeline for Odierne as soon as he'd had the chance.

"Besides, why should Gnat care who his mother is?" Frog Eyes put in. "It doesn't matter where you're from. All that matters is that you're a Crown."

Yes, the old Crown motto, which Duck had always found inspiring: Who cares who you were before? Who cares where you came from? Who cares what's in your past? They'd left all that behind to be Crowns.

But Gnat was the one who had come up with this rallying cry, and this had been another clue for Duck. "Gnat wants us all to forget about our pasts . . . only because he couldn't find his," she offered quietly.

Gnat smirked.

But Duck spotted the alertness in his eyes. He'd been found out.

"Gnat . . . you said my parents probably drowned in the flood that took our farm," Fingers chirped, her digits fluttering with nerves. "Did they? Did they drown?"

"Who cares?" Gnat said. "Who cares who you were before you became a Crown? Isn't being a Crown better than anything else you could do as the daughter of some poor tiller? You've seen half of Avilogne; the queen herself could never be this free."

"Did they drown?" Fingers repeated, her jaw clenched. "Or are they still alive?"

Gnat shrugged. "They never found you, did they? So they're as good as dead."

Fingers inhaled, her gaze falling to the ashes on the floor.

"And my parents?" Frog Eyes said. "What about mine?"

"You want to know about your folks?" Even with Gnat's bruised face, his authority was menacing. "Your folks had another baby as soon as they realized you weren't coming back—another boy. Guess they really thought you were a changeling."

"And you—" He turned to Le Chou. "Your father went all the way back to Telgary before he realized you weren't in the apple cart anymore, and then he drank himself into a stupor and lost his orchard."

He pointed at Spinner. "And your grandparents told their village that you'd been sent to a fancy artists' colony instead of admitting they'd lost you at the spring fair."

Now to Drippy: "Your family was sick with plague, and most of them kicked off before they even noticed you'd left. If any are still around, I doubt they remember you at all."

"You," Gnat said, looking at Ash. "Your folks were too ashamed to abandon you properly. Instead of dropping you off at a church, they let you climb up a tree in a village green . . . and then they left."

Ash swallowed, but Duck could see his muscles tensing—one tiny answer, and a hundred more questions had popped up in its place.

He angled his harsh gaze at Duck. "And you. You want to know where you came from?"

She pursed her lips, defiant. "A baby fell in a river," she recited, "and Ash fetched it out—"

"That's how it ended." Gnat lifted his chin. "I know how it started."

Duck did not speak.

Inside, her chest billowed with jitters.

She could cover her ears. If she didn't want to have a past, she could cover her ears right now.

It didn't matter where Crowns had come from. It only mattered where they were right now.

"Your mother," Gnat said, "was running from the watch. That's right—she was a thief, and not a very remarkable one. Not clever enough to escape arrest and death in the same night—"

"How would you know?" Ash cut in. "I was with you that whole time."

"And you were too busy fussing over your squawking new garbage to notice," Gnat snapped. "It was all anyone talked about around here for weeks—how the watch chased her up to the top of the cathedral in the storm, how she took a flying leap with you in her arms and landed right in the river. Who knows where she went after that? Maybe she was broken up by the currents, sent down every tributary in Avilogne like flotsam.

"So you see, Garbage, it's in your blood. No matter how much you try to scrub up and pretend to belong . . . you'll always be garbage."

Her mother, a thief.

Duck didn't know whether to laugh or cry. *The family trade,* she thought, and wondered if that qualified her as an apprentice or a master.

But she'd been running from the watch, and Duck wondered what she'd think if she knew that her daughter, too, had spent a lifetime running.

Running, on the run, ready to run—until Griselde.

Gnat leaned against the banister, surveying the wreckage. Some Crowns were trying to hide their sniffles; others were gritting their teeth. Frog Eyes breathed in and out through his nostrils, which whistled, making him sound like an angry teapot.

"So," Gnat said, "are you happy now? Are you glad that you know exactly how you were abandoned, left behind, forgotten?

"No," Duck cut in. "No, we weren't abandoned. We were stolen."

She could see it now—Gnat, searching the underbelly of Avilogne all those years, not for lost orphans in need of a merciful home, but for possible comrades.

He could have turned them all over to a church. To a home for children. He could have found them new loving homes with parents who had been hoping for such a miracle—

But instead, he'd been the first one to find each kid when they were all alone . . . and then he'd kept them for himself.

Gnat couldn't find his own family, so he stole one.

The systematic cobbling together of the Crowns—it was Gnat's greatest scam of all.

He shook his head now, chuckling. "See why it doesn't pay to care about these things? Look at you all—a bunch of milksops, crying for your mommies. So no, I don't care about whatever you have in that parchment. I know all I want to know."

"Gnat," Duck said. She thought of things that made her feel calm: the warmth of a fresh mug of tea, the crunch of a baguette, the softness of Ash the cat when he decided she'd earned the privilege of petting him. She breathed in the burnt air and tried to embody the stoniness of the gargoyles: eternal, patient, wise. "I found her."

Gnat glanced at her like a cornered kitten, inhaling sharply. "Found who?"

Duck held out the slip of parchment. "Your mother."

Somewhere in the bakery, water dripped off the roof, plinking onto an overturned cast-iron pot.

Duck bit her cheek, waiting.

And then Gnat burst into a cruel laugh.

"Oh, that's rich!" he cried. "You really think you found something! Don't get excited, Garbage. I know all of it! My mother was a coward. She plopped me on the front stoop of a bishop's house when she decided she didn't want me, and then she walked away. She left me. Five years old, and she left me for dead, didn't matter to her. I wasn't her problem anymore."

Duck's heart panged. "Maybe she had good reason—"

"Is there ever a good reason to throw your five-year-old out with the pig slop?" Gnat's eyes burned holes in Duck.

Something within her turned to water. "She did look for you," she said. "She searched everywhere—"

"She could have tried harder!" Gnat belted out. "She could still be looking, but she gave up—and so I've given up on her." He came down the stairs, clutching his right arm against his chest. "Now that you've delivered your big news, Garbage, kindly get out of my way."

Duck crunched the parchment in her hand—yes, everything Gnat had said was in her notes. A small boy was taken into the children's ward of the local parish, and by month's end, he had run away. And then Gnat had disappeared from the records—but those same records had told Duck the answer.

"I have her name," Duck announced. She unfolded the parchment and held it out to him so he could see what was written on it.

Gnat started to shrug, his signature movement, dismissing everything in the world that was not bread and coin—

"More than just her name: I know where she is."

The other Crowns murmured, their sentences indecipherable. Gnat locked his gaze on Duck.

Duck had never been able to read Gnat the way she and Ash could read each other, but there was something in that swirl of emotions behind his eyes that she recognized.

Longing. A need, deep and desperate.

She'd seen it in Griselde's eyes, and she'd felt it for herself—and she watched it surge through Gnat, despite his best efforts to stop it, as he looked at the parchment.

Duck lifted her hand, motioning to the Crowns to keep quiet. She wanted to give Gnat the time he needed.

"All right," Gnat finally said, glaring up at Duck. "I'll say hello. I'll let her look at me. But that's it. And if she tries to hug me, I'm leaving." He twitched once, tucking his right arm into place by his side. "Lead the way."

The Last Rite of Gnat

They moved as one down the streets of Odierne.

Every Crown was either chewing on their lips or peering at the windows they passed with glazed-over eyes, all of them solemn, thoughts swirling in their heads.

Duck left them alone. They'd all need to think things through on their own—Gnat had thrown some fireballs at them when he'd called out their stories.

Stories they'd all probably wondered about now and then, stories they'd dismissed as irrelevant when Gnat had told them that being a Crown was the only important ending in their lives.

It was unfair of him to do that. To hold those tales back and then release them all at once like weapons.

But now at least they knew. Knowing was better than wondering, Duck decided. She'd never again look at the sparkling Sarluire and feel like it was holding back secrets.

Yes, there were more holes in her own story than in Telgarian cheese: What had her mother stolen that night? Had the watchmen known she was holding a baby when they'd pursued her, when she'd jumped into the river?

Didn't she have anywhere to run to? Anyone who could keep her safe?

A sanctuary?

All answers she might never get—

But right now, Duck was only concerned about one story.

When she looked over her shoulder at Gnat, he was shuffling along, his hands in his pockets. She'd never seen him like this, staring down at the ground instead of glancing suspiciously at the city all around him.

He peered up at her, narrowed his eyes, and Duck quickly looked ahead again.

They arrived at the abbey, and Griselde stopped first, the rest of them bumping into her like baby ducklings following their mama.

"Go and fetch the abbess, please," the baker requested of the nun who was on gate duty. "We've got someone here who wants to speak to her."

Duck's palms itched. She shifted her feet, exchanging a wordless gaze with Ash.

The other Crowns, too, seemed nervous for Gnat's sake. All their lives, they'd heard him dismiss moments just like this, but here he was, about to meet his own past.

Pre-Crown Gnat.

"Sister Baker?" Sister Ernestine approached the gates, tugging at her veil until it lay flat. "You needed me?"

Duck's stomach twisted.

Now that she was looking for it, she could see that Sister

Ernestine had the same sharpness to her eyes that Gnat did, the same hunger.

"All right, Sister." Griselde Baker wrung her hands, excited, the grin on her face exactly like Christmas morning. "Brace yourself. We found him."

"Found who?" Sister Ernestine crossed herself as she unlocked the gate. "And who are all these children? They look . . ."

Duck watched it happen—watched the realization dawn on the sister, and her face went white as pastry. Her mouth opened and closed. "No," she whispered. "No, you couldn't mean—"

"Yes." Griselde was surprisingly solemn when she made the reveal. "We found your son."

"Holy bones," Frog Eyes whispered, "Gnat's mom's a black-and-white?"

"Yes," Duck answered. Nuns were not born nuns. Thieves were not born thieves. Everyone was on a journey to becoming who they would someday be.

Sister Ernestine covered her mouth with her hands, her eyes tearing up. She crept forward. "Sebastian?"

The Crowns parted down the middle, clearing a path for the nun—

But when Duck peered behind her, wanting to see Gnat's face when he saw his mother for the first time in years, there was no one there.

Just the dusty street and the road to the market square behind them.

Duck's chest squeezed.

He was gone.

"All right, then." Griselde frowned, squinting her eyes. "Where'd the little wisecracker go?"

The Crowns looked at one another, silently refusing to be the ones to deliver the news, and so Duck piped up.

"He . . . left." She was sorry to say it, and even sorrier that she wasn't surprised. She didn't even want to glance at Sister Ernestine. To have this emotional buildup, all these years of longing, and then your own son decides not to face you . . .

But this was Gnat, after all. Some things changed . . . and some things did not.

"Where on earth did he run off to?" Griselde thundered. Then she reached into her pockets. "And—and wait a minute! I had a coronet and some pennies—no. No, he didn't."

"Of course he did." Frog Eyes grinned wickedly.

"Took the money and ran." Le Chou said this as if it were the most natural conclusion in the world.

"Can't say I blame him," Spinner added. "A whole coronet to his name? It'll get him far, especially if he's on his own."

"It's for the best." Sister Ernestine, when she spoke, sounded clear as the abbey bells. She'd wiped her cheeks and straightened, looking once again like the stern and dignified abbess Duck had come to know so well. "If he isn't ready . . . then there's nothing to be done."

Griselde put a hand on her old friend's shoulder. "At least he knows where to find you now."

A small comfort, Duck thought darkly, considering how stubborn Gnat was.

"In some ways, I'm relieved." Sister Ernestine's hand flew to the rosary suspended from her belt; it was a chain of subdued red crystals that caught the sunlight and broke it into little panes on the dirt. "God forgave me my sins long ago—but I'm not sure I have. It would be wrong to ask my son to forgive me when I haven't forgiven myself."

A dozen questions popped into Duck's head—questions about baby Gnat, why Sister Ernestine had left him, what she had hoped would happen if she ever found him—but she set them aside.

This was not her story.

This was Gnat's.

And if someday he wished to hear those answers, Sister Ernestine would be waiting.

"Sister Ernestine? Can I ask you something?"

Duck hid from the brightness of the sun beneath the clouds of lilac, letting the sister handle trimming the fat purple bunches off the branches.

"Of course."

"How do you get someone to forgive you?"

Sister Ernestine pressed her mouth into a long, tight line. "I don't think you can," she said at last. "You can apologize and you can repent, but you cannot change someone else's heart."

A pigeon fluttered loudly past, and Duck tracked it all the way up to the blue sky. An image flashed in her mind: Petrus's face when he'd come into the bakery to find her there with the Crowns and the Swords. The disbelief. Betrayal. Heartbreak. "How do you let them know that you've changed?"

The sister tilted her head, thinking. "When I arrived here ten years ago, my heart was broken. Cleaved in two. I'd had to make the most difficult decision of my life—we had nothing to eat, nothing, and my Sebastian, my . . ." She grew silent, her eyes closing. Duck waited until Sister Ernestine's breathing started again, but secretly, she was startled; when the sister closed her eyes, she looked just like Gnat.

"I've spent the last ten years regrowing my heart. Here, in the garden, I've learned how to feed myself and feed others. I had nothing when I arrived. Less than nothing—I'd given away a piece of my soul—but the abbess put a trowel in my hand and showed me to the dirt. I learned how to fill the holes I'd dug. I learned how to let new things grow."

Sister Ernestine regarded the cut lilac in her hands with fondness. "You change for yourself and yourself alone. If it's a true metamorphosis, if your heart has really shifted, then those around you will see it. What they choose to do after that? It's up to them."

The sister took the flowers back to the abbey, leaving Duck in the garden alone.

Duck had never thought much about repentance. It was one of those church words that had no place in the Crowns' lives.

But something Sister Ernestine said stuck out like overproofed dough.

A true metamorphosis.

If Duck wanted to show Petrus that she was sorry for what she'd done, she'd have to change.

Real transformation.

A sinking feeling filled her belly as she realized what she should do to make things right.

Inside the abbey, Duck borrowed a bit of parchment and a pen and locked herself in a room, where she stayed for hours, working.

She wrote her words carefully, burning a candle down to the stub, and with every dip of the pen, her dread parted, giving way to a tiny bud of hope.

Transformation would be painful, she knew—but there was no growth without pain, without heat. She was ready.

Ready to take another step toward becoming who she was meant to be.

She rolled up her letter and passed it under Sister Ernestine's door. The abbess was awake still, Duck noted by the flickering light in her chambers, but Duck wanted this written down. She wanted her request there in black and white, a record of her willingness and her efforts. A record of everything.

And then she waited nervously, sitting on her hands in the abbey chapel, until it was time.

Duck stood on the porch of a small green cottage, the second-story bedchamber jutting out over the door.

Petrus's house.

Behind them, near the front gate, Sister Ernestine waited, her veil freshly pressed, a wooden cross centered on the white bib of her habit. Her hands were laced patiently around a wrinkled roll of parchment. Master Griselde was beside her, her wounded leg bound in a cast, her smile encouraging.

Duck wiped her sweaty hands on her baker's whites. Maybe this wasn't a good idea. What if Petrus yelled at her, or slammed the door in her face, or refused to speak to her at all? Duck wouldn't put any of that past Petrus. Not with the way she'd behaved.

But she deserved it. She'd brought thieves into the bakery and then burned it down. Whatever Petrus wanted to do to punish her, Duck deserved it.

And so she let out a long, slow exhale . . . and knocked loudly on the door.

And promptly felt her stomach wring itself out when the door opened.

There was Petrus, looking sullen, Hugo on his hip.

"What are you doing here?" he demanded. He glanced curiously at his master, standing at the gate, but the baker said nothing. Duck was on her own.

She searched for that part of her, right in the center, that was warm and brave, and tried to hold on to it. "I'm here to make things right." She motioned to Sister Ernestine, who approached the porch and unfurled the parchment.

Duck had deliberated about what form her plea for forgiveness should take. She'd considered throwing herself at Petrus's feet, offering to scrub his whole house and be his servant until she'd restored her good name. Or taking out a loan somehow, maybe begging Master Frobertus for the cash to pay the bakery in full for what had been taken, so that Petrus would know justice had been served. She'd even thought about fetching Constable Deveraux so he could hear her guilty plea and let the law take care of her—perhaps Petrus would see that Duck was truly chasing redemption after she'd spent a few days in the stocks.

In the end, Duck decided to speak Petrus's language.

The language of the church.

The best way to change your heart, if Petrus had anything to say about it.

Sister Ernestine cleared her throat as she approached the porch, scroll in hand. "I am here to witness the recitation of the full confession of one Duck . . . Duck."

Duck kept her eyes on the ground. No last name. Nowhere to hide.

When she took the scroll from Sister Ernestine, she lifted her trembling finger to the things she'd scrawled, pointing to each word as she read aloud:

"I stole a pear from a farmer back in Perpinnet. The pear cannot be returned; it has been eaten. I stole a leather quiver from a peddler's cart in Illyon. The quiver cannot be returned; it was pawned, and the money was used to buy bacon, which has been eaten."

Duck had stayed up all night, trying to remember everything— every item she had ever taken, every coin, every sin.

As she read, Duck puffed up her chest, trying to act tougher than she felt.

Griselde Baker had already heard a shorter version of this list, but it was clearly unsettling for her to have all the specific details; her mouth gaped open when Duck read about how she had aided the Crowns in stealing an entire outhouse.

Petrus, on the other hand, remained stoic. Unyielding. *You can't make him forgive you*, Duck reminded herself as she kept reading. *All you can do is transform yourself. Your own heart.*

Metamorphosis.

When Petrus let out an impatient sigh, Duck paused and considered the parchment, the end of which dangled near the ground.

"It . . . it goes on like that for another hundred items or so, but I'll skip to the last one." It was important that Petrus hear that one at least.

"I stole money from the baker—lots of it, and lots of bread, and a few tools that were pawned as well. I am also responsible for the fire."

There it was. The truth.

Enough that Duck was lightened by her confession, and also terrified.

She'd committed crimes enough to convict an adult many times over—but knowing Griselde was close by, silently supporting her, gave Duck a burst of courage.

"What are you playing at?" Petrus growled. He passed Hugo off to Raina and stepped onto the porch, leaning over Duck, his eyes blazing. "Do you expect me to feel sorry for you? All that thieving and lying—"

"I don't expect anything from you." Duck inhaled deeply. Expectation was different from hope. "I know you'll probably never be able to trust me again. But I have changed."

"You've confessed," Petrus fired back. "That's only the first part of repentance."

"That's true," Duck agreed. "I'm making amends. I'll work around the clock, and when I become a journeyman, all my salary will go toward paying back the bakery—"

"That's monetary restitution." Petrus folded his arms. "You've broken the law. And according to the law, restitution comes in the form of punishment—"

"The stocks," Duck cut in. "Or prison, more likely." A zip of chills went down her spine.

Prison. A dark dungeon. Locked inside for a few years if she was lucky, or a lifetime if they wanted to make an example of her. She swallowed hard, reaching for her courage. "Very well. Call for the constable."

"Oh, come off it," Petrus griped. "Surely not—not prison." He looked across the yard to Griselde Baker, who shrugged.

"Duck knows the laws. She's only trying to right a wrong, and for that, I think she's showing her true colors."

"True repentance requires a broken heart and a willing spirit," Sister Ernestine said. "Duck's transformation is slight so far, but even the smallest changes have rippling effects. And I believe she will continue to remake herself into a good and decent citizen, again and again, as we all must remake ourselves. We all make mistakes. I leave it up to you, Petrus," Sister Ernestine concluded, "to decide what restitution is acceptable for our Duck. As for God . . ." The sister lifted her rosary up for Duck to kiss and gave her a kind smile. "He forgives you."

Duck bowed with gratitude. It made no difference to her whether God forgave her or not—she knew so little about God and His proceedings—but it was nice to be forgiven by someone.

Then she turned to Petrus, awaiting her fate.

If he decided she needed to be clapped in irons and marched off to prison in order to make things right . . . so be it.

Duck was on a path now toward true transformation—and

425 •ₒ•˙ ˙ ˙

that could happen in the coziness of a bakehouse or in a dark, drippy prison.

Crowns were good at the dark.

Petrus's face was scrunched with bewilderment. He took the parchment from Duck and scanned it, but asked softly, "Who are you, Duck? Who and what are you?"

A Crown.

A scoundrel, a pickpocket, a thief.

A baker's apprentice with a nose for rosemary.

A liar.

An orphan.

A dozen other things, hiding within her like secret peas in horse bread, waiting to be discovered.

"I'm not sure," she replied after a moment. "I'm still deciding. But I know that I am sorry." She'd said she was sorry already so many times. She'd keep saying it forever, if that's what he needed to hear.

Petrus scanned the parchment, and his eyes were unreadable.

Duck swallowed. "I know I shouldn't have done it—"

"No." Petrus's voice was weary with emotion. "No. You stole pears, bacon, breakfast rolls, eggs . . . You stole cups and wigs and sold them to buy food . . . You stole shirts and shoes and then wore them to holes . . . And I'm guessing any purses or coins you stole went to buy food as well. Stealing to eat, stealing to stay alive . . . you did what you had to do. You survived." When he gave Duck a restrained smile, she knew she'd truly earned it.

"Now for your penance." Petrus rolled the parchment tight and passed it off to Sister Ernestine. "If you are truly seeking forgiveness, you must find someone to speak for you, someone who will guide you onto the path of righteousness. Someone to watch over you. And you must watch over them in return. You're a bit of a handful, if you ask me. It might be tricky to find someone willing to overlook your sins and steer you toward goodness."

"I'll speak for her," Griselde boomed. "I'll keep her out of trouble."

"Absolutely not," Petrus answered, and Duck tensed. "You're far too forgiving of her, Griselde—she needs someone much more discriminating. Someone to keep her on the straight and narrow path." After a long pause, his face cracked into a kind smile. "I suppose I'll have to take up the task."

Warmth spread through Duck's chest. Unafraid now, she stretched out her hand in earnest professionalism; Petrus considered it for a moment, then gave it a sturdy shake.

"You are a lucky one indeed," Sister Ernestine said, her eyes twinkling with sadness, "to have so many willing to love you." She kissed Duck's forehead and excused herself, heading back to the abbey, and Duck gave a thought to Gnat, his wise mother, the gap between them. Perhaps someday Gnat would come around. Perhaps someday Gnat would let someone love him.

Duck's lungs relaxed as she reached the gate, and Griselde Baker pulled her into her side.

She had people to speak for her. People to keep an eye on her. People to watch over her, far more people than she ever thought she'd have, a rascal like her. She had the Crowns and would always have the Crowns—though some things had changed, certainly. But to have so many people who loved her on any terms was an embarrassment of riches, and something she'd never have been able to swipe for herself.

She'd grown herself a family—two families, in fact, because Duck would always be a Crown, even if she decided to live as an inside cat for a while.

The stink of the streets was more than skin deep; it was in her very blood. But underneath her fingernails was flour and yeast.

Bread, the stuff of life.

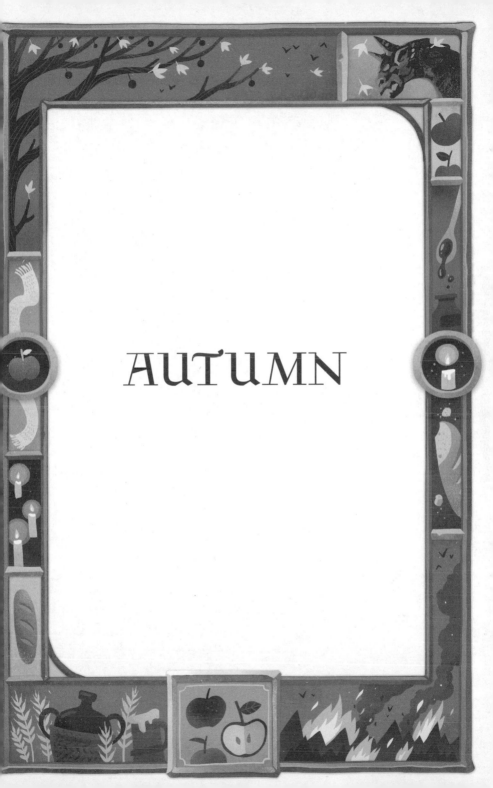

AUTUMN

Our Daily Bread

"All right, knaves, line up!"

In the hollow space beneath the shortest of the canal bridges, the one reserved for merchants with handcarts and lone donkeys, a group of dirty kids scrambled to form a row before their leader.

If you thought they were mere farmers' children, enjoying the blue sky and the autumn daylight streaming through the branches, you should check your pockets.

If you crossed the bridge and spotted an errant shadow, you should take care that the shadow didn't follow you home and pick every apple in your orchard.

But if you were an old friend, approaching with a couple of unclaimed loaves from this morning's batch, you might be safe—it all depended on what kind of mood Gnat was in.

And today, judging by the wry grin on his face and the way he tied his rope, slowly, masterfully, Duck thought she just might be in luck. Damp leaves squelched beneath her boots; overhead, a murder of crows watched her every move.

"Someone's here!" called one of the kids, pointing at Duck. The rest of them made for their hiding places along the bank, behind boulders and clumps of reeds.

One of them was familiar—Drippy, who had decided to follow Gnat into a new gang and was trying hard to keep from waving to Duck as he vanished behind the stones of the bridge.

This wasn't the only new gang in Odierne. Fingers had left to start her own gang, a bunch of wild-haired girls who mostly prowled around the north end of town, cutting the purse strings of the noblemen and ladies who came through the city gate. Duck had spotted them a few times at the Cheap Wife, sneaking into the stands to see the Green Dragon fight.

But this was the first time Duck had actually seen Gnat with his new crew.

She'd been expecting to be gutted to see Gnat thriving without her or the rest of the Crowns.

Instead, it felt right.

Everything was slotting into place, everyone finding where they fit best.

Ash had gone straight—not just straight, but ultra clean as well. He'd been taken in by Master Frobertus, who had immediately spotted Ash's potential bookish brilliance and decided it was time the notary took on a true apprentice. Ash wasn't as quick with his letters as Duck had been, but he was bright and clever with words, and thoughtful. Maybe he'd work in the clergy someday. Or maybe he'd be the best-read thief in all of Avilogne.

Either way, Duck was just glad she got to see him twice a week when she came to the notary for her own lessons.

Frog Eyes and Le Chou she saw every day—and every night, too—because they were working as delivery boys for Griselde, pocketing tips and eating more bread than they could possibly handle. They were well kept, too, sleeping in the counting room, which Griselde had converted into a sort of orphans' bunk. On more than one occasion, Duck had come downstairs on those early pink mornings to find Ash piled in there, too, the remnants of their late-night pegs and crosses game scattered on the floor.

Spinner wanted to be on her own for a while. She wanted to travel, so she'd skipped town with a bag full of rolls and a few spare pennies in her pocket. She had promised to come back when she was done looking around. She'd always been smarter than the rest of the Crowns anyway, Duck figured. Maybe out in the world, she'd find somewhere worthy of her brains.

And Gnat.

He'd disappeared after that day at the abbey.

When he resurfaced, he already had a new place to hide out and some recruits under his command.

Duck and those Crowns who had opted not to join his new campaign had given him a wide berth, letting him settle into whatever new life he wanted to swipe for himself, but soon the seasons would turn.

Soon it would get cold.

And Duck had to make sure Gnat and Drippy were all right before the first snowfall.

They were family.

"I'm here to see Gnat," she called out under the creaky wooden bridge, a drop of brackish water falling onto her crisp baker's whites.

There were whispers, then footsteps.

And then Gnat emerged from under the bridge.

Duck's first thought was that he looked smaller than she remembered. She worried that he wasn't eating enough, but he wasn't bony or anything. There was color in his cheeks, his hair had grown long enough that he now twitched to shake it out of his eyes, and his left arm seemed well muscled and strong.

Then she realized that Gnat hadn't grown smaller; she herself had grown.

Grown taller. Outgrown him.

She no longer fit under his thumb.

"Well?" he said after a good ten seconds of silence. "What do you want?"

"I heard you had moved here," Duck started. She wondered if she looked as different to him as he looked to her—though the Gnat she'd always known would never admit this. Not in a hundred years.

"Home sweet home." Gnat spat into the leaves, then glanced at her expectantly.

A pair of faces loomed from the shadows beneath the bridge, faces that hadn't been wiped or washed in ages, but the eyes were bright, curious.

Young.

"You have a name for yourselves yet?"

Gnat paused, then said, "We're the Bread Boys. Funnily enough," he added.

A smile tugged at the corner of Duck's mouth. "So you're all right?" As soon as she asked it, she regretted it—of course he was all right. As long as Gnat was alive, he was all right. Winter was coming, yes, but there was no more formidable opponent to the elements than Gnat.

He would out-survive them all.

"What are you doing here, then?" Gnat straightened, finding his rope in his pocket, twirling it in his fingers. "Trying to start something?"

"No." Duck offered him her basket. "I had deliveries. And these were extra."

The hungry eyes in the shadows followed the bread as she set it down on a rotted stump in the mud.

Gnat sneered. "We're perfectly fine without your charity, thank you."

"It's not charity," Duck countered. "It's just a bit of leftover bread—"

"We. Don't. Need. It." Gnat pronounced every word on the edge of his teeth. "Now leave before I let Drippy practice his punches on you. Go on."

Duck opened her mouth to speak, but turned around instead.

She used to be an outside cat. She remembered.

"All right." She deliberately left the basket right where it was. "I guess I'll see you around."

"I guess so." Gnat narrowed his eyes, but when she'd nearly reached the road, she heard him call out her name:

"Hey, Garbage! Bring some of that horse bread next time! Drippy likes the onions!"

Her smile tasted a little sad as she traipsed back to the bakery. Gnat with a new gang. Still, she couldn't be upset with Gnat, not for any of it.

He'd given Duck her first family, and for that she'd always be grateful.

Duck reached the bakery just after the church bells pealed out the afternoon chimes.

Griselde sat on the porch in a patch of sunshine, a bowl of cream in her hands.

The only one unaccounted for was Ash the cat, who had apparently moved on to another, better place to steal milk and sardines.

"Still no sign of him?" Duck asked, taking her place on the steps beside the baker.

"Oh, don't you worry," Griselde crooned. "I have every reason to believe we'll see him again this winter. Just you wait. He always comes back."

The two of them sat in silence for a moment.

Griselde sniffed. "What's that? Rosemary?"

"Rosemary." Duck smelled her fingertips, the oils from the herb-filled dough on her skin. Delicious.

Griselde chuckled. "Funny thing, that. I've been thinking . . . we used to have a woman who came and bought a rosemary loaf every Saturday, right at eight, on the button. For the better part of a year. I was always in the kitchen, handling the ovens, but my Symon—he would always sneak her an extra trencher or two because the poor thing looked ravenous. With child, too."

Duck's skin prickled.

"Her coins were always hot, like she'd been clutching them in her palm for days, and her clothes were always ragged. Symon thought perhaps she was a vagrant, or an outlaw on the run." The baker smiled. "I don't remember when she stopped coming, exactly, or if my Symon simply stopped mentioning her. That happens sometimes, as you know. Sometimes people stop becoming so remarkable, so new. They become fixed in your lives—just another customer."

No, Duck thought, *they become family.*

"But she loved that rosemary bread. Once, I thought I saw her answer to it. 'Rosemary,' someone called from the line, and she lifted up her head. I loved to think it was her name—though maybe they were just calling out their order. But still. A beautiful name, isn't it? Rosemary? Makes you wonder."

All up and down Duck's arms, goose bumps made her skin prickly. "Do you recall what she looked like?"

Griselde grinned. "Indeed I do. This was before my eyes really started to go. She had big red hair, a quiet smile, and dark gray eyes. The color of ash."

Duck wasn't sure what she'd been hoping to hear. She wasn't even sure what to believe. "So, then . . . I don't look like her at all."

"No," Griselde said. "No, you're your very own person." She reached for her cane and used it to stand, but Duck stayed where she was.

Rosemary.

That scent always found her.

And that story had found her again, the story of where she'd come from—but Griselde was right.

Duck was her own person, every day. She got to choose, every day.

No one got to choose where they came from. But everyone got to decide where they were going.

"Sister Ernestine said they're overrun with basil," the baker said. "We'll head over there tonight after supper, if it isn't too chilly." She glanced up at the sky. "Looks like it's going to be a beautiful night."

"Looks like it is," Duck agreed.

SUMMER

BENEDICTION

All the gargoyles in the garden of the Glorious Sisters of Mercy face north.

From our spot in the sweet grasses near the edge of the cobbled pathway, we can see the sinking sun and the morning light. We can see the moon rest on the tops of buildings, and the stars.

We no longer have a rooftop view of Odierne, but it is so much better to be down here. Down in the city. Down on the ground, down in the thick of it.

All of the gargoyles in the garden of the Glorious Sisters of Mercy are covered in pigeons at any given moment, because all of us gargoyles are no longer just gargoyles.

We are birdbaths, every single one of us.

Rescued from the river and the rubble, transformed into the finest yard art, we protect the birds that land in our basins. We gargle water and let them clean their feathers. We allow them to drink their fill. We protect them from the cats that threaten their lives. We keep watch.

Forever.

Well, perhaps not forever. I do not know if the sisters will one day move out, and the abbey will one day crumble, and the plants here will dry out, and the dirt will grow pale and unusable. But I am here now, and I have my flocks to protect, and it is enough.

As a gargoyle, I saved one person, and it is enough.

One morning, I am surprised to see Chirp diving for my stone. Chirp is a full-grown pigeon now, and I cannot tell if it remembers me from its days as a nestling.

It makes no difference. I will provide respite. I need not be remembered. I would much rather do the remembering.

Across the garden, Harpy is eyeing me as the sun sets.

"It was rather warm today, wasn't it?" I call, and she sneers and turns her attention to the stew pond. I chuckle to myself.

Perhaps there are not enough lifetimes to become friends with Harpy. Perhaps we are just too different—different stone, different makers, standing at different ends of the garden. Perhaps we are fated to glare at each other from our perches forever as the sisters sing and pray and the children and the baker's apprentice pick their herbs and throw dirt clods and run around the plants.

There may not be time for us to become friends. But perhaps we might at least become *friendly*.

I can wait. I can wait lifetimes if that is what it takes.

I was made to wait.